continued...

More praise for
MURDER IN GRUB STREET

Praise for Bruce Alexander's first
Sir John Fielding Mystery
BLIND JUSTICE

"Blind Justice is as much fun to read as it must have been to write. Bruce Alexander has done a fine job of depicting mid-eighteenth century London, and moves easily into the classic mode of the detective genre, always mixing his shady characters, likely suspects and dubious dealings with some of the more notable personages of the day, such as Samuel Johnson. And he has a good deal of fun; indeed, one can almost sense the author rubbing his hands in satisfaction."

—*Washington Post Book World*

"A shocking solution . . . Lively characters, vivid incidents, clever plotting, and a colorful setting . . . A robust series kickoff."

—*Publishers Weekly*

"A marvel."

—*Chicago Tribune*

continued...

Berkley Prime Crime Books by Bruce Alexander

BLIND JUSTICE
MURDER IN GRUB STREET
WATERY GRAVE

WATERY GRAVE

Bruce Alexander

BERKLEY PRIME CRIME, NEW YORK

WATERY GRAVE

A Berkley Prime Crime Book / published by arrangement with the author

PRINTING HISTORY
G. P. Putnam's Sons hardcover edition / 1996
Berkley Prime Crime mass-market edition / October 1997

The Putnam Berkley World Wide Web site address is
http://www.berkley.com

ISBN: 0-425-16036-X

Berkley Prime Crime Books are published
by The Berkley Publishing Group,
a member of Penguin Putnam Inc.,
200 Madison Avenue, New York, NY 10016.
The name BERKLEY PRIME CRIME and the BERKLEY PRIME CRIME
design are trademarks belonging to Berkley Publishing Corporation.

PRINTED IN THE UNITED STATES OF AMERICA

10 9 8 7 6 5 4 3 2 1

For
Tony and Susan Luraschi

WATERY
GRAVE

A NOTE TO
THE READER

*In which witnesses
interpret an action
most different*

If you would be so good as to put your mind to it, you might try to imagine a storm at sea. Yet perhaps, reader, I ask too much, for unless you are a veteran of many voyages and have endured consequent dangers of fierce weather on shipboard, you could not conceive of such a storm as this one, which many an experienced seaman claimed to be the worst he had known.

The sky in midafternoon is darkened by clouds so that it be as deep night. From those clouds pours a rain which, though constant, is unsteady, for it often comes in great rushes near drowning the sea itself, then slacks in intensity for minutes at a time, only to explode once again in vast inundations of wet. The waters of the sea rise and fall in mountain-sized swells so that a ship of good size, a frigate of the Royal Navy, is tossed up and down, to and fro, like some small button box with sails.

Aboard that frigate, those of the crew on deck struggle to do what they can to keep the ship afloat. It slides precipitously down to the bottom of wave after wave to crash at the bottom, often taking on water, laying about port and starboard in the trough and taking on more water still. Those of the crew belowdecks pray, curse, and stay close to the lad-

ders that they may not be last to the boats should the ship
begin to break apart.

Into this hellish scape two figures appear upon the poop
deck, which, as the ship's uppermost level, is in such circumstances also its most perilous point. Having emerged
from below, they make their way slowly across the wind-
swept space. Only one of them proceeds under his own
power; he supports the other, who, though his feet touch the
deck, can hardly be said to be walking at all. The two move
most uncertainly. He who bears the load of the other goes
stiff-legged with the weight of him.

Thus slowly they make their way across the poop deck to
the starboard ladder. But in the midst of their journey the
frigate drops low into the trough of a deep swell, and the
weaker of the two is torn from the grasp of the stronger. He
is thrown against the taffrail just opposite the starboard ladder. Quite miraculously he keeps his feet—but not for long.
His companion extends his arms—and the other man dis-
appears overboard.

That final movement is seen by two men on the quarterdeck below. The first, who stands wrestling with the helm,
glances across at the crucial moment and perceives it as a
futile attempt to hold the doomed man back. The second,
holding tight to the stout rope which secures a cannon in
place, later describes it as the final push which sends the
unfortunate to his watery grave.

Rescuer or murderer? That question would occupy us profoundly in time to come. And even to this day, this question
of intent remains matter for heated discussion, even bitter
argument among those many whose lives it touched.

ONE

*In which I meet
my prospective
stepbrother*

On a day in July 1769, I had been sent by Sir John Fielding to accompany Lady Fielding to the Tower Wharf, where we were to meet her homecoming son, Tom, returned from near three years' duty on the India station. I had been told by Sir John that the official welcome ceremonies for the H.M.S. *Adventure* were not to begin until noon, and our departure from Bow Street left ample time for a prompt arrival. Yet the hour precluded the possibility that Sir John might have attended the occasion, as he would have liked, for he must sit his court in Bow Street that day, as he did every day, barring sickness or some unforeseen occasion. Therefore had he taken me aside, given me a proper allowance of shillings and pence, and charged me to convey Lady Fielding to the Tower Wharf and, with her son, back again to Bow Street. It was a considerable responsibility for a fourteen-year-old boy, as I was then, yet I was grown a pair of inches in the past year and was the size of a smallish man.

As we descended Tower Hill, the driver of our hackney carriage reined in with a call of command to the horses. "This is as far as I can take you," called he to us. "You take the footbridge yonder." He pointed ahead. "Cross it and up the stairs, and you will be at the bottom of Tower Wharf."

And thus we proceeded, the moat on our left, in the direction of the Thames, down to the bottom of Tower Hill. It seemed certain to me that we were in no wise tardy for the proceedings. Yet just then, with a great roll of drums, a too-tling of fifes, and a call of the clarion trumpets, an invisible band struck up beyond the stairs—and Lady Fielding shot ahead and disappeared up the staircase. By the time I caught her up, she had joined the crowd on the wharf and was push-ing into it like any Covent Garden housewife at the green-grocer's stall.

There, above the hubbub and shouting, the band which had assembled only ten paces or so across the cordoned open space before us made an even greater din. There, too, near the front of the crowd, I had my best view of the Thames. As I now recall, I had some dim notion that the H.M.S. *Adventure* would be firmly docked at Tower Wharf, side by side with it. Yet it was not so. It lay far out at anchor some distance up the river, sails furled, pennants flying. The reason for this was evident. The ship was surely too big to fit the wharf. As I learned later, it was also the custom for ships of war to maintain a discreet distance from the shore. A frigate the *Adventure* was, as I had heard. I knew there were bigger vessels in His Majesty's Navy, yet I could not, for the life of me, imagine such.

A boat of good size, manned by eight oarsmen, had set forth from the frigate. There were many more within the boat, so many in fact that the men at the oars made slow progress toward the wharf.

"Oh, Jeremy," said Lady Fielding by my side, "what shall I do if I do not recognize him? He was but a boy when he left. Now, by his letters at least, he seems a man."

"Surely a mother will know." It seemed the right thing to say.

She considered that a moment, then gave a firm nod. "Yes," said she, "surely."

The boat had disappeared beneath the height of the wharf. I expected its passengers to pop up at any moment. Yet first there was a courtesy to be observed. I heard a voice boom forth from the river below.

"Permission to come ashore."

A man in uniform stepped forward on the wharf and, in

lieu of words, he responded with a long blast in several notes on a whistle.

Then, after a pause, crew members of the H.M.S. *Adventure* appeared from below. I supposed they had come up a ladder. The crowd applauded at the appearance of each mariner—and indeed that seemed appropriate, for there was something theatrical in all this. As the men came, one by one, they formed a ragged line along the wharf. By the time they had all assembled, they were fifteen in number. Once there together, standing in the same stiff attitude, they were forced to wait as a stout man of senior years came forward and stood before them.

He made a speech of some minutes' duration. By throwing his voice back and forth, he managed to address both the seamen and the crowd that had come to welcome them. He was richly dressed in uniform, bemedaled, beribboned, and red of face. Without knowing his rank, I judged him to be a rear admiral at least. The speech he gave, though in no wise memorable, praised the men before him for keeping the trade routes open against attacks by pirates and privateers. He cited some twenty-odd separate engagements in which the officers and men of the H.M.S. *Adventure* had acquitted themselves admirably—prizes taken, trade tonnage saved, and so on. All this was quite beyond me, as I believe it was to most of us there. Yet he continued—and here he addressed members of the crew only, commending them for remaining firm in their duty in the face of apparent dissension in the upper ranks and reports of violent attack.

All this struck me as passing strange, as indeed it seemed to do Lady Fielding, as well, for we two exchanged puzzled glances at his remarks. The crewmen seemed less puzzled than disturbed. A few dared turn their heads, exhibiting sullen looks to one another. One or two appeared downright angry.

"If any of you has information on these matters," said the speaker, "I invite you to step forward now."

He waited. None stepped forward.

"So be it," said he. "But know that my office is open to any and all. What I am told in private will be kept in confidence." Again he paused, this time no doubt to give weight to what he had said. Then he resumed: "All this aside, I wish you to know you have done your duty to your ship, your King, and your country. We are proud. Boatswain?"

As the man with the whistle stepped up to pipe another tune, the speaker moved forward, broke the ranks of the crewmen, and disappeared down the same ladder they had ascended. The last I saw of him, he was sitting in the boat conveyed by its eight oarsmen back to the frigate.

That struck me as odd. And odd, too, that he had not mentioned the captain as another for whom they had done their duty.

Then the boatswain whistled another tune and the band struck up again. With that, all thoughts of what was odd, strange, or puzzling in what I had just seen and heard suddenly left me, for crew members and the waiting crowd swarmed together. I was buffeted away from Lady Fielding and near knocked down in the rush.

When I managed again to locate her, she had attached herself to a young man of fair aspect some inches taller than I was then. He quite dominated his mother, who was even shorter than I, yet she clung to him, embracing him, squeezing him so tight that I thought she might rob him of his very breath. He took it well. Smiling and laughing throughout her attack, he pulled away at last and, holding her hands clasped in his own, began talking earnestly to her. She responded passionately, pulling a hand away to wipe the tears from her eyes. All this I saw, but none of it I heard, for I thought it best to keep a polite distance from this touching occasion until such time as my presence should be wanted. Through it all the band played on.

Lady Fielding had remarked to me but two evenings before that her last sight of her son, Tom, had been at the Old Bailey. When he was led from the courtroom in the company of two others, she'd been sure—because the judge had declared it—that he would be hanged.

I recall that we were in the kitchen, drinking a last pot of tea. Mrs. Gredge, cook and housekeeper, had retired for the night. Sir John was below, conferring on some matter with Mr. Bailey, the captain of the Bow Street Runners. Though I knew the circumstances regarding her son from Sir John, she had never before discussed these things with me, so painful were they in her memory.

"You may believe me, Jeremy," she had said to me, "when I tell you that when I saw my son, my only child, taken from the courtroom in chains to what seemed his certain death—*that,* my dear young friend, was the darkest moment of my life. He was but a boy, younger than you are now, and his young life was to be taken—and for what? For a few shillings, perhaps a pound, that he intended to give me, his mother, so that we might not starve further. In all truth, I cared not then whether I lived or died. Nay, I wished to be dead and would, I'm sure, have ended my life—had it not been for Jack."

She referred to Sir John. So she called him, and so had the first Lady Fielding, as well, during those few weeks I knew her before her death.

Sir John Fielding had urgently petitioned the Lord Chief Justice for the lives of the three boys, out of respect to their young years—the eldest was but fourteen. He had managed to save others as young for a life on the sea in the Royal Navy. Queen Charlotte herself had expressed her royal approval of this form of clemency, and the King had knighted the Magistrate of the Bow Street Court in recognition of it. And so the Lord Chief Justice was well prepared when Sir John brought his petition and arguments before him; yet he resisted them powerfully.

He resisted not from pure obduracy, or hardness of heart, but because in the course of the robbery bodily harm had been done to the victim, a shopkeeper. When the victim resisted, the eldest of the boys had dealt the shopkeeper great blows with a stout club he carried. A wound was opened on the man's scalp and his leg was broken. He was quite unable to pursue them, of course, but the boys, frightened at their crime, had run from the shop. The hue and cry was raised, and they were apprehended.

In the end, it was the shopkeeper's testimony that proved the salvation of two of the three. He gave it in court that the younger two of them were quite horrified at what the eldest had done and had wrestled the club from him ere he did further hurt to the poor man. Sir John had argued to the Lord

Chief Justice that in this way two of them had demonstrated that while they were party to the robbery, they could not be blamed for the bodily harm inflicted upon the shopkeeper. The Lord Chief Justice had reluctantly admitted the point had some merit and signed an order remitting Jonah Falkirk and Thomas Durham to duty in the Royal Navy. Thus they were saved. John Dickey, aged fourteen, was hanged at Tyburn two days after his fellows set sail from Portsmouth on the H.M.S. *Adventure.*

All this I had heard from Sir John, yet in the year I had shared the same roof with Lady Fielding she had never made direct reference to the matter, and indeed had never discussed her feelings regarding it until that recent evening in the kitchen over our pot of tea. She had continued only a bit further, explaining that Sir John had not informed her of his efforts on her son's behalf until they were successful.

"He wanted to arouse no false hope in me, should they fail," said she. "It was probably best so, yet had he known the depths of my despair he might have thought otherwise. Yet when he summoned me to Bow Street and informed me of his success—that is, his partial success—it was as if he had given me my life, given me a reason to live. It was the kindest act ever a man could do for a boy and his mother."

She was silent then for more than a minute, so long in fact that I rose from the table and gathered my cup and the empty teapot and began to prepare for washing up.

Yet she resumed one last time: "And to think that that same good, kind, generous man should take me for his wife, knowing my history—that is, to me, a fair marvel of fortune. There is no telling, Jeremy, what fate has in store for any of us."

"And well I know that," I said to her.

She smiled then at me the most serious of smiles. "And well you must," she had agreed.

So it was we had had our talk two evenings past. How was I then to interrupt her reunion with her son there on the Tower Wharf? I held back until Lady Fielding looked around her, clearly wondering where I had got to.

Only then did I come forward. The wharf was emptying quickly. The crewmen who had been landed formed a line before an officer who sat at a table right there on the wharf.

"I must join the tail end of the pay line," said Tom to her, "else my three years will be for naught."

"Go, Tom," said she to him. "Jeremy will collect our hackney, and I shall wait for you here."

He smiled and nodded at his mother as he backed off in the direction of the pay line.

To me he said: "Jeremy, take my ditty box with you to the hackney. It is all the baggage I have." He pointed down at the object at my feet.

To her credit, Lady Fielding stepped forward and said, "Tom, Jeremy is not a servant. Please form that as a request, and I am sure he will be glad to oblige."

"Oh, you do it, Mother. Make it right with him. I must collect my pay and my leave ticket." And with that, he left us and took his place in the pay line.

If I was not a servant, then what indeed was I? I seldom gave thought to my station in the household of Sir John Fielding, Magistrate of the Bow Street Court, so glad was I to be included in it. He had been master and friend to me ever since that day only a little more than a year before when I, Jeremy Proctor, had appeared before him falsely accused of theft. Though blind, he had seen through the lying devices of those who had perjured against me, and then kept me, an orphan, as a helper in his house and court and occasionally as an assistant who served as his eyes in criminal inquiries.

For the most part he treated me as an adopted son. The first Lady Fielding had expressed the hope from her deathbed that I would be a good son to him. Kate Durham, whom I had known and loved as a friend before her marriage to Sir John, was less maternal to me. But as the second Lady Fielding, she gave me good counsel, friendship, and had a continuing interest in my welfare. She it was who suggested that it might be proper to send me off to school. In his opinion, there was no need for it, so long as I kept reading as voraciously as I had done hitherto. Yet she took charge of my reading, directing it, questioning me on the contents of each book I finished, requiring me to write essays upon diverse

subjects. I daresay she was as exacting as any schoolmaster
or tutor.

As for my duties about the house, it seemed only right
that I should help Mrs. Gredge, for in the past year she had
grown more infirm—and more crotchety, as well. And I
found it a joy to do whatever Sir John required of me in his
official capacity. There were errands to run, letters to take
and deliver, and a myriad of other tasks too varied to mention. I was, as he had once dubbed me, in a jocular mood,
his "man Friday." Having read Defoe's *Robinson Crusoe*
more than once even at that young age, I took that gratefully,
for I knew Friday to be a willing and resourceful worker.

So there I was, something less than a son, something more
than a servant. The order given me by Tom Durham and his
mother's quick response had served to remind me of my ill-
defined state. I did not wait for Lady Fielding to make it
right with me, as he had asked her, but with a smile picked
up the case, which was neither heavy nor bulky, and set off
down the wharf toward Tower Hill.

"I shall sort it out with Tom," Lady Fielding called after
me.

I turned, again smiling, and waved in response. And as I
did so, it occurred to me to hope that when she had sorted
it out with her son she might also make it all clear to me.

The Magistrate of the Bow Street Court had had a most
eventful twelvemonth past. Not only had he sprung a trap on
the perpetrators of the "great massacre in Grub Street," as
it was known in the broad-sheets and gazettes, he had also
wedded the widow Durham at St. Paul's, Covent Garden.
Their lives together in the ensuing months had been peaceful
and quiet, marred neither by rancor nor by discord. They
smiled often, and always to one another, and were given to
long evening talks in Sir John's darkened study. Not many
came to visit; those who did not were not missed.

The only difficulties that had arisen were caused by Mrs.
Gredge, the cook. I have said she had grown more infirm
and crotchety. Tetchy might be the better word. She would
sulk for long periods of time, then give vent to an outburst
of anger—usually directed at me, which caused no hurt, for

I was accustomed to her ways. But twice or thrice she lashed out at Lady Fielding; on these occasions there was little that could be done to mollify her. She seemed to resent any changes that were made in the conduct of the household, even when they were made to benefit her. Sir John was perplexed by her and confided in me that he believed she harbored some hostility toward the second Lady Fielding out of loyalty to the first. It seemed to me that there was very little could be done about that.

Yet Mrs. Gredge was barely mentioned when, as was my wont, I visited him that day of Tom's arrival in his chambers after his court session. In answer to my knock he called me to enter. I found him as he was usually at such times, waistcoat unbuttoned, wig off and placed upon the table before him, and both feet up on a chair nearby.

"Well, Jeremy," said he, "is it you who come, looking for tasks?"

"It is, sir, and I am."

"You are quit with Mrs. Gredge for the day?"

"Oh, indeed," said I. "She chased me from the kitchen, so taken up is she with preparations for dinner."

"So soon? We'll not eat, surely, for three or four hours."

"It seems she has much baking to do before she even thinks of cooking the meal. Or so she said before she pushed me out."

"Ah," said Sir John, "the mysteries of the kitchen. And what of mother and son? Their reunion goes well?"

"Oh, yes, they are deep in discussion in the sitting room."

"And things went well at Tower Wharf?"

"Oh, yes sir. A band played, and a speech of welcome was made by one who must have been an admiral, at very least. Oh, a grand ceremony it was, in truth."

"And what was this admiral's name, Jeremy?"

"That I could not say, sir. He did not give it."

Sir John laughed at that. "No, I suppose he did not. But tell me, boy, did he have anything to say that struck you as odd or unusual?"

How could he have known that?

"Well . . . yes, or it struck me as odd at the time. There was something that was known to him and to the crew—but not to the rest of us. He spoke of dissension in the upper ranks and a violent attack. He asked any who had information on this to step forward. When none did, he told them that his office would be open to them and . . . and that anything said to him in private would be kept in confidence.''

"Until the court-martial, of course." He said it as if to himself.

"How was that, Sir John?"

"Oh . . . nothing." Sitting in silence for a moment, he turned neither right nor left but lifted down his feet and seemed to lean slightly to the front, where I stood before him. Then: "You used a certain phrase a moment or two ago that struck me as having some particular meaning. You said that Kate and her son were 'deep in discussion.' Have you any idea as to the nature of that discussion?"

"But Sir John, the sitting room door was closed. I would not eavesdrop."

"Of course not. I would not have you do so. But was anything said, let us say, prior to the time the door was closed, said openly in your presence, that might give indication of what was discussed?"

"Well . . ."

I was made a bit uncomfortable by this. It seemed like spying to me—or the thing next to it.

"What you tell me in private will be held in confidence," said he.

"Until the court-martial?" I asked, perhaps somewhat impudently.

At that he laughed again. "Oh ho! You did hear what I muttered, did you? Well, I assure you, Jeremy, there will be no court-martial. I have good and sufficient reason to ask. It is not base curiosity that prompts me in this."

I accepted what he said, of course. And so, not unwillingly but without much enthusiasm, I told him of a conversation that had taken place in the hackney coach during our return to Bow Street: of Lady Fielding's offer to buy Tom a proper suit of clothes and his firm negative response. I quoted Tom—"A seaman is what I am and proud to be"—and told Sir John that Lady Fielding had ended things by telling her son that they would talk about it later.

Sir John took all this as he might have in court, with no noticeable change in expression and with a moment of reflection after I had ended. Then he slammed down the palm of his hand on the table with such force that his periwig was made to jump.

"Hah!" he crowed. "Just as I thought! I told Kate, told her again and again, that once the lad had had a taste of salt water he would never willingly return to life on shore. But being his mother, she would see it only her way, talked of the advantages he would have here, supposed he might return to Westminster like a proper little schoolboy. Nonsense! The lad's sixteen years old, near a man—more a man, by God, than any clerk or secretary in the City. What do you think of him, Jeremy?"

"Pardon, sir?"

"What do you think of Tom Durham? What sort is he?"

"Oh . . . well, a good sort."

"Is he manly?"

"He's good-sized."

"Well, yes, of course, he would be at that age, but what about his manner? His voice? His bearing?"

"He's deep-voiced, sir." Of that I was painfully aware, for mine was at that time still a bit unreliable; I was never quite certain which octave would sound when I opened my mouth to speak.

"Has he an attitude of command?"

I thought of the ease with which he ordered me to take his things to the waiting hackney. "Yes sir," said I, "I would say he does." Then, hesitating: "And . . . indeed he has the speech of a young gentleman in which is mixed all manner of seaman's terms. He talks rough, but as a gentleman might."

"Ah," said Sir John, "excellent, excellent."

He drummed his fingers on the table, thinking hard upon some matter which obviously concerned Tom Durham, his face quite animated. Had it not been for the black silk band that covered his eyes, I fancied I would have seen them shining with excitement. Clearly, he had a plan.

"You'll be going to meet him soon?" I asked.

"Not for some time, no. I think it proper that I let them

have their talk and bring it to a close. Then perhaps Kate will be willing to listen to my plan.'' Feeling about the tabletop, he found a bulky letter—sealed and ready for delivery. ''What I have here is for the Lord Chief Justice. You know the way to Bloomsbury Square, of course.''

I took the letter from him. Indeed I did know the way. I made the trip to the Earl of Mansfield's impressive Bloomsbury residence once or twice a week. ''Will an answer be required?'' I asked.

''No, none.'' And at that point he delved into the voluminous pocket of his coat, brought up some coins, and felt them to assess their worth. He offered me the whole handful. ''Take these,'' said he, ''and take the rest of the afternoon for yourself. Go to Grub Street and buy a book or two. Do whatever you like, Jeremy.''

He urged them toward me, and I took them. ''Thank you, Sir John,'' said I. ''I believe I'll do just so.''

''We simply must get you onto some regular system of payment. Remind me, please.''

''Oh, I shall, Sir John.''

''Go now, but be back early for dinner.''

So it was that I returned not much after five and found Mrs. Gredge quite in a state. She was running about the kitchen aimlessly, wiping her hands on her apron.

''Oh, Jeremy, where was you, boy? I needed you so!''

''But you told me to leave! Pushed me out, you did.''

She sighed. ''Oh, I may have,'' said she. ''Yet when I need you, I need you.''

''What is it that you want, Mrs. Gredge?''

''You must put the roast in the oven for me,'' said she. ''I built the fire up hot. It's all ready to go, but I'm fearful I may not have the strength for it.''

''Just open the oven doors, Mrs. Gredge, and I shall do what needs be done.''

She scurried to the oven and, using a good, thick rag, did as I asked. The oven fire was indeed hot—I hoped not too hot to cook the roast proper. As for the roast itself, I knew it was not near so heavy as she had made it out to be. I had bought it from Mr. Tolliver myself and carried it home. I knew well she could lift it, iron pan, potatoes, and all; I had lately seen her lift heavier loads. I wondered at her game.

Yet I did not challenge her. I simply asked why she had not sought the help of Tom Durham in my absence.

Her answer struck me as queer: "Oh, I would not do that. Is the dinner tonight not in the young gentleman's honor?"

And so, reasoning that what I had put in the oven I should also be called upon to take out, I took a place in the kitchen, opened the book I had bought at Boyer's in Grub Street, and settled down to read. Mrs. Gredge continued to fly about in a most distracting manner, doing the many other tasks that needed to be done. Sir John came at last from below, where he had been in a long conference with Mr. Marsden, the court clerk. Offering perfunctory greetings, he made his way through the dining room to the sitting room.

The book I had got was Lord Anson's *A Voyage Round the World*—an old edition, got at a good price. Lady Fielding had urged me to learn more of the world's geography. Sir John seemed eager that I learn more of the sea. And the book dealt at some length with China, so perhaps it would give me something to discuss with Tom Durham; I hoped so, for indeed we seemed to have precious little in common. I had but read through the introduction by the true author of the book, one Richard Walter, the chaplain of the *Centurion*, the vessel on which the voyage had been accomplished, when, much to my astonishment, Mrs. Gredge suddenly grasped the table where I sat, cried out with something like a moan, and quite collapsed into the chair next mine, breathing with difficulty in great gasps.

Was she unconscious? Was this an attack of apoplexy? I had no idea. What was I to do? Having no better thought, I brought her a cup of water. Surely that would help. I asked her to drink a bit of it. She obliged me and moaned out her desire to talk with Sir John. Having heard that, I ran on through to the sitting room. There I banged rather peremptorily on the door, threw it open, and announced that Mrs. Gredge had collapsed.

There was a great rush to follow me back to the kitchen. "Has she fainted?"

"Did she fall to the floor?"

Then, beholding her, her head lolled over the back of the chair and her hands knotted uselessly in her lap, Lady Fielding flew to her side, exclaiming, "You poor, dear woman, what is it has failed you?"

"My strength," said Mrs. Gredge, in a voice which proved her weakness. "Sir John?"

"I am here, Mrs. Gredge."

"I think I should go to my bed. Could Jeremy help me up the stairs?"

"Certainly," said he. "Jeremy and Tom will carry you up."

We struggled up with her to the floor above and returned hurriedly to the kitchen.

There I was met by two stern, unsmiling faces.

"Jeremy," said Sir John, "had you no earlier sign Mrs. Gredge was so near collapse?"

"None, sir," said I. "She was fluttering and flying about the kitchen till the moment she slumped down in the chair."

"And where were you at the time?"

"Right there at the table."

"Doing what, if I may ask?"

"I was reading, I . . . thought to be nearby if she asked for further help."

"*Further* help? Explain yourself, please," said Sir John, most solemnly. It was his court voice. There was no holding out against it.

I took a deep breath and told the truth: "She had asked me to put the roast in the oven for her. She said she feared she had not the strength."

"And did you not take that as a sign she was weakening?" Again that solemn tone—and I so frightened and ashamed I thought I could not speak, though I knew I must.

But at last: "At the time, sir, I thought she was shamming. I . . . I can see now I was wrong."

"And why did you think that, Jeremy?" asked Lady Fielding.

"Because I had often seen her lift heavier loads quite recent."

"I'm sure," said Sir John, "you can see the failure in your reasoning."

"I can, sir, yes."

"Well, now you must run and fetch the doctor—that man Carr, who treated Kate—that is, Lady Fielding—some time ago."

"Yes, sir," said I, grabbing up my hat and making quickly for the door.

Then, quite to my surprise, Tom Durham stepped forward and said to them: "I believe I shall accompany Jeremy. A walk would do me good just now." And in three quick steps he was by my side.

With that, we went—and swiftly—I preceding, leading the way past Constable Baker and the empty strong room, down the hall and out the door to Bow Street. We said nothing to one another for some time as we moved along toward Drury Lane whereat Amos Carr kept his surgery in his rooms.

"There was something I wished to say to you," said Tom to me at last.

"Oh?" said I, keeping step with him. "And what might that be?"

"You mustn't take it hard the way they came down on you there. When things go wrong, people look around for someone to blame it on. It's quite natural. I'm sure it was just as you said—that you stuck close to help her. I got cobbed twice on the *Adventure* just because I was the nearest. She's a very old party, that one we carried up the stairs. She was headed for something like this."

"You're right about Mrs. Gredge. I'm sure of it."

"Course I am," said he confidently. "They're decent people, my mum and your Sir John. And you were right to answer honest. They'll think over what was said and consider the old bawd's condition. You'll not be cobbed this time out. Mark my words."

Amos Carr examined Mrs. Gredge and pronounced her sudden attack no more than simple exhaustion: he prescribed bed rest. On his way out, he asked her age; no one seemed to know.

"Well," said he, "she's no babe. That's plain to see. She can't carry on as she once did." He smiled wisely, as if

convinced he had just imparted great wisdom to us, his lis-
teners. "That will be five bob, Sir John."

Seeing him to the door, Sir John dipped into his pocket,
paid him off, and all but pushed him out.

"Remarkable!" said he to us. "Five bob to tell us Mrs.
Gredge needs a rest! Well, come all, let us at last sit down
to dinner."

Yet before we were to do that, Lady Fielding had taken
me aside and gave a quiet speech to me there in the kitchen.

"Jeremy," said she, "we feel we dealt with you a bit
severely. You've looked after her interests. Sir John is the
first to admit she is a difficult woman. She has her ways, as
of all of us, you best know. In any case, Sir John and I agreed
that your response to her behavior was not as unreasonable
as we first judged it to be. After all, you remained in the
kitchen. You were there to tell us of her collapse. Had you
not been, who knows how long she would have suffered
without our knowledge."

Tom Durham, who had heard his mother through, though
he pretended not to, made no comment to me—save for one.
As she turned away from me, with her back to him, he offered me a most prodigious wink.

I carried in the roast and saw that it was somewhat the
worse for wear. In her uncertain state, Mrs. Gredge had
hoped to hurry things along by building a fire that would
well have burned Number 4 Bow Street to the ground if it
were not well contained within our stout kitchen stove. As a
result, it was burnt crisp and near black on the outside but
was near raw on the inside. I knew that before the rest, for
it fell to me to carve it. Lady Fielding made apologies, yet
neither Sir John nor Tom Durham seemed to find fault.

The former, after a judicious bite or two, pronounced it
"a good piece of English beef," adding, "It is near impossible to spoil such a good piece of meat. You chose it, did
you not, Jeremy?"

"I did, yes, sir."

"Well done, boy, well chosen."

And as for Tom, he seemed quite in a transport of delight.
"I had near forgotten how beef in its natural state tasted,"
said he, most enthusiastic, "so long have I endured salt beef.

Jeremy, do please cut me another, a thick one, eh?''

Indeed he had finished the first in no time at all. I jumped
to my task and cut a whole joint for him.

"Kate, dear girl, do these boys have wine to wash it
down?"

"Enough, I'm sure," said she.

"Well . . . fill their glasses. What can it hurt?"

Resigned, she did as he bade.

"Let me assure you, Tom Durham, I recall the taste of
salt beef—and its texture, as well," said Sir John.

"Hard as a rock!"

And the two laughed heartily together, as if sharing a great
joke.

"Then you, Sir John," said Tom, "you've been to sea?"

"Indeed I have!"

"His Majesty's Navy?"

"H.M.S. *Resolute,* seventy guns, no longer in service."

"But tell us about it, sir. When was that?"

Sir John waved his hand, dismissing the matter. "All too
long ago to remember," said he. "I would far rather know
a bit of your experiences. The *Adventure* was detached to
protect East India shipping, was it not?"

"Aye, sir."

"But the East Indiamen are armed—well armed—are they
not? Can they not protect themselves?"

"The East India Company asked for help. The *Adventure*
gave it," Tom declared proudly, "privateers, pirates, frig-
ates, sloops, grabs. What we could not take as prizes, we left
sinking, sir."

"That sounds a proper report. You must give it me in
detail now. But tell me first, Tom, what in the name of God
is a 'grab'?"

"Ah, well, that will take a bit of explaining, and then a
tale to tell."

"Then explain and tell your tale."

Sir John leaned forward in anticipation, drained his glass
of wine, and lifted it toward Lady Fielding for refilling.

"A grab," said Tom, "is a sort of galley—oars and
sails—small and lightly armed, much favored by Angrian
pirates. Now in itself it is nothing, a few small swivel guns,

less than fifty men aboard. Yet they operate in fleets of five or six, sometimes more, along the Malabar Coast. They come in alongside under your guns and make to board. They've taken two East Indiamen just so. Now to the tale . . .''

''By all means the tale!''

''We were sailing just out from the coastline, at dusk it was—and I not much older than Jeremy here. We rounded a point of land protecting a cove, or a small bay—and we found them waiting for us. Of a sudden there came a swarm of these grabs about us, from either side, six at least. In no time they were under our guns—only our own swivel guns were of any use at all then.''

''What, then, did you do?''

Sir John felt about and found his wineglass. He took a great gulp of claret as Tom held him for a moment in suspense.

''We fought them, by God, we fought them!''

What followed was a swiftly told narrative of the battle in which bits and details came forth as on a huge canvas which may seem in whole to be all ajumble. Tom gesticulated wildly over his joint of beef with his knife and fork. He cut the air with them, this way and that. He became quite carried away with the telling of it—the steady musket fire kept up by the marines, the heavy cutlasses handed out quickly to the crew, pistol fire, resolute determination, desperate bravery. Though I had read such tales, I had never heard one told. I was all alive with the excitement of each moment he described. Sir John, too, listened close, held in fascination to the glorious end of it, in which all that had managed to board the *Adventure* had been killed or captured. And the grabs from which they had come were burning and adrift in the night—though one or two had got away—and the British ensign flew yet high above.

Nevertheless, sometime during Tom's recital I happened to glance at his mother. She was neither excited by the tale nor fascinated by his telling of it. Her jaw was set. Her lips were pursed. Her face expressed an attitude of stern disapproval.

Thus it was that when at last it was quite concluded, I was not entirely surprised, as Tom and Sir John seemed to be, when Lady Fielding rose to her feet and announced that she was for bed.

"I'm afraid the powerful sentiment of this day has exhausted me," said she. "Jeremy, you'll clear the table?"

I promised and declared I would do the washing up, as well.

"Good night then, Jack, Tom. Stay up as long as you like. I can see you have much to talk about."

We three stood as she departed. Tom stepped to her, bestowed a kiss on her cheek, and whispered a few words to her just as she made her exit from the dining room.

Resuming our places, we sat in silence for many moments until at last Tom Durham spoke up.

"I fear I was the cause of that," said he.

"Your story?" ventured Sir John. "I thought it a good one."

"Oh, the story, I suppose—yet even more, my refusal to listen to her pleas for me to remain here ashore. I mean to ship out again on the *Adventure*. She thinks she can hold me here by persuasion, and that you, Sir John, will make it right with the Navy. Mine was a seven-year enlistment—and lucky I was to get it. I haven't thanked you properly for that—I never can. But obligation or no, I would return to the sea. It is the life for me."

"Your mother spoke to me of this whilst you and Jeremy went forth after the doctor."

"You understand my feelings perhaps better than she."

"Oh, I understand very well," said Sir John.

"Your own time at sea, of course," said Tom.

"Indeed," said the magistrate. "Those years were happiest in my memory. But tell me, what has happened to that other lad who shipped out with you on the *Adventure?* I believe his name was Jonah Falkirk."

"It was, yes. I regret to say he fell in the very battle with the Angrians I described. He caught a ball in the throat. Though I was separated from him in the fight, I'm told he comported himself well." Tom hesitated but a moment; then he added, "I thought it best not to include that in my account with my mother present."

"You thought well," said Sir John. "But hear me, Tom

Durham, I've a plan to put before you. First, let me ask you, did you return a landsman?''

"No sir, I was made ordinary seaman shortly after the battle with the grabs. Toward the end, with much of our crew Lascars, I was made a foretopman.''

"A foretopman, is it? Well, indeed! I think that excellent, Tom. I commend your progress. And it is specifically that I wished to address—your progress. I may have it in my power to beg for you an appointment as midshipman. What would you say to that, lad?''

Tom Durham was quite overwhelmed. "I know not what to say,'' he blurted, then fell silent as he considered the matter.

"You would then,'' said Sir John, "have an officer's career ahead of you. You would have the advantage of your age, your maturity, and your experience as a seaman on a frigate. But I would not seek for you a midshipman's berth until I were to hear from you that you wanted it.''

"Oh, sir, I want it certain sure,'' said Tom Durham. "You may have no doubt of that. My only concern is this: If indeed you were to win for me a midshipman's berth, I would not wish to return as such to H.M.S. *Adventure.*''

"Tom, I understand entirely, and I think your attitude commendable. You would not want to be in a position of modest command above your former mates belowdecks— indeed commendable.''

"But do you think they would take me as a midshipman with my—with my history?''

"That is my problem, is it not? Remember, I said I *may* have it in my power. I make no promises. I had to know, first, however, if you would accept such a boon if it were offered you.''

"I would, sir, with great thanks.''

"Then with that step done, I may proceed. I believe, by the by, that it would ease your mother's mind considerable if you were a midshipman. She no doubt has the mistaken notion that an officer—even the most junior of officers—is safer aboardship and in particular in battle than are ordinary members of the crew.''

Tom Durham smiled then with knowledge I did not have—

and indeed would never have. "No doubt she does, Sir John."

"It would ease her mind some—and make her proud of you." Then, with an emphatic nod: "I shall see what can be done. But again, I have a question, or perhaps more than one, to ask of you."

"I shall answer as well as I can."

"I am sure you will."

He tapped the table, as if deciding from which angle to attack the problem. Whilst he was thus engaged, Tom gave me an inquiring look, which I answered with a reassuring nod of my head. Then at last Sir John began again at the point where he had left us:

"It is not a usual thing for a ship such as the *Adventure* to return from near three years in the Orient and dock at Tower Wharf. Do you know why you have come to London and not to Portsmouth?"

"But a day ago," said Tom, "I would have said no. Yet last night a most astonishing bit of news ran through the forecastle—near unbelievable, it was. To wit, sir, that one of our officers, Lieutenant Landon, had been confined to quarters and would stand before a court-martial."

"What is the charge against him?"

"Murder—murder of the captain of the *Adventure*."

Sir John seemed somewhat taken aback at this. "Murder, is it?" said he. "And when did this supposed murder take place?"

"That is a thing that struck us all as most peculiar, sir. The captain was washed overboard in a fierce storm more than two years ago. It had gone down as an accidental death until now."

"And why not now? What has changed?"

"Little that we know, except that Lieutenant Hartsell has lodged charges against Lieutenant Landon, an officer well loved by all, a decent man."

"And who is Lieutenant Hartsell?"

"Oh, yes, of course, sorry, sir. He is the first officer of the *Adventure* and has been our acting captain."

"He is not so well loved by the crew?"

"Lieutenant Hartsell is not so popular," said Tom, leaving the impression that he could have said more.

"I see. Jeremy has told me that upon landing at Tower Wharf, the leave party was addressed by an officer of considerable rank."

"That was Admiral Sir Robert Redmond, sir."

"And he asked that any who know of this matter might step forward. None did, said Jeremy."

"For the good reason, sir, that none of us knows anything of it—or so I believe. There were no rumors at the time of the captain's death, no sly suspicions whispered. This came to us as if from the blue."

Sir John said nothing, merely pushed his glass forward to be filled from the bottle of wine which stood nearest me. I obliged him. He sipped at the glass and waited, almost as if he hoped to hear more from Tom. Yet the young seaman apparently had nothing more to tell.

"It may interest you, Tom," said the magistrate at long last, "to know that Sir Robert has written me regarding this matter, asking my opinion in it. Yet he was very parsimonious of details. I find, for instance, talking to you, that a charge of murder is involved here. He alluded simply to a troublesome matter aboard the H.M.S. *Adventure* that would likely result in a court-martial at which he must preside. He and I are old friends. We were shipmates on the *Resolute*. As I said, he has asked for my help. What this will entail I cannot guess, yet as a friend I am bound to give it. Jeremy and I will see him tomorrow afternoon at Tower Hill."

"We will, Sir John?" said I, quite amazed.

"Indeed we will," said he. "I had neglected to mention it to you, I fear. But you are willing to come?"

"Certainly, sir—oh, most certainly."

Not long afterward, whilst their talk continued I made to clear the table, knowing that if I did not attend to it soon, I should be unable to keep my promise to Lady Fielding. The little wine I had drunk had gone to my head, and while it had not made me drunk, it had made me powerful drowsy.

I shuffled the dishes out, as well as the near-consumed roast, leaving only the wineglasses before Tom and Sir John.

As I made my last trip from the table, the young seaman was uncorking one of the bottles of claret held in reserve as he narrated the taking of a privateer along the dangerous coast of Coromandel. He told the tale with the same keen spirit he had shown in telling of the battle with the grabs.

Somehow I managed to do the washing up, or most of it, for I left some for the morning. And as I dragged past the dining room, I heard them talking still, Sir John joining his voice with Tom's to question him on some matter of armament, or other such. These were stories Sir John was eager to hear. I had never known him to be so completely in the thrall of another as listener.

At this distance in time, near thirty years it is as I write this, it seems strange to consider that a matter which caused greater controversy and contention than any of Sir John Fielding's inquiries should have begun thus, with domestic matters and family considerations—a dinner in celebration and welcome. But it is so that we can none of us tell when or how the great events in our lives will begin, nor if, once they have transpired, they will affect us for good or ill. There can be no doubt but that Sir John himself was deeply touched by the series of happenings that began that day so modestly. He spoke of them ever afterward with great bitterness. Yet in my view, if he lost something, he gained much, as well, for we must always count it a gain when we are given the chance to look upon our lives, take stock, and consider what of our past we should put aside.

TWO

*In which friendships
are renewed and
tested*

I know not the time Tom Durham retired, yet when I woke next morning, I found him my bedmate. Having no need to waken him, I slipped quietly from beneath the quilt, dressed hurriedly, and silently left the room, leaving the door ajar behind me. In all probability I need not have been so careful, for my bed companion slept as sound as any man slept this side the grave.

Yet I continued quiet down the stairs, shoes in hand, making my way on tiptoe. Most days I was the first up and about. It was my regular duty to set the oven fire for Mrs. Gredge. Due to her sudden incapacity, which was confirmed by the sounds of labored breathing that issued from her room, I had decided that morning to cook breakfast for the household in her stead. Yet who should I find in command of the kitchen but Lady Fielding? She scurried about most efficient, doing all that needed be done in the cause of breakfast. From her progress, it seemed to me she must have been at work near an hour.

"Am I so tardy rising?" I asked, as I stood before her, rubbing my eyes. "What is the hour?"

"No, no," said she, "nothing of the kind. I was early awake and thought to make myself useful, merely—as you did last night."

"Ma'am?"

"The washing up, I mean."

"Oh, well, that," said I, with a shrug. "I do that always for Mrs. Gredge."

"I, for one, was most grateful to find the job done." Then she clapped her hands in her manner of command: "But sit, Jeremy. Eat your porridge. Have a cup of tea. Then, if you will, you may take a tray to our ailing cook."

So sit I did and ate my fill, as well. She fed me bread and porridge, with a dollop of butter for each. And when she put a cup of tea before me, she poured another for herself and sat down at the table to watch me eat. It seemed a curious thing to do. Though it caused me some slight embarrassment, it clearly gave her pleasure.

"This porridge is ever so good," said I, thinking to flatter her labors.

"Oh, come now, Jeremy. Porridge is but porridge. You may butter it and salt it, both of which I have done—but there is little more that can be done to lend it savor." Yet then she added, relenting, "But I vow it is a pleasure to see you eat it with such relish. It was just so that my young Tom used to do not so long ago." She sighed. "He is not my young Tom now."

"Is he so much changed?"

She bobbed her head most decisively. "Indeed he is," said she. "Not so much for the worse or better—simply altered so that I scarce know him. I believe that Jack understands him now better than I—and I, after all, am Tom's mother. *You*, Jeremy!"

She gestured broadly at me—pointing.

What did she mean? What had I done? "Yes, ma'am?"

"You probably also understand him."

"In what way?"

"Well," said she, "you must tell me. Can *you* understand why he is so eager to return to that . . . that vessel?"

"The H.M.S. *Adventure?*"

"Call it what you like. Why does he wish to go back?"

"If I have it aright from what he said," I began, "it is not so much the ship that attracts him, nor those aboard, it is rather the life upon the sea that moves him so."

"But *why?*"

"Well, ma'am, the physical rigors, the dangers, the chance to prove himself a man."

"As a *man!*" She gave a most joyless laugh at that. "He is but a boy. I do not comprehend, nor have I ever, this pell-mell rush to manhood, this love of danger. It may be," said she, musing upon the matter, "that Tom nor any other has much control upon it; that at some appointed hour in each boy there is an alarum that sends him off in pursuit of who knows what folly whose achievement marks manhood, be it martial, intellectual, or car—" She broke off, as if just having come to a realization of some sort. "Jeremy?"

"Yes, ma'am?"

"I wonder would you do me a special service?"

"Gladly."

"I have a great jumble of clothes that I have so far collected for the Magdalene Home. Perhaps you can help me load them in a hackney carriage. The ladies will unload them swift enough, I'm quite sure. I had intended to ask Tom to do this and accompany me so he would have some notion of what it is has involved me this past year. Yet why not let him sleep, eh? I take it he was deep in the arms of Morpheus when you left him?"

"Oh, indeed yes. He was like unto a dead man."

"Very good," said she. "Well then, after you have brought the tray to Mrs. Gredge, I should like you to go out to Bow Street and flag down a hackney carriage. Bring it round, and we shall load it up together. No need even to mention Magdalene to Tom."

The Magdalene Home for Penitent Prostitutes had been the better part of a year a-birthing, midwifed into existence jointly by Sir John and Lady Fielding. Her idea it was, and his the energy and practical planning that brought it forth to substantial reality. Even I had made a modest contribution, for who but me had carried Sir John's begging letters about town?

Thus was the plan circulated and thus was the money collected. If those first donors did not perhaps shower guineas down upon Sir John and Lady Katherine, they were at least sufficiently generous so that a sturdy house could be bought and rebuilt within as she would have it done, a small staff could be hired, and the doors thrown open at last. The truth was that many were curious what would be made of the place before they were willing to give freely for its support. Most, ladies as well as gentlemen, seemed to question the very existence of *penitent* prostitutes—thus, it was said, the place would go empty. On the same principle, the blades averred the opposite, declaring that the Magdalene Home would no doubt become London's most crowded brothel.

Neither prediction, of course, proved out. Indeed there were, and still are, penitent prostitutes, for the Magdalene Home filled early and, though none of its residents stay for more than a year, remains full to this day. It is not, as some call it to this day, a club for fallen women. Lady Fielding insisted there were those who, given the chance, would leave the life on the streets. If they had a trade, or other means of earning money, every effort would be made to place them in positions where they might earn their way; this was ever accomplished in a few months' time. If they had no trade, as most had not, then they were taught one and given a rough apprenticeship while resident at the Magdalene Home; there is, after all, little work done by women in this world that cannot be learned in a year.

It was hence to the Home, located in Westminster, that she would go on that morning. I brought the hackney carriage round to Number 4 Bow Street. Then, with no help from the driver, I made to fill it with the great pile of dresses, skirts, and shifts I had hauled up from the cellar. There was bare enough space inside for Lady Fielding when at last she emerged, apologizing for her tardiness and showering me with praise for doing all without her assistance (which, in any case, I should have declined).

"I shall be gone a good part of the day," said she. "I mean to inquire among the ladies in the Home for one to help out in the kitchen."

"Mrs. Gredge may soon be able."

"And again she may not." She sighed. "Well, Jeremy, no need to tell Tom much about all this—simply that I shall return when I can do so. I'm sure you can keep him entertained."

"I will do my best, of course."

"And out of trouble."

To that I made no promise but simply waved a goodbye as she mounted into the carriage, and the driver pulled away.

"You must tell me more of this place," said Tom Durham. "A charitable home for young women, you say? Have I understood that aright?"

"I think I should not say more," said I to him.

"Oh? And why not?"

"Because," said I, "your mother wishes you to be kept ignorant of it."

At that he let out a loud yelp of amusement, then continued walking in silence with me for a good long space.

It had been his notion, after all, that we go off on a ramble through Covent Garden. I did a bit of buying out of a list Lady Fielding had provided—vegetables for the stew she would make from what was left of the roast. But most of our time in the Garden had been spent wandering about in no particular pattern from one end of the grand piazza to the other. It contented him so.

As I had expected, his seaman's duds caused quite a stir among the layabouts and lazy boys. They called after him; he smiled merely and waved a greeting. One stepped out before us and attempted to execute the steps of a hornpipe as a kind of jeering salute to Tom, who nimbly demonstrated in his turn how the dance was done proper. The women of the street, too, gave him note with calls, cries, snatches of song, and open invitations. To these he was quietly unresponsive. He did indeed cause quite a stir.

"Ah, Jeremy," said he (following a warm solicitation by one of their number—black-haired and blue-eyed, she was), "I suppose what I should do is pick out the prettiest of the lot and get the awful deed done with. I've money enough for it. I've the appetite, God knows."

Here was a disappointment. I had supposed Tom Durham to be well past me in carnal experience. I had hoped he might supply me with knowledge, even perhaps a bit of wisdom, in these difficult matters. Yet I was certainly sympathetic to his situation and attitude, so like my own they were.

Yet I gave him a matey reply to his complaint: "What is it prevents you then?"

"Lack of opportunity, I suppose."

How could that be? Half the easy women in London seemed to have established themselves here in Covent Garden and the streets surrounding it.

"And the pox," Tom added. "I may as well own up. I am frighted of the pox."

"I share that same fear." I confided it to him in little more than a whisper.

"Well, what do *you* do?" It was as if sixteen-year-old Tom were seeking advice from fourteen-year-old me.

His question was so direct that it left no room for equivocation or subterfuge. I had no choice but to fall back on the truth: "I'm afraid I abstain."

"I'm afraid that's what I have done, too. My messmates think me a freak. The ship's surgeon insisted upon examining me. Hints were dropped from on high. And all this came as the result of my refusal to go with my mates on a sorrowful expedition to a Bombay brothel, from which three did, in fact, return poxy. Strange, don't you think, that my mother means to keep me away from her home for young women and girls because she believes me to be like some ravening wolf who will prey upon her poor lambs?"

"Now there I believe you wrong her," said I.

"What then do you say?"

"They are not lambs, and well she knows it. Perhaps she fears *they* will prey upon *you*. You are, after all, her son. She wishes to keep you from harm—at all cost."

"Well, with that last I agree," said Tom, "at all cost, certainly."

After much back-and-forth through the Garden, we had come to rest at the pillar, which then stood at the exact center of the piazza but now stands there no more. We leaned against its base as we conversed, and though impassioned by our frustration, we spoke in quiet tones. Indeed we spoke so quiet, our heads so close together, that there in the daylight, with the marketing crowd all about, we must have had the look of conspirators. For when Jimmie Bunkins spied us and approached, he hailed us thus:

"Here's a rum sight for me peepers! Tom, the village hustler of yore, decked out natty in a sailor suit, selling me pal Jeremy into a life on the scamp!"

At that, Tom Durham let forth a guffaw, jumped down from the pillar base, and threw his arms open to Bunkins.

"Jimmie B.! The hornies ain't got you yet? I figured you for a scholar on Duncan Campbell's floating academy. Or worse. Your heaters kept you out of the clink, have they?"

I was doubly surprised: first, that the two were obviously well acquainted; second, that Tom should know Covent Garden's flash-talk so well, much less remember it, as he did, after an absence of near three years.

They embraced, as proper friends might. Tom, much the taller of the two, pulled poor Bunkins off his feet. There followed a bit of back pummeling and hand shaking with shouts of "How be ya?" "You've grown to man size," and so on.

Then Bunkins, the reformed thief, turned to me and again expressed his surprise at seeing Tom and me together. I explained, as best I could, our relation. Then Tom gave to me his history with the one he called Jimmie B.

"We were scamps together," said he. "My year in the Garden he was a proper chum. He taught me nap prigging, tick squeezing, and all the dark arts practiced in the precinct. Ain't that so, Jimmie B.?"

" 'Pon my life," swore Bunkins, "and I never had no better student. Just listen how he learned the flash!" Bunkins stepped close and, with an eye toward Tom, spoke quietly to me: "In fact, had he stuck to napping, as I advised, he would not have gone bad with the Beak-runners." Then to Tom: "It was the Beak hisself saved you, was it?" (He referred, reader, to Sir John.)

"It was," said Tom Durham.

"A rum cove," said Bunkins.

"A rum cove," Tom agreed.

"Where's your mate Jonah? You two was shipped off together."

"Well, keep a dubber mum, 'cause all who get a chance at the sea should jump at it, but pal Jonah crapped on the Malabar Coast."

"Mum's the word. But . . . did he get caught napping?"

"Oh no, we left all that ashore, the two of us. Jonah Falkirk died a fair seaman's death in a battle with Indian pirates."

"*Injun* pirates, is it? Crikey, Tom, you got some stories to tell, ain't it?"

"A fair few."

"My cove *was* a seaman," said Bunkins proudly. Then whispered: "They say he was a pirate, but he don't talk none about such."

"*Your* cove, is it? And who might he be?"

"John Bilbo, so he is."

"Black Jack Bilbo? Him who has the gaming house in Mayfair?"

"The same, on'y he don't let just everybody call him that. He asks me to call him Mr. Bilbo, and I obliges, for he treats me fair and looks out for me."

"I'd noticed you'd come up in the world," said Tom, "and not just that you'd grown a few inches. You've a proper suit of clothes on you, and I see your face clear and unsmudged for the first time in memory. It's a new Jimmie Bunkins I see before me."

"Chum, you don't know the half. Mr. Bilbo's got me learnin' to read and to do sums!" He looked craftily about. "How would you like to meet him, Tom Durham? Walk right up and give his daddle a wiggle? He's a good sort, ain't he, Jeremy?"

"Oh, he is indeed," said I. "A friend to Sir John—though it's true they have their differences."

"Well, then, come along—you, too, Jeremy. He speaks good of you, always askin' after Sir John and yourself."

Shaking my head with a show of regret, I held up the bag of vegetables I had bought at the stalls. "If we are to eat tonight," said I, "then I must return with these. Go, Tom, and on the way tell Bunkins the tale of the grabs."

They said their goodbyes and waved. As they started off together, I heard Jimmie Bunkins ask, "What, for Gawd's own sake, might a 'grab' be?"

Walking on by myself across Covent Garden in the direction of Bow Street, I reflected that Tom Durham and his

Jimmie B. seemed an odd pair—but then, so must Bunkins
and I appear equally ill matched.

I had not realized Tom had quite such a history in petty
crime. The two were reformed villains and each had done
his separate form of penance. It would be best, I decided,
not to tell Lady Fielding where her son had gone and with
whom. She might indeed draw the wrong conclusions.

Upon my return, I visited Mrs. Gredge, and then I was free
to seek out Sir John. He had asked me to be ready as soon
as he concluded his court session, and we would travel to
the Navy Board office for the meeting with Vice-Admiral Sir
Robert Redmond. Only minutes before, I had tested the door
to the courtroom and found him engaged in the examination
of a witness. It seemed likely then that this would continue
for quite some while, yet when I left Mrs. Gredge and returned to the courtroom, I found it empty.

Quite in a panic, for I did not wish Sir John to make such
a long trip alone, nor did I wish to lose the chance to meet
an admiral, I went searching and found him directly in the
little alcove that served Mr. Marsden, the court clerk, for an
office.

Yet before I spoke, he had turned his head in my direction.
"Jeremy," said he, "is that you?"

"It is, sir."

"Good, then let us be off. I believe our business is complete, Mr. Marsden?"

"Yes, I shall have the letters on your desk for your signature before I leave tonight."

"Shall we go then, Jeremy?"

Mr. Marsden or Mr. Fuller, or one of the other daytime
gentlemen, had seen to the matter of the hackney carriage.
One stood waiting on the street just outside the door.

As we ascended into the carriage cabin, Sir John called
out our destination to the driver. "Tower Hill," said he.
"The office of the Navy Board."

I brought the carriage door shut behind me and turned to
Sir John with a question:

"Sir, when I came up to you just now at Mr. Marsden's
desk, you knew quite immediate it was me. I had not even

spoken, yet you knew. It has happened just so more times than I can remember. If I may ask, Sir John, how are you able to tell?''

He smiled. ''Oh, it was partly a matter of anticipation,'' said he. ''I was expecting you, after all, for we had agreed to go off together to Tower Hill. But then, too, I may have noted your step. It is a bit quicker and lighter than most heard in Bow Street.''

Then he hesitated but a moment, frowning, as if weighing the wisdom of proceeding. Yet eventually he did:

''There is another matter to be taken into consideration, as well.''

''And what is that, Sir John?''

''You have a smell.''

''I . . . I stink?'' Surely I washed clean enough to rid myself of those noxious odors of the body which so many disguise with perfume.

''No, no, do not take offense, Jeremy. Each of us has a distinctive odor. That is how dogs tell us apart—not by our clothes, which matter little to them, nor by our faces, which they seldom see, but rather by our odor. Their sense of smell is much superior to their sight.''

''And yours is also so keenly developed?''

''Oh, I am no hunting dog, yet I can pick up a scent when the situation requires.'' He laughed at his little joke.

We rode in silence for a time; then I thought to ask:

''What is my smell like?''

''Oh, what indeed?'' said he. ''What makes one face different from another? A longer nose, perhaps? A chin stronger or weaker? It is, rather, the combination of all the elements, their balance, that gives the look of a face—or so I recall from my days with sight. Is that not so? Well then, just so, your smell is compounded of a good many elements—sweat, yours has a rather high odor; milk, you drink a good deal of it; and—oh, other things I suppose. It is not, in any case, an unpleasant smell, if that was your fear. Simply *your* smell.''

''And each has his own?''

''Precisely.''

That silenced me, giving me much to consider, for a good piece of our journey. Sir John kept his quiet, as was often his way. Not until the Tower was in view did he speak up.

"Did you have an opportunity to look in on Mrs. Gredge?"

"I did, sir, yes."

"How did she seem to you? Better? Worse?"

"In some ways better. She was awake and alert, but I noticed some difficulty in her speech, as if her tongue had grown too big for her mouth."

"I noticed that. Apoplexy may be the cause. She must not work again. I fear it would be the end of her. I shall try to contact her sons. There are three, I believe—two in London."

All discussion of Mrs. Gredge's sorry situation ended at that point, for the hackney driver pulled up before a large, imposing building in a row of such imposing buildings. Although they stood within sight of the great rampart and moat, I had not noticed them on my previous day's visit, so taken was I by the prospect of the Tower.

These buildings housed the offices of the Navy Board. In one of them Vice-Admiral Sir Robert Redmond awaited our visit. Up the stairs and inside, we presented ourselves to a petty officer, who chose a seaman from three on a bench nearby and detailed him to accompany us to the proper office. It was then up a good many more stairs and down a long hall. Sir John had no difficulty keeping up but had as little notion as I just where we were headed. There were two unanticipated turns at which we nearly collided with our guide, but at last we found ourselves before the proper door.

The seaman rapped smartly upon it, then bawled forth, "Permission to enter, *sub!*"

Then, from beyond the door, in a voice near as strong: "Permission granted!"

The door was thrown open before us and we two, Sir John and I, entered an outer office at which a young lieutenant presided. The door slammed behind us. We were left in the lieutenant's charge. He stood rigid in full-dress uniform, hat folded beneath his arm, and spoke forth in an unnatural nasal singsong tone, as if issuing orders to us.

"I take it, suh, you are Sir John Fielding?"

"I am he."

"And the young man?"

"My companion."

That seemed to baffle him. He hesitated, then nodded sharply, about-faced, and made for the large door that stood behind his desk.

We were ushered into an inner chamber twice the size of the one we had left. In size and furnishing, the room reminded me of the one occupied by Sir Percival Peeper at the East India Company in Leadenhall Street, not too far away from this very building. Yet where Sir Percival's was a dark room made darker by drawn curtains, the admiral's was all light and bright, the rear wall but one wide window by which I was near dazzled by the sunlight reflected upon the great river below. The Thames was there in full view, its docks and wharves bustling with activity, ships and boats, large and small, plying its streams in both directions.

The man who stood in the midst of this vast picture was of course the same who had addressed the seamen on Tower Wharf. Yet he did not stand long, but rather shuffled quickly around his wide desk and came out to greet Sir John. They managed to shake hands, embrace, and pound one another on the back all at once—no easy feat, as it seemed to me then. And all the while, they kept up a steady chaunt of friendship, braying enthusiastically at one another of the great length of time it had been since they had last been together; delighting in this opportunity to renew their relation; in short, saying all those things that grown men will when reunited after a long separation.

"Yet Jack, who is this lad?" asked Sir Robert. "Is he your son?"

"No, but he will do until such time as nature provides one. His name is Jeremy Proctor, and he aids me in every way possible."

I was so overcome at Sir John's eulogistic presentation of my humble self that I scarce knew what to say—nor do I. I stared so long at him that I near missed Sir Robert's outstretched hand as it was offered. Yet not completely, for at last I grasped and shook it enthusiastically, if perhaps a bit tardily.

"I noticed," said Sir Robert, "that you were quite taken

with our view of the Thames, Master Jeremy.''

"Yes sir, indeed.''

"Well, just to the right there, the largest ship in sight, is the H.M.S. *Adventure*, just returned from duty in India. Do you see it?''

"I do, sir,'' said I. "Yes, I do.''

"Well, that, Jeremy, and that, my dear friend, Jack, is the cause of my problems. But here, sit down, both of you, and I shall make all this plain.''

He gestured in a rather lordly manner toward a couch which stood against one wall. With a touch at Sir John's elbow, I assisted him back toward it. We took our places just as Sir Robert began. He proved in the minutes that followed a talker much given to perambulation, pleased to move around and about the grand space provided him as he told his tale. It struck me later that this habit of restless pacing must have been developed on shipboard; this office seemed to serve him as his quarterdeck.

"I was much dismayed,'' said he, "when I discovered that my promotion to admiral meant the end of my career on the sea. What I liked most about the Navy was life on shipboard, and now that was all over. I was put in charge of Naval Stores at Portsmouth, made certain changes in accounting and inventory that were helpful, all of which led to my nomination to the Navy Board and my arrival here in London. Now, I am greatly in favor of a strong representation of Navy men on the Navy Board. Matters of acquisitions, supplies, and stores are far too important to be left in the hands of politicians and clerks. Don't you agree, Jack?''

"What? Oh? Oh, yes, of course I do.''

Which was said by Sir John in such a way that I half suspected he had not been paying close attention. That, of course, surprised me no little.

"Yet when I arrived to begin my duties less than a month ago I was asked—nay, ordered, for I could *not* refuse—to serve as chief judge on what I was assured would be those *rare* courts-martial that come to be held in London, rather than Portsmouth, since they deal with capital offenses—piracy, mutiny, and of course, murder.

"Well, indeed it turns out that such courts-martial may

not be all that rare, for what do I find waiting for me but a letter that has been passed from hand to hand and office to office for a year or more. When I read it, I quite understood why none had wished to take responsibility in the matter.''

At this point the admiral paused, halting his restless feet at one and the same moment. From the way he peered at Sir John he seemed to be soliciting a comment or a question. Yet the magistrate would grant him only a nod.

"May I read it to you, Jack?"

"By all means, Bobbie. Is it so difficult a matter?"

"Sticky, rather, damned sticky. There are so many irregularities, so many questions suggested by what is said that I for one would like to know what is *not* being said. If you follow?"

"I may," said Sir John, "but I cannot be truly certain about that until you read me the letter in question, can I?"

"What? Oh . . . oh no, I suppose not. I have it here somewhere. If I may . . . just a moment."

He turned his back to us then and rummaged hastily through the papers piled on his desk. He found the letter in question after a brief search and turned back to us, a pair of spectacles perched upon his nose.

"It is addressed," said Sir Robert, " 'To him who is judge in His Majesty's Navy's courts,' and it proceeds thusly: 'Let the following stand as a formal statement of charges against William Landon, Lieutenant, R. N., who did, upon the evening of April 12, 1767, off the Cape of Good Hope and during a fierce storm, push and propel Captain Josiah Markham, R. N., over the taffrail and into the ocean waters where he did drown himself, such act constituting murder and homicide of Lieutenant Landon's superior officer. This act was witnessed personal by the eye of the undersigned, to which he swears by almighty God.' And it is signed, 'Lieutenant James Hartsell, R. N., acting captain, H.M.S. *Adventure*.' ''

"Well," said Sir John, after a moment had elapsed, "it is not very gracefully writ, but he has got the important points in. If you want my opinion on the matter, it will stand as an indictment."

"*Except*, Jack, for the date attached, which is 25 November, 1767—near seven months after the event it describes.''

"And where was this Lieutenant Landon all that while?"

(It seemed to me, reader, as it must seem to you, that Sir John was asking questions to which he knew the answers. He must have decided to say nothing of what he had learned of the matter the night before from Tom Durham.)

"You would suppose, would you not," said Sir Robert, "that he would have been clapped in irons aboard ship, or cast into some Indian prison for keeping until such time as a court-martial could be assembled there in India—would you not?"

"Something of the sort, yes."

"Well then, you would be wrong—as I, too, was wrong, for that also was my supposition. This Lieutenant Hartsell kept Landon on as his acting first officer for the *Adventure*'s entire tour of duty. Landon was not notified of the charges against him until the ship was to anchor off Tower Wharf. Only then was he confined to his cabin."

"Most unusual," said Sir John. "But why, specifically, did this Hartsell make no effort to have the fellow tried earlier in India?"

"Since shortly after the French War the Royal Navy has had no regular presence in India. The East India Company has taken it upon itself to arm its ships heavily that they might protect themselves and their precious cargoes. Perhaps you were unaware."

"And so now those greedy bankers on Leadenhall Street have their own navy, as well?"

"You might say so, yes. But the Admiralty was quite willing to let them have their way. We are, as you must know, cutting back our naval force in near every way possible. Not my wish, nor that of my fellow officers, but the politicians have overruled us. However, having lost one or two of their precious merchantmen to pirates, the barons of the East India Company called upon the Admiralty to send a frigate to seek out those sea-robbers and destroy them. The H.M.S. *Adventure* was the frigate sent. All told, I understand the mission was carried out rather well."

"So what you say, Bobbie, is that there could be no proper court-martial in India for want of Royal Navy officers, captain or above?"

"Exactly so. I did rather lose the point there, didn't I?"

"According to the old Articles of War," said Sir John, "this fellow Hartsell could have tried Landon on the spot, served him up in canvas, and had him tossed overboard—he, after all, being both judge and chief witness for the prosecution. He would not have doubted his own testimony, I daresay."

"I daresay. Yet he must have feared others might, for he told me that he felt he had not the power to proceed in such a way, since he was not captain—only acting captain."

"So you have talked to him already?"

"Indeed I have."

"And to Landon, as well?"

"To him, as well."

"Well, what do you think, Bobbie?"

"What do I think? I think it is, as I said at the start, a damned sticky business. I think that Hartsell's conduct of the matter—the late charges, the fact that he did not immediately relieve Landon of his duties and confine him in some way—leaves him open to question and the charges open to doubt."

"And what does Landon have to say in his own behalf?"

"Very, very little beyond simple denial. But then . . ."

Vice-Admiral Sir Robert Redmond trailed off glumly at that point, quite unable to continue.

"What is the trouble, old friend? Do speak up, please."

"The trouble," said Sir Robert, "is my own inadequacy in this matter, Jack. I know damned little of the law and even less of questioning witnesses, weighing testimony, and so on. I am wholly unprepared for this burden, and I wish profoundly that it had not been placed upon me. Jack, could you—" Again he broke off, but immediately resumed: "As I wrote you in my letter I need help. Could you see your way clear to giving me a hand in this?"

"In what way?"

"Well, I have no art in questioning. I know not how to draw a man out, to trip him up, if need be. To you, I'm sure, this must all be second nature. I had intended to go back to the *Adventure* today to interrogate both men, since I got so little from them yesterday. Would you accompany me—you and the boy? Put questions of your own to them. You know far better than I how it is done.''

''Bobbie, it is many years indeed since I was on shipboard.''

''Is that a yes or a no?''

''A very strong affirmative.''

THREE

*In which accuser and
accused each has
his say*

The same eight-oared pinnace that had conducted the
crewmen of the H.M.S. *Adventure* to shore awaited us
there at the deserted Tower Wharf. A petty officer attended
us there and snapped sharply in salute at the admiral's approach. Sir Robert returned it carelessly in the weary fashion
of high authority.

"At your command, suh!"

"There are three in my party."

"Right this way, suh!"

"Jack," said Sir Robert, "can you manage the ladder?"

"I did it earlier often enough," said Sir John, "and if
memory serves me aright, it was done more by feel than by
sight."

"As you say. Perhaps the lad can precede you and I position you so."

"That should work well enough. Jeremy?"

He placed his hand upon my shoulder, and I led him to
the point indicated by the petty officer. It looked like any
other spot in sight but for the two ropes spiked down into
the timbers of the wharf. I leaned forward right careful and
looked down. Sure enough, there was a good-sized boat there
bobbing below in the Thames at the foot of the ladder. But
it looked to me well filled already with its eight oarsmen—
and good God, it did seem a great distance down! Would
the ladder hold me? Would it hold Sir John's considerable

weight, as well? It did seem so flimsy—and what if the boat should move away just as I had reached the bottom of the ladder? Perhaps I should tell them I had never learned to swim. Perhaps I should be excused from this perilous exercise altogether!

"Jeremy?" prompted Sir John.

"Uh . . . yes sir?"

"You simply turn about and find the first rung with your foot," said he quietly. "Then hold on to the ropes with your two hands and go down rung by rung. The men in the boat will pull you in."

"Yes, Sir John," said I, but hesitated still.

"Turn about now and take my two hands. I shall hold you until you are on your way."

And so held by the blind man, I clambered down, feeling my way with my right foot on one of the wooden rungs, then my left. The strength in his hands gave me courage. He knelt, still holding tight, then released me as I sought the ropes with my hands. With my four extremities engaged, I found it all went much smoother.

I was near down when the ladder suddenly stiffened with added weight. I looked up and found Sir John had begun his descent. There was naught to do but put my faith in the flimsy thing that now supported us both. I scrambled down quick as I could and found myself taken into the brown arms of one of the oarsmen. He said nothing but pointed to a spot forward in the boat where I was to put myself. Somehow, though the rocking of the boat unbalanced me with each step, I managed to find my way to my designated perch betwixt two of the dark crew.

These, I told myself, must be the Lascars of whom Tom Durham had spoken. The fellow to my right, who seemed not much older than myself and no larger, nodded and smiled broadly, revealing a row of teeth of the brightest white. Nodding, I returned his smile, though I'm sure a bit less certainly.

Then, a moment later, Sir John took his place behind me, and moments after that Sir Robert and the petty officer descended into the boat. We cast off and were on our way. Though all eight oars were manned by Lascars, and not many were larger than the fellow beside me, we made swift pro-

gress toward the *Adventure*. And as we approached, I saw
what I had not before noticed: A flotilla of four or five small
boats had preceded us—simple rowboats they were, heavy
laden with goods and ... yes, women. What could women
want aboard a warship? What could a warship want with
women?

Puzzled, I watched as first one and then another of them
ascended a ladder tossed over the side, skirts aflutter yet
moving with surprising nimbleness.

"Ahoy, the bumboat!" shouted the petty officer from his
place at the tiller. "Pull away from the ladder!"

"I will," shouted back the boater, "soon as I'm paid for
hauling the bawds."

"Pull away, or we'll ram you proper!"

Since ours was much the bigger craft, and since we were
bearing down straight upon him, he had no choice but to
obey the petty officer's command. That he did, letting flow
a stream of curses as he went. For some reason this occa-
sioned great hilarity among the other boatmen and their fe-
male passengers. He could but glower in response to their
guffaws and giggles.

The Lascars paid them no heed but pulled up hard against
the H.M.S. *Adventure* in the space occupied a bare minute
before by the rowboat. This time I felt not so intimidated by
the ladder that hung down and, in any case, wished to get
the ordeal over with. I started to rise, but was caught in
midmotion by Sir John.

"Sir Robert precedes us," he whispered in my ear.

Then bellowed forth the petty officer: "Boatswain, pipe
the admiral aboard!"

We waited but a moment until one of those queer tunes
was played on a whistle up above us on the ship. And as the
last notes died down, I felt the boat shift slightly. Casting a
glance over my shoulder, I saw Sir Robert moving up the
ladder with admirable agility. Still I was restrained by the
hand that remained upon my shoulder. I understood the reason when, after another brief pause, a miniature band of fife
and drum started up a martial ditty. There would be a deal
more of strutting and saluting on deck ere we were allowed
aboard.

"The Navy does love its customs and ceremonies, does it not, Sir John?"—this in a whisper over my shoulder.

"All too much," said he to me.

At last things quietened above. The petty officer came forward and whispered in Sir John's ear, who allowed himself then to be led to the ladder. I followed. The next bump of the pinnace against the ship, he was handed the ladder, fixed his foot on a rung as in a stirrup, and started upward. He proceeded confidently, his stick tucked through one of the large buttonholes of his coat. And when he was near the top, the petty officer beckoned me over. He grabbed at the ladder and held it for me as I mounted—then up I went.

Though I had farther to go to reach the top, I found it not near so hard going up as it had been coming down. Life on the deck above seemed to have returned to normal. Seamen crowded the rail and called out in rowdy style to those in the little boats that circled behind me beyond the pinnace—from which they were answered in kind:

"Hey, you, Jolly Jack Tar, I've enough spirits to keep you drunk a week, or a month, or a year!" Another voice: "Rum or gin or beer!"

"And a woman to share it with," piped a husky soprano, "who'll bring you good cheer!"

"Just look at these bubs," cried a fourth. "You'll hold them ever so dear!"

Thus they rhymed their pitches and were answered rudely from the deck with catcalls and whistles. It was Covent Garden on the Thames! Indeed, I had no notion of the commerce carried on around and about the great ships anchored in the river. (It continues thus, or so I am told, unto this day, reader.)

When at last I reached the rail, there was none to help me over, so intent was that gang of seamen on the hucksters below. Yet I threw a leg over and came down light upon the deck with what I reckoned to be good shipboard style.

There were sounds of music from a lively fiddle, raucous singing, and the clop-clop-clop of dancing from below. Through a large open space in the deck I spied men and women carrying on in most outlandish fashion, cutting figures among the tethered cannon. In no wise had I expected such merriment aboard a warship. The admiral had done nothing to dampen their fun.

Where was he? Where was Sir John? Not below, surely. I surveyed the level whereon I had dropped and saw no trace of them there, none but common seamen and a few marines. Yet there was a deck above this one to the rear of the ship— "aft," as I was to learn soon enough was how one said it rightly. There was a narrow stair ("ladder") leading upward. I hied over to it at good speed and hopped up to the top. My way was barred at that point by another whom I would have called a boy, though he may have been a year older than me. He wore a uniform that was certainly not seaman's dress, yet was not quite that of an officer's. I was not sure, in other words, just who he was, nor what authority he had. However, I was sure that Sir John, Sir Robert, and another whom I took to be the acting captain stood together only a bit beyond him. I wanted past this bothersome boy.

"Here, you," said he to me, "get down where you belong. Such as you is not allowed up here unless summoned—as you should well know."

Not merely his words but his manner, as well, were most arrogant. I sought to explain just who I was and why I should be allowed to join those I had come with. He gave no ear whatever to what I said, but simply thrust out his chin and continued bullying at me in a low and threatening tone of voice:

"A landsman, are you? Just pressed into service? Call me Mr. Boone and be sure that I shall make life aboard ship hell for you if you do not get belowdecks damned quick."

"But you do not *understand*," said I. "I am *not* one of your crew. If you would but listen to—"

"Must I thrash you on the spot? I'll have you cobbed. I'll . . . I'll . . ."

Then he signaled his intent by setting his jaw and raising his two open hands before him. Just as he leaped at me across the three feet that separated us, I jumped neatly to my left, leaving an empty spot where I had been and a free passage down the narrow stairs—which he took, headfirst, then heels over head, tumbling quite uncontrollably to the bottom, where he lay in a moaning heap.

Though I found it difficult to feel great sympathy for him, since he had clearly intended to put me down on the deck in a similar state, I did regret the incident and hoped blame would not be put to me. However, I was quite unprepared for the response of the crewmen. They gathered round silently. Then, as he attempted weakly to rise, there were a few giggles from the crowd, one right hearty guffaw, then suddenly all joined in and the ship rang with laughter at Mr. Boone's misery. They came from belowdecks to see, and then these, too, became quite panicked with hilarity to see the boy struggling painfully to his feet. None moved to help him. I could only surmise that young Mr. Boone was not much loved by the crew.

"What is this? What has happened here?"

I looked up and found, standing beside me, that officer I took to be the acting captain—which is to say, the author of that statement of charges which Sir Robert had read aloud to us. He was, as the admiral, of a rubicund complexion but appeared to be in a high emotional state, as if choleric by nature. Tall he was, as well, with a loud, commanding voice.

"He seems to have fallen down the stairs, sir," said I, all innocent.

He gave me a sharp look but made no reply to me. Instead, he addressed himself to the crew: "You men, leave off that laughing. It is goddamned unseemly is what it is."

The merriment ended more sudden, even, than it had begun.

"Now, two of you—you and you—" He pointed them out of the crowd. "Help Mr. Boone down to the surgeon."

"No longer with us, sir," spoke up one of the designated helpers.

"Then take him to the surgeon's mate, you fool!"

"Aye-aye, sir!"—with a salute.

And then, suddenly solicitous, the two seamen gently brought Mr. Boone erect, and he hobbled off between them toward belowdecks.

With that, the acting captain turned abruptly on his heel and in a few long strides returned to Sir John and the admiral. I trailed along after him and quietly took a place next Sir

John. I felt his hand grip me strong upon the shoulder. I was certain I should have some explaining to do.

"I suggest," said the acting captain, "that we continue our discussion in my cabin—that is if you are agreeable."

Sir Robert murmured his assent.

"Mr. Grimsby," said—yes, his name was Hartsell, as I remembered at last—"send down for one of the other midshipmen to take Mr. Boone's place, will you?"

At that request, a young officer stepped forward, whom I had not before noticed. He seemed to have stood apart from the rest, as if to distance himself from the discussion.

"I'll attend to it, Mr. Hartsell," said he.

"Gentlemen?"

All moved forward as Lieutenant Hartsell showed us the way, Sir John and I bringing up the rear. As another, even narrower stairway presented itself, my blind companion kept his hand firmly upon my shoulder. Just as we were about to descend, he held me back a bit.

"Had you anything to do with that?" he whispered sharply. "Did you push that midshipman down the ladder?"

"Sir John," said I, "I give you my word most solemnly that I did not touch the fellow."

He hesitated but a moment. Then: "I accept that, Jeremy."

Then a pat on the shoulder and we began our descent.

"Careful here, sir, it is quite tight."

"You need not tell me," said he. "At your age I had walked many a ladder such as this one. I allow, though, I was closer your size then than mine today."

We were brought into a cabin, the first of a few along a very narrow corridor, which by shipboard standards was most spacious. It was the captain's cabin, which, Lieutenant Hartsell explained, he had occupied since the death of Captain Markham. There were chairs enough for all, but out of respect to Sir John, I chose, rather, to stand beside him, as if in attendance.

"Now that we are seated here in the privacy of your cabin, Mr. Hartsell," said Sir Robert, "I wish you to repeat the story as you told it to me the day past."

"Must I?" He sighed. "It is all put plain in the Statement of Charges."

"Nevertheless."

"Ah, well, as you will. We were hit by a gale a day out of Cape Town so that our position was direct south of the Cape of Good Hope. And—"

"If I may interrupt you at this point," said Sir John. "I noted when Sir Robert read your Statement of Charges against Lieutenant Landon, while it was specific in most particulars, it was curiously vague as to your exact compass position at the time of this lamentable occurrence. In fact, none at all was given. Why was that?"

"Indeed you have interrupted me," said Lieutenant Hartsell most coldly. "I will allow the interruption and answer your question if you will tell me on whose authority you ask it. You were introduced to me, Sir John Fielding, as the Magistrate of the Bow Street Court. Since these events occurred many thousands of miles from London, I cannot, for the life of me, understand what interest you should have in them."

With that, the acting captain of the H.M.S. *Adventure* folded his arms and waited for a reply. For his part, Sir John sat with a tolerant smile upon his face and waited also for the reply, for he knew that indeed it must come from one other than himself.

Vice-Admiral Sir Robert Redmond cleared his throat a bit sententiously. At last he spoke up: "Sir John is here on my invitation," said he, "and you may accept it that he speaks upon my authority. He is an experienced investigator in criminal matters."

"But this is a matter for a naval court."

"And the matter is murder, which is most certainly an act criminal in nature—I'm sure you agree. So please answer the question, Lieutenant Hartsell. I am curious about it myself, now that it has been raised."

"Very well then. A compass reading was taken at the beginning of the day, April 12, 1767, and recorded in the ship's log. As the day went on, the storm increased in intensity until it reached full gale condition sometime in the afternoon. The waters off the Cape of Good Hope run high even in the best weather, as you know, Sir Robert, and we were fighting waves of near ninety feet. The *Adventure* laid along so perilously on that fateful day that we were moving horizontal port and starboard through most of the worst of it. We were taking on water. There was no opportunity to take a second reading to mark the event under such conditions—though I allow it should have been done. There was no reading taken, in fact, until next day when the storm had abated. We had made virtually no progress on our course, for most of the time we were simply riding out the storm."

"Quite understandable," said Sir John. "But tell me, Lieutenant Hartsell, was the captain on deck during all this— that is, during the worst of the gale?"

"No, he was not." The reply came in a somewhat guarded manner.

"And where was he?"

"In his cabin—in *this* cabin. Captain Markham was ill. In fact, he had been ill through most of the voyage. I acted in his stead a good bit of the time. He trusted me to do so. I held the rank of captain myself during the last two years of the French War."

"Oh?"

"Reduced in rank in order to remain in the service," said Sir Robert. "Only the best were kept. Lieutenant Hartsell was captain of a frigate at twenty-six. He, better than most, could wait out such a reduction. His record during the war and after has been exemplary."

"I'm sure it has," said Sir John. "But I am curious about Captain Markham's belated appearance. When did he make it? Why did he make it?"

"I sent for him. It seemed to me we were about to lose our foremast. I wanted his judgment as to whether we should take it down. I was reluctant to make such a decision on my own. In the event, it held—though it showed splintering. We replaced it in Bombay."

"Was that what Captain Markham counseled?"

"I had not the chance to talk to him before he—before he was pushed overboard."

"How was he summoned?"

"I sent Lieutenant Landon for him."

"Mmmm. Interesting. And he returned with him?"

Lieutenant Hartsell had begun to show signs of exasper-

ation at Sir John's close questioning. I had little doubt he
would show more as this line continued. Sir Robert, though
he had little to say, seemed quite upset by all that passed
between them.

"Yes, after some delay they made their appearance. That
was when—"

"Beg pardon if I interrupt again, but at what hour was
this?"

"*How should I know*? Good God, I had my hands full just
keeping the *Adventure* afloat. I had a foremast I feared might
not last the blow. I had a hundred separate causes for concern. The least of them, you may believe me, was at what
precise hour and minute the captain made his appearance on
the poop and was pushed into the sea by Lieutenant Landon!" This was delivered in such a state of agitation that
Hartsell was near panting by the time he got it out. But,
recovering his composure, he added: "Put it in the afternoon,
midafternoon, whatever that might be in shore time."

Sir John nodded thoughtfully. "Very well," said he, "put
it at that. Yet what concerns me is just how, when you were
in the distracted state you have just described, you could be
so certain of the act you saw Lieutenant Landon commit."

"Well, Sir John Fielding, let me tell you what I saw."

"No, I think not," said Sir John. "It would be far better
if you *showed* us. With your permission, Sir Robert, I should
like us all to return to the poop deck that we might see a
demonstration."

"What? Well, I . . ." Caught off guard somewhat, the admiral fumbled a bit before agreeing that it seemed quite a
good idea to him. "No time like the present I always say,
eh?"

And so we returned the way we had come—Sir Robert
leading the way this time, we following, and Lieutenant Hartsell bringing up the rear. Once on the poop deck, the other
two looked to Sir John for directions.

"Now," said he to Hartsell, "will you fix as near as possible the place you occupied on the poop when you observed
Lieutenant Landon commit the alleged act?"

"I was not on the poop. I had been, but I went below to
the quarterdeck."

"Oh? Then you were not very near."

"I was near enough."

"Well and good. Let us go down to the quarterdeck. Find your position there then. Jeremy, you stay here, and play the role of Lieutenant Landon. But who can play Captain Markham? There is another officer here on deck, I believe?"

The officer detailed earlier by Hartsell stepped forward.

"Yes, sir, Lieutenant Grimsby—at your service."

Sir John turned in his direction with a smile of welcome. "Ah yes, Lieutenant, would you be willing to take part in our little charade?"

"Of course, sir."

"Very good. If you will then remain here on the poop with my young assistant, Jeremy Proctor, we three will descend to the quarterdeck, and Lieutenant Hartsell will place you two according to his memory. Does that satisfy all here?"

Although Hartsell offered no disagreement, his objection to this exercise was writ plain upon his face. Nevertheless, he brought them down and after a false try or two, chose a place for himself on the right ("starboard") side of the deck up close to a cannon.

As this action took place, the crew left off its banter with the bumboats on the river below and quietened down. They looked on at a distance, evidently mindful of the meaning of all this shifting and moving about there on the quarterdeck. Mr. Grimsby and I watched, as well, ready to play our roles as we were directed. That came soon enough.

"Now, Mr. Hartsell, if you will tell our two actors where to go?"

"Over here, close," said Hartsell, "at the corner of the poop nearest the starboard ladder."

We moved to the place he had appointed. Mr. Grimsby knew precisely what was meant.

"Next the taffrail," added Hartsell.

We stood then close to the polished rail that rose as a barrier and ran all around what they called the poop deck. I noted that the starboard ladder just to my left was the one where I had met Mr. Midshipman Boone and down which he had tumbled.

In level distance, Hartsell was no more than ten feet away, perhaps less. Yet standing on the poop deck, we were elevated a good six feet above him.

"In which direction were you facing, Mr. Hartsell?" asked Sir John.

"Why, towards them, of course." Yet he stopped and considered. "I see your point," he added. "No, as they approached the point where they now stand, I was facing for'd. But, wondering at their delay, I turned, and that was when I saw them just as they are now."

"Just as they are now?"

"No, no, of course not. Captain Markham had his back to the taff, and as I looked, Lieutenant Landon thrust out with both hands and sent him straight into the sea."

"Amazing," said Sir John. "But the taffrail presents a considerable barrier, does it not? It would not be easy now for Jeremy to push Mr. Grimsby into the Thames."

"Yes, but we had laid hard along to starboard. The two were near horizontal at that moment."

"As you were, too."

"Certainly, as I was, too. I had grasped onto this eighteen-pounder to hold myself steady."

"Tell me, Mr. Hartsell, as you mentioned before, the approximate time all this happened was midafternoon—that being the case, what were the conditions as to light? I take it the sun was not shining?"

Hartsell threw a wild look at the admiral, as if questioning Sir John's sanity. "With all due respect, sir, have you ever been in a full gale on the sea before?"

"As it happens, yes, I have."

"Then you must know how deep dark it gets. It was almost as night in the daytime."

"And it was raining?"

"Yes, dammit, it was raining."

Sir John remained silent for a good long moment, and when at last he spoke, he did so in a deep, resonant tone that could be heard by all: "Then, sir, I question that you could see anything at all as clearly as you say. Let me remind you of what you have said. It was near as dark as night. Rain was coming down. And you viewed the poop at an angle so

queer that you yourself were holding on to a gun to keep
from going over the side yourself. How can you be so sure?"

Hartsell hesitated not a moment, but spoke out clear that
all might hear him too: "I saw what I saw."

"Jeremy!" the magistrate called to me. "Are you still up
there with Mr. Grimsby?"

"I am, sir," said I.

"Extend your hands against him, as if to push him overboard. But leave them so, in that position."

I did as he told me. Perhaps carried away by the moment,
I landed with a mite too much force against Mr. Grimsby.

He let out an "Ugh!" and whispered, "I do believe you
could push me into the river, boy. Ease off a bit."

That I did and whispered my apology, though keeping my
open palms against his chest.

"Is it done so?" Sir John inquired.

"Just so," said I.

"There then," said he to Hartsell, "look upon that, if you
will. That must approximate what you say you saw, sir.
Could Lieutenant Landon not have been reaching out to Captain Markham to pull him back? Could his intention not have
been, rather, to save him?"

To that Hartsell did no more than repeat: "I saw what I
saw."

An angry murmur started among the crew. Sir Robert
heeded it, frowning, and murmured something in Sir John's
ear. In response, Sir John did naught but shrug.

"That will be the extent of our questions," said the admiral to Hartsell.

"I should hope so. Will you require anything more of
me?"

"As it happens, yes," said Sir Robert. "In these extreme
circumstances, I must request that you hand over the ship's
log."

"That will be put in your hands ere you leave the *Adventure*. Am I dismissed then? I wish to return to my cabin. This
has, as you may suppose, been most trying."

"You are dismissed with my thanks, Lieutenant Hartsell."

Saying nothing to Sir John, Hartsell saluted the admiral
smartly and made for the poop deck, avoiding Mr. Grimsby

and myself by choosing to ascend the port ladder.

"Jeremy?" Sir John called out. "Would you come down here a moment? And Mr. Grimsby, if you will remain where you are."

And so it was. Mr. Grimsby, a friendly sort by any measure, gave me a pat on the back and a "Good fortune for you," as I left down the ladder. Sir John awaited me, somewhat apart from the admiral. I went to him, and he pulled me close.

"Jeremy," said he to me, "I wish you to position yourself behind the helm and tell me if you can see all or any part of Mr. Grimsby."

"The helm, sir?"

"The great wheel with which the ship is steered."

"Ah, yes."

There was no missing the helm once he had described it to me. The thing stood, unattended, just away from the wall of the poop deck. I stepped behind it and looked up to my right. There was Mr. Grimsby, or most of him—cut off at the knees he was. He saw me as I saw him and gave me a mock salute. I returned to Sir John and gave my report. As was so often his way, he merely thanked me, giving me no idea what the significance of this might be.

Vice-Admiral Sir Robert summoned us then and took us through a short corridor. As he pounded stoutly on the door, I looked about me and realized that Lieutenant Hartsell was only a few steps away in the captain's cabin. Strange place a ship such as this one was, wherein accuser and accused resided in such proximity. Indeed it was not even locked from the outside. Lieutenant Landon had nothing but his word of honor to keep him prisoner there.

The door opened, and he was revealed to us, a young man not yet twenty-five I should say, spare of build and lean of face. His dark hair he wore long. The dark expression in his eyes brightened only a bit when he recognized his visitor.

"Sir Robert," said he, "kind of you to look in on me again. Come in, all of you, and please seat yourselves."

His manner struck me as quite informal, considering his situation. He was introduced to Sir John, told of his qualifications, and the reason for this visit. Yet as he eased himself down into a chair and put aside the Bible he had been reading, the light seemed to fade from his eyes, as if merely to discuss the charges against him with others were to remind him that his case was quite hopeless. He seemed almost to accept his state. He gave the impression of a man already condemned, one simply awaiting his appointment with the hangman.

Had he been present during Sir John's interrogation of Hartsell he would not be in such a state, I told myself. Had he heard him trip up the acting captain with his own words he would have taken heart. Of that I was sure certain.

Nevertheless, as they began to converse on the matter, he talked as listless as he looked. When Sir John asked him if he was on the poop deck with Captain Markham at the time the captain went overboard, he agreed that he was and added that he was there on the orders of Lieutenant Hartsell.

"Would you describe for me the action that led to the captain going into the sea?"

"We, the captain and myself, came up top," said Lieutenant Landon, "and I looked for Lieutenant Hartsell on the poop, where he had been. He had specifically told me to bring him there, yet he was then on the quarterdeck. I struggled to assist the captain in the direction of the starboard ladder, yet then we laid along hard to starboard, quite flattened against the sea we were. I thought it likely we would be swamped and sink. The captain flew out of my grasp and against the taffrail, and I saw him lose the deck with his feet and begin to slide over the side. I grasped at him first at his coat, then at his feet as he went. There was no holding him. I was left with naught but his shoe in my hand."

"Have you a notion why Lieutenant Hartsell is convinced you were pushing the captain, rather than attempting to pull him back?"

"None, none at all. All I can do is insist I did not push the captain. I tried, rather, to save him."

Had this last been said with force and certainty, it would have stood as an impressive denial. As it was put forth by Lieutenant Landon, however, the words seemed to drop from him indifferently, uncertainly. He did, in fact, end the speech with a shrug, as if to imply that it made little difference whether he denied his guilt in the matter or accepted it.

"Young man," said Sir John sternly, "you must do better than that in your own behalf, or you are sure to hang."

Perhaps it was the prospect thus put before him, or perhaps it was merely Sir John's tone of voice, but the effect upon Lieutenant Landon was such that he immediately sat up straight in his chair, gave a sharp nod, and said, "Yes, sir." Had he been standing, I daresay he would have given the magistrate the salute he had denied the admiral.

"I have but two more questions to put to you," continued Sir John. "First, since you do not deny your hands were outstretched toward the captain, the question becomes simply one of interpreting your action. Can you consider why Lieutenant Hartsell should interpret your action in a manner so negative?"

As in the captain's cabin, I had taken a place beside the chair wherein Sir John was seated. From that vantage, I saw a look, or perhaps better stated two looks, pass between Lieutenant Landon and Sir Robert. The lieutenant's was inquiring; the admiral's was cautionary. All this went between them so quickly that there was only the briefest pause before Landon's reply came.

"I have given thought to it, of course, sir," said he forthrightly, "but I can give no good reason."

"Well, think on it more, for it is an important matter. My second question is like unto the previous one. Is there any reason for you to have moved with violence against Captain Markham? That is to say, had you any motive to do him harm?"

"None. In fact, I doubt that the captain even knew me."

"You *what*? That is a most odd thing to say. You were his second officer, were you not?"

"Yes sir, but as you may already have heard, the captain was ill through most, if not all the voyage. He barely ventured from his cabin."

"In what way was he ill?"

"Since I am no medico, my opinion would be worth little. You had best take that up with the ship's surgeon, Donald MacNaughton. I understand, however, that he has left the ship."

"We shall do that, I presume. But for now, I have done with questioning you, Lieutenant Landon."

So saying, Sir John rose and tapped his stick smartly on the cabin floor. I took his side and we began moving toward the door of the cabin. Somewhat surprised by this quick exit, the lieutenant and the admiral got swiftly to their feet and were only beginning to say their goodbye when I had the door open and Sir John had stepped out into the corridor. As I followed him, I heard Sir Robert inquire if the young lieutenant was well fed and if he was allowed from his cabin for exercise at some time during the day. That seemed to me curiously solicitous under the circumstances.

It seemed to me curious also that bare ten words passed between Sir John and Sir Robert once they were together. Sir Robert remarked upon his need to return to his office at the Navy Board. Sir John agreed that it was growing late. The ship's log was delivered to the admiral by a midshipman at the ship's ladder. At that Sir John did no more than emit a skeptical grunt. And nothing more was said the length of our voyage from ship to shore in the pinnace of the *Adventure*.

Again, at the Tower Wharf I was last up the ladder. Considering the silence they had kept, I was somewhat surprised to hear them, as I reached the top, talking loudly and in such animated fashion that I could have sworn that the two old friends were arguing. In fact, they were. Whatever passed before I cannot say, but as I crawled up and over, I saw the admiral butt his fist into his open palm.

"By God, Jack," he was saying, "it wasn't proper, the way you talked to him. He knew it wasn't. I knew it wasn't. And he knew I knew."

"What does it matter?" replied the magistrate. "I treated him as I would have any witness."

"But he was not *any* witness. He was the captain of the H.M.S. *Adventure*."

"Acting captain."

"Don't quibble with me. He has served as captain de facto for over two years. And to talk to him as you did before his crew—expressing *doubt*. What was it you said? 'I doubt you could see anything as clearly as you say.'"

"Well, I did doubt it, Bobbie, and I do still."

"But to say as much before his crew is tantamount to inciting mutiny."

"Nonsense," said Sir John. "A captain who does not have the confidence of his crew is no captain at all."

"So we were once taught. But the truth of it is that a man in Hartsell's position must deal with criminals and cutthroats, whatever the press gangs scrape up from the bottom of society. To keep *their* confidence, a man must sometimes be hard, may sometimes seem inflexible and capricious, but above all, he must *not* allow them to doubt him."

"I deal with such as you describe every day at Bow Street, and in my experience, fairness and consistency do far more to win their respect and confidence."

Clearly, Sir Robert had grown weary of the argument. He took Sir John by the arm and moved him to the wharf stairs, as he beckoned me also to come along. Well did I know that my chief and master seldom allowed himself to be led in such a way; a touch at the elbow was all he would put up with as a rule, for he liked not being thus reminded of his blindness. Yet from his old chum he would tolerate it.

Thus they walked in step half the length of the long wharf, I following close behind. At last, as they descended the stairs, the admiral spoke up in tribute to the magistrate:

"I give you credit, though, Jack. You got far more out of Lieutenant Hartsell than I could have done, whatever your method."

"That is my job, Bobbie. I fear, however, I did not do near so well with the accused. You seem to be on good terms with the young man; you must encourage him to think and speak more forcefully in his own defense. He seems almost languid, as if given in to despair. Have you named a counsel for his defense yet?"

"Not as yet, no. There are not many to choose from here in London."

"He would be Navy, of course?"

"Of course."

"I would advise him—and I *will* advise him, if you like—but I would tell him to attack Hartsell's story and to seek other witnesses among the crew."

"None yet has come forward from the crew—at least not from those let out on leave. But as for what you propose as regards Lieutenant Hartsell . . ."

"What? You suggest it might create doubt? That, if you'll pardon me, is precisely what should be created. And don't tell me about the crew. None will be present."

"But Jack, Hartsell *is* the captain."

"And all he need do is repeat, 'I saw what I saw'—is that it? He seemed almost to be saying, 'I am who I am,' did he not?"

"He *is* the captain."

"Ah, Bobbie, Bobbie, the law of the ship is something quite apart from the law of the shore. I begin to appreciate that more and more. But let us not part with the slightest rancor between us, old friend. We have too many good memories for that. Let me propose something. Come to dine with us tomorrow evening, and we shall not say a word of this matter—not one word! It will be humble fare, but there will be plenty of wine, I promise."

They had come to a halt there on Tower Hill. The building which housed the offices of the Navy Board lay close by. The admiral grasped Sir John's hand and clasped it warmly in both of his.

"I should be happy to, Jack," said he. "The mess at the Tower leaves much to be desired, even for an old bachelor such as myself, yet since I have not yet taken up permanent lodging, I have little choice."

"Tomorrow night at eight then? Number Four Bow Street above the court."

"Tomorrow at eight—and I look forward to meeting your good wife. Till then."

He pulled away then and hurried across the street, a considerable figure in his long coat and bouncing epaulets. He had not taken notice to say goodbye to me—but after all, he was an admiral, was he not?—and I but one of Sir John's crew.

"Now, Jeremy, if you can find us a hackney, we shall be on our way."

"One waits just ahead," said I.

"Well, signal him forward. I have had enough of up and down ladders and tramping about."

Moments later, we were settled inside the carriage and Sir John was bemoaning the necessity that had driven him to invite Vice-Admiral Sir Robert Redmond to dinner.

"Kate will not be happy," said he glumly, "not with this matter of Mrs. Gredge hanging fire. Perhaps the old soul will be sufficiently recovered to help out a bit. Perhaps not."

"But you said you were driven by necessity, sir," said I. "I don't quite . . ."

"Ah, well, the matter of Tom Durham's appointment as midshipman, of course. I hope to enlist Sir Robert's help. I became so caught up in the interrogation of those two— damned rude I was, I admit it—that I quite forgot I had come to beg. Then that final wrangle with Bobbie, it would have been impolitic to mention it then as an 'Oh, by the by.' No, tomorrow evening it will have to be. We must begin on the matter as quickly as ever we can."

We rode along in silence a good long way, and as we went, Sir John began tapping on the floor of the carriage with his stick. Was he deep in thought or merely impatient? Since I had a matter to broach I waited a bit, but in the end thought it best to come out with it.

"Sir John?"

"Yes, boy, what is it?"

"When you asked Mr. Landon if there was any reason why Mr. Hart-sell might have thought ill of his motion to grasp at the captain, I saw that young lieutenant give a look—oh, with eyebrows raised—to the admiral, and the admiral answered with a frown and a slight shake of the head."

"Just so, eh? Permission requested, permission denied. Well, that is interesting, is it not?"

"And they did seem to be on somewhat informal terms."

"Yes, indeed. Like those mountains of ice that float in the north seas, there is more to all this beneath the surface than above, and far more than I would like."

A surprise awaited us upon our return. Lady Fielding had returned from the Magdalene Home for Penitent Prostitutes and had in tow a girl to help in the kitchen. Since she had

declared her hope to find one such, this was no surprise. But
what quite astonished me was that the girl in question was
none other than Annie, the saucy and flirtatious slavey from
the kitchen of the late Lord Goodhope. I recalled that Sir
John had expressed the fear she might wind up on the streets,
and it was by that devious route she had come to our kitchen.

When Sir John and I made our entry we found the two
women engaged almost gaily in the preparation of our dinner—peeling, chopping, talking as women will in the
kitchen. It was to be a stew from the leavings of last night's
beef—rich stuff that was for stew meat—and the good smell
of it quite permeated the place. Mrs. Gredge was nowhere to
be seen.

Lady Fielding presented her—Annie Oakum—as a girl
from the Magdalene Home with some skill in cooking. And
she added: "Annie tells me the two of you met a year ago,
Jack, in the course of the infamous Goodhope matter." All
smiles she was, like a teacher presenting her best pupil.

"Why, indeed!" said Sir John, offering his hand. "Of
course I remember you, Annie—and pleased I am that our
paths have crossed once again."

Thus he greeted her as an old friend. She, for her part,
was the very exemplar of politesse, curtseying, giving him a
"sir" every third or fourth word. She seemed determined to
make a good impression upon him, and by and large she
succeeded. To me she threw a wink.

Inviting Lady Fielding upstairs for "a talk," Sir John left
us for his small study. I knew better than she the matters he
wished to talk to her about. She seemed perplexed and a bit
puzzled.

"Can you keep a hand on things till I return?" she asked
Annie.

"I'm quite capable, mum, I swear, you've no need to
worry."

"I shan't, Annie. You're in charge now."

Then she turned to me with a frown and said, "Jeremy,
have you any idea where Tom has got to? He seems to have
been gone quite some time."

In truth, I did have an idea, yet the one I had would only
have distressed her. (How could I have told her he had gone

off to meet an ex-pirate?) And so I simply reported to her the facts as I knew them.

"When last I saw him he was off with an old chum a-walking through Covent Garden."

"I do hope it was not one of those who led him into crime."

"He's all right," said I. "I know the fellow myself."

"Would you vouch for him?"

I gave that a moment's thought. "Yes," I told her at last, "I would."

"Very well," said she, "but if Tom is not back soon, I shall send you out to fetch him home."

Having said that, she gave a firm nod and headed for the stairs. We two watched her go. Once Lady Fielding was out of sight and safely out of earshot, Annie burst forth with a great giggle.

"You shoulda seen your face," said she, "how your mouth hung open when you spied me. It was all I could do to hold m'own face together."

"Well," said I in a bit of a pout, "I was surprised to see you."

"Oh, I daresay you was." And she giggled again. "But best you get used to seeing me here, Jeremy, old friend, for I'm your new cook."

"Are you as certain as all that? Mrs. Gredge may soon be up and about."

"That ain't how her ladyship sees it. She said she'd give me a chance, and a chance is all I ask. I've no wish to go back to what I left."

"Why?" said I, all too naive. "Is life at the Magdalene Home so insufferable?"

"That ain't what I meant."

"Oh." I considered for a moment what she *had* meant. Then my young mind turned to more practical matters. "But Annie, forgive me for asking, but can you cook? I thought you and Meg were but washers of pots and pans."

She pulled herself erect and raised her chin. "Well, Mr. Jeremy Smartyboots, it shoulda been plain to you that Meggie and me did all the cookin' in that house—or most of it—as well as the washin' up. Cook called us her 'prentices and taught us a good bit, yet she never signed papers for us. I'm not sure she could, being a woman. Still and all, we learned a thing or two from her, we did.''

"Have you . . ." I began timidly. "Have you heard anything from Meg since she left for Lancashire?"

"So you fancied her just as she fancied you?"

I ignored the question, for it was one to which she expected no answer.

"No, I ain't heard a word from Meg, nor am I likely to. She can't write, and I can't read."

It was then that Tom Durham saved himself from the indignity of being fetched back from the pirate's lair. He came tramping up the stairs and into the kitchen, wearing a broad smile which bespoke a pleasant afternoon spent in the company of Jimmie Bunkins and his cove, Black Jack Bilbo. To me he seemed in no wise exceptional, nor different from the fellow I had been with earlier that day.

Yet when I greeted him and turned to Annie to manage an introduction of sorts, I found her who was usually so quick with her tongue quite struck dumb. Her face wore an expression akin to awe.

Tom, too, must have noticed. Yet with the good manners which seemed to come natural to him, he put out his hand and gave hers a squeeze.

"Annie Oakum, is it? Well, I am most pleased to make your acquaintance. I hope you will be with us for a while."

"Oh," said she with a deep sigh, "I do, too. Indeed I do."

FOUR

*In which we learn how
Sir John Fielding lost
his sight*

In point of fact, Annie went back to the Magdalene Home
for Penitent Prostitutes that evening after dinner. Yet she
had proven herself thoroughly in managing and improving
upon the meal that Lady Fielding had begun, for the discussion undertaken by Sir John lasted far longer than could have
been predicted so that she had ample opportunity to spice
the mélange to her taste. She went so far as to pour the
leavings of a bottle of claret into the stew pot, quite amazing
Tom and myself who had never seen wine put to such use.

"The Frenchies do it all the time," she explained confidently to us. "It's for the taste, it is."

Whether it was the claret, or the diligent peppering and
thyming she followed it with, the stew was quite memorably
good. As we five seated ourselves around the kitchen table,
Sir John and Lady Fielding dipped their spoons into their
bowls and tasted. The smiles that lit their faces cheered Annie and reassured me. Sir John simply dipped again and continued eating with great gusto. Lady Fielding leaned to her
young protégé and conferred upon her a most emphatic nod
of approval.

"My dear," said she, "this is quite the most savory stew
I have ever put my tongue to. You've done a few things to
it, I hazard."

"I took a few liberties, mum."

"All to the good, I assure you."

"Hear, hear," said Sir John, "hear, hear." Then did he return to the business at hand.

Thus, in her absence, was the fate of Mrs. Gredge sealed. After a visit to her, it had been discussed, along with Tom Durham's future, during the conference in Sir John's study. That they had a replacement for her in Annie Oakum, it was readily agreed after the two of them had downed dinner. Annie, of course, would be more than willing. It remained for Mrs. Gredge, poor soul, to be informed. That they prepared to do as I cleared the table. Lady Fielding filled a bowl with the last of the stew, which she would carry up with her. Then she turned to me with another of her emphatic nods.

"Jeremy," said she, "I wish you to take Annie back to the Home in a hackney. Have you money enough left from yesterday's outing?"

"I'm sure I have."

"Well then, see her safe inside and then return. Tell the driver to wait for you." And to Annie she said: "Gather your things together tomorrow, my girl, and in the afternoon you may return with me here and move into Mrs. Gredge's room."

"I'm ever so grateful, mum."

"You'll be paid, of course. Sir John will work that out with you."

"Thank you, mum."

With that, Lady Fielding said her goodbye to us and, with the bowl of stew for Mrs. Gredge in her hands, ascended the stairs with Sir John.

And so I came, not long afterward, to accompany Annie to the Home in a hackney all to ourselves. All the exuberance that was pent up within her came out in a rush of eager questions; yet all of them, it seemed, had to do with "that dear, lovely fellow" to whom I had introduced her, Tom Durham.

I told her much, though not all, about him: that he was the son of Lady Fielding; that his father's death had considerably reduced their circumstances and ended his schooling; that he had gone to sea in the H.M.S. *Adventure* over two and a half years ago and done service in India; that he had every intention of returning to the sea, but that (and here I may have overstepped myself a bit) Sir John hoped to win for him an appointment as midshipman. What I omitted, of course, were the circumstances of Tom's enlistment in the Royal Navy: his life in crime and his near brush with the hangman.

Annie sat beside me quite enraptured by all the details I divulged. When there was no more to hear about him, she simply fell silent and stared out the window of the carriage. What could she see? That mattered little, for, as I rightly perceived, her head was filled with naught save thoughts and fantasies of her now dear Tom. I knew not what to make of this, for I had not encountered such an emotion on the rough streets surrounding Covent Garden. What passed between Sir John and Lady Fielding seemed more to me in the nature of great friendship than this display of sudden obsession. Was this an inflation of those tender feelings I had for her kitchen chum, Meg? Or was it the great thing the poets wrote about? Was it Juliet's love for her Romeo that saucy Annie felt for Tom? Surely not. Indeed, considering the hard life that had brought her to us, I hoped not.

Sooner than I expected, the hackney came to a halt before the Magdalene Home. I instructed the driver to wait for me if he wished to be paid, then accompanied Annie to the door. The fearsome directress greeted her in a rather hostile manner.

"Back again, are you?" said she.

"Yes, but not for long," said Annie, her back up once more. "I'm to return tomorrow to stay."

"Well, Miss Uppish, we'll see how long you lasts."

To that Annie made no reply, simply kissed me light upon the cheek and said, "Thank you, Jeremy," and disappeared into the place, past the large figure in black.

I sulked a bit upon Annie's simple thank-you, on my return trip to Number 4 Bow Street. Were we not old chums? Was she so besotted with Tom Durham? Ah, but what did it matter, I consoled myself, so long as it turned out well? For, in truth, I was as much beneficiary as them all. Though I had eaten much of Mrs. Gredge's cooking the twelvemonth past—and eaten it gratefully—it seemed always to me to be more than a bit bland.

And so I came to the house on Bow Street I knew so well. Inside, I gave a wave and a greeting to Mr. Baker who, of all the Beak-runners, was the only one present at that hour—then up the stairs and into the kitchen, wherein a pleasant surprise awaited me. I discovered that in my absence, all the washing up had been done, and done well. Seeing no one about, I continued up the stairs, heard a deep drone of talking behind Mrs. Gredge's closed door—Sir John's voice—and went on higher to the attic room which I shared, for the time being, with Tom Durham. He was stretched across the bed, reading my newly purchased copy of Lord Anson's *A Voyage Round the World*. He looked up, smiled, and raised the book that I might see what he read.

"Ho, mate," said he, "is this your book?"

"It is," said I. "I bought it only yesterday. But you may read it. Of course you may."

"Ah, that Anson, he was a seaman—and was he not?"

I agreed—how could I disagree?—and listened then to an intelligent disquisition of some minutes' duration on the feats of George Anson as sailor, navigator, fighter, and First Lord of the Admiralty. At the end of it, he smiled a sad smile.

"Do you know who taught me of him? It was Lieutenant Landon of the *Adventure*—that selfsame Lieutenant Landon who now is restricted to quarters as to some dungeon, falsely accused of murder. He it was who raised me from scullion to deckhand, then made me foretopman."

"You say he is falsely accused. Could you give evidence that might help him in his situation?"

"If only I could! No, I declare it and know it to be true, for a man as decent as he could never do what he has been said to do. I know the man. I know him well, for he and I spent many a night hour in talk along the Coromandel and the Malabar. It was through him and because of him I came to love the sea."

"I met him today," said I, which was not quite true since I had not been introduced—yet it was essentially so.

"How is he? How does he bear up?"

I answered honestly: "He is weak in his own defense—or so thinks Sir John."

"You were there today, with Sir John—and you went

aboard the *Adventure*. Tell me all you saw and heard. Please, Jeremy, I must know.''

Thus I came to give Tom Durham as full and true a report as ever I had given Sir John on any matter. He listened quite attentive as I told how the magistrate, in his clever questioning, had near forced Lieutenant Hartsell to admit that he could see little in that moment he now confidently claimed to have seen so much. I told him too of the dark rumblings of the crew as Sir John interrogated Hartsell before them. Then I jumped ahead and quoted the admiral's misgivings, his talk of inciting mutiny, et cetera.

"And what did Sir John say to that?" asked Tom, interrupting for the first time.

"He said," and I deepened my voice somewhat in imitation of him, " 'A captain who does not have the confidence of his crew is no captain at all.' "

Tom laughed heartily at my performance. Then of a sudden he grew quite somber.

"He is quite right, of course," said he. "Yet the truth of it is, Lieutenant Hartsell does *not* have the confidence of the crew. And so the admiral was not wrong to suggest the possibility of mutiny."

"In port?" I asked, sounding quite incredulous. "In London?"

"Not likely," said he, "but anything can happen on the open sea. I would wager that had he made his accusation against Lieutenant Landon earlier, and had the crew learned of it, there would have been mutiny on the *Adventure*. At the very least, Hartsell would have met with a fatal accident. That, I am sure, is why he did not confine him to quarters and let out the charge until the night before we anchored."

"Was Lieutenant Landon really so well liked?"

"He was the ablest, bravest, fairest, and best officer we had. Hartsell may have been acting captain, but Landon was the leader of the ship—but what of him? Tell me now."

And so, very shortly, I did just that. Would that I could have given Tom a more favorable picture of his favorite. Yet what had I to describe but a melancholy man who greeted us, Bible in hand, and was apparently resigned to his fate? All he could offer in his defense was that he certainly had not pushed the captain overboard but was attempting to pull him back—which, in any case, Sir John had already perceived.

(You will note, reader, that I withheld from Tom any mention of the peculiarly personal relation between Vice-Admiral Sir Robert Redmond and Lieutenant Landon of the *Adventure*; nor especially did I mention the looks which passed between them at a certain crucial moment during Sir John's questioning of the lieutenant. Such information I considered to be the property of the magistrate—and his alone.)

That Tom Durham was saddened by my account I had no doubt, for he remained silent for quite some time after I had finished, though his face was as near without expression as could be. He seemed to me to be deep in thought.

At last he turned to me and said: "I wish there was a way I could help him."

"Perhaps one will present itself."

"Perhaps."

We talked of many more things that night: of Black Jack Bilbo and Jimmie Bunkins; of the admiral's coming visit; of the strange lives both of us had led—orphaned, uprooted, thrown to our own devices—but it was only toward the end of the evening, as we were yawning and about to take ourselves to bed, that Tom happened to mention Annie. He asked me about her—who she was and how I had come to know her. Briefly, I told him something of the Goodhope matter, and said merely that Annie had worked in the kitchen of the great house in St. James Street.

"Really?" said he. "I was in just such a house in St. James today—Mr. Bilbo's it was."

"The same one," said I.

"Was it indeed? Well, I suppose Lord Goodhope had little use for it, being dead and all."

We sniggered together at Tom's rough joke like the careless boys we were.

"But Annie is a fine cook, little doubt of it," he added. "Pretty, too, when you think of it. I should like to know her better."

We were beneath the blanket, the candle out, and near asleep in the bed we shared when a thought occurred to me.

"Tom," said I, "was it you did the washing up tonight—
all those pots and pans?"

"Think nothing of it, mate," said he in his drowsy state.

"Well, I thank you for it."

"Anything for a chum." And moments later, I heard him
breathing deeply and regularly in sleep.

He had called me mate and chum. That meant, I was sure,
that we were now friends. I mulled that over happily in my
mind until pleasant dreams overtook me.

My Lady Fielding determined, and Sir John agreed, that one
thing that must be got ere the admiral visited us for dinner
was a suit of clothes for Tom. Since Sir Robert was sure to
appear out of naval habit, it would be improper for one of
their number to make an appearance so dressed.

"No, lad," said Sir John to Tom, "it will not do. Your
mother has described to me that costume of bits and pieces
you now wear. Proud you may be of your sailor's garb, but
it would be an affront to the admiral to ask him to sit down
at table with an ordinary seaman."

"But—"

"And *since*," continued Sir John over Tom's attempted
objection, "and *since*, I say, the object in inviting him here
is to seek his help in elevating you from seaman to midshipman, it would be best to present you as the young gentleman
you might have been had not fortune turned against you."

"But surely you will tell him of . . . of the circumstances
of my enlistment!"

"I will in due time, perhaps not tonight. What I wish to
do tonight is offer you in the best light—well dressed and
well spoken—then plant in his mind the notion that such a
fine young fellow as yourself would make an excellent midshipman and a superb officer."

Tom gave a sigh of capitulation. "As you say then, Sir
John."

"Precisely."

And so it was by these circumstances that Lady Fielding
got her wish. She would not, as was her hope, see him in
bespoken clothes, tailored to his new dimensions, yet there
were respectable shops in Chandos Street that sold ready-

made of fair quality and castoffs of high quality that might
be altered to fit. It was decided she would take him there.

Before they left, however, she passed to me a list of co-
mestibles to buy in Covent Garden for the admiral's dinner.
At the top was "a side of lamb fit for roasting."

"Lamb is hard to find," said I, mumbling my dissent.

"Go to Mr. Tolliver," said she. "He is sure to have it this
early in the day. If not, I fear you must make a trip to Smithfield Market."

"All right then," said I. "I'm on my way."

And so I was, running as I did most days through the
crowded piazza, making my way from vendor to stall, picking over the stock to find the best they had to offer. I had
become a wise buyer in the year or more I had been with
Sir John. Satisfying Mrs. Gredge was no easy matter, yet
taught by Lady Fielding, I had learned that to buy the biggest
was not always to buy the best, that the brightest color did
not always assure the best taste.

Yet in our trips through the Garden, Lady Fielding had
surprised me by avoiding the butcher stall of Mr. Tolliver.
Situated as it was in the far corner of the piazza, it was not
difficult to avoid, but well I remembered that it was she who
had first taken me across the wide Garden and introduced
me to Mr. Tolliver and assured me that his was the best meat
available there, that he gave the best cuts and the best values
for pence and shillings. All this, however, was before her
marriage to Sir John. During their brief courtship, I had
borne a message to her from him, and afterward seen Mr.
Tolliver emerge from her lodgings all dejected and forlorn.
I know it now, though I did not perceive it then, that the
Covent Garden butcher had himself been a suitor for her
hand. Therefore, after her marriage to Sir John, she must
have thought it more seemly and certainly less embarrassing
to avoid his stall altogether. Thus, taught by her example and
with a word or two to direct me elsewhere, she diverted my
course from Mr. Tolliver's place of business and sent me to
his lesser competitors. When something special was wanted,
such as that grand beef roast we had eaten at Tom's homecoming and the next night, too, I was sent traipsing off to
Smithfield Market. Yet not on this day. Why was it so? Even

now, I can only guess that perhaps a matter of time was involved, or perhaps even quality, for his meat was equal to any I bought at Smithfield—as she must have known.

In any case, it was to Mr. Tolliver I went on that warm day in July 1769, to seek "a side of lamb fit for roasting." He was there at his post, serving a great swarm of buyers. I took a place in line, and as I waited I was recognized. He acknowledged me with a nod of his great head, and when my turn came, he waited not for me to speak but, blurting out a bit uncertainly, gave forth his greeting.

"Well, Jeremy lad, it's been a bit since I seen you, ain't it?" said he.

"Yes sir," said I, "though I'm not quite sure why."

"Well, I've a good idea of it."

"I've been often to Smithfield."

"They've good meat there, though no better than mine, as I'll be pleased to show. What will you have?"

I told him, and he went off to the meat, uncovered a small carcass hanging apart from the rest, and with a few expert turns of his big knife cut it near in half—and then he remained to cut some more. He sent away the flies, wrapped the remains of the carcass in its cloth, and my meat in paper. This package he delivered to me.

"This is true lamb," said he, "not young mutton. It makes a smaller piece than you might suppose, so I gave you a leg, as well, at no charge. Call it a gift to bring you back again."

"Well, thank you, sir." I counted out his payment into his palm.

"The fact is, I'd see you whether you bought from me or not. You're a good, plucky boy, Jeremy. Remember that day we chased them black-suited devils away?"

"Oh, I do, sir," said I, most enthusiastic.

"We showed them, didn't we?" He shook his head in thought, giving a most queer smile as if the memory he had called up gave him both pleasure and pain. "Remember me to your mistress. Next?"

And I was pushed aside by a cook in a great hurry. The package of meat under my arm, and my other purchases filling my hands, I started back to Bow Street. I knew not altogether why, but I felt quite filled with emotion by the encounter. Could we, when young, but understand as well as we feel, how wise we would be.

Arriving home, I found a stranger in our kitchen giving his attention to Sir John. He was a small man of no particular distinction, perhaps the keeper of a little shop, or a clerk. He held his tricorn tight in his two hands before him and gave me a quick, nervous smile as I went silently to the kitchen table and unloaded my packages. Mrs. Gredge was seated there, fully dressed, in an attitude of waiting, looking no better nor worse than she had the day before. She threw me a glance, no more, then lowered her eyes as she continued to listen to Sir John.

". . . and since, in regard to her many long years of service in my household, I feel an obligation—nay, a duty—to provide for her in her declining years, I have decided to settle upon her an amount of one pound a month."

"Oh, but that is most generous, sir," said the small man. He squeezed his tricorn even tighter. I feared he might crush it altogether.

"You are married, are you not?"

"I am, yes sir."

"And you have children?"

"We been blessed with three."

"And a noisier trio of rascals you never heard," squawked Mrs. Gredge in her inimitable jackdaw manner. Her tongue still seemed a bit large for her mouth.

"Aw Mama," protested the small man, quite evidently her son, "you ain't been by for a couple of years. They ain't like that now."

"That's as may be," said Sir John, "yet the question is, how large are your lodgings?"

"Two rooms, sir."

"That being the case, this added pound per month will enable you to move to a larger place, one in which your mother may have a room of her own, a privilege she has always enjoyed with us. I shall depend upon you to do that. Is that understood, Mr. Gredge?"

"Oh, aye, sir, quite well understood—and agreed! And when Will Gredge gives his word, sir, he keeps it. I'm well known for that in the tailoring trade, sir."

"Very good," said Sir John. "And you may use the remainder to raise your general situation. She will benefit from that, of course, but you and your family deserve something for keeping her, as well."

"I likes my sweets!" crowed Mrs. Gredge with sudden vehemence.

At that Sir John chuckled most heartily. "Indeed she does," said he, "perhaps too well. See that she gets them from time to time. Far more important, however, that she get her meat and vegetables. You'll see to that?"

"Oh, I will, sir."

"Good then. All that understood and agreed, here is the first payment on my debt to your mother for her service to us."

And with that, he presented him with the one-pound banknote he had held throughout their conversation palmed in his right hand. Mr. Gredge took it eagerly, near too eagerly it seemed to me, and pocketed it. Yet he sounded most sincere in his response.

"I'll not let you down, sir." Then, to Mrs. Gredge: "Nor you, either, Mama. I'll take good care of you."

She rose from the chair whereon she sat, struggling a bit to make it to her feet. But she won the struggle and was encouraged by her victory to limp over a few steps to Sir John. She took his hand.

"You've been a good master, Sir John Fielding," said she. "None could want better. And you've provided for me well. My only sorrow is that my old body failed me, and I could not go on serving you the rest of my days."

Sir John groped a bit but found her shoulder with his left hand and drew her to him in an embrace.

"Thank you, Mrs. Gredge. And from the bottom of my heart I thank you for my poor, dear dead Kitty. You were the best and gentlest nurse that ever she could have had. None could have treated her as well as you treated her. I shall always remember you for it."

With that, she pulled away, tears streaming down her old, slack cheeks.

"I'm ready, Will," she announced. "Take my chest down."

"When . . ." Sir John began, then cleared his throat and began again: "When the first of the month comes, another one-pound payment will be delivered to you, Will Gredge. I hope by that time you will have settled in larger quarters. Be sure to communicate the location of your new place to us."

"Yes, sir. I'll do that, sir. Thank you, sir"—bowing and scraping a bit.

"Jeremy," said Sir John, knowing full well that I was also present, "help Mrs. Gredge down the stairs. Her son will have his hands full. Then get them a hackney carriage." He gave a great nod to us then. "Goodbye to you all." He turned and made his departure across the kitchen he knew so well and started up the stairs.

Will Gredge lifted the chest filled with his mother's belongings, which in truth was not so heavy but bulky and clumsy and difficult to carry. "Come on, Mama."

He went down the stairs with it. Mrs. Gredge and I followed, she leaning upon me so that we went quite slowly, one step at a time. By the time we arrived at the bottom, Mr. Fuller, the day constable, had come to help Will with the chest. Between them, it was no job at all to move it out and through the door to Bow Street.

"Jeremy," said she to me as we made our way together, "I have to say that Sir John was righter about you than I was. I admit I had my doubts, but you turned out better than I ever thought you would. I want you to take care of him, boy. Take care of him, obey him in all things, and love him as you would your own father if he was alive."

"I will do it as you say, Mrs. Gredge."

"He has great faith in you, Jeremy, and high expectations."

We had reached the door to Bow Street. I helped her through and saw that Mr. Fuller had already brought a hackney to us. As he and Will handed up the chest to the driver, Mrs. Gredge kissed me on the cheek.

"Goodbye, Jeremy. Take care now."

"Goodbye, ma'am. I'll see you again soon."

"God willing."

I helped her up to the door of the carriage, and Will, who was already inside, pulled her through. It was done awkward between us, and she tripped once going in; but in she was, and the carriage door shut after her. The driver stirred his horses to life, and the hackney pulled away.

Alone I stood on the walk, for Mr. Fuller had left us as soon as the chest was loaded. I thought that just as well, for tears had welled in my eyes and begun to course down my cheeks. I wiped at them, of a sudden quite embarrassed that those walking by might see me so. In my own mind, it seemed to me I was far too old to weep.

This bleak farewell had brought me so low that when I returned to the kitchen, all I was able to do was sit and mope at the table. I know not how long I sat thus, but when ascending steps came on the stairway below, I roused myself at last from my lethargy and stood to my task, unpacking the things I had brought in from Covent Garden some time before.

In the first moment of his appearance, I did not recognize Tom Durham, even though he entered the room with his mother, and sense dictated it could be none but he. He looked that glorious in his new apparel. Yet it changed him in ways I could not have foreseen. He looked distinctly older, more settled and capable. The serious expression he wore, I later discovered, was due to his discomfort in this new costume. Even so, it added to the impression of maturity, giving him the look of a young gentleman of affairs. I had seen such on their way hither and thither in the City of London.

"Does he not look elegant?" asked Lady Fielding.

"Oh, indeed he does!"

"Quite lubberly is how I look," said Tom stubbornly. "I know that full well, for I've spent a good long time before the looking glass this day."

"We were *most* fortunate," said she, quite aflutter with excitement. "The breeches are ready-made and of quite good stuff. They look well on him, don't you think so, Jeremy?"

"Oh, yes."

"Ah, but the coat—the *coat!* True enough, it was owned before, but barely worn at all—you can tell. Just look at the trim on it, the good work on the buttonholes, *feel* the stuff of it. And it fits quite perfect just as you see it."

Obediently, I grasped where she directed me. Tom seemed

to fight an impulse to jerk away. In a way I pitied him being tugged and tucked at all morning, but much more did I envy him. The fabric seemed both soft and strong. It was indeed an elegant coat.

"I should like to get into my old duds, Mother," said Tom, hefting the package he carried, which contained them.

"Not until I show you to Jack!"

"But he cannot *see* me."

"I can describe you to him exact, and he can form a picture in his mind. He is quite good at that, Tom. Sometimes I think he can see more than we do—quite uncanny, really. Do you not have that feeling at times, Jeremy?"

"More often than you know, my lady."

"Is he about?"

"Upstairs—in his study, perhaps."

"We shall look for him there. Come along, Tom."

She led the way. As Tom left me, he rolled his eyes most expressive, as if to marvel what a fellow had to put up with.

Thus the rest of the day passed in preparation for the visit of Vice-Admiral Sir Robert Redmond. When at last Lady Fielding returned from above, she inspected my purchases and approved them, though she registered surprise that I had taken it upon myself to add a leg of lamb to the side of lamb she had asked me to buy.

"That was given gratis by Mr. Tolliver," said I, "to tempt us back to his stall."

She smiled then a smile that was near as odd as the one I had seen on the butcher's face.

"That was dear of him, was it not? Perhaps we have been neglecting him. Henceforth, Jeremy, you may go always to Mr. Tolliver unless I specifically tell you to go elsewhere."

"His meat's as good as any at Smithfield Market," said I. "So he says, and I believe it to be true."

"Well and good. We'll try him again, shall we? But now, I must run off to the Home. I have much to attend to there before I return with Annie, and we get properly under way. So goodbye to you."

She started for the door, then stopped to turn and exclaim: "This is all so exciting! Imagine Tom a midshipman—an officer!"

Then she disappeared down the stairs. For all concerned, I hoped it happened just as she supposed.

Sir John's departure was much quieter and less hurried. He made his way at the usual time downstairs across the kitchen on his familiar journey to his courtroom.

"I take it Tom's new clothes met your approval, Jeremy?"

"Oh, yes, he will present a fine figure to the admiral."

"That's as we would like it."

And then he strode on, tapping the door to the stairs to determine whether it was open or shut, then opening it to descend.

Since Tom had remained above, I took it he was in the attic room we shared, perhaps pouting at the indignities that had been forced upon him by his mother; perhaps reading Lord Anson's *A Voyage Round the World*; perhaps both. In any case, I thought it best to leave him alone. Left to my own devices, it was not long until I myself found my way down to Sir John's courtroom.

It seemed to me that I had neglected it of late. With the shopping and the cleaning and the general hurly-burly that preceded Tom's homecoming, there seemed little time or opportunity to attend to those things I like best. And best of all did I like those hours I spent in the Magistrate's Court on Bow Street.

As a magistrate, Sir John Fielding had power to try lesser crimes, adjudicate lesser suits, and bind over for trial at Old Bailey capital crimes, of which there were then a great number and are still far too many. It was in that last capacity that his famous powers of investigation and interrogation came to the fore. I had seen him, on a number of occasions, turn a witness quite inside out, forcing him to admit that he had not actually *seen* what he claimed to have seen—only heard it, heard about it, or supposed from other factors that it had taken place. It seemed one of life's ironies that he, a blind man, should give such paramount importance to the evidence of the eyes. (You may thus imagine, reader, the frustration felt by the magistrate at the end of his questioning of the acting captain of the *Adventure*.)

Having said all this, I must now disappoint by informing

you that during the court session I visited on that day, Sir John performed no great feats of interrogation, turned none inside out, nor taught any to say what he had seen—and that, only. It was, as days go in Sir John's courtroom, a rather humdrum session. There was a dispute between a blacksmith and the driver of a hackney carriage over the shoeing of a horse and repairs of the conveyance, which involved the payment of a sum of two pounds; Sir John settled it amicably by persuading the blacksmith to accept three-quarters the amount, which the blacksmith agreed was a bit high, and taking it in two installments. There were two men who appeared before Sir John, one charging the other with assault; yet he who made the charge was much the larger of the two, and the smaller looked as if he had got much the worst of it. Since, according to Constable Baker, who had come upon the scene and taken down the accusation, no weapons were involved but bare fists, Sir John called it a matter of mutual combat and dismissed the charge; he warned them, however, that if they appeared before him again, he would find them both guilty of assault and fine them equally.

And so, you see, even on quiet days in court there was much to interest a lad of my years. To see Sir John thus in action day after day gave me a growing understanding of the workings of his remarkable mind, an understanding which benefited me greatly afterward in the pursuit of my own career in the law.

The last case of the day's light docket was one of public drunkenness, and it proved to be of interest not just to me but also to Sir John.

The two men so charged shuffled up before Sir John in a state of embarrassment and proper chagrin. Mr. Marsden, the court clerk, read the complaint against them, naming them as Isaac Banneker and George Stonesifer, both seamen in the Royal Navy. The arresting constable, Constable Cowley, was called forward, and he gave a brief account of his apprehension of the two past midnight in Bloomsbury Square, wherein they had made "a remarkable lot of noise, sir."

"Were they fighting, loudly quarrelsome?" asked Sir John.

"Oh, no sir," said Constable Cowley. "Quite the opposite. They was happy and singing loudly, serenading the entire square, as you might say but there was complaints. In fact, sir, I was summoned by a footman of Lord Mansfield's household to the scene.''

''On Lord Mansfield's order?''

''Yes, sir.''

''Oh, well,'' said Sir John, ''I suppose the Lord Chief Justice needs his sleep as we all do. Did these two happy serenaders give you any trouble when you invited them to Bow Street?''

''None at all, sir. They had finished their bottle of gin. Their only problem was walking the street. They was a bit weak in the legs, sir, found it difficult walking a straight line, they did.''

''It sometimes happens so,'' said Sir John—then to Banneker and Stonesifer: ''What have you two to say for yourselves?''

''M'lord,'' said the first, ''we can't make no dispute with the constable, sir—''

''Who is this now who speaks?''

''Isaac Banneker, m'lord.''

''Continue.''

''As I say, we got no quarrel with the constable. He treated us right. It was probably just as he said. The truth is, George and I don't remember much about it. We came ashore from our ship, was paid, and given our leave tickets. By then,'twas right late. And we thought to save our money by buying a bottle and staying out of the grog shops. Which we done and walked till we found us a nice, quiet place to drink it. Well, we drink a bit of gin, and we were feeling ever so good, and George says to me, 'Isaac, do you know this one?' And he sings to me the ballad of 'Molly on the Shore,' and then—''

''That will be all for the moment. I should like to hear from your companion. Is this as you remember it, Mr. Stonesifer?''

''Just so, sir. I sung it to him and he sings me another. I don't rightly recall which, for we sung so many that night. It was grand while it lasted, but then the constable come and took us away.''

"So you plead guilty as charged."

The two men looked at one another, shrugged, and responded, "Yes, m'lord," and, "Yes, sir," in ragged chorus.

"Before we go further," said Sir John, "I wonder if you two gentlemen would satisfy me on a point. You are both seamen in the Royal Navy, are you not? Tell me please, what is your ship?"

"Same as you were on yesterday, m'lord, the *Adventure*," said Isaac Banneker. "You did a right job on Mr. Hartsell, you did. All us in the crew were for you, be sure of it."

Sir John, slightly taken aback by the response, gave a tardy wave of his hand to silence Mr. Banneker.

"Please, Mr. Banneker," said he, "what I may have done yesterday or any other day on the *Adventure* is not a proper matter for this court. I am but curious on the matter of the leave you were given. You said, I believe, that it came late yesterevening?"

"Well, our turn did, m'lord. See, they started running the boat back and forth between the dock and the *Adventure* not all that long after you left, m'lord, and took the whole crew off. We was all quite surprised, for they was to do the usual and let us off fifteen at a time, that party come back, and another fifteen go on leave. We was all surprised when they emptied the ship, for they'd let ladies aboard and booze, as well, just to keep us happy. But no, they sent us all off the *Adventure*. I ain't sure how many they will get back, in truth, sir. George and I were the last boatload but one."

"So now I shall have a crew of drunken sailors roistering about my precincts of London. Is that your information?"

"Well, not quite *all* the crew, m'lord. They kept the Lascars on, about fifty of them in number—and officers, midshipmen, and petty officers, of course. We came back a bit shorthanded. I'd say you had about two hundred of us to deal with, sir, till the *Adventure* weighs anchor."

"Most interesting," said the magistrate. "I wish I had been told. But now, I have you two to deal with, have I not? I have two choices. I may toss you in Newgate and let you serve a term of thirty days for your public drunkenness, which might indeed put you out of jail after the *Adventure* has sailed, making you, in effect, deserters—and you know how the Navy treats deserters . . .''

"Oh, yes sir. Could we but—''

"Silence, please, for I have not finished.''

"Yes, m'lord.''

"That is one choice. The other is this: I could fine you and allow you to go on your way if you were to promise me faithfully that you would seek out your fellows, and tell them for me that I shall not tolerate rowdy and riotous behavior in Westminster or the City of London. I shall deal with it quite severely. Now, gentlemen, I shall let you help me decide. Which would you have me choose?''

"Oh, the second, m'lord,'' said Isaac Banneker.

"Please, sir, the second,'' said George Stonesifer.

"Very well, the second it is. But I shall send you out not entirely as free men, for you are under an obligation to me to spread the word as I have instructed you. Is that understood?''

Both men agreed quite solemnly to his terms.

"Then you are fined each a pound. Pay Mr. Marsden.''

The small crowd in the courtroom seemed to find a bit of entertainment in this last little drama. As Sir John gaveled that session of his court to its conclusion, the spectators filed out laughing and smiling to one another, amused at the outcome, though perhaps puzzled a bit at details discussed dealing with the frigate *Adventure*. They were ignorant of their significance; I was not.

For if the release of the frigate's crew meant that two hundred extra souls had been added to the number who populated the dives, alehouses, and grog shops, it also meant that someone—Lieutenant Hartsell or perhaps even Vice-Admiral Sir Robert Redmond—had taken the threat of mutiny quite seriously. They feared the crew, even in the Port of London. Tom Durham's appraisal of the situation had proved, in some sense at least, accurate.

While I felt drawn to Sir John's chambers to ask him about this, a contrary impulse kept me away. Beneath his commanding exterior, he seemed quite disturbed by the events that had happened, and were happening still, aboard the *Adventure*. And so, wisely, I went not to visit him, but rather above, where I busied myself cleaning and polishing in the sitting room, wherein, as I had been told, our party for the admiral would begin.

It was late afternoon before Lady Fielding arrived from the Magdalene Home with Annie, who carried with her a small bundle of clothes and miscellaneous belongings. After inspecting and approving my work in the sitting room, Lady Fielding hurried up to the attic room to urge her son back into his new-bought finery. This left me alone with Annie in the kitchen. She fixed me with a critical stare.

"Awright," said she, "let's see what you brought me to cook."

The vegetables satisfied her, but what she was most interested in was the package of meat I had brought back from Mr. Tolliver's. I unwrapped it, and she gave it a hard appraisal.

"Mmm, a rack *and* a leg," said she, thrusting out her lower lip and nodding. "You'll not leave the table hungry tonight. You buy this at Smithfield, Jeremy?"

"No, in the Garden at Mr. Tolliver's."

"And good meat it is. But tell me, did the old party who had my position previous keep any mint sauce about?"

I had seen a jar, I thought, while cleaning the cupboards not so long ago. I went and pulled it down. Finding it unopened, I managed with considerable effort to pull off the top. Annie dipped her finger in it and tasted.

"That'll do," said she. "But I know they've no garlic or spices about, so you must hurry off swift to Covent Garden, while the stalls are yet open and buy me a whole garlic and a good bunch of fresh marjoram. Have you got that clear? If I'm going to do this—by God, I shall do it right!"

"I thought you promised naught but humble fare, Jack," said the admiral. "Strike me dead if this is not the best lamb e'er I tasted. I *know* I never ate better."

"You do me honor, Bobbie."

"We have a new cook," ventured Lady Fielding. "She was formerly in the kitchen of Lord Goodhope."

"Well, you may give her my sincerest compliments."

"Thank you," said she. "I shall certainly do so."

"Lord Goodhope . . . Lord Goodhope," muttered Sir Robert, sucking to call up the memory. "He came to a bad end, did he not? Why, I do believe I heard that you yourself had something to do with that tawdry affair—an investigation of some sort, was it not?"

"Indeed I did conduct an investigation," said Sir John. "And you are right, it was a tawdry affair, probably not the sort of thing my dear Kate would like to hear discussed at dinner table—another occasion, perhaps."

"Certainly, certainly. My apologies, Lady Fielding."

"Quite unnecessary, really. Tom, I see that Sir Robert's glass needs replenishing. Would you attend to it?"

Her son poured with a heavy hand, filling the admiral's glass near to the brim.

"Thank you, lad," said Sir Robert; then, taking a deep draft of the wine, he spoke out to the table, though in name he addressed his host: "Jack, I do envy you so. Here you have a lovely wife, two fine boys to assist you and give you comfort—in short, a real home. While I, who have never married, must return to my humble quarters in the Tower and eat my next dinner alone in the officers' mess."

"Never married?" echoed Lady Fielding. "What a pity!"

"No, all those years at sea, after all. It would have been unfair to any woman to ask her to endure absences of two or three years for a month or two of true married life. Now that I am seaborne no longer but shoreborne, my quarterdeck an office, I have come to wish my life had been otherwise—most specially when I find myself in such company as I find myself in at this moment."

"But surely it is not too late to marry," said she. "You are still a young man, still vigorous."

"The Navy seems to disagree with you on that, dear lady, else I would not have been put in the position I now hold. But alas, in any case, I fear I am too set in my bachelor ways to be a proper mate for any woman." Sir Robert gave a light, dismissive laugh. "Oh, I confess that in seeking your sympathy, my lady, I have painted a rather bleak picture of my state," he continued. "I am only recently come to London. When I have found proper lodgings my situation will be much improved. Then I shall be in a position to return your kind hospitality, Jack.''

Yet Lady Fielding pressed the point: ''Have many naval officers decided as you have to remain bachelors?''

''Not most, certainly, but a goodly number.''

''I should not like to think that I should be deprived of grandchildren. My son, you see, seeks a career in the Navy.''

At this point the admiral raised his eyebrows and looked across the table toward me. ''Do you mean Jeremy here? He is certainly a likely-looking lad. He would make a proper midshipman.''

Before Lady Fielding could correct his error, Sir John raised his hand toward her and spoke forth.

''No, Bobbie, Jeremy's for the law—or so he has told me. Kate refers to her son by her first marriage, Tom Durham, who sits at your right.''

And of course, the admiral then turned to his right and gave Tom close inspection. He seemed unsure in his assessment.

''I would not be altogether discouraging,'' said he, ''but the matter of age might . . . How old are you, young man?''

''I am sixteen years of age, Sir Robert,'' answered Tom right smartly.

''Sixteen, is it? I would have taken you for at least two years older—oh, at least that. But indeed sixteen would not be judged too old for an appointment as midshipman. How do you feel about it, young sir? Life on the sea is the roughest sort of life you can imagine. There are dangers at every hand. There are not only dangers of war, but also dangers of the elements. No landsman can begin to suppose the rigors of a storm at sea.''

''I believe I am up to it, sir.''

Then did Lady Fielding break in most impulsively: ''Tom has already experienced the dangers you describe, Sir Robert.''

''Oh? And how did that come to pass?'' The admiral continued to address Tom Durham.

Though for different reasons as curious as Sir Robert as to how that question might be answered, I turned my attention to Sir John, who had earlier voiced some hesitation with regard to bringing up the circumstances of Tom's naval service. Although Sir John's eyes were covered, as always, with a band of black silk, and were therefore unreadable, I saw that his brow was furrowed in a frown, and his fork had stopped midway in its passage to his mouth.

And then the answer from Tom: "I have served as an ordinary seaman on the H.M.S. *Adventure*, the last year as foretopman, sir."

Far from being put out of sorts by the blunt response he'd been given, the admiral chuckled heartily.

"You don't mean it!" said he. "I had wondered at your dark color and your nautical gait. But young sir, you wear clothes as a proper gentleman, and you certainly talk as one." He broke off then and looked from Tom to Lady Fielding and back again. "I hope you did not wound your mother by running away to sea, as boys sometimes do . . . ?"

"No, sir, I—"

"Tom is a court boy." Sir John interrupted in a voice low but commanding; Tom fell immediately silent as the magistrate continued, explaining the dark circumstances which had led to his enlistment in the Royal Navy. He mentioned that it had taken the personal intercession of Queen Charlotte herself to rescue Tom and another boy from the hangman.

Sir Robert, who had maintained a respectful silence throughout Sir John's long explanation, nodded seriously, and withheld comment for a long moment.

"I see," said he at last. "And now his mother wishes to see him an officer?"

"No," said Sir John, "I must make it clear that it was my idea and mine alone to seek an appointment for Tom as midshipman. When I met him off the *Adventure* two days past, I met a lad who loved the sea and its life with a great passion. I found that he had risen from galley scullion to ordinary seaman to foretopman in the space of the frigate's duty on the India station. Though but a boy, he had participated in battle with pirates and privateers—close battle, for you know how such do their villainous work. He earned his promotion from the galley by his conduct under fire. I found a young man who had been well educated to the age of thirteen at Westminster School, one blessed with natural gifts of intelligence, strength, and endurance. In short, I found one who would make a superb officer in the Royal Navy, one who would gladly have been accepted as midshipman three years ago, save for the single mark against him. It is my contention that he would still make a fine officer, and that his experience as seaman would make him an outstanding midshipman.''

"You make a strong case, Jack."

"I mean to, Bobbie."

"I won't pretend that such an appointment would not meet opposition. If his background were known, and in all fairness to the process it would have to be revealed, some Member of Parliament would say, 'Why not choose instead the son of Squire Whosomever in Northampton, who is a positive angel?' No, it would not be easy, but I believe Tom Durham to be as you describe him and I will give him—and you— all support possible in your suit for his appointment. That I promise you.''

"I could not ask for more, dear friend."

"However, Jack, let me give you a bit of advice. I would at the same time, if I was you, explore another channel to gain your goal. You said that you had gained the help of Queen Charlotte herself in your original effort to send this lad off to sea. His success on the *Adventure* proves the good sense of your plan of enlisting boys into the Navy. Why not write her of Tom here and of your wish to see him a mid-shipman? His success as an officer would further validate her faith in the enterprise. There are, you know, so-called 'King's-letter' boys—not many but a few—who receive their appointments as midshipmen direct from the King. There could be no arguing against Tom's appointment if it came from such a source.''

"On high, as it were? But aren't such King's letters only granted to the sons of the nobility and lesser lords?"

"Usually—but not always. I think you would be remiss to neglect that avenue.''

"Then I shall certainly do as you suggest."

There the matter ended between the two men as they finished their plates. My Lady Fielding directed her attention downward to a few choice morsels of lamb left on the bone before her; yet she could bare hide the pleased smile that played upon her lips, having heard the matter she had brought up settled so much to her liking. Only Tom and I were left to rove about with our eyes. We looked up the table and down and finally across the table at one another. He winked at me. I winked at him. Thus we commented favorably upon the proceedings.

Both the admiral and the magistrate passed down their plates to be refilled.

"A bit more of that lamb, if I may," was the request from one.

"Yes, I'll have more, as well," from the other.

They were duly served by Tom, who provided each with a second chop and a slice from the leg. Each fell silent again as they fell to the work of chewing and swallowing with great earnestness. Minutes passed thus. Vice-Admiral Sir Robert was the first to speak.

"My lady," said he, "I take it you, too, favor this career for your son?"

"I do, yes," said she. "Let me assure you, Sir Robert, that my son will have his life on the sea, whether it be as seaman or officer. He has made that plain to me. If my husband believes Tom would make a proper officer, then naturally I favor that."

"As a good wife would and should, no doubt. Yet my lady, I would not let you hold illusions as to the safety of an officer in the Royal Navy. When a ship goes down in a great storm, as happens now and again, officers perish along with the crew. When in battle, officers are obliged to stand fast and offer good example to the men; their uniforms make them grand targets for enemy musketry. In short, they run *greater* risks. Let no one tell you otherwise."

Throughout this oration Sir John had listened and eaten undisturbed, his expression unaltered; at the end of it, he beckoned with his empty glass, and Tom left his chair with the bottle to fill it.

His wife, for her part, looked the admiral straight in the eye and nodded her understanding of each grim possibility that was put before her.

"Nevertheless," said she when he had done, "my son

wants it, and my husband wants it for him. There is little more to say, is there?''

"Perhaps this," said Sir Robert, "and I shall make it as brief as I can. It is a story that is worth telling on three counts, I believe. First of all, it illustrates that not even midshipmen are immune to such dangers as I have described. Secondly, it is an instance of bravery from which young Tom here may take inspiration. Thirdly, I think it is not a story well known in this company."

"All this happened during the siege of Cartagena in the war with the French and Spanish near thirty years ago. Now, Cartagena was the great port of the Spanish on the Carib Sea in the southern part of the Americas. Gold and silver flowed through it, and the Spanish kept a fleet of warships there. Its capture would no doubt have made a quick end to a war which went on for many years afterward, for we would have cut the Spaniards' purse strings. Yet this campaign, which brought together both Army and Navy, generals and admirals, was both ill conceived and badly executed.

"There were fleet marines on every one of our ships, of course, and full battalions of Army on the big men-of-war, most of them—marines as well as soldiers—raw recruits never before under fire. There were two fortresses guarding the entry to the inner harbor, Boca Chica, which mounted eighty-four guns, and St. Joseph with thirty-six; both also mounted mortars, as was soon to be discovered. The generals insisted on holding back their soldiers for the assault on the inner harbor and the town, and as it was up to the Navy to blast a path past these two fortresses and to take them by storm, marines were landed at Boca Chica and a detachment of armed sailors at St. Joseph. Our ship, the *Resolute*, landed its marines under cover of darkness from a position in cannonade range of the fort. The marines numbered a hundred, and what with equipment and armaments it took several trips by cutter to transport the landing party from ship to shore. By the time the last of the marines had been landed, dawn had broken, and the bombardment had begun. The midshipman who commanded the cutter saw that return to the *Resolute* would be impossible, and so he ordered his oarsmen to take up their pistols and powder horns, and he took them to join the marines on the beach.

"The midshipman reported with his cutter crew to the ship's lieutenant who was in charge of the landing party. The lieutenant immediately put this young lad, who was but a year older than Tom, in charge of a battery of mortars which they had brought from the ship, for though the marines were not great in number, they were well armed. They had set up behind a hastily thrown-up parapet of sandy earth and beach wood covered by hides. Thus they were reasonably impervious to musket fire from the Spanish in the fortress—yet not to mortar fire, for as they, from behind the rampart, rained down shot from their small cohorn mortars upon the fortress, the Spanish responded in kind with their larger ones. Thus they dueled as the grander duel took place between the guns of the fleet, a great many in number, and the eighty-four cannons of Boca Chica fortress. It continued thus for the better part of the morning—a frightful din there on the beach—and there were casualties among the landing party. Among them was its head, the lieutenant from the *Resolute*; he was quite blown apart by a mortar round from the Spanish.

"When informed of this, the young midshipman, who was up for his lieutenant's examination within a month, ran to take the place of the dead officer, and he left in charge of his mortar battery a marine sergeant. It was from this marine sergeant that I got the whole of the story. Toward the end of the morning, a breach was opened in the wall of the fortress by the ships' guns. It was then the midshipman knew that it was time to act. He took up the musket of a fallen marine and ordered all to fix bayonets. He jumped atop the parapet, and as a signal to advance, he fired the musket at the fort. Now, it sometimes happens that in the heat of battle a man lacking experience and composure may unintentionally double-load his musket. The dead marine who gave up his weapon to the midshipman must have been so rattled that he loaded his thrice, for as the sergeant told it, there was a great flash as the midshipman fired. The young lad staggered, recovered himself, and drew the officer's sword, which he had buckled on. He waved it, pointed it, and led them forth, bayonets fixed, at a quick march.

"It is my experience that the mass of men are capable of surprising bravery, but they must be led. They were truly *led* across that expanse of beach by that midshipman. The Spaniards, knowing not what to think of this sudden advance, nor if indeed a second or even a third line of marines might follow over the parapet, began to desert their cannons, which were in any case useless against a foot assault, for they were trained out into the harbor. The bombardment from the fleet was lifted. Soon the marines, led by the midshipman, reached a point where the mortars could do them no harm. Yet musket fire rattled down upon them from the rear guard left by the Spanish to cover the cannoneers' hasty exit out the rear. The midshipman stopped their advance twice to order return musket fire and reload. After the second fusillade they were but steps from the breach in the wall of the fortress. With a sweep of his sword and a great yell, the midshipman bade them through the gap at double time. They overtook him, ran beside him and beyond, yet he crashed into the wall.

"He lay dazed as the marines and his cutter oarsmen swept by and through to the consternation of the remaining Spaniards. Those of the defenders who did not surrender escaped. Boca Chica had fallen. The marine sergeant, believing the young midshipman to be wounded or dead, went back to the wall, and there he found him on his feet, still dazed but unable to see. He had been blinded by the flash from that overloaded musket. They had been led across the beach in that brave assault by a blind man."

We listened to that gripping account quite transfixed by the teller. At its astonishing conclusion Lady Fielding shuddered. Tom and I exchanged looks of amazement. Only Sir John sat quite unmoved.

"And that young midshipman is in our midst tonight," concluded Sir Robert. "In fact, he sits at the head of the table. His name was and is still John Fielding."

All heads turned to him who had been named. Sir John kept silent. When at last he spoke out it was in a calm voice, near colloquial in manner.

"Ah, Bobbie," said he, "I do hate to spoil a good story,

but the truth of it is, I had a bit of vision in my left eye, which I had shut sighting down the barrel of that exploding musket. I could make out the general shape of the fort, and I thought if I could lead them there, they would do the rest. And so they did. They were brave, plucky lads."

"And yet you ultimately lost that bit of vision you had left, did you not?"

"Yes, I fear I did," said Sir John. "It left me on the hospital ship on the way back to Jamaica. I believe I lost it to the maggots. I lay untended there for the length of the voyage. Can you imagine a hospital ship without a single surgeon aboard?"

"Ah, Jack, they did what they could, I suppose. Had the remainder of the battle gone to us, they would have sent you home bemedaled and beribboned."

"Though sightless."

"Though sightless," Sir Robert agreed. "Yet they did promote you to lieutenant, did they not?"

"Yes, and immediately retired me on half-pay. It was all I had until my brother Henry took me in hand."

"We were all proud of you on the *Resolute*. You were ever after a hero to us, your fellow midshipmen. The captain and the chaplain arranged a special service in your honor."

"For which I am grateful, of course. But let us talk of other things, shall we?"

That proved to be difficult. The weight of Sir Robert's story put a pall upon the rest of the evening. The pudding Annie had baked was eaten in near silence by our little party at the table—and not eaten at all by Lady Fielding.

The offer of an after-dinner port was made as Lady Fielding excused herself, though Sir Robert declined it. He rose from the table and thanked her profusely for the excellent meal and the kindness she had shown him. He assured her, too, that he would do all possible on her son's behalf. For this she thanked him warmly and then departed the room toward the kitchen.

At that, all made toward the sitting room and the seldom used front entrance to Number 4 Bow Street.

"Jeremy," called out Sir John, "will you fetch Sir Robert's hat?"

"I will, of course, sir," said I.

And off I went to the kitchen, where I found the richly braided thing where I had hung it on a peg. I also found my lady sitting at the kitchen table, weeping, as Annie did her best to comfort her. I wanted to comfort her too, yet what could I but return with the admiral's tricorn?

Once back, I found the two men deep in talk as Tom Durham stood respectfully to one side.

"Even so," Sir John was saying, "I wish you had not told it—not in her presence, at any rate."

"But Jack, women should know what happens in war—what it is like."

"Why?"

"So they will not cheer so enthusiastically when we sail off to it."

"Would you have crying and weeping instead?"

"It might be more fitting."

"It might indeed."

Sir Robert took his hat from me with an indifferent nod.

"Jack," said he, "I know we promised not to discuss the matter which concerned us the day past, but that ship's surgeon, MacNaughton, has been located in Portsmouth about to ship out."

"So soon?"

"I, too, thought it strange. I wonder, would you accompany me to Portsmouth, say tomorrow, so that you might question him?"

"I have not been out of London for an age, it seems. So yes, Bobbie, if I can arrange with Mr. Saunders Welch to handle my docket, I shall accompany you—and Jeremy, too."

FIVE

*In which we go to
Portsmouth, and I
am briefly enlisted*

T he next day began calm—but ah, how quickly it went!
In the morning Sir John dictated to me a letter to Mr.
Saunders Welch, magistrate of the districts beyond of Sir
John's. It was a simple request that Mr. Welch assume responsibility for the cases, civil and criminal, that were sched-
uled before the Bow Street Court the next day. Dictated, it
was signed by Sir John at that place on the paper where I
placed the pen in his hand. Signed, it was sealed with wax.
And sealed, it was delivered by me to the hand of him to
whom it was addressed.

Saunders Welch was a handsome man who gave the impression that he was quite pleased with himself. He took the
missive with a languid hand, as soft and clean as a noble-
man's, opened it without difficulty, and read it through.

"Ah, so he wants me to fill for him, does he?"

"Perhaps, sir. If that is what the letter says." Of course I
knew the contents of the letter very well, for I had served as
Sir John's amanuensis.

"Do you know, is he leaving town?"

"That he did not tell me, sir." In point of fact, he had
told Vice-Admiral Sir Robert Redmond; I had merely been
present at the time.

"Pah!" said Mr. Welch, exclaiming in dismay at my ignorance. He turned quickly on his heel and strode to a writing desk in the corner of his office. Without bothering to sit,

he dipped a quill in ink and scrawled a brief message on the bottom of the letter. Then, taking a moment to blot it and fold it up again, he handed it back unsealed.

"On your way then, boy."

"Yes sir," said I, only too glad to be gone.

I skipped out of the magistrate's house and court, both of which were accommodated in a building which seemed twice the size of Sir John's on Bow Street. Once safely away and out of sight, I opened the letter—reasoning that if its contents had truly been confidential, Mr. Saunders Welch would have sealed it—and read what had been written in reply: "Glad to oblige, S. W."

My heart leaped within me. Sir John would be traveling to Portsmouth, the home of His Majesty's Fleet, and I should be traveling with him!

In all fairness, Mr. Welch could hardly decline the request that had been made him, since Sir John had filled so often for him. I had learned from Mrs. Gredge that there had been bad blood between the two magistrates in the beginning. When in 1754 Henry Fielding made known his plans to retire from Bow Street and journey to Portugal for his health (from which he never returned, for he died there less than a year later), Mr. Saunders Welch expected to be named as his successor. But his half-brother, John, was given the position of Magistrate of the Bow Street Court in his stead. Mr. Welch fumed in envy and acrimony and passed remarks that a blind man could never do the job (even though Sir John had already proven himself on the Bow Street bench). He set up shop beyond John Fielding's jurisdiction, and soon found it was in his own interest to make peace, for he frequently absented himself and needed a substitute. Requests for such assistance between them were quite uneven; it had been near a year since Sir John had last asked.

But with the news I carried in my hand, and the growing anticipation I felt in my breast, I ran back near the whole distance to Bow Street. I found the magistrate with his clerk and could bare contain myself until they had finished. But at last they did, and before I could present the letter, Sir John turned abruptly to me and spoke up.

"And now what *is* it, Jeremy? You have been perspiring

and hopping about on one foot and then another from the moment you arrived. I daresay I have never known you so excited."

"Mr. Saunders Welch said yes, he would be glad to oblige."

"And how do you know that? Surely he sent back a written acceptance."

"Well, he wrote it on the bottom of your letter—and, well, he did not then seal it."

"And what is not sealed is fair game? Is that your rule?" It was said teasing, for he often plagued me thus, and I read the smile on his face.

"Does that not seem fair, Sir John?"

"I shall remember your rule in the future and warn my correspondents of it. But as it happens, I anticipated Mr. Welch's agreement, and dear Kate packed my portmanteau. I am quite ready to leave as soon as my session is done. I advise you also to pack and be ready. You would not want to be left behind, now would you?"

"No, sir!"

And with that I was off and running for the stairs to the sound of his laughter.

When I burst into the kitchen, I found Tom sitting at the table and Annie leaning against a cabinet. Although there seemed nothing untowardly in their posture, manner, or tone, they seemed to start guiltily from their places at my appearance. (Did I truly notice that then, or has time given me this wisdom in retrospect?)

"I must pack," said I, all breathless.

"Where are you going?" asked Annie.

"To Portsmouth. But Tom, what shall I take? I have never packed before."

"Well, you need not take much—a clean shirt, a—"

"I thought to wear my clean shirt today."

"No, the one you have on will do. Always best to save the clean for the second day. And stockings—have you clean stockings?"

"I think so. I must see."

"And you must take along that waistcoat Mother got me yester-morning."

"Oh, I cannot do that."

"But you must if it fits. And bring it all in my ditty box. Things should fit well inside if we fold them proper. We cannot have you traipsing off to Portsmouth with all you own in a bundle on a stick. What would the admiral think? Come along, mate, I'll help you."

I gave in to him completely. He had traveled the world over and knew of such things, while I had made but one journey in my life—and that to London with little to my name but the clothes on my back. As we started up the stairs to the room we shared, I could not but think how good it was to have a wise and generous friend at a time like this.

It seemed we had bounced and been shaken about for an eternity, yet since the sun was still well up in the July sky, it could only have been four or five hours. Though Sir Robert had promised a fairly pleasant trip in his coach-and-four, I myself would as soon have walked. The cushions were soft enough, but below them there was something hard and unyielding which punished the spine yet left the buttocks undamaged.

My travel companions seemed not to mind so much, but then they were all much heavier than I and bounced not near so often, nor so high. We were four in number. Besides the admiral, Sir John, and myself, there was that lieutenant from the admiral's office, himself a rather corpulent man of about sixteen stone. The lieutenant—Byner by name—had been chosen by Sir Robert as the defendant's counsel. As we traveled slowly through London early in our journey, and it was still possible to talk within the coach, Sir John asked the lieutenant if he had had any legal training. He answered in the negative with a great loud "suh!" but said he would be happy to learn whatever the magistrate wished to teach him. This must have seemed a bad beginning to Sir John, for he did not pursue the matter further.

Once we were out on the road, conversation became quite impossible. What with the turning of the wheels, the galloping hoofbeats of the horses, the bucking of the conveyance, and the shaking of the passengers, nothing could be said at less than a shout. It was only at those intervals when the horses were walked and rested that once more talk could resume. At one of them, the admiral remarked that he had planned a stop along the way at an inn just ahead.

"Surely not to overnight there?" said Sir John.

"Oh no, Jack, we'll stay at the George in Portsmouth. Even though we make a late arrival, they will have room for us, I'm sure."

Sir John grunted his approval.

"No, I thought a bit of dinner might go well. Though it is early to eat, there is no better place between it and our destination. Nothing approaching that feast you laid on last night, I fear. That was indeed memorable—the tenderest, tastiest, best-seasoned lamb that ever was."

I wondered if word had been passed to Annie.

"Just so we are not too long in the dark, Bobbie. There are highwaymen aplenty on all these roads leading south."

"Surely they would not dare!"

"They dare much, for they are very saucy fellows."

And so, not much later, with great dash and flash and reining in of horses we came to a halt at the inn by the roadside which Sir Robert had designated as our stopping place. It was an ordinary-looking sort of place, no doubt of it. I had seen many like it on my way to London—two floors, rambling, a survivor from the last century, or perhaps the one before it. There were two horses tethered in front and a coach smaller than our own pulled up to one side, where the horses might be watered.

The inside of the place was no more impressive than its outside. The dining room was dark and tight, without seeming in the least cozy; it crowded us close with the passengers from the smaller coach, a most respectable-looking married couple, and in the darkest corner of all, two men of low, slouching appearance who seemed to have spent a long time drinking at the table. As we sat down next the man and his wife, I noted they seemed to be finishing their meal, such as it was, of bread and cheese and a bottle of wine.

"They make a good stew here," said the admiral.

"Well then, Bobbie, that is what I shall have—and Jeremy, too."

"Did you hear that, innkeeper?" Sir Robert shouted to the

man behind the bar. "Dip four stews for us, but bring us also a bottle of wine and a bottle of brandy."

The innkeeper hopped to, serving the drink before the food, placing four glasses before us, then popping the cork on the wine. He sloshed it out into our glasses and left the bottle at the table.

"A man develops a terrible thirst on the road," said the admiral, downing half the glass before him. "Do you not find it so, Jack?"

"I am so seldom on the road, to give you the truth, that I could not say."

"Well, here's to good health and long life for all at this table."

"And for Lieutenant Landon, as well," said Sir John, raising his glass.

"What? Ah yes, of course."

I tasted the wine; it had a raw, sour taste, quite unlike any I had had at Sir John's table, yet the admiral did not seem to mind. Lieutenant Byner, who merely sipped at his, did not seem to find it to his liking.

As the innkeeper served up our stew, I saw that those at the table next ours had risen to leave. The man tossed a few coins down on the table and led his wife to the door. There was a swift movement at the table in the corner. I looked sharp and saw the one fellow pulling the other back. They talked for a moment in low voices and one of them, it seemed to me, nodded in our direction.

"Bobbie, a most curious thing came about yesterday during my court session."

"Oh, and what was that, Jack?"

"I had two seamen from the *Adventure* before me for public drunkenness."

Sir Robert burst out laughing at that with so little restraint that he lost a bit of stew down his chin. He wiped it off, drank the rest of the wine from his glass, and filled it up again.

"What is curious about a drunken sailor?" he said at last. "I should think that a drunken sailor was the *least* curious thing ever. Put a seaman on shore, and he's bound to do two things—get drunk and catch the clap.'' He laughed again, though a bit more tidily.

"That's as it may be," said Sir John, "but these two fellows astonished me by saying that they had been given leave from the *Adventure* on the very night of their arrest, that in fact the ship had been emptied of its crew.''

"Not so! Not so! The Lascars are still aboard. It would not do to let fifty niggers loose in London.''

"Yet two hundred white-faced drunks bent on whoring should be no worry at all—do you believe that, Bobbie?''

"Well . . .''

"Frankly," said Sir John, "it worries *me*. We manage to keep the peace in Westminster, thanks to my constables, yet it is a precarious business at best.''

"But Jack," said the admiral in a tone of mild censure, "I fear you must take a good part of the blame onto yourself. The mood of the crew was ugly after that show you put on with the captain. I feared mutiny. And so I gave permission that all be put on leave.''

"Permission in advance, I take it.''

"I gave Lieutenant Hartsell an option, and he took it. Damned difficult it was, too, to get leave tickets and pay for them all. Put quite a strain on the bursary, it did. Is that not so, Lieutenant Byner?''

"Oh, indeed, sir!'' said the plump lieutenant.

"He was up half the night counting out pounds and pence by candlelight there on Tower Wharf. But here, Jack, let's have no more of this on our little ramble. I see you've finished your stew. Why not drink up and let me fill your glass with brandy?''

Sir Robert hefted the flask and pulled out the stopper. He held it at the ready.

"I fear not," said Sir John. "I can hold my wine, but spirits are dangerous to me.''

"And you used to be the greatest toper of us all! Ah, well.''

He gulped the remainder of the wine in his glass and filled it with brandy. Then he downed that in short order too.

"What about you, lad?'' said he to me. "Would you like to try a little brandy?''

"Ah, no sir, but I thank you for the offer, sir," I replied to him, most polite.

Vice-Admiral Sir Robert Redmond was showing a side I had not seen before. Already he seemed half in his cups. I wondered at the restraint he had shown the night before. It would be most inconvenient if he were to drink himself unconscious here at this inn. What would we then? His lieutenant seemed most concerned, and I could tell by the stern set of Sir John's mouth that he would not welcome that possibility.

I glanced at the two at the corner table. They seemed both interested and amused at the admiral's state and our unhappiness. But why not? Sir Robert was in full uniform, as was his lieutenant. How often, I reasoned, did one have the opportunity to behold a drunken admiral?

(The answer to that, reader, as you yourself may know, is far *too* often.)

Sir John rose firmly to his feet, indicating with his hand that I should follow his lead, which of course I did.

"I think we should be going, Bobbie."

There was a great scramble off to my right as the two men at the corner table tossed coins down on the table and departed. Why were they of a sudden in such a great hurry? Ignorant as I was, that boded ill even to me.

"Oh, sit down, Jack. We've plenty of time. Even if we arrive late, I'll have them rout a pair of lieutenants from their rooms. The George would not dare to let me down."

"We must be losing daylight, Bobbie. We should be on our way."

"I suppose so—go if we must. Innkeeper! What do I owe you? I'll take the flask of brandy along with me. But give me a good price, or I'll malign your name from Portsmouth to London."

As Sir Robert settled up, insisting on a ticket of receipt for his expense record, I guided Sir John through the tight passage between tables with a few touches at his elbow and a word or two in his ear. But when we reached the door and exited outside, I saw the two tethered horses were now gone. I decided it would be wise to mention to him what I had observed.

"Sir," said I in a low voice, "there were two men drinking in the corner who left in a rush when you stood up and said 'twas time to go."

"That was well noticed, Jeremy. I was aware of them. I even managed to hear a bit of what they said between them. But come, take me to the coach. I would have a word with the driver and the footman."

Have a word he did, yet he directed me inside the coach, and I heard none of it. The footman, a young Navy man as was the driver, wore a troubled expression as he assisted Sir John into the seat beside me. We were joined soon enough by the admiral. Lieutenant Byner had scrambled atop the coach where the baggage was stored. He descended after a minute or two.

"So, Jack, you think there is danger of robbers on this road?" said Sir Robert.

"Yes, I believe there is. This road is no different from any other in England."

"Come inside, Mr. Byner. Let's be on our way."

The lieutenant hauled his bulk through the coach door and closed it after him. I noted he had something of leather and straps under his arm. He collapsed into the seat beside the admiral just as the coach lurched forward and the horses began to pick up speed.

"If it's robbers ahead," said Sir Robert, "then I came right well prepared."

He patted the space on the seat between him and the lieutenant, and Mr. Byner placed his burden there, unfolding it to my view. It was not one but two very large pistols, a brace of them, each slung in what I now know to be saddle holsters.

"I take it," said Sir John, "that you are now displaying some manner of firearm."

"Two of them, as fine a brace of pistols as e'er was made. You think that a just description, Mr. Byner?"

"Oh, I do, sir."

"I won them at whist from a captain of cavalry. Proper horse pistols, they are, each near two feet long—heavy enough to fire a huge ball but well balanced so they seem much lighter than they are. Would you like to try one, Jack?"

"I would not, Bobbie. I have had no use for firearms since one exploded in my face."

"What? Oh . . . yes, of course." The admiral was given pause by that for but a moment. "I have had them only a short while," he continued, "and I have been hoping for a chance to try them out. Let the villains come, say I!"

"I wish they would not," said Sir John. "And I wish you would stop the coach and have the lieutenant pack those things away again."

"Are they loaded, Mr. Byner?"

The lieutenant did what I would not have been brave enough to do and, leaning toward the window, took the light to look down the barrel of each in turn.

"They are loaded, sir."

He replaced them in their holsters.

"Good," said the admiral. "Now I shall have someone to blame if they should misfire."

The lieutenant frowned at that, yet restrained himself from examining the pistols a second time.

This last exchange with Lieutenant Byner was carried on at shouting level, for the coach had reached its full road speed. I could but look at the other three passengers to judge their attitudes and thoughts. Sir John, whom I beheld in profile, was unsmiling and most frightfully serious. The lieutenant was openly apprehensive, casting his eyes about the interior of the coach, then down at the huge pistols, then out the window. Sir Robert, in a show of swagger, opened the flask of brandy, from which he took a deep gulp, then stoppered it and tucked it close by his side.

We jolted on for many minutes more through a country of fields and woods. From the position of the sun in the sky I judged it to be some time past seven o'clock, post meridian. There were yet some hours of daylight left, but whenever the road cut through woods, some of which were long and deep, we were plunged into a counterfeit night, so dark was the shade of the tall trees at roadside.

It was as we passed into just such a shaded stretch and had rounded a bend in the road that all of a sudden and quite unexpectedly the driver reined the horses to a halt.

We inside were tumbled about. The pistols were thrown

down to the floor. The lieutenant, all in a panic, bent to retrieve them, then dropped them again.

"Why are we stopping?" cried the admiral.

"Because there are two armed men in the roadway, sir," came the reply.

"Footman, you have a fowling piece and a brace of pistols. Use them."

"I cannot, sir."

"Why not?"

"One of them has a pistol pointed at my heart. I can do nothing, sir."

At that I heard rough laughter from the highwaymen and slow, close advancing hoofbeats.

"Well, by God, I can," said Sir Robert sotto voce.

He grabbed a pistol from the lieutenant, who had at last recovered them. Then he threw the door open, and taking bare a moment to steady himself and aim, he pulled the trigger. There was a great roar, followed by what can only be described as a screaming whinny from a horse, and then a roar from above.

I strained forward to see what had happened. Sir John threw me back hard against the back of the seat and held me there.

"Damn! I hit the horse."

More sudden than we had stopped, we started up again. Yet the wheels of the coach could not have made more than two revolutions when I caught a glimpse through the window of the poor, dying beast by the side of the road, and the admiral slammed shut the door.

"Duck!" he yelled.

The lieutenant cowered. Sir John and I sat frozen. The admiral grabbed for the other pistol.

The window broke. Something hit hard into the seat cushion beside my head. I looked at Sir John quite fearfully, yet he seemed unhurt. He went so far as to release me from his grip.

"I believe you will find the ball directly between our two heads, Jeremy," said he.

I looked and poked into a hole larger than my finger and felt something hard and still warm to the touch.

Sir Robert was all for opening the door and trying again.
Yet a pat on the knee from Sir John restrained him.

"Damn, Jack, I shouldn't have hit the horse. A shame to
shoot an animal like that."

He threw himself back on the seat, panting and perspiring
and muttering to himself.

"Shouldn't have killed that horse."

He grabbed up the flask of brandy and took another gulp.

It was some time before the driver felt it safe to stop. And
when he did so, it was in an open spot with wide fields on
either side. The footman climbed down and opened the door.
He had in his hand a fowling piece with the longest barrel
e'er I'd seen.

"All safe here, sir?"

"A near miss, but all safe."

It developed that when the admiral's shot had felled the
horse, the second highwayman was so distracted that the
footman was able to aim the fowling piece at him and blow
him quite from the saddle. Yet the rider at whom Sir Robert
had shot had jumped clear of his dying mount and was
poised by the side of the road with his pistol leveled when
the driver wisely started his team of four. He it was who put
the shot between Sir John and me.

The footman, a petty officer, had redeemed himself in the
eyes of his chief by murdering one of the robbers. He accepted Sir Robert's congratulations quite modestly.

"Just doin' me duty, so to speak, sir." Then he added:
"You'd be interested to know the two stopped us was the
same two as was at the inn. Didn't even wear masks, they
didn't." He saluted. "Well, all safe then. We'll be on our
way, sir."

He shut the door to the coach, and a few moments later
the driver kept the footman's promise. The coach moved
ahead at a moderate pace, resting the horses.

"Did you hear, Jack? Didn't wear masks—and in broad
daylight, too."

"Indeed I did hear."

"These roads are no longer safe."

"I did warn you they were not."

"You should do something about that."

''My jurisdiction does not reach near so far, Bobbie. But in point of fact they have approached me to set up some sort of horse patrol on the roads around London—constables on horseback, as it were. I think it a bad idea.''

''But why? Something should be done.''

''Most of my constables cannot ride. They can bare sit on a horse and say 'Giddap' and 'Whoa.' I should have to recruit some who are expert on horseback, and for that neither Parliament nor the Lord Mayor are willing to grant funds. I think myself the job should be done by the Army. Let the cavalry stop parading and do some work.''

''The job of the Army is to fight wars, Jack.''

''There are, at this blessed moment, no wars to fight.''

Sir Robert had no ready reply for that, and so he pulled forth the flask of brandy once again and took another swig from it. In fact, as daylight faded and dusk came on, he drank at regular intervals from it until he had near emptied the good-sized bottle. By nightfall he was fast asleep, his head resting and bouncing upon Mr. Byner's shoulder.

Still the horses plunged on through the dark until clusters of lights began to appear. These I saw were more than the villages through which we had passed along the way. I sensed quite rightly that we had reached the outskirts of Portsmouth.

The admiral slept on, though his dreams seemed to trouble him. He grew restless on his lieutenant's shoulder, tossing his head to one side and another, adding considerably to the uneasiness of Mr. Byner, who shifted this way and that to better accommodate him. Sir Robert began muttering in his sleep, though not talking aloud in any manner that might be judged comprehensible. I strained to understand what I could, but only a few words came through—''judgment,'' ''cannot plead,'' and a woman's name, ''Margaret''—of the great multitude that he mumbled. Sir John, beside me, seemed also to take interest in these occult communications from the realm of dreams. He leaned forward slightly in an attentive mode I had come to know well from watching him in court. The lieutenant, however, seemed merely embarrassed by the unexpected garrulousness of his superior officer.

Then, as the horses slowed and we entered Portsmouth proper, Sir Robert seemed to come to a kind of terrible climax in his dream state. Still asleep, he began talking—nay, shouting—quite intelligibly.

"No, no, no," said he, "you cannot blame me, you cannot!"

And thus he continued protesting, as Sir John began slapping him sharply on the knee and thigh.

"Wake up, Bobbie, wake up! It is but a dream, only a dream."

Then came the dreamer's eyes open, even as he shouted a final "No!" He blinked. He looked about.

"A dream?" said he in a timid, confused voice. "Oh, such a dream—a nightmare, it was."

He leaned forward of a sudden across the gap that separated them and grasped Sir John by both hands.

"Jack, you must save my nephew. Do what can be done. Find witnesses. Teach Byner your tricks. Do what you must, but save him."

"Lieutenant Landon is your nephew?" The magistrate spoke not in astonishment but as if seeking confirmation from a witness.

"Yes! Yes! And in my dream he sat in judgment on me—on *me!* He and his mother—my sister Margaret—and another who kept his face hidden from me until the end, when I saw it was none but myself. They sat in judgment upon me—and they condemned me—to what I do not know. Ah, but it was something horrible, horrible. I, the judge, joined in the verdict. I condemned myself!"

"Bobbie, listen to me. You must disqualify yourself. You cannot head a panel of judges sitting in court-martial upon your own nephew."

"But I must. I must see it through. It's expected of me. This is the Navy, not one of your courts of law."

"I daresay it's not."

Through all this, the lieutenant—and I confess, I as well—looked on and listened in amazement. Surely his lieutenant would know of this—yet apparently not. As for myself, it made clear to me the informality of the admiral's relationship

with Lieutenant Landon. Yet not quite all questions were
answered—no, not all.

And then the driver reined to a halt. Sir Robert, having
slept so long, seemed to have no idea where we were, and
perhaps feared another encounter with highwaymen. He
turned and looked sharply out the window of the coach.

At just that moment came a cry from the driver: "It's the
George, sir. We've arrived."

I woke next morning to bright sunlight and a glorious smell
of the sea. This was not the dirty, refuse-and-ordure-laden
Thames beneath our window but the great, broad, shining
sea. I bounded out of bed and went as swift as silent feet
could carry me to that window that I might look upon what
I smelled.

Indeed I found it there before me, but upon it—what a
sight, what riches to the eye!—rode at anchor what seemed
to me to be the entire Royal Navy. (It was not, of course:
there were ships at Spithead, a few at Bristol, and others on
duty at every point of the compass.) I, to whom the frigate
Adventure seemed uncommonly large, was quite unprepared
to find two or three others of its dimensions and shape so
close at hand. Even less was I ready for the great men-of-
war, giant ships of seventy-four and eighty guns that were
anchored farther out in the harbor. But there were others—
sloops, dinghies, cutters, skiffs—boats and ships of every
size and shape. Some smaller boats moved here and there
across the great mouth of the port, but most were relatively
stationary, bobbing in the morning sun. To my mind, the
naked masts, the spars whereon were fixed the furled sails,
gave the harbor the appearance of a lightly moving forest. I
had no idea it would look so.

Wanting to see more than the window could reveal, I
washed and dressed quickly, remembering Tom Durham's
advice and pulling on my clean shirt and stockings. I did
what I could to subdue my wild hair, surveyed the results in
the looking glass hanging on the wall, and decided they were
satisfactory. Then I sat down to wait.

Sir John had slept soundly through all my preparations and
gave every sign of sleeping on through the rest of the morn-

ing. Well, he couldn't do that, of course: he must at least be
present during the interrogation of the ship's surgeon who
had lately served on the frigate *Adventure*. And if I knew Sir
John well, he would do more than listen. I thought perhaps
I should wake him. Could it be done discreetly? I let out a
quiet cough. His slow, deep, regular breathing continued undisturbed. I coughed again louder and managed to stir him—
but only that. Perhaps it would be too early to wake him, in
any case. I only wished to ask his permission to go out and
take a better look at the harbor. Surely he would give it.
Why wake him at all? Perhaps it would be best to leave
quietly and see the time on the clock downstairs. Then, if it
was time to wake him, I would return and do the job proper.
And while downstairs, I might just go out and take a peek
at the harbor. What could it hurt?

And so I left quietly, unlocking the door, pulling it shut
silently after me. Then down the stairs and into a kind of
sitting room that I had bare noticed when we arrived the
night before. The George, as it was called, was a large inn,
with a floor above our own and as many rooms as one would
find in one of the grand inns of London. I wandered about
the sitting room and found the clock easily enough, a great
standing thing taller than myself.

"Well, young sir, you *are* an early riser."

It was then, standing before the clock, I saw that it was
but half past six.

The gentleman who had spoken, surely the innkeeper himself, was a healthy-looking fellow with a round belly and a
rubicund face. He had in hand a large tray upon which he
gathered glasses and bottles which littered the sitting room
and beyond.

"I had not known it was quite so early," said I.

"Nothing to be ashamed of," said he. "I'm the early riser
in my family. My son closes up at night, sells spirits and
wine to all the young lieutenants who drink the clock around.
Since I'm up at five, no matter what, I do the tidying up.
But you—what about you? What brings you down so
early?"

I gave that some thought. "Since it is to me falls the job
of building the stove fire each morning in our household,"

said I, "then I must be customed to it so that I wake at six, no matter where or what the circumstance."

"We are all of us creatures of habit," said he.

"I thought to go outside for a better view of the harbor."

"Aye, we have a good one." But then he considered a bit and added a caution: "I would, however, stay close to the inn if I was you. The gangs have been about these past days, and a boy alone, such as yourself, is just what they seek."

"I'll remember what you say, sir."

"Do that, young fellow," said he, turning to his work, "and a good morning to you."

I walked out the front door of the inn a little puzzled. What were these gangs who sought young boys such as myself? There were gangs aplenty in London which assembled to rob and do burglary. But to steal boys off the street? No, I had never heard of such a thing. What would they do? Sell them in slavery to the Turks? Surely the Royal Navy would not allow that—and Portsmouth was then, as it is still, the Navy's home. Perhaps I should have inquired more of the innkeeper.

Yet so taken was I by the view and the smell of that sea air that I did not return to ask questions. I took it in and walked a long walk around the place for still a better prospect. This was the side of the George that faced direct upon the harbor. What I saw was that the port was even larger and wider than I had first thought—and there were even more ships anchored about, some of them in corners quite close in. Some were docked off far to the right. I looked and looked and breathed in the air. Ah, but it was grand!

But would it not be even grander if I were to see it closer? I was not far from the seawall there at water's edge. Surely I could see more and even better there. So, putting my trust in the Royal Navy that order would be maintained at its home, and assuring myself that I had never heard tell of a gang of any sort that did their villainy at half past six in the morning, I ventured away from the inn and headed down toward the seawall.

Reader, I never reached it. For halfway there, at a corner of the street, I was set upon by a group of men lying in wait

for one just such as me—naive, innocent, and ignorant of
their foul tricks.

They were remarkably quiet for so many. I had no warning
whatever. As I cleared the corner where they had sequestered
themselves, I was quite swarmed upon. They were five in
number—grown men, armed with battens with which they
threatened me as I was grabbed and dragged back. Oh, I
fought—indeed I did! And I yelled out in protest so loud I
must have wakened all in the surrounding houses who still
slept, which of course was my intention. Yet none rushed
out to save me. How could they be indifferent to the predicament of a poor lad? What manner of people were these who
resided in Portsmouth?

I was pushed, pulled, and dragged back to a sixth in their
party. And what then should I discover but that he wore the
uniform of a lieutenant in the Royal Navy? Astonished,
amazed I was that one in such a position of trust and authority should take part in criminal practices. But as I stood
panting before him, silenced by my surprise, it occurred to
me that those who now held me were themselves in rough
seaman's dress. Could there be villainous gangs organized
within the Navy?

"Will this one do, sor?" asked one of the seagoing ruf-
fians.

"Let me have a look," said the lieutenant dubiously.

And he began prodding and poking me about, squeezing
me here and there.

"Stop!" said I, who was in no wise customed to be treated
as so much meat upon the hoof. "I am a freeborn Englishman."

"Oh, are you?" said he with a proper sneer. "Well, this,
my lad, is how we treat such impudence as yours."

He then gave my ears a thorough boxing with the palms
of his hands. It had never before been done to me (and for
that matter never was again). Held tight as I was, there was
naught I could do but suffer the indignity and endure the
ringing of my ears afterward, as he intended.

"He will do, I suppose. He's certainly no plowboy, but
lean as he is, he might one day make a topman."

"I'll say this, sor. He's stronger'n he looks."

"Well, that is reassuring." Then to me the lieutenant said: "Tell me, Mr. Freeborn Englishman, are you resident of Portsmouth?"

"Indeed I am not," said I hotly. "I am a Londoner and proud to be."

"Perfect," said the lieutenant. "Take him to the boat."

With that, my captors turned me round and began shoving and pulling me along toward the seawall, where, I presumed, a boat waited. I thought to break away and outrun them to the inn. Yet with two on either side, hands grasping my shoulders from the rear, and the chief of the seamen in front with a firm hold of my wrist, escape seemed quite impossible. I thought then perhaps to reason with the lieutenant.

"Sir," I called back to him, "I am an assistant to Sir John Fielding. We came to Portsmouth with Vice-Admiral Sir Robert Redmond."

"Ah, tell me another, lad. Why not the Lord High Admiral himself?"

"We stay at the George. You may go there and ask if you do not believe me."

"No time for that. Must be on our way."

And so, having no choice in the matter, I marched along silently a few steps; then hearing a solitary walker behind us, I hung back a bit, allowing myself to be pushed and dragged along, yet slowing us down so that I could tell by the steps on the cobblestones that we were about to be overtaken. Then I threw back my head and yelled out lustily:

"Help! I am being kidnapped. Raise the hue and cry!"

And so I got a sound thwack with a batten on the backside for my trouble, then another. Yet I had succeeded in stopping the party while I took my punishment, and I aroused the curiosity of the passerby.

He turned out to be none other than the admiral's adjutant, Lieutenant Byner.

"Mr. Byner! Sir!" I called to him.

He looked at me with mild curiosity, said his hello, and started on his way again.

"But tell them who I am!"

He stopped again and made the face of one in a sudden agony of thought.

"Oh, what *is* your name?" he asked himself. "Jeremy, isn't it? As for your surname, I know it was given me when we met, but I'm just not good at names at all. So 'Jeremy' will have to do. Hello, *Jeremy*."

"But did I not ride with you and the admiral here to Portsmouth?"

"Yes, of course." Then he frowned. "Ah, I see! You're in some sort of difficulty, are you? Like me to vouch for you?"

"Indeed I would!"

By this time I had at least managed to create a bit of confusion among this gang of villains. The seamen looked at one another uncomfortably, and their chief in crime, the lieutenant, stepped forward and introduced himself to Mr. Byner. Lieutenant Byner introduced himself, as well, and the two shook hands like gentlemen. They chitchatted for a couple of minutes, then in low voices discussed my situation. I was at last relieved when I heard Mr. Byner say something about the admiral not liking that at all. "Cause him a bit of embarrassment, you know."

"Ah, well, you may have him then. I confess he did say something about all that, but I chose not to believe him. We hear so many stories, you know—a wife and seven children to maintain, that sort of thing."

"Oh, I'm sure you do."

"*But* can't embarrass the admiral, can we?" The villainous lieutenant looked to his partners in crime. "All right, fellows, back where we were. It worked well for us once. It may work again."

They left me reluctantly and without apology as I gave Mr. Byner profuse thanks for his intercession.

"Well," said he, "that was quite a near thing for you, wasn't it? If I hadn't come along when I did, you would not have been heard from for three years—two, at least."

"Would the Turks then have let me go?"

"Turks? What have they to do with it? Don't you understand who those fellows were? That was a recruiting party from the H.M.S. *Steadfast* out in the harbor. Damn shame it was you they picked up and not some other. That's the very ship I'm off to in order to fetch that fellow MacNaughton back to the George so we may question him. I could have gone out with them. I suppose I'll find a bumboat about which'll work just as well. So I'll be off now.''

''Again, with my thanks, sir.''

He started away, then called back: ''This should take a while. Tell them not to expect me for at least an hour.''

And he continued on his way.

I ran back to the George at full speed, not wishing the recruiting party to suffer a change of heart and pick me up again. Inside the inn, I did not stop to thank the innkeeper for his kind warning which I had so carelessly ignored. But rather, I went straight to the room I shared with Sir John and burst in to tell him what had happened.

''Who is there?'' said he in mild alarm. ''Is it you, Jeremy?''

He was out of bed and half dressed.

''It is, sir. And I have something remarkable to relate.'' I was quite out of breath.

''Well, first fetch some hot water, for I need you to shave me. You may tell me your story as you attend to it.''

And that, of course, is what I did. As I lathered him up, I began my tale, which, with a multitude of details, I made last through one of my special twice-over near shaves. In response, at certain points in the telling he would let out a grunt, yet he attempted to say nothing until I had wiped his face dry with a towel.

''Well, you have learned a thing or two, haven't you?'' said he. ''Primarily, I suppose, you have learned not to ignore a warning, even when it is not fully understood.

''Ah, but more important, and all too sadly, you have learned something of one of the most execrable practices of the Royal Navy. Such recruitment parties, or to give them their more popular and accurate name, 'press gangs,' operate freely wherever magistrates permit them. I will not allow them in my jurisdiction. They pull men off the streets indiscriminately and press them into service. They stop merchant vessels and take their pick of the crew. It all began in wartime—which war I cannot say, for it is such an ancient practice—when the need for men was desperate, but now even in peacetime it continues whenever they are in need of men;

it is a form of slavery, certainly. Mr. Byner was quite right. Had they succeeded in sailing off with you aboard the *Steadfast*, you would simply have disappeared for at least two years, more likely longer. We would have grieved, thought you dead, until such time as you could get a letter back to us.

"I love the Navy greatly. I gave it my sight, but I love it still. Yet I know that it is not without faults. This one, which you have now experienced at first hand, is probably its greatest. I make no excuses for the practice. I only thank God you managed to evade the press."

Donald MacNaughton was a Scotsman, and he shared with a good many of his countrymen that habit of mind which busies itself making endless distinctions, raising objections, and arguing points for the sake of argument. I myself have found them to be a contrary people, much given to needless controversy. And just so was Mr. MacNaughton, one whose very physical being seemed to display these qualities. Lean he was and tall, near six feet above the ground; and though his mouth was downturned and his brow furrowed more often than not in a frown, his eyes glinted bright each time he felt he had won some small intellectual victory—thus his eyes seemed always to be smiling.

As had been agreed, Mr. Byner brought Mr. MacNaughton into the dining room of the inn, which, though not empty, was not near so full as it might have been. (Those who drink the clock around next day have a tendency to sleep the clock around.) Sir John and I came first, ate a good and proper English breakfast of porridge, hen's eggs, and smoked fish, which was more than either of us might have eaten at home; yet this was half a holiday to Sir John and more than half to me. Sir Robert came stumbling in near an hour later, much the worse for his adventures on the road, the bottle of brandy he had drunk and the nightmare he had had in the coach. I wondered if he had had more bad dreams during the night; if so, he did not speak of them. In fact, he spoke very little at all and ate even less. He ordered coffee for our table (for which I blessed him since I had come to love the drink) and sat sullenly waiting for his lieutenant and the ship's surgeon, who at last made their appearance well after ten by the clock perched on the fireplace mantel. Sir Robert called for more coffee.

After introducing the surgeon to the admiral and the magistrate, Mr. Byner announced cheerfully that in their discussion of the matter of the captain's death on the *Adventure*, Mr. MacNaughton had convinced him during their voyage across the harbor that he had nothing to contribute.

"Well, I wouldna' say that exactly," said Mr. MacNaughton. "Not perhaps nothing but very, very little."

"Why not let us be the judge of that, Mr. MacNaughton?" said Sir John.

"That is your right, sir, since, as I understand, you *are* the judge. Yet who, better than me, knows my own mind?"

"What little—very, very little, as you have said—do you have to contribute on this matter?"

"Well, there's no denyin' I was aboard the ship at the time."

"During the storm?"

"You may call it a storm, sir, but I call it an act of God. I have never experienced the like of it." Then he checked himself: "Well, perhaps once five years ago in the Caribbee."

"And were you on deck at any time during the storm?"

"Never once," said he, which seemed to me the first unqualified statement he had made.

"And where did you choose to ride the storm out?"

"Most of the time in my quarters, praying to the Blessed Virgin Mary that I might be delivered from that terrible storm."

"You are of the Roman Church then?"

"I am from Aberdeen, sir"—as if that settled the matter.

"You say you were in your quarters 'most of the time,' implying you were elsewhere part of the time. Where were you that rest of the time?"

"In the cockpit, attending to my surgery."

"Oh? There were casualties in the course of the storm then? Only Captain Markham had been mentioned to me."

"They were recorded in the ship's log by Mr. Hartsell," said Sir Robert.

"Ah, yes, Bobbie," said Sir John. "We must discuss the contents of the log."

"I have not yet concluded my reading of it, Jack."

"Very well," said Sir John. Then turning back to Mr. MacNaughton: "Do you recall who you treated and for what?"

"I do no' recall the names, sir, only the disorders."

"And what were they?"

"Two seamen with broken arms, which I set. Another with a broken leg, which was so badly broke, with splintered bone sticking through the skin, that I was forced to amputate, for it could not be set so. His name I do recall, Bartle it was, for he took it ill that he was to lose his leg at the knee. He made a great fuss, he did, and had to be held down." He paused in his inventory. "And, ah yes, there was another who was lost early, a topman who fell to the deck. His mates saw him still breathing and carried him down to me. Unknown to them, he had broken his neck, and the trip down to the cockpit was what killed him. Yet I could hae done little to save him. His was the first death caused by the storm."

"And the other was Captain Markham?"

"And then there were the four in the boat launched at Mr. Hartsell's orders to save the captain."

"Oh? I had not heard of that."

"It is mentioned in the log, Jack," said the admiral.

"Very well, but even by Lieutenant Hartsell's account, at the time the captain went overboard, there would have been no hope of retrieving him. Launching a boat? Was that not excessive zeal on the part of Lieutenant Hartsell?"

It was unclear whether Sir John had directed the question at Mr. MacNaughton or Sir Robert Redmond. Therefore an awkward silence followed.

"Some members of the crew thought it excessive."

"Some?"

"All to whom I talked. It was a general complaint, sir. All except . . ."

"All except who?" asked Sir John.

"All except the officers, of course—neither Mr. Landon, nor Mr. Grimsby, nor Mr. Highet."

"Who is Mr. Highet?"

"He *was* the fourth officer, sir. He fell in battle against the Dutch privateer *Haarlem* a year later. Quite young, good young lad, a pity and a shame it was."

"It always is."

"You mentioned the opinion of Lieutenant Landon as regards Lieutenant Hartsell's action in launching a boat. You must then have talked to him about the incident—Captain Markham's fall into the sea, et cetera. When was that? What did he say?"

"Why, he was quite distraught when we spoke the night after the storm, when things ha' calmed down. Blamed himself he did, but I wouldna' say he felt guilt."

"You are making a distinction which I do not quite follow."

"Well, I think it plain enough," said Mr. MacNaughton, a bit loftily. "In any mishap, him who tries to give aid or remedy may feel afterward he should have done more or different. As ship's surgeon I feel it full many a time. In this way, you blame yourself, still knowing you were not the cause of it all. To feel true guilt, it seems to me, you must indeed feel you yourself were the cause. And so I say Mr. Landon blamed himself, but I wouldna' say he felt guilt."

"I accept your distinction," said Sir John. "Do you remember what he said?"

"No." Yet having said no, he reconsidered. "Well, perhaps . . ."

"Perhaps? Please, sir, we must hear. We have traveled down to Portsmouth to glean what we can of your knowledge of this matter. We deserve better than perhaps. Mr. Landon deserves better than perhaps."

"Aye," he agreed. "Well, the first thing he said was of little importance, something to the effect that if he had grasped Captain Markham by the belt of his britches he might have saved him—the sort of thing we always tell ourselves as we look back on such situations." Mr. MacNaughton laughed abruptly and rather inappropriately at that point. "I recall tellin' this to Tobias Trindle, what Lieutenant Landon said. Tobias is a proper old salt who was at the helm that terrible day, and he saw it all. When he heard that about grabbin' the captain by the belt of his britches, he said, 'Had Mr. Landon done that, he would hae wound up with the captain's pantaloons in his hand, 'stead of his shoe. There was no savin' him.' Or so said Tobias."

"Would you repeat that, please?"

"What Lieutenant Landon said?"

"No, what Tobias Trindle said."

Donald MacNaughton repeated it, as requested, realizing as he did that what he had said was of some significance. His eyes glinted shrewdly, and in him seemed to kindle, for the first time, the beginning of respect for Sir John.

"Now," said his interrogator, "you indicated that something else said by Mr. Landon was of greater importance. What was that?"

"He said that the captain should not have been up on the poop deck in any case. He was far too ill. Mr. Landon said he had returned to Lieutenant Hartsell and told him that, but that Mr. Hartsell ha' simply repeated his order to bring him forth."

"When I talked to Lieutenant Landon—when was that, Bobbie?—but three days ago, he indicated that you would be the best source to reveal the nature of the captain's illness. Did Captain Markham consult you? Did you treat him?"

Mr. MacNaughton let out a sigh and for the first time showed some degree of discomfort at a particular area of questioning. He hesitated long and said at last: "Yes, he consulted me early in the voyage."

"And what was the nature of his complaint?"

"He ha' a swelling in his innards that gave him pain."

"What was your diagnosis? A tumor?"

"In my opinion, no. It was his liver was swollen. I advised him to give up drink. He . . . He did not take my advice."

"Am I to take it that Captain Markham was something of a tippler?"

"A good deal more than that, I fear. He seemed to me to be in the last stages of alcohol addiction. Probably he was wise not to follow my advice and give up drink. Had he done so, the shock to his system would no doubt hae killed him. He was past saving. The death he got was probably the best one he could hope for."

"Again you make a distinction. What would be the difference between frequent drunkenness and what you call alcohol addiction?"

"One of degree, I suppose—but more important, the condition of the body. His color was yellowish. His liver, as I said, was swollen and painful. I observed him at the officers' mess, and he did not take food, used it only as an occasion to take wine. He could be depended upon to down two bottles each meal. Soon he gae up the pretense of eating. He simply kept to his cabin and drank his brandy. I wouldna' hae given him six months. I canno' understand how he could hae been given a command in his condition."

Vice-Admiral Sir Robert Redmond coughed loudly at that as a warning to Mr. MacNaughton that he would countenance no criticism from him of the Fleet's decisions.

"This must have put a great strain upon the other officers," said Sir John.

"Aye, oh aye! And on Lieutenant Hartsell most specially. Him it was who charted the course, kept the ship's log, and stood double watches on deck. He took his duties serious, oh, a bit too serious, it seemed to me."

"Oh? How so?"

"Well, perhaps not so. After all, he'd had command in the French War, as I understand. He knew probably better than any of us what was required."

"What are you trying to say, man?" For the first time Sir John showed some slight exasperation with the surgeon.

"Simply that as we sailed down the coast of Africa, Lieutenant Hartsell took it upon himself to stand near every watch, every day. He complained that on those rare opportunities when he might allow himself to sleep, he was unable to do so. He'd become a proper insomniac."

"What in God's name is an in-som-ni-ac?"

"It's a medical term," said Mr. MacNaughton, with a quick upward movement of his eyebrows and a flash of his eyes. "An insomniac is one who finds it difficult to sleep."

"But you had already said that. I understood you quite well. Why should it be necessary to—" Sir John broke off, gained control of himself, and began again: "I take it that he sought help from you?"

"Of course. To whom would he go but me? I offered to administer him sleeping drafts. He found that inconvenient, since his chances to sleep came at odd hours. He thought it better if he had the contents at hand. And so I gae him a quantity of the seeds of the poppy I had carried with me from India, and I instructed him in how he might make a tea from them."

"And did that solve his problem?"

"Aye, it must have done, for he never had occasion to ask me for more. In fact, sir, his sleeplessness seemed to vanish once the captain was overboard."

"Did it indeed? How remarkable."

"He became more dependent upon his brother officers—Landon, Grimsby, and Highet. They supported him well."

There was a pause then of near a minute. The silence became a bit awkward—then somewhat unnerving to Mr. MacNaughton. He looked to the others at the table—the admiral, Mr. Byner, and even briefly at me, as if to ask, Has he done with me? Then, with a great phlegmy rumble, Sir John cleared his throat and spoke up once again:

"What is your opinion of Lieutenant Hartsell?"

"A good officer," said Mr. MacNaughton, "somewhat strict, but a first-rate sailor and steady in battle."

"And as a man?"

"Well, you know what the Good Book says."

"What is that? It says many things."

"Judge not that ye be not judged."

"Nevertheless," said Sir John, "it falls to some of us to judge—to me, for instance, when I am on the bench. And to you, sir, when asked the question I have just put to you."

Again an awkward pause. Mr. MacNaughton's eyes glinted no more. They were downcast as he shifted in his seat and squirmed a bit. Yet who but Sir Robert should come to his rescue?

"Jack," said he, "I must remind you that Lieutenant Hartsell is not the issue here. It is not the condemnation of the accuser but the defense of the accused that concerns us."

Sir John glowered. I thought certainly he would speak out in anger, yet he did not. He spoke with great control:

"Then if that is the case, tell me, Mr. MacNaughton, what is your opinion of Lieutenant Landon?"

"William Landon is the finest officer and Christian gentleman I have met in my fifteen years as ship's surgeon with the Royal Navy. It is my deepest conviction that he could never hae committed the act he is accused of."

Sir John's anger flashed out at last: "Is that, sir, why you turned tail and ran like a frightened rabbit for a berth in Portsmouth the moment the *Adventure* anchored in the Thames? So that you would not be called upon to testify in behalf of this finest officer and Christian gentleman at his court-martial?"

"Jack! Please! Mr. MacNaughton has been most co-operative."

"Yes," said Sir John, rising from the table, "and I shall ask his cooperation for twenty minutes more, while Jeremy and I go upstairs and prepare a statement drawn from the interrogation of this pusillanimous Scot. Do not worry, Donald MacNaughton, I shall put no words in your mouth. It will contain no more than you told me. But then, sir, you must sign it. You must."

He waved briskly at me, who had risen by his side. "Come along, Jeremy."

SIX

*In which we receive a letter,
and
again visit the* Adventure

There was a curious silence in the kitchen when Sir John and I returned from Portsmouth. It was near the dinner hour and indeed we hoped to be fed. Yet as we ascended the stairs, we heard no hustle and bustle, no rattle of pots and pans, nor none of Annie's loud laughter. We, or at least I, presumed that the kitchen was empty; but when I, struggling with Sir John's portmanteau and my ditty box, managed to open the door at the top of the stairs, I was surprised to find both Lady Fielding and Tom Durham sitting quiet at opposite sides of the kitchen table. Her arms were folded. His head was hung low. There was no sign of Annie about.

Tom jumped up immediately to help with the portmanteau.

"I'll just take this upstairs," said he, seeming most eager to be away.

Thus he made his escape, bag in hand. And though his mother seemed about to call him back, she checked herself and raised no objection.

Sir John entered the kitchen, came forward a few steps, stopped, and sniffed the air.

"What," said he, "no smells of dinner? Nothing in preparation? I persuaded Bobbie to go through without a stop except to water the horses. I hoped that we might eat what Annie cooked us. Where is she?"

"Annie Oakum has returned to the Magdalene Home, John."

"Oh?"

"Yes."

"I see," said he, in such a way as to make it clear he did not. "But couldn't you . . . ?"

"I was detained with matters at the Home. I only just arrived here myself. There was no one about to do the buying."

"But . . . Tom . . . ?"

"Tom is in disgrace."

"But in disgrace or no, could he not . . . Ah, well, what then have we to eat in the house?"

"All I can offer is bread and cheese."

"Well, then, bread and cheese it shall be."

"And tea, of course."

"Of course." He ruminated a moment, then said he to me: "Well, Jeremy, I reckon a pair of hungry travelers can fill their bellies on a simple meal as easy as a grand one."

Yet before I could make polite agreement, my lady raised her arm in a manner almost threatening and pointed to the stairway.

"Jeremy," said she, "up to your room, please. You and my son will be called when dinner is put out. Sir John and I have matters to discuss."

Having no choice and no proper reason to argue, I picked up the ditty box, excused myself, and marched up the stairs. Tempted though I may have been to stop halfway and eavesdrop, I continued to the top, assured that I would hear the whole story from Tom.

Yet he proved evasive. I found him in a posture not unlike that in which I had first seen him in the kitchen: he sat upon the bed, elbows on his knees, chin in his hands. He seemed the very picture of melancholy there before me, as he glanced up and acknowledged my presence with but a nod. I put the ditty box down on the floor and threw myself down on the bed next to him.

"What is it?" I asked him quite direct. "What has happened?"

"Oh, please, Jeremy, let it be."

"Well, I will if you insist, but you might at least tell me what has happened to Annie. I believe I deserve to know, for I'll probably catch some blame myself. It was I spoke up for her in this household, more or less. Why was she sent away?"

"She is in disgrace."

"So are you—or so says your mother."

"Oh, well I know, well I know. She has done nothing but remind me of that, ever since . . . Never mind, Jeremy. Let it be."

"As you will," said I.

Then, half in annoyance, I jumped up from the bed and went to where I had left the ditty box. I unpacked it in a trice, for there was little of mine inside it, and thanked him for its use. In response, he merely nodded, annoying me further. So then with nothing better to do, I went to the books piled against the wall to search out one I had not yet read. Though they numbered near a hundred, this was becoming more and more difficult each time I looked. What should I do when I had read them all?

It would be disingenuous for me to play the complete innocent with you, reader. If Tom was in disgrace, and Annie was in disgrace, it was very likely they had together committed some disgraceful act. And I knew full well that what men and women did together was held to be immoral, unless done within the bounds of marriage. It might to some then seem all the more reprehensible if undertaken by such as young as Tom and Annie. Yet I wanted to hear this from Tom. Above all—and I burn with shame to admit it—I wanted instructive details.

But then of a sudden Tom spoke out to me in a manner most accusing: "Why did you not tell me of the true nature of this 'Magdalene Home'? Penitent prostitutes, after all!"

"Your mother told me not to."

"Why did you not tell me Annie was one of these former prostitutes? That she had been on the streets for near a year?"

"Well," said I, "if I did not tell you of that about Annie, neither did I tell her that you had been a thief."

That seemed to me to be a reasonable retort, yet I admit I meant to sting him with it. What had become of us—we two mates, we chums—that we should now speak so sharp to one another?

"She could have given me a disease—the pox or some other!"

"Who? Annie?" It seemed a strange idea to me. "She seems healthy enough to me."

"Mother says you cannot tell. She has scarce talked to me of anything else. She has me frightened as I was back in Bombay."

"But what about Annie? You could have given her a baby."

"I could?"

"Well, isn't that how it is done? I admit I don't know much about it, but that much, at least, I heard from Jimmie Bunkins."

Tom seemed quite awestruck by the notion:

"By God, I suppose it's possible."

"It may be growing inside her this very moment."

"But she's so young."

"Well, so are you."

After that, he quietened down somewhat, perhaps brooding upon the pox or his unintended fatherhood. Time passed. I began to wish that Sir John and Lady Fielding would soon conclude their discussion, no matter how grave, so that I might have my portion of bread and cheese. Oh, I would miss Annie long after Tom had gone, I knew full well I would. She was a remarkable good cook—and a good companion, too. Having gone back to the books, I dwelt upon that a bit as I shuffled through them desultorily.

"It was in this very bed," said Tom, unbidden, giving the mattress a slap.

"Truly?"

"Yes, it was all arranged beforehand, it was. The girl is quite daft, Jeremy. Said she loves me . . . would do anything I liked . . ." He hesitated. "I'd no idea, really."

I frowned in my effort to comprehend. "What was it you didn't understand?" I thought she had made her feelings quite plain.

"Well, none of it. What a lot of doing there is to that business, mate! Why, we did and did all night until we fell

asleep quite exhausted in one another's arms. And that, you
see, was our mistake.''

"Falling asleep, you mean?"

"Well . . . yes. We had chosen this bed quite wisely because it was well away from where my mother slept. But I
had been chosen to set the fire in the stove in your absence.
When Mama rose in the morning and found neither me nor
Annie about, she must have suspected the worst, for she
came directly here and found us all atangle, as naked as ever
could be, dozing away there where I now sit.''

"What happened then?''

"What do you suppose? She let out a terrible roar, sent
Annie away to get something on her, and as I tried to cover
up she began preaching to me that I might now have the pox,
and such other terrible things as I do not wish to mention.
And then—''

Just at that moment the summons came from our kitchen.
Lady Fielding called us down in a manner much less genteel
than was her usual.

"Bread and cheese," said I.

"Ah, well," said he, "at least it is something. I'm quite
famished.''

And so, together we answered the call, descending to the
kitchen not as two hungry lads in a great hurry to eat, but
with the slow measured tread of two who know not what to
expect but expect the worst.

In the event, what we experienced was far from the
worst—thanks, in large measure (if not completely), to the
efforts of Sir John. He delivered a long report on our trip to
Portsmouth which, all in all, was a most eventful journey,
what with the attack upon our coach by marauding highwaymen, and my near recruitment into His Majesty's Navy.

Even Lady Fielding was impressed by this last. She roused
herself from her unhappy musings and reached across the
table to clasp my hand.

"Oh, Jeremy," said she, "how terrible! You would simply
have disappeared. We would have had no notion of what had
become of you.''

"A goodly portion of the men on the *Adventure* were

pressed," said Tom. "It was them who were left aboard when we anchored."

At that his mother gave him a critical look. Apparently those in disgrace were not allowed to contribute to table talk.

"Indeed," said Sir John, "and it was them who Hartsell allowed ashore with Sir Robert's permission—or connivance, better put—to cause mischief in my jurisdiction."

"Not likely to see them again aboard the *Adventure*," said Tom.

"We are likely, though, to see a good many of them in my court."

A knock came upon the door. I jumped up from the table and went to it, throwing it open, and there I found none other than Benjamin Bailey, captain of the Bow Street Runners.

"It is Mr. Bailey, Sir John," I called back to the table.

"Well, have him come in, by all means."

"No need, sir," said he. "It's just as I was making my first round of the night I was stopped by a drunken seaman who gave me a letter addressed to you. Sealed it is and in a good hand, so I'm sure it were not the sailor who wrote it."

"Was he off the *Adventure?*"

"He didn't say, Sir John. Just stuck it in my hand and asked me to give it you. From the look of it, he's been carrying it about for a while. I'll just hand it over to Jeremy here and be on my way. Pleasure to see you, my lady. Sorry to interrupt things."

"Nice of you to come by, Mr. Bailey," said she, waving in good fashion.

And with that he touched hand to brow and started back down the stairs. I put the letter in Sir John's hand, and he laid it carefully by the side of his plate.

Though modest by our household standards, the meal was in no wise stingy. There was near a pound of Stilton set out upon the table alongside a good-sized loaf with butter aplenty and a bowl of pickled cucumbers. We ate well, though after Sir John finished his tale of our travels, we ate mostly in silence. It was indeed only after he had finished that I noted that he had omitted any mention of his interview with Mr. Donald MacNaughton and had said nothing of Sir Robert's startling revelation of his kinship to Lieutenant Landon. In fact, nothing was said of our purpose in making the journey to Portsmouth.

After we had done with the meal and drunk the last of our tea, Sir John pushed back from the table and belched appreciatively. "Thank you, Kate, that was indeed as good a meal from scratch as has ever been got together." Then: "Tom, dear boy, I wonder, would you be willing to take on Jeremy's usual washing-up duties on this occasion? He and I have a bit of work to do."

Then, rising, he took up the letter Mr. Bailey had brought and signaled me to follow. We climbed the stairs to his small study. He took his accustomed place behind his desk and laid the letter between us.

"Let us hear what Mr. Bailey has brought us," said Sir John.

There was still light from the window, yet it was growing dim from the lateness of the hour. "I wonder, sir," said I, "if I might light a candle to read by?"

"Of course, Jeremy. Light or dark are much the same to me. There are matches there? A tinderbox?"

"Yes, sir."

I lit the candle nearest me, took the letter, and broke the seal.

"The letter is signed Jonathan Grimsby, Lieutenant, R. N.," said I.

"Hah! Well, the third officer of the *Adventure*—or perhaps acting second officer, since Lieutenant Hartsell styles himself 'acting captain.' What has Mr. Grimsby to say to us, Jeremy?"

Holding it close to the candle, I read the following letter aloud to Sir John:

To the Hon. Sir John Fielding, Bow Street Court, No. 4 Bow Street.

Sir John,

   Whereas I, with the unfortunate Lieutenant William Landon, am become as a virtual prisoner upon the H.M.S. *Adventure*, it is impossible for me to visit you, which is unjust as I have information to give. I wish to

impart it to you for you seem most truly interested in
helping my brother officer. Would it be possible for you
to return to the H.M.S. *Adventure*, so that I might speak
to you direct?

Since we are extremely shorthanded as to officers
with Mr. Landon confined to his cabin and Mr. Hartsell
remaining in his by choice, I serve as officer of the deck
through all the daylight hours. I cannot be sure when,
or even if, this letter will reach you, since I am entrust-
ing it to one of the crew, and so I shall not request that
you come on any specific day, which would be rude and
presumptuous of me in any case. All days are the same
to me here aboard the *Adventure*. I shall be eager to see
and talk with you whenever you can come.

> Yours & c.
> Jonathan Grimsby
> Lieutenant, R. N.

After taking a moment or two to digest the contents of the
letter, Sir John brought himself upright in his chair, planted
his elbows on the desk, and leaned toward me.

"Well, Jeremy, what do you make of that?"

"Only good," said I. "He wishes to help Mr. Landon. He
has information to impart. I see only good in that."

"Yet why write to me? Why insist on speaking to me and
only to me? Why not to Lieutenant Byner, who is, after all,
Mr. Landon's counsel in this terrible matter? Why not to Mr.
Landon himself?"

"I cannot suppose why not to Mr. Landon," said I, "except what Mr. Grimsby wishes to tell may not be something
Mr. Landon wishes told."

"Or cannot tell himself."

"Yes sir, you felt Lieutenant Landon might indeed be
holding something back."

"Under instructions from his uncle."

"But as to why Mr. Grimsby chooses not to tell Mr. Byner, I can only suppose that he may not yet know that he is
now acting as counsel."

"Or if he knows, he may feel that Mr. Byner is too closely placed to Bobbie . . . er, Sir Robert."

"Yes, sir."

"Damn all, Jeremy, this matter has more convolutions than a snake, and like a snake, you know not where to grab it. I feel that Bobbie is all for helping the young man—he was near in tears when he told me Mr. Landon was his nephew and begged me to save him. *There* was a surprise, eh? His sister's son! Imagine!" But then he lapsed into silence a moment before he added: "Yet he often seems to be blocking my way, telling us, in effect, that there are certain paths of investigation open to us and others that are not. Why did he call me into this matter if he would put such restrictions on me?"

"What do you plan then, Sir John? Will you accept Mr. Grimsby's invitation?"

"Oh yes, but it will have to be done behind Bobbie's back, so to speak. We'll go tomorrow afternoon following my court session. How does that strike you, Jeremy? You'll have an errand in the morning, and I'll have a task I don't look forward to, so afternoon it will have to be."

Since he had not been specific regarding the errand or the task, I knew not to ask him. I accepted it that I would find out soon enough.

"In any case, we have our witness. Mr. Landon's case is not lost."

"Sir?"

"You caught it, surely, in the course of MacNaughton's rambling, bladdering responses? We did leave it out of the statement he signed, however, for it was hearsay. Remember?"

"Oh yes, of course—the helmsman, Tobias Trindle."

"Exactly! Him who said that if Mr. Landon had grasped the captain by the belt of his breeches he would surely have been left with those breeches in his hands, rather than a shoe."

"He gave it as his opinion that no man could have saved the captain."

"We have our witness," said Sir John, "but now we must find him."

I gave a moment's thought to that. "Perhaps Tom and I could help there better even than Mr. Bailey or the constables. Tom must know Trindle by sight. And perhaps I know better where to look for him."

(And, I thought, Jimmie Bunkins might know best of all.)

"You make a good argument, lad. Let me discuss it with Tom. I must now talk to him, in any case. I heard him but a moment ago climbing the stairs to the room he shares with you. Go now. Tell him that I wish to talk with him."

Excusing myself and wishing him a good night, for it was grown late, I did as he bade and proceeded to the attic room. There I found Tom stretched out upon the bed, hands clasped behind his head, staring up at the rafters in the ceiling. His eyes shifted to me as I entered; he offered me a muttered hello and nothing more.

"Sir John wishes to speak with you," said I. "He's in the little room below he calls his study."

Tom rose from the bed and planted his feet firmly on the floor.

"Now I *will* get a proper cobbing," said he. "I suppose I should dismiss all thoughts of the midshipman's appointment."

I knew not what to say to that. I could do no more than shrug. And so he left, and I took his place on the bed. I knew not how long their talk lasted, for whilst reading in some book chosen from the pile against the wall, I dozed. Yet from the deep dark of the night and the guttering of the candle, I judged it must have been a very long talk indeed. In fact, I barely woke sufficient to ask him how he had fared.

"What?" said he. "Oh, we barely talked about that at all. It will come tomorrow. We talked about life aboard the *Adventure*. It turned out I had much to tell him."

"He made a witness of you then."

"Yes, I suppose he did."

Constant was my amazement at Sir John Fielding's knowledge of London. How could he have known where bumboats were to be hired? Yet all he had to do was call to the driver of the hackney, "St. Catherine's Stairs," and we were off on another adventure. Our destination lay just beyond the

Tower of London, as I found, so I was able to view sides of
the great castle that I had not seen before. Down Little Tower
Hill we went to St. Catherine's Street, where we came within
sight of the church. It was there the driver reined up and
called down that we had arrived.

I was relieved to see no wharf at the bottom of the stairs:
there would be no rope ladder to descend. No, the stairs
simply led to the river's edge where a half-dozen boats of
various shapes and sizes were pulled up upon the bank. As
soon as the boatmen saw us coming, they surrounded us and
began shouting out their prices that bargaining might begin.
Sir John dealt expertly with them and soon we were on our
way out into the broad river.

"Don't know why you'd wish to go out there, sir," said
the boatman between manful tugs at the oars. "Ship's all but
deserted now."

"We've good reason."

"We had great trade out there for a time—drabs, doxies,
booze. Many's the trip I made."

"And then they sent off the crew on leave."

"Aye, all of a night it was. By the morning there was just
some Lascars and the ship's officers. Lascars got no money."

Sir John said nothing to that.

"That being the case," said the boatman, "strangest thing
is, you're the second haul I made today out to the *Adventure.*"

"Oh? Truly? Who was your first?"

"Naval officer, a lieutenant he was. Took him out this
morning and waited, just as I'll do for you, then took him
back—though he asked for Tower Wharf on the return."

"Interesting."

"Why they did not send a boat from the ship I cannot
guess."

"Perhaps he was not expected."

"Must be so," said the boatman.

And then the conversation between them, tenuous at best,
lapsed completely.

With but a single oarsman, the longer trip from St. Catherine's Stairs took longer still. It gave me time to consider
the surprising morning I had spent. The errand I had been

sent on took me to the Magdalene Home. From there I was
to take Annie back to Bow Street. She was as surprised at
this as I was and full of questions on the return trip. Yet I
had no answers for her, and hearing no answers, she soon
gave up questioning. She was quite anxious by the time of
our arrival and demonstrated her state with much wringing
of hands and a tear or two which she bravely wiped from
her eyes. She was no longer the saucy Annie of old.

The solemn-faced trio who awaited us in the kitchen
seemed to frighten her more. She met them with eyes cast
downward and when they bade her come with them she as-
sented with a nod. When I made move to follow, I was
sternly instructed to remain there in the kitchen. They went
direct to Sir John's study, as I could tell by their footsteps,
and once there one of their number shut the door. They must
have talked near an hour, and when they emerged and returned to the kitchen all was changed.

I did not know then, though I was to learn later from Tom,
that Sir John and Lady Fielding faced the two young mis-
creants and lectured them on the gravity of their act. Sir John,
of course, did most of the talking. He did not dwell overmuch
on the dangers of disease, for he must have felt that his Kate
had covered it sufficient; he did, however, give weight to the
possibility of pregnancy. He asked Tom if he was in a position to support a child; Tom admitted he was not, acknowl-
edging at the same time that it would be his duty to do so.
What had they to say for themselves in defense of their actions? Annie said that she had done what she had done for
love, the first time ever it was so, that she loved Tom with
all her heart. Sir John pointed out that because she was the
more experienced of the two, she might be said to bear the
greater blame, but that there was an extenuating circumstance. He then asked Tom if he loved Annie. He admitted,
his face averted from her, that while he liked Annie and was
attracted to her, he could not say that what he felt was love.
Then Sir John pointed to Annie's poor crumpled, weeping
face, and said that Tom, knowing her feelings for him, had
used them to have his way with her. And then said he, most
solemn, "It is a terrible thing, my boy, to use another human
being so." And Tom was sore ashamed. In the end, a grave

promise was extracted from each that what had happened
would not be repeated. And Annie was told that as long as
she kept her promise she might stay.

Yet none of this I knew when the four returned to the
kitchen. And when I was told that Annie would stay with
us, I could not suppose why such happy news should make
them all look so sad—and Annie most sad of all. But thus
the crisis passed, and it was not long before she had recovered herself sufficiently to sit down with me and call out a
list of edibles for me to buy at Covent Garden Market. She
confided that she would make this a meal for all to remember. . . .

"You shall have to precede me up the ladder, Jeremy,"
said Sir John, rousing me from my ruminations, "and ask
permission of Mr. Grimsby for me to come aboard."

We were quite near the ship, coming hard along the dan-
gling ladder.

"But," said I, "you were invited by letter."

"Of course I was. It is but a formality, but one that is
rigidly observed."

And so, at the right moment, with a proper signal from
the boatman, I grabbed hold the ladder and began my ascent.
Going up was never a problem for me, after all. The problem
came when I reached the top.

For who should I find waiting for me but Mr. Midshipman
Boone, that nasty young fellow who, in attempting to push
me down the poop deck stairs, had tumbled down them himself.

"Away, you pissy little lubber," said he. "I'll not let you
aboard."

Ignoring him, I attempted to throw my leg over the deck
rail. But he pushed it back, and I near lost my balance for a
brief moment. I grasped the rope ladder tight.

"I am come for Sir John Fielding," said I with all the
authority I could muster. "He waits in the boat below."

"I care not who waits. This is His Majesty's Ship *Adventure*, and we let no lubbers aboard."

"You had better," said I. "He is Magistrate of the Bow
Street Court."

And so saying, I went up the ladder again. He, in turn,

pushed down at my head with such strength that he near unseated my hat from its perch on my head and forced me down a rung or two.

"I care naught for your magistrate," said he. "Get down and get away, or I shall push you into the river."

I admit that his threat had some effect upon me. Though I have since conquered my fear of the water and can now swim a fair distance, I was at that time quite incapable except in a wading pond. Nevertheless, I had bested him once and was determined to do so again. And so I set my hat firm upon my head and started again up the rope ladder. Yet this time when his hand came down toward me, I was ready for it and grabbed him tight around the wrist. He fought to get loose—but to no avail. Then, pulling with all my strength, I descended one rung of the ladder, stretching him down over the deck rail, perilously threatening his balance. He had been flailing at me with his free hand, but now he was forced to grasp the rail with it and hold on for dear life. Then, tugging downward with all my strength, I began to move down to the next rung. His round face wore a fearful expression. His eyes bulged from the effort of resistance. He looked in pain. Perhaps he could swim no better than I!

If I could force him down one more rung I'd have him overboard.

But then another face appeared above that reddened, sweating one upon which I concentrated all my energy. It looked familiar, yet I was in no state to try to put a name to it.

"Ah, Mr. Boone, I see you are about to take a swim," said the familiar face. "I would advise against it. The Thames is much too dirty for that sort of recreation. And Mr. Proctor, I'd advise you to let loose your grip, for if he goes swimming, he may take you with him."

The face belonged to Mr. Grimsby. I loosed my grip, and Mr. Boone collapsed out of sight on the other side of the rail. My hand was so weakened by the struggle that it was near useless on the ladder. Yet somehow I managed to get up and over, only then noticing that our combat had attracted an audience of smiling Lascars along the rail. They waved their approval, saying nothing. One or two applauded. I had to jump wide not to come down feet-first on Mr. Boone.

"Sir John," called out Mr. Grimsby loud and clear, "you have permission to come aboard."

"I heard a bit of difficulty up there," Sir John called back.

"Nothing your assistant couldn't handle, it seems."

Mr. Boone righted himself and rose slowly to his feet. The look he gave me was the evilest I had e'er got from man or boy.

"I know you have other duties, Mr. Boone," said the lieutenant. "Go now and attend to them."

"Yes, sir," said he, and went limping off, perhaps still bearing reminders of our encounter three days before. He was the sort of fellow on whom it would be unwise to turn your back.

And then it seemed that in no time at all Sir John's face appeared, his heavy leg also, and he hopped on deck more artfully than I should ever have expected.

Mr. Grimsby came to him, grasped his arm, and shook his hand. They spoke together in low tones, and Mr. Grimsby led him off across to the starboard side of the deck. Much as I would have liked to follow and listen in, I knew I could not. Ah, well. Taking heart in the words of the poet—"They also serve who only stand and wait"—I looked about for a proper place to pass the time.

I was approached by one of the Lascars. He, like the rest, was thin and small of stature—no bigger than my fourteen-year-old self—but unlike the rest he spoke a kind of English.

"Good day," said he to me.

"Good day to you, sir." Though I could not judge his age, he was plainly older than I was.

"We all like you. Inja boys all hate Mr. Boone. Oh yes." There was a most peculiar rhythm to his speech—quite rapid and a bit up and down the scale. "I think we go to sea, and there is a storm, he fall overboard. Oh yes."

He flashed a great smile at that, as if he had just told a great joke.

"Why do you hate him? What has he done?"

"Oh, many things, many things. He like to beat Inja boys with bamboo stick for no reason. Just he like to. Oh, very bad boy. Best he die, start a new life, do better next time. Oh yes.''

(This seemed to me such a peculiar notion that I wondered had I heard him aright. But reader, I have since learned that this business of living successive lives is part and parcel of their strange religion.)

''And what of Lieutenant Hartsell?'' I asked, remembering what Tom Durham had predicted.

He flashed his smile again. ''Same storm. Oh yes. For Mista Landon. Silly man Mista Hartsell, makes girls of boys, thinks nobody knows. Very silly.''

That struck me as a most peculiar thing to say. I wanted to question the Lascar gentleman further to ascertain his meaning, yet before I could do so, he had pointed to the shore and changed the subject.

''That is London there?''

''Yes sir,'' said I with a citizen's pride. ''It is the largest city in the world, sir.''

''Many big houses, yet I think Bombay is more big. More people in Bombay. Oh yes.''

Footsteps behind me brought me swiftly round. (Did I fear that it might be young Mr. Boone, the ''very bad boy,'' with his bamboo stick or a knife to plant in my back?) But just a few paces away I found Mr. Grimsby and Sir John returning. Their conference had not lasted near as long as I had expected. The Lascar gentleman to whom I had been talking snapped a sharp salute, and Mr. Grimsby returned it in the casual manner common to most officers.

''Ah, Mr. Singh,'' said the lieutenant, ''are you keeping our young guest entertained?''

''Oh yes, sir. We finish to sand the quarterdeck, sir. Wait your look, sir.''

''You shall have it. Oh, Mr. Templeton!''

Mr. Grimsby called up to the poop deck where a boy who looked bare twelve years old strutted about as though he himself were master of the *Adventure*. He answered with a salute and a ''Suh!'' sung out in high soprano.

''I should like you to convey these two visitors from the city to Mr. Landon's cabin.''

''*Suh!*''

As he descended, Mr. Grimsby said softly to Sir John: "For appearance' sake, I think this necessary."

"I quite agree," said Sir John. "And who knows? With Sir Robert absent, the poor fellow may be willing to speak more in his own behalf."

Moments later, Midshipman Templeton appeared among us, saluting again, and Mr. Grimsby sent us off with him.

"Will Mr. Hartsell be available to us?" Sir John asked the young midshipman.

"I think not, sir," said the boy. "He spent a restless night, on deck most of the night. He retired to nap but an hour ago."

He was quite the young gentleman. Mr. Boone could and should have taken lessons from him in deportment.

Having brought us to the door of Mr. Landon's cabin, the midshipman rapped sharply upon it.

The door opened and there stood William Landon, somewhat in a state of dishevelment. He had doffed his coat and unbuttoned his shirt against the heat and closeness of the small room. His long hair was damp with sweat.

"Visitors, sir," said Midshipman Templeton, and stepped aside.

"Ah, Sir John Fielding, is it not? But your name, young man, eludes me for the moment."

As he shook our hands, I took the opportunity to inform him. He seated Sir John, and I took my place to the side of the magistrate's chair. Then, looking about before seating himself, Mr. Landon found the door still open and the midshipman standing at an attitude of attention.

"That will be all, Mr. Templeton. Please shut the door."

The boy did as he was told, and Mr. Landon seated himself opposite the magistrate.

"This is indeed a surprise," said the lieutenant, "not so much seeing you as seeing you unaccompanied."

"By your uncle?"

"Ah, he told you then."

"He did indeed," said Sir John, "in the course of our visit to Portsmouth."

"You have been and come back so quickly?"

"Yes, and had we not, we might have missed your de-

clared admirer, Mr. Donald MacNaughton, altogether. He
had snagged a berth on a ship of the line, the *Steadfast*,
bound for the Mediterranean.''

"That was his choice and his right."

"Perhaps, but to my mind, it showed a deficiency in moral
courage, especially in one who purports to hold you in such
high regard. In any case, we got a statement from him. It
may be helpful." Sir John paused, then said to him rather
severely: "But tell me, Mr. Landon, why are you so forgiving of those who run from you?"

The lieutenant was silent for a moment; then he burst out
as one in anger: "Because my cause is lost! Because the
noose is already tight round my neck!''

"Let me rephrase what I said on my earlier visit to you,
young man. Your cause is lost only if you think it so. If you
do not fight, if you do not do all you can, *tell* all you can to
help yourself, then you will surely hang. But if you tell me
or your defense counsel, Mr. Byner, all you know, then you
have a chance and a good one, I believe. Now, please inform
me, has Mr. Byner visited you?"

"Yes, this morning."

"I thought as much. Did you tell him any more than you
told me three days past?"

"No sir, I did not.''

"He seems a bit dull, but we must work with what we
have. To be quite frank with you, Mr. Landon, I believe,
though I cannot seem to convince your uncle or Mr. Byner,
that you know very well why Lieutenant Hartsell has lodged
a charge at you which we both know to be false. Why can
you not give it forth?"

Again, silence from the lieutenant. Then: "Not here."

"Do you fear for your life?"

"That is all I can say."

"Well . . ." Sir John stopped, exasperated. "At least your
man MacNaughton gave us something—the name of a witness."

At that, the lieutenant caught my eye and put a finger to
his lips and pointed to the door. I gave Sir John's shoulder
a squeeze in an attempt to persuade him to hold his tongue
and began across the short space to the door on my tiptoe.

"What? What did you mean by that touch, Jeremy?"

I had reached the door. I flung it open in one swift motion, exposing young Midshipman Templeton. Though he threw himself immediately erect, he had been caught in that classic posture—ear to the keyhole.

"Who is there?" roared Sir John.

"It . . . It is I, Midshipman Templeton. I wished only to ask if there was anything you would require, sir."

"Yes, that you absent yourself far from here, young man, and do not return."

"Yes, sir!" And so saying, he left in a great hurry.

"You see the difficulty in talking here," said Lieutenant Landon.

"I do, yes. Jeremy, I must ask you to close the door and stand guard outside it. I am quite disappointed in myself. My ears are such that none can approach without my knowing. At least as a rule."

"He was in stocking feet, Sir John," said I. "He had removed his shoes."

"Then he was a proper little sneak, wasn't he? But I'm afraid, Jeremy, you must guard the door."

I shut it behind me and took a place in front of it, arms folded, a sour expression on my face. Let them come—Templeton or Boone. They would have me to deal with. Then came my second thought.

Though I saw the need for this task and could not, in any case, have refused it, I nevertheless regretted having to leave the lieutenant's cabin at a time when it seemed likely that he might at last have something substantial to say. Sir John was indeed most persuasive. Yet why should Mr. Landon resist at all? Why should his uncle forbid him, with a shake of his head, from discussing certain matters? His *uncle?* Ah, it was all most perplexing. Perhaps, I thought, if I made my mind still and concentrated all my attention to the door behind me, I might be able to discern what was being said in the low, muffled voices behind it. In any case, I would not stoop to listening at the keyhole.

But then, quite surprising me, the door behind me opened. I had been leaning against it, and it unbalanced me, though I did not embarrass myself by falling upon my backside.

"Oh, sorry . . . uh . . . Jeremy, I should have tapped upon the door before opening it, something of the sort, to give you warning."

Lieutenant Landon was most apologetic, and I most forgiving. The two men took leave of one another, and I saw Sir John out onto the quarterdeck.

There, waiting for us, hands clasped behind his back, erect, in a studied posture of command, was the acting captain of the H.M.S. *Adventure*, Lieutenant James Hartsell, R. N. I muttered the news in Sir John's ear as Mr. Hartsell approached.

"You, sir, are not welcome aboard my ship."

"Oh?" said Sir John. "Mr. Landon certainly seemed to welcome me."

"Mr. Landon is a prisoner awaiting court-martial."

"And therefore entitled to counsel."

"His counsel, Mr. Byner, visited him this morning. We had a long talk. You, Sir John Fielding, have no standing in a naval court."

"Perhaps a little as an amicus curiae. That has not yet been settled."

"Quoting Latin will do you no good with me, sir. I will give you no access unless accompanied by Vice-Admiral Redmond. Lieutenant Grimsby was wrong in granting you permission to come aboard. He assumed you came with the authorization of the admiral. He was wrong in doing so—and thus I have informed him."

"How can you be so certain that I have not Sir Robert's authorization?" asked Sir John, all innocent.

"That was one of the matters that emerged in my discussion with Mr. Byner. And so, sir, I will accompany you and the young street ruffian with you to the ladder and thank you both to leave my ship."

"Then leave we must. Come along, Jeremy."

The acting captain bumped along ahead, his boots thumping the deck loudly with each step. He seemed to wish to sound important, since Sir John was denied the sight of his commanding appearance.

"By the by, Mr. Hartsell," said the magistrate, "since we may not be coming back this way again, I wonder, sir, if you would answer two questions I neglected to put to you on our earlier visit. The first is why you waited so many months to lodge charges against Lieutenant Landon in that letter to the Admiralty Court. The second is why, having lodged them, you allowed him to continue serving in active duty on the *Adventure*."

I saw that we had come to the ladder on the port side of the deck. I plucked on Sir John's sleeve as a signal to stop. He came to a halt and waited calmly for a reply.

Mr. Hartsell seemed quite affronted that Sir John dared to persist. He had thought, it was plain, to intimidate him, having no idea how difficult that would be. But then a smile of the most supercilious sort appeared upon his face. He had no doubt had an inspiration of sorts.

"Though I have no need to answer the questions you ask and do not recognize your authority to ask them, I shall do the charitable and gentlemanly thing and give you a response, sir. In fact, I shall give you two.

"The answer to your first question is that to charge an officer of my ship with the murder of its captain was indeed a very serious matter, and I felt it necessary to give such a serious matter long consideration. In fact, I took months to think about it before writing the letter to which you refer.

"As to why I continued Mr. Landon in active service, the answer is simple. He was a good officer in all respects but one. He had murdered his captain. Why should I have deprived myself of the services of a good officer? Good day to you."

With that, he turned on his heel and left us there by the port ladder—though not quite alone. Mr. Singh was there to assist me in guiding Sir John onto the ladder. It was done without much difficulty. The boatman below gave a wave; all was well at his end. The Indian gentleman and I watched his swift descent. I wanted to ask him to explain the peculiar thing he had said—yet now was not the time. All I could do, when my turn came, was to say, "Thank you, Mr. Singh."

It was not until we were settled within the hackney and on our return journey to Number 4 Bow Street that Sir John showed any inclination to talk of our visit to the *Adventure*. He had been silent in the bumboat—silent and within himself in such a way as to forbid discussion. Once more the loquacious boatman sought to inspire conversation by prattling on and asking questions. Yet he heard only grunts in response and soon gave up his enterprise.

We had gone but a little distance in the hackney coach, however, when Sir John chuckled of a sudden and gave my knee a touch.

"Jeremy," said he, "did you hear what that popinjay of an acting captain called you? He called you a 'street ruffian'! I'd no idea you'd acquired such a reputation—and on a warship, too. You must indeed be a nastier fellow than ever I had guessed."

I knew not what to say: "Well, I . . . sir . . . that is . . ."

"Or perhaps we had misjudged Lieutenant Hartsell. He may be a gentler soul than we thought him—especially with regard to Mr. Boone, whom I understood from Mr. Grimsby to be a particular favorite of the acting captain. He made him an acting lieutenant, more or less at fifteen—isn't that remarkable?"

"Was Mr. Grimsby's information worth the trip to the *Adventure*, sir?"

"I would say so, yes—though it did no more than confirm what I heard from Tom last night. He did give us a name, however—another frightened rabbit who fled the frigate— though not so far as Portsmouth, praise be. We shall pay him a visit tomorrow."

I considered a moment, then decided. "Sir John," said I, "there was a Lascar seaman assisted you to the ladder; he—"

"Ah, that explains it!" said he, interrupting. "I caught a most exotic odor from him—the most remarkable spices. But proceed, Jeremy. Pardon my intrusion."

"He speaks English of a rather curious sort, yet for the most part quite comprehensible. We talked while you were with Mr. Grimsby, and he said the strangest thing about Lieutenant Hartsell."

"Let me hear it then, by all means."

SEVEN

*In which I meet a man
of the cloth and later find
a drowned man*

As Sir John and I made our way together through the bustling morning crowd in Covent Garden, he pulled me close and exclaimed the difficulty in negotiating a way through such disorder.

"There is no pattern to their movements," he grumbled. "It is all back and forth, this way and that. Some simply dawdle and chat. My stick does me no good, for it seems always to be colliding with something or someone, nor can that something or someone be depended upon to then move from my path. I'm afraid I shall have to depend upon you completely through the piazza, Jeremy, until we make our destination."

"What is our destination, sir?"

"Oh? Did I not tell you when we started out? Sorry. I meant to keep no secrets. We're for St. Paul's."

"In the Garden?"

"Of course! I would not subject myself to this chaos if I was headed for the other. The din here is intolerable!"

It was, in truth, loud, chaotic, and disordered, and yet I quite liked it for the very reasons Sir John found it repulsive. It was indeed no place for a blind man to venture unaided. But the piazza pulsed with the life of London, and most specially in the mornings when the cooks and kitchen slaveys and boys such as myself came out to do the buying, or some simply to wander about and listen to the cries of the hucksters and the sellers. It seemed the liveliest place in the city at such times.

Yet I said nothing of this to him. I simply held tight to his right arm and muttered my instructions in his ear: "A little to the left here," "A crowd ahead, let us give them a wide berth," et cetera.

Thus we made our way until the church was mere steps away. It was then Sir John informed me that it was not the church proper to which we were headed but the rectory.

"You see it, Jeremy? It should be just to the right, unless I am mistaken. It must be a largish building, for it accommodates many visitors and guests such as him we visit."

Indeed it was a large building, of red brick construction. It was, as I later discovered, maintained as a kind of hostelry for clerics of the Church of England who visited on various matters whilst their bishops were in London during the sessions of Parliament. I guided Sir John round to the entrance and up the two steps to the door. We stood before it for a moment.

"Just here?" said he.

"Just here," said I.

Then he banged upon it stoutly with his stick. I believe he enjoyed doing that. I had never known him to make use of an ordinary door-knocker. Just as he was about to repeat the summons, the door opened and a woman of some years and wide dimensions appeared. She seemed rather formidable.

"Sir John Fielding," said he, "to call upon the Reverend Mr. Andrew Eagleton."

"What is your business with him?" she asked most suspiciously.

"That is of no concern to you, madam. Leave it that I am Magistrate of the Bow Street Court, as you no doubt know, and I wish to talk to him in my official capacity."

Still she held on stubbornly: "He has committed no crime."

"That's as may be, madam, but he may have been witness to one, and that I can only determine by talking with him."

Though her hard face became no softer, she relented at last and swung the door wide.

"All right," said she, "you may wait in the sitting room whilst I fetch him."

Together we moved inside. I ushered him through the next door to the left, which she had indicated with a sharp wave of her hand. Once in the sitting room with Sir John ensconced in a chair and I beside him, we heard the housekeeper's heavy tread upward upon the stairway which I had glimpsed on my way in.

"Why is it," remarked Sir John, "that women are so much more difficult to intimidate than men?"

For that I had no answer and gave none.

The room was empty but for us two and quite silent. The thick walls of the building and the well-fit glass of the windows kept out the hullabaloo of Covent Garden. Only the ticking of a clock upon the mantel could be heard until, through the sitting room door, came the sound of two descending sets of footsteps on the stairs.

As they continued, Sir John said to me, "I want you to watch this fellow carefully, though not obviously. In my experience, preachers show a great talent for dissimulation."

"I shall, sir."

Then, only moments later, the door opened and a man in black entered, one of about the age of thirty, tall and fair. He seemed the very picture of what a young cleric should be. Sir John rose, introduced himself and me, and shook hands with the Reverend Mr. Eagleton. The latter pulled a chair near, and both men sat.

"This," said the young man, "is an unanticipated honor."

"Oh? How so?"

"Why, sir, as long ago as my time in Oxford your name was known to me. All Queen's College was alive with talk of you and your Bow Street Runners. Now I have the opportunity to meet you, as it were, in the flesh. I count myself lucky and indeed honored, as well."

"Well, and I, Reverend Eagleton, find myself somewhat abashed. I'd no idea my modest reputation would reach so far. Oxford, you say?"

"Certainly, sir, and even in the little country parish of Stanton Harcourt, where I served for a time as curate, your

name was heard, though not as oft as at the university—
simple country folk, after all.''

''Of course,'' said Sir John, ''yet they are the very salt of
our English earth.''

''Amen and amen. May God bless them all.''

By this time, reader, you may be as dismayed by your
reading of this exchange as I was in listening to it. On the
part of Reverend Eagleton it seemed the most unctuous sort
of flattery; while I can here but quote his words, I cannot
convey the tone of voice in which they were uttered, which
was honeyed but somehow solemn and boyishly eager all at
the same time. Perhaps more surprising was Sir John's response, for he seemed to consume these candied words and
puff up upon them before my very eyes. Could his natural
vanity be fed so easy on such sweet pap?

''You say you were a curate,'' said Sir John, ''but your
title tells me you have been ordained to the priesthood.''

''I have been, yes, and that but three years past. Though
I come from modest stock, my dear father somehow found
money enough to defray the expenses, may God bless him
for it.''

''Indeed,'' said Sir John, ''yet how did it happen that,
newly ordained, you accepted a place as modest as chaplain
on a Royal Navy frigate?''

''Ah well, yes, that,'' said he with a most serious smile.
''For two reasons, chiefly. The first was that there was no
vicarage open to me at the time. And you may not credit it,
sir, but I craved a bit of adventure. I had lived so sheltered
a life up to that point—and I thought that, after all, I might
do some good among those rough seamen. In all modesty, I
believe I did.''

''I'm delighted to hear it,'' said Sir John. ''Are those the
two reasons then—the lack of a suitable vicarage and a crav-
ing for adventure?''

''No, I count them as but one and the same. The other
reason, the greater reason, was this: I had had bubbling inside
me during my last two years as a curate . . . a book!''

''A book? Do tell.''

''Oh, yes sir, with your kind permission I shall. I had taken
many, many notes there in Stanton Harcourt, gone so far as

to write out a prospectus strictly for my own use that I might better understand what ought to go into the book when I should have time enough to write it. And upon consideration of my options following ordination, which I confess were not many, I decided that on shipboard my opportunities would be much greater to write—and indeed they were!''

"Bravo! And were you able to finish?''

"I was, yes. I brought my notes, my prospectus, and the necessary books along on the voyage, and the two and a half years we were away proved more than ample time.''

"What is the nature of the work?'' asked Sir John, leaning forward on his stick, as if truly eager to know.

"Theological,'' said Reverend Eagleton. "In style it is hortatory, and in content Latitudinarian.''

"Ah,'' said Sir John, "Latitudinarian—how exciting.''

(I must remark here that I hadn't the slightest notion what Reverend Eagleton meant by that—nor, do I believe, did Sir John. Yet the magistrate encouraged him by a smile and a nod of his head to continue; that, of course, was all that the cleric needed.)

"I reach out on one side to pull in the Church of Rome,'' said he, throwing out one arm, "and on the other to pull in the Methodists,'' and out went the other arm. He drew his arms together in a kind of self-embrace. These gestures, though eloquent, were lost on Sir John, I fear.

"For what have we all in common?''—resuming. "Why, the Holy Scriptures, of course!'' He gestured with his left hand to an invisible Bible he held in his right. "I argue from the Scriptures against dogmatical intolerance, of which, going back to the last century and the one before, we were as guilty as they.''

"I had not realized the Methodists had been around so long,'' said Sir John.

"Well, no, naturally not. Here I refer to the Church of Rome, but . . . well, you get my drift—a nautical term. I mean to say, you understand?''

"Oh, indeed I do. It sounds a worthy work indeed. And you are in London to find a publisher for it?''

"Yes,'' said he, "with the right dedication to an influential patron, this book could win me preferment. I could secure a chaplaincy to a noble household, a prebendary!"

"A bishopric," suggested Sir John.

A glint came into the eye of the cleric for just a moment—
but then he laughed in a deprecating manner. "Oh," said
he, "I aim not so high so soon, yet who knows what the
future might bring? I am no less worthy than others."

"I'm sure, I'm sure. But, you know, I have acquaintances
within the world of publishing."

The Reverend Mr. Eagleton nearly jumped from his chair,
so eager was he.

"Could you . . . well, would you consider putting in a
word for me?"

"I would consider it certainly, but let us talk of other
things for a moment, shall we?"

"Oh, yes, as you wish, sir."

"Let us talk of life aboard the H.M.S. *Adventure*."

"Ah, the *Adventure*! Well, I admit I was puzzled when
the housekeeper told me that you thought I may have been
witness to a crime. You referred, naturally, to that lamentable
matter involving Lieutenant Landon. I know the man, of
course, and respected him greatly. I was as astonished as any
on board to learn of the accusation against him the night
before we anchored. But as for being a witness to the crime
he has been charged with, I'm afraid I can't help you there.
During that dreadful, dreadful storm I was belowdecks in my
cabin the entire time, praying that we might survive. I don't
mind telling you, sir, that I have never been so frightened in
my entire life. But no, Sir John, I saw nothing—absolutely
nothing."

"I thought that might be the case, yet it was only proper
of me to ask."

"Yes, but . . . well, I'm surprised that you are involved in
this case. Is this not before the Admiralty Court?"

"Indeed, yet I am assisting, more or less in an advisory
capacity."

"Assisting the prosecution or the defense?"

"Would it matter? I'm for the truth, Reverend Eagleton.
I always am."

"To be sure, to be sure. Of course it does not matter."

"I believe that in addition to serving as chaplain on the

Adventure, you were also schoolmaster to the midshipmen.
Is that correct?''

"Well, yes, it is not unusual for the chaplain to hold the
position of teacher also—or so I was told."

"How many were in your class of midshipmen?"

"There were four, but about a year into the voyage one
of the boys was killed—an accident, fell from the top rigging
onto his head and died immediately. Terribly sad. I preached
a lovely sermon at his funeral. Though short, it was one of
my best, I believe. I wrung a few tears from those hardened
old seamen."

"Jeremy and I have met but two of the remaining three—
Midshipman Boone, who is a bully and not liked by the
crew."

"Poor Boone!" said the cleric. "He is so pitifully inept
at maths that navigation is simply beyond him. I fear he will
never pass his lieutenant's examination. Perhaps he takes out
his frustration on his inferiors—not commendable, of course,
but understandable."

"And we also met Midshipman Templeton, who is a
sneak."

"Goodness, Sir John, you do judge them harshly. They
are but boys, after all."

"That I grant you. Now tell me, who was the third surviving member of your class?"

Reverend Eagleton did not like the turn taken in the interrogation. The questions and comments were harder-edged
and now put to him with increasing rapidity. He responded
by pouting.

"Midshipman Fowler, and he is a perfectly fine young
man."

"While you were their teacher, you were also their spiritual adviser, were you not?"

"As chaplain, I was spiritual adviser to all aboard the *Adventure*."

"Yet since the midshipmen were presumably the youngest
aboard, did you not feel a special responsibility toward their
spiritual welfare?"

"I suppose so, yes."

"Did any of the midshipmen ever come to you with complaints, asking for advice, or moral guidance?''

''Well, they must have done. Yes, over two and a half years, of course I'm sure they did.''

''Of what nature?''

By this time Reverend Eagleton sat most uncomfortable in his chair. Beads of sweat stood out upon his domed brow. His lips were pursed in a tight line.

''I'm afraid I cannot answer that.''

''And why not, sir?''

''Because what is said to me in my capacity as spiritual adviser should not be repeated. Don't you see? It is much the same as the seal of the confessional in the Church of Rome.''

''Is it now? But you are not a Roman priest.''

''The principle is the same.''

''There are bishops and theologians who would argue with you on that point, I'm sure. Yet you are a clever fellow. I'm sure you could hold up your end of the debate. But let me press the question, being more specific. Let me put it to you thus: Did the boy who fell to his death—What was his name, by the by?''

''Midshipman Sample.''

''Did Midshipman Sample ever come to you alleging unnatural conduct against him by one of the officers?''

''I cannot answer that because it was discussed in confidence.''

''Then it *was* discussed.''

''I cannot answer that.''

''What about your Midshipman Fowler, whom we have not met but you say is a fine boy? Did he ever come to you with a tale of unnatural liberties taken against him?''

''I cannot answer that.''

''Boone? No, not Boone. He is so much the pet that he must never have complained.'' Sir John sighed. ''I tell you, Reverend Eagleton, you disappoint me. I should think you would have shouted to the high heavens. I should think you would have gone to that officer and faced him down, called on the Almighty to strike him down. But no, you remained in your cabin and wrote that book of yours, did you not?''

With that, Sir John rose swiftly from his chair and just as

swiftly I was at his side to start him toward the door. Yet he
held back, not yet ready to leave.

"I did not lie to you, sir. I do have acquaintances in the
world of publishing. And I will gladly put in a word for you
and your book if you will stand up in Admiralty Court and
answer the questions you have refused to answer me. Nay, I
will do more than that. If you will name the acts and name
the name of the perpetrator, I will see that the book is published, whatever its quality, even if I have to pay the costs
myself. Those are my terms—quid pro quo. Nothing more
or less. What say you to that, sir?"

The Reverend Mr. Andrew Eagleton had nothing to say to
that. He sat with his face averted, his eyes on the window,
concentrating on some distant object.

"I thought not," said Sir John. "But should you change
your mind, you will find me at Number Four Bow Street
nearby. Good day to you."

And he was off for the door at a quick step. It was all I
could do to catch up and get it open before he crashed
through it.

Outside in the piazza, he continued his swift pace, making
it difficult for me to keep up. He threw his stick before him
in reckless arcs, shouting, "Make way! Make way!" He
seemed not to wish my assistance at all. Yet when he had
bumped once or twice, he slowed a bit so that I might catch
him up.

"Guide me through this, Jeremy," said he. "My rage is
spent, though my anger persists."

I took him by the elbow, guiding him this way and that,
saving him from at least one collision. Thus we proceeded
at a more reasonable pace, threading our way through the
clusters of buyers and idlers.

"I take it, sir, you will need no report from me on his
reaction to your questions," said I.

"Oh no, I read him well enough—a flatterer, a young man
filled with himself and his ambitions, a moral coward. Not
a rare combination of qualities, certainly, but seldom are they
advertised so plain. He must *learn* dissimulation. And he
will."

"You baited the hook cleverly," said I. "He must choose

between losing your assistance in getting his book published
and standing up in court to give testimony."

"Jeremy, he would never give testimony willingly in Admiralty Court or any other—not on the matter we discussed.
To do so, he must needs reveal himself as the craven wretch
he was at the crisis. But I shall give his name to that dunce
Byner. Perhaps a subpoena can be issued." He paused
abruptly, then asked himself, "Does the Admiralty Court
even have the power to summon to witness those no longer
attached to the Royal Navy? Good God, I must find out.
Don't let me forget, lad."

"I promise, Sir John."

We walked on, by now nearly to Russell Street and out
of the Garden. The flow of the crowd had eased to the point
where I thought it a good time to put to him a question that
troubled me.

"Sir John?"

"Yes, Jeremy, what is it?"

"There is something I should like to know. I understand
that serving both as chaplain and schoolmaster to the midshipmen, the Reverend Eagleton had a special responsibility
to the boys. They were in a sense his charges."

"That is correct."

"I understand, too, that when some special harm was done
to one or more of them, he evidently sinned by omission in
failing to confront the doer of the harm and defending his
charges."

"Yes, by doing nothing he tolerated it, even accommodated it."

"But what I don't understand is the specific harm done to
them. What is unnatural conduct? What are unnatural liberties?"

He said nothing for a goodly number of steps, then he
made an uncertain beginning—clearing his throat, uttering
an "uh," then clearing his throat again.

"Ah, well, yes," said he at last, "unnatural conduct is . . .
uh . . . conduct that is not natural. That is to say, well, the
Lascar seaman you talked to put it simply but rather well.
He said . . ."

"Yes, sir?"

"Well, you remember what he said. You told me in the hackney coach."

"Yes sir, but you did not explain it to me."

"True, Jeremy, I did not, but I shall . . . in due time. Yes, I will explain it all in due time."

"Well, is it that—"

"But not now."

"As you say, Sir John."

So it was with Sir John Fielding. Some explanations came easily and readily from him. Others came late, if at all. Still others did no more than obscure what they sought to illuminate. I was indeed not hopeful of learning more from him.

Turning from Russell Street onto Bow Street, we walked at a good pace, he having shaken off my hand at his elbow and I once again challenged to keep up with him. We had not gone far until Number 4 was well within view, and I spied before it a coach-and-four. A little closer and, identifying driver and footman from our journey to Portsmouth, I realized that this was the conveyance of Vice-Admiral Sir Robert Redmond. Of this I informed Sir John, and he gave a deep grunt of satisfaction, though little more in response. Yet when we came abreast of the coach, he seemed to be aware and paused.

"Good day to you, gentlemen," said he to the coachmen.

They greeted him in kind most respectfully.

"And where is your master? Inside the coach?"

"No sir," said the footman—petty officer. "He waits you inside your place of business."

Sir John chuckled at that. "I had never heard it so described, but it will do, it will do. Has he waited long?"

"No doubt longer than he would like, sir. Near half of an hour's time, I should judge."

"Thank you," said Sir John, and turned away, moving his stick about until he found the right stone, the right step, and finally the correct door of the two that stood side by side giving separate entrances to the building. His capabilities often amazed me still.

The one he had chosen led back to the strong room, where the day's harvest of offenders awaited their appearance in court. Mr. Fuller was there, keeping order among them, and

so was Mr. Marsden, who was preparing the docket for Sir
John, and so, finally, was Vice-Admiral Redmond.

He was in full-dress uniform, a sword at his side, pacing
in such a way that his back was to us as we entered. His
manner betrayed impatience.

"If he has waited this long," said Sir John to me, "then
it must be something of importance he wished to discuss.
And that, my lad, is good, for I have much that is important
to discuss with him."

Then came the admiral bustling toward us, all red-faced
from his exertions.

"Jack," said he, "where have you been? We must talk."

"Good, Bobbie. Where I have been is one of a number of
matters I wish to talk to you about. Into my chambers, shall
we? It's that door just ahead."

Yet Sir John held back, took me aside, and whispered in
my ear.

"You recall, Jeremy, that you put yourself and Tom forward to search for our witness, Tobias Trindle? The time has
come to look in earnest. Stay out as long as you must, but
find him. Now get Tom and go."

It had been over a year since I had been inside the grand
house on St. James Street that had formerly been the London
residence of Lord Goodhope. It had been transferred grudg-
ingly, though out of necessity, by his widow to Mr. John
Bilbo, the somewhat notorious proprietor of London's most
fashionable gaming house, in settlement of her late husband's
gambling debts. Tom Durham had been there recently, taken
by Jimmie Bunkins to meet his master, the dark, black-
bearded man rumored to have once been a pirate and known
to one and all as Black Jack. Tom came back quite taken
with the man, as all seem to be, even and including Sir John
Fielding, who with some slight reluctance counts him as a
friend. The house on St. James Street had awed Tom, as well.
Yet his description of its interior was so inexact I could get
no sense of how it had been changed—though changed I
knew it surely had been.

It was none other than Jimmie Bunkins himself who answered the door when Tom, decked out in his shore duds,

banged hard upon it with the brass knocker. Black Jack Bilbo kept no servants, as I knew from Bunkins, except a cooking staff, a server, and two coachmen. Instead, he housed a few of those in his employ at his gaming house; they were expected to work for their keep, so whoever was nearest when a knock came upon the door was at that moment appointed butler. Thus was Bunkins nearest.

"Well," said he, "if it ain't me two old rum chums! *Entrez vous!* That's Frenchie talk which I am learning from a Frenchie lady who dorses here."

He pushed the heavy, oaken door shut after us.

"What's the word? You two look right queer, you do."

"It's a queer matter, Jimmie B.," said Tom. "We've got us a hard lock."

"We're looking for a witness," said I.

"Ah, Beak business! Best tell me plain and see can I help."

And so, as shortly and quickly as I was able, I laid out before him the task given us by Sir John. I told him of Mr. Landon's situation; that he stood accused by Mr. Hartsell, who was the only witness against him, but that we had learned of another who had seen it all and could speak in Lieutenant Landon's defense.

"He's an old salt sailor," put in Tom, "and sure to be out on a tear for as long as he's got bobstick to his name. Where would he be, my Jimmie B.?"

"Why, in some stew or dive on the river beyond London Bridge, taking a flash of lightning with his mates, t'be sure."

"You know the where of it?"

"I know the lay near as good as I know Covent Garden. I filched many a guinea and napped many a bob from sleeping sailors in the gutter thereabouts. You know the cull by sight, Tom?"

"I know him well."

"Then I can help—but I must first ask the cove of the ken. Come along, you two. He'd want to see you both."

And so we followed Bunkins down the hall which I remembered well from my earlier visits to the house. How different it seemed! Walls that were painted white were now a deep gold yellow. Over the fireplace which was situated

midway down the long way was a painting of a Venus, all
lush and pink, with an attendant Cupid. I thought to give it
closer study yet saw that this was not the proper moment.

Then to the library wherein the Goodhope affair had got
its beginning. Bunkins knocked stoutly upon the door and
waited right patiently until a familiar rough voice from beyond barked out an invitation to enter. Once inside, I found
that it was a library no longer, though there were indeed a
few books about. The shelves had been removed, the walls
painted a light blue, and the room had been converted into
a picture gallery of sorts. Nautical pictures and prints were
everywhere the eye might look—the prints hung in sets, the
paintings large upon the wall. There were more pieces of
furniture about the room than I recalled, but, as before, the
large desk dominated all else, perhaps Lord Goodhope's
same desk, and behind it sat the master of the house, "the
cove of the ken," Black Jack Bilbo. He rose and beckoned.

"Well, come in, come in, all of you—and if it isn't my
old friend Jeremy! Come forward and let me have a look.
You've grown an inch or two, I swear. How long has it
been?"

"Near a year, Mr. Bilbo. 'Twas at the little wedding party
when last we met."

"So it was," said he. "Sir John I have seen here and
about. We've dined together once or twice—but you . . . a
year, you say!"

"Yes sir, nearly that."

"And Mr. Durham, I'm glad to see you've returned in
such good company. Always welcome here, both of you.
Now, what can I do for you lads?"

"I came seekin' permission to go with them, sir," said
Jimmie Bunkins ever so politely.

"Go with them where, young sir?"

"Down to the places on the river where the drunken sailors is to be found."

"*What?*" roared Black Jack, who could truly roar when
it suited him. "Have I not spent a year of my life trying to
keep you from such places? And now you wish to return to
your old haunts to corrupt these two good lads?"

"Oh, no sir," said Bunkins. "You misunderstand, sir.

They're searchin' a witness off Tom's ship, the *Adventure*. They asked me help to show them where to look. I, uh, know the territory from, uh, earlier days.''

''I see. Well . . . perhaps I should know a little more about this. Pull those chairs over and seat yourselves. Jeremy, suppose you tell me what you can of this matter.''

We did as he bade us, and once settled, I retold the tale and at greater length than before. At one point Tom interrupted to testify how much liked and respected was Mr. Landon by the crew. But then I went on to describe Sir John's interrogation of Mr. MacNaughton in Portsmouth and how he had mentioned in passing the name of one who during that fearful storm had witnessed the fall of the captain into the sea and Mr. Landon's efforts to save him.

''And it is him you now seek?''

''Yes, sir, it is,'' said I, as Tom seconded me.

''Well, first of all, Jimmie Bunkins, you have my permission to go and be part of this search. But mind, be back for dinner for you must go to my establishment for to make a delivery of the usual sort. Is that agreed?''

''Yes, Mr. Bilbo,'' said he most properly.

''But let me tell you, too, Jeremy and Tom, your Mr. Landon is in a right tight corner, for the way His Majesty's Navy works is this: The captain is king aboard the ship. His word is law; his judgments as from the Almighty. Would you not agree, Tom, that that is the way of it?''

''I would, sir. No question of it.''

''I'm surprised,'' said Black Jack, ''that your fellow— Hartsell is his name?—that he did not make his accusation on shipboard before the crew, pass judgment upon him, and have him sewed up in a canvas and tossed overboard. That was the punishment for murder given in the old Black Book.''

''To that, sir,'' said Tom, ''I could say that he was acting captain and no more.''

''Still and all,'' said Bilbo, ''he was the captain.''

''And had he acted so in summary judgment, it might well have worked against him. Mr. Landon was so much the favorite of the crew that there could have been mutiny, retribution at least.''

"But your witness has not stepped forward, and he has had the chance, am I not right?"

Tom gave sober thought to that. "Yes, Mr. Bilbo, what you say is true."

"Then he may not prove a very willing witness."

"If so, I shall persuade him."

"Well, I wish you all good fortune. You, Jimmie Bunkins, have your orders."

"Aye-aye, sir."

"Show them where to look. Stay with them till it be time to return. Here—" He dipped into his pocket and tossed some coins out on the desk. "You'll need money for a hackney coach, to and from. Take this, Jimmie."

Bunkins jumped up and scooped the money from the desk.

"And for you two, a warning. Where you are headed is indeed a dangerous territory. I think you will need these."

So saying, he opened a drawer in the desk and pulled from it a box of leather with brass strapping. He opened it, revealing a pair of what I took to be dueling pistols, each silvered and engraved like one I had myself once had occasion to fire.

"Both of these are loaded," said he. "But I'll not give you powder and balls to reload, for I don't want them fired. To show them and threaten should be enough to get you out of any bad situation. Is that clear enough?"

"Yes sir," said Tom and I in chorus.

"Now, you, young Mr. Durham, have fired such in battle. You know the dangers and the precautions to be taken. About you, Jeremy, I am a little less sure. But you proved once you could shoot. Now you must prove you know when to hold back."

He dug the two like weapons from their resting places and, taking each by its barrel, handed them to us.

"They should fit in your pockets. Get them back to me as soon as you have found your man or given up the search. And if ever Sir John receives from you any hint that I have lent you these, I shall be your enemy for life. I make a good friend but a terrible enemy. Now be on your way."

•   •   •

Dear God, this was indeed an ugly section of the city. It was all docks, wharves, keys, and storehouses, and in between them all were nestled some of the lowest dens and dives I had seen. All that made it tolerable was the bustle of the crowd and throngs of workmen at some locations along the way. When docks or wharves were empty, or ships stood empty of their cargoes, then there was no work to be done and all was deserted—except for those dark places where gin, rum, ale, and beer were sold. Such locations were far beneath any in Covent Garden. Some that we visited—and we visited quite a number—had not even tables and chairs. Patrons had their choice of standing at the bar, sitting on the floor to drink, or lying drunk upon it among their mates.

Our plan was simple enough. We would begin at Custom House Stairs and work our way westward along the river, stopping at each such place as I have described so that Tom might see were there any of the crew of the *Adventure* inside, that he might inquire of them the whereabouts of Tobias Trindle. Since these grog shops were nearest the anchorage of the frigate, just off Tower Wharf, they were the likeliest in which to look. We would go as far as London Bridge and no farther, for the tall-masted, seagoing ships themselves could not travel beyond it. Bunkins, who seemed to know the territory quite as well as he had boasted, had authored the scheme. Tom concurred, and I, having no preference in the matter but simply wanting to get on with our search, fell in with them.

The Gull and Anchor, with a crudely painted sign hanging above the door, was the first place in which we looked. Hard by the Custom House as it was, this one was not near so crude as others we would visit. But it was as dark as any and smelled as bad of stale beer and ale. Jimmie Bunkins and I held back near the door and let Tom roam free through the clusters at the bar, then turn away, shaking his head in a negative. Just as he did, he was hailed by a loud voice from a table in a nearby corner.

"Avast there, Tom Durham, ain't you the one in your suit of lubber's clothes!"

Tom started over to the table whence the cry had come, beckoning us to follow.

"Well, if it ain't old Bristol Beatty!" shouted Tom in a tone near as rowdy. "And Mizzen Trotter Tim and Ol' Isaac. Imagine finding you three here."

"They like our bobs as well as any place along the river," said one of them. I was never sure which exactly was which.

"Just started our day's drinkin'," said the second.

"Seat yeselves, boys. Have one on us," said the third, waving frantically at the serving maid, as fat as a country sow, who came waddling over to the table.

"Give these lads beer. That's a proper drink for lads."

"Where did you get them duds, Tom?"

"Aw," said Tom, "from my ma. She would have me out of my seaman's suit or know why."

"Well, if a body must wear shore clothes, them's the kind to wear. You look a proper gentleman."

"Who're these two mates of yours?" I believe the questioner was Old Isaac; he was, in any case, the eldest of the three, white-haired and near toothless.

"This here is Jimmie Bunkins. We were thieves together, but now we're well reformed. And this is Jeremy Proctor, sort of a brother like now my ma got married again."

There was a great deal of hand shaking all around the table. Then came the fat serving maid and banged down three tankards before us. Money changed hands. Then Tom bade the woman bring his three mates from the *Adventure* a round of what they were having. She scampered off as quick as ever she could waddle.

"No, no, no, Tom lad, it's us as should be treatin' you."

"I've not spent a farthing all the days I've been in London," said Tom. "Living at home I am, eating at my stepfather's mess. I've plenty to spare."

"Always said you was a good boy, Tom," said the one I suspected to be Old Isaac.

"Besides," said Tom, "I've something to ask that would help us if you knew the answer."

"And what is that, lad?"

"Where is Tobias Trindle? Have you seen him? Where might we seek him?"

The three exchanged looks. Such questions seemed to disturb the seamen.

"Oh, don't you worry," said Tom. "We mean him no harm. The fact is, there may be a reward in it for him when we find him."

A reward in heaven perhaps, thought I. That was the only possibility that I saw. But let him say what he would to them.

"A reward, is it? Well . . ."

Old Isaac pulled out a clay pipe and began filling it with tobacco from a pouch on the table. He tamped in the crushed leaves of the stuff as he considered.

Just then the serving maid returned with three glasses of water-clear liquid—gin from the smell of it. The trio from the *Adventure* raised their glasses as Tom paid her with a shilling and collected a whole pocketful of copper in exchange. When they set their glasses back down upon the table they were but half full. The liquor seemed to loosen their tongues.

"Well, if you're lookin' for Tobias in such a place as this," said one of the other two, "then you're lookin' in the wrong place."

"Why is that, sir?" I asked, at last shrugging off the burden of silence I had heretofore accepted.

"Because, lad," put in Old Isaac, pointing with his unlit pipe, "she's the only woman here, and old Tobias would say, 'She ain't worth bothering with.' In fact, he said so just yesterday at this very table, didn't he, mates?"

"He did."

"Yes, he did so."

"Now, some men, they get their leave tickets, and they like to take a little holiday with a bottle. Others, they might take to the drink, but if a woman comes along who's to their liking, they might take a roll with her, as it's a bit of pleasure a man can't get on shipboard. But Tobias Trindle is the onliest man I know who's got only one thing on his mind when he comes ashore—and it ain't gin or rum. Ain't that so?"

The last lines he delivered with a great leer, which brought guffaws from his mates.

"No, lad, if you're searching for Tobias, you must go where the doxies are in the greatest number, for that's where he will surely be."

"But where does he dorse?" put in Bunkins.

"Dorse? What language is that, boy?" Old Isaac seemed somewhat offended.

"Cant, flash-talk," said Bunkins in his old pugnacious way. "Where does he sleep? Ain't he got no proper lodging house?"

"None at all, just as where the whore has her crib."

I looked at Tom across the table. He gave a slight shrug, as if to say, What more can we get from these fellows? Then I felt a nudge from Bunkins at my left side.

"You goin' to drink that?" he asked, knowing full well I quite loathed beer and would only take coffee or wine as strong drink.

I gave the tankard a little push in his direction, and he grabbed it up. He guzzled its contents in a trice.

There was a general murmur of approbation from the three old seamen.

"Now there's a lad knows how to drink!" exclaimed one of them, as Old Isaac at last brought out his tinderbox and made ready to light his pipe, giggling his tribute.

When Bunkins responded with a colossal belch, there was even greater merriment.

"Well done!"

"Let's put another in front of him, see can he do it again."

But at that Tom jumped to his feet, and I followed. Bunkins rose a bit reluctantly.

"No," said Tom to them, "we must be off and continue our search. If you see Tobias, tell him I seek him, will you?"

"Be sure of it, lad."

"And remember what I told you," said Old Isaac through great billows of smoke. "Look for the doxies, and you'll likely find Tobias Trindle."

"Try the Ship Tavern downriver. There they got whores aplenty and rooms above. That's where he spent his first night ashore."

As we departed with goodbyes and thanks, I could not but wonder why they had not told us that earlier.

While Tom was all for getting on direct to the Ship Tavern, I, knowing that a proper search should be conducted in orderly fashion, insisted we stop at the places between and search through them, too. Bunkins had no opinion in the matter; he simply wanted more beer, it being a hot day and the air most heavy.

We must have stopped at six or seven dives along the way. In some there were women, and in some there were not. Yet having given in to my judgment, Tom was most thorough. He circulated through these dark dens and found other seamen from the *Adventure*. All had seen Trindle at some time or other since coming ashore; none knew his present whereabouts. In the two drinking places that were without the most rudimentary comforts of table and chair, as I have previously described, Tom turned over those stretched out upon the floor—but without purpose, for even though he found two of the crew in one such place, they were in no condition to tell him anything. Bunkins, on the other hand, took advantage of these stops along the way to feed his apparently unquenchable thirst. He would bang upon the bar and call for beer as Tom moved through the room. Nor would he leave a tankard unfinished, for he prided himself on his ability to quaff one off in two or three great gulps.

By the time we reached the Ship Tavern Jimmie Bunkins was in a rather sorry condition. We had stopped thrice along the way so that he might relieve himself against a wall. But with our goal in sight, he begged our help that he might vomit into the river and give some help to his bursting belly. There was an empty wharf nearby. We supported him between us over to the edge and held him by his belt as he leaned over and let gush the brownish-yellow contents of his stomach in great repetitive heaves until there was no more. We pulled him back up and Tom gave him his handkerchief. Bunkins wiped the sweat from his face and the vomit from his mouth; then he spat twice into the river.

"That should help," he said at last.

"Why did you drink so much, Jimmie B.?" asked Tom.

"Don't know," said he. "Start, can't stop."

He stood, panting a bit, swaying, looking dizzy in the head.

"Listen, chums, you'd best go on without me. The cove, he won't like it if I'm late. But I should tell you, there's more such as we been in beyond the Tower. They start at St. Catherine's Stairs, but be careful, for that's the worst part.

Keep your daddles on your barking irons there.''

"I know St. Catherine's Stairs," said I.

"Good," said he. "You're a right pair of rum chums. But keep your dubber mum about this, would you? The cove wouldn't like it, and I'm tryin' hard to please him. Uh ... Tom?"

"Yes, Jimmie B.?"

"I wonder, could I beg a bob for the hackney. I drank up my return."

Tom quickly thrust a coin into his hand.

"I'd best shove my trunk. Goodbye to both of yez.''

And shove his trunk he did, taking each step most purposefully up Fresh Wharf in the direction of London Bridge. He would find a hackney likely enough there. Still and all, his condition troubled me.

"Will he be all right, Tom?"

"He'll be fine. He'll throw some water on his face, dab some cologne smell on to take away the stink of his puke, and nobody will know.''

"He slurred his words a bit."

"Then he should keep silent."

"As you say then."

Tom was, after all, something of a man of the world.

"Well," said he, "are you for the Ship Tavern?"

"I am indeed."

"Then let us find Tobias!"

And together we set off across the empty wharf toward the Ship Tavern, walking in step at a swift pace, like the two boldest lads in all London. We were fair upon it when, of a sudden, the door of the place flew open and five or six men came running out, all of them in jumbled seaman's dress. Great excitement there was. We stopped and stared. For a moment they seemed to be running right at us—but no, they veered off toward the river in the direction of the bridge.

"Jeremy," said Tom, "they're my mates from the *Adventure.*" And then he hailed the last of them: "Hi, Harry! What is it? Where are you off to?"

Harry did not answer. He simply turned and beckoned for us to follow. Tom and I looked at each other, and without a word between us, we started out at a run in pursuit of them.

We were close, near catching them up, when they suddenly disappeared down a flight of steps to the riverbank. By the time we had descended it, we found them grouping around a bumboat pulled up onto the bank. The boatman stood by, talking earnestly to one of the crew, while the rest stared in dumb amazement at the boat's contents. The body of a man lay in the bow, water-soaked, hair plastered to his face, a drowning victim, no doubt.

"No," the boatman was explaining with obvious irritation, "I did *not* pull him out of the water. He weren't afloat, anyhow. He'd got stuck at water level on one of the bridge supports. No telling how long he was there, and no telling how many spied him there before me. But it was me rowed out and pulled him into the boat. I done my good deed, and that's all I'm going to do. You know him, you take him."

"He drowned, did he?"

"Must have."

"Any marks on him?"

"Indeed there's marks on him. You bump up against London Bridge for hours and hours, you'd have some marks on you too."

"But wounds, any such like?"

Tom pulled away from me, and drawn by more than curiosity, he pushed forward through his mates and was now staring down at the body in the boat.

"If you want to know about wounds," said the boatman, "then you must pull his clothes off and look for yourself."

Then I pushed up next to Tom and saw what he saw. Though the face of the corpus in the boat was somewhat bloated and marked, it was nevertheless recognizable as that of Lieutenant Grimsby of the H.M.S. *Adventure*.

EIGHT

*In which Sir John fails
to read the Riot Act
to the crew*

Though there was much interest in the body of Lieutenant Grimsby by the crew members present there on the
Thames bank, and much speculation as to the cause of death,
none seemed to know quite what to do next. One suggested
he be carried to the Navy Board and dumped on the doorstep
of Vice-Admiral Sir Robert Redmond. Another thought the
generous thing might be to hold a wake for him at the Ship
Tavern.

The boatman showed his indifference to the matter by
hauling out the dead officer from the bow and bumping him
down in the river mud. He then pushed his boat into the
water, jumped in and settled himself behind the oars. When
last seen, he was out in the channel, dragging oars left and
right, steering expertly on his way to his next landing.

"P'rhaps if we just left him here someone would be by
and know just what should be done."

There were a few grunts of assent to that suggestion. Feet
shuffled. It was clear that they, too, meant to be quit of the
corpus.

"You cannot do that," said Tom most severely. "Leave
him here in the sun, and he will bloat and stink something
horrible in an hour or two. It ain't the decent thing to do."

"Tom's right," said one, nodding sagaciously.

"Aye, 'tis so."

I cleared my throat and pushed my voice down to its deepest.

"If you will pardon me, gentlemen," said I, "there is but one way to treat this matter."

I was eyed suspiciously by all but Tom.

"Who're you to tell us, lad?"

"I am assistant to Sir John Fielding, Magistrate of the Bow Street Court."

"Aye! So he is, so he is. Remember, Bert? The boy with the blind man who made a fool of the captain."

"Now I recalls. He's the one knocked Mr. Boone down the stairs, ain't he?"

"You're awright with me, lad!"

"Aye, tell us what then. We'll hear you out."

I declared that he should be taken to the Raker, who was the keeper of all bodies found in curious circumstances such as these. I would then notify Sir John, who would then learn how Mr. Grimsby died and when and all sorts of other things a competent Doctor of Physick could tell him. (Alas, in truth, he knew only one such, Mr. Gabriel Donnelly, who was far away in the Tibble Valley, wooing a reluctant widow.) I made every effort, in short, to create the impression that there was a proper manner in which to handle inconvenient matters such as this, and of course they would wish to do it properly.

They looked at one another and scratched their heads.

"How far is it?" asked one at last.

"Not far," said I, "just beyond London Bridge some."

"Well . . . I suppose we could do that. They's enough of us. We could share him out between us, two by two."

There was a general murmur of agreement—but then came an objection:

"I don't know, sounds like mighty dry work on a hot day like this."

"By Gawd, you're right, Harry. Why don't we take a couple of bottles with us? What say? Gin or rum?"

"One of each!"

They made a collection. I myself gave a few pence in the spirit of fellowship. Tom donated, as well. One of their number was delegated to do the buying, and I urged Tom to go along to look for Tobias Trindle within the Ship Tavern.

"Had he been inside, he would be out here with us now," Tom objected.

"Well . . ." I hesitated. What he said was perfectly reasonable, of course.

"Let me ask," said Tom to me. And to them: "Hi, mates, is that old goat Tobias about? Was he in the tavern?"

"No, he ain't been there for days. He was in the Gull and Anchor a day past, howsomever. Saw him with Isaac and Bristol Beatty."

"An old goat he surely is, Tom. Remember how he led us all off to that wog whorehouse in Bombay?"

"All but me," said Tom.

"And wise you was to stay on board. How many of us was it got the pox? Three?"

"No, more—five. You're forgettin' Cherrupin' Sam and Ned Tobert."

"Aw, but they got kilt in the fight with the grabs, so we can't be sure about them."

"Well, they *thought* they had it. Damn, that was a fight, weren't it—with the grabs? Bastards just kep' swarmin' aboard."

Thus they passed the time in reminiscence until their messenger returned with the bottles for the journey to the Raker's. The bearer had generously supplied another from his own pocket. Since gin was what he preferred, gin was what he bought. He pulled the cork and passed the bottle around. I declined my chance at it, but Tom took a swig and handed it on.

"Well," said one—call him the leader, for he was the first to fall in with my plan, "I s'pose we'd best get on with it. Harry, you grab t'other end."

Harry did as his mate had bade, and off we went, up the stairs and across, and then up a bit of a hill along Fresh Wharf. Though there was no ship moored, there were yet a few men about at the storehouse door. They looked at us rather queer when they saw Mr. Grimsby swinging free between his porters. The group at the door may have thought him an officer overcome by drink, until one leaned over for a closer look as the corpus passed and gave a solemn shake of his head to his fellows. Not a word was heard from them in comment, however.

"Damn all, they do get heavy when they're dead, don't they?" said Harry. He it was who led the way, supporting the lieutenant's feet.

"He ain't half so heavy where you are as where I am," said his partner. And it was true enough, for proceeding up-hill as they were and supporting the weight of the trunk, he bore the greater weight.

The rest of us were grouped before and behind. Tom and I led the strange funeral procession, looking back frequently to see just how the others were getting on.

"You know where this place is—the Raker's? What kind of a name is that?"

"It's not a name," said I. "It's a . . . a description. He rakes in the dead, you might say." I hesitated, then plunged on: "But yes, I've been there before—not often, but I can find it. It's not the sort of place you'd visit by choice."

"I can imagine."

"No, you can't."

We reached Thames Street, wherein a great crowd of pedestrians thronged. What might be thought of us and our grotesque burden I could not so much as guess. Yet there was no way of reaching our destination but to travel it for a distance, and so I led them off to the left in the direction of the bridge. Those we met along the way seemed to shrink from us, giving us a wide berth. Some turned away in disgust. One or two simply wrinkled their noses and walked on. A lady, accompanied by a gentleman, quite collapsed in his arms. Yet how was one to move a dead man, if not by these rude means?

"By God, this is far enough," said my first volunteer. "Let's put him down here."

He and Harry dropped Grimsby's body roughly on the steps of St. Magnus Church.

"Give me that bottle of rum."

As he uncorked it and took a deep draft from the bottle, I looked uneasily about at the passing throng. I read shocked disapproval on each and every face, and for the first time I felt truly embarrassed by this rough crew. I could make no

excuses for the uncaring manner in which they had tossed
their burden down, nor for the way they stood now, passing
their bottles back and forth. Tom, I noticed, stood uneasy
and apart from them too; he seemed to be avoiding my
glance. His mates were a bit like children, bad boys, were
they not? I had often seen such in Covent Garden, drinking,
carrying on loudly, courting the displeasure of the crowd—
and they not much older than I. These were men of some
years. Yet all they had to exchange among themselves were
their bottles and their tales of killing and whoring.

(Did I truly think so deeply of the misbehavior of these
half-wild seamen? Perhaps thirty years has given me a degree
of wisdom with which I now generously endow my fourteen-
year-old self. I do recall, however, the keen sense of embarrassment I felt there on the steps of St. Magnus. Such
feelings are to some of us the most lasting and the least easily
forgotten.)

I thought perhaps that a reminder that the task was un-
completed might return them to it.

"It is only a bit farther," said I mildly during a brief
recess in their tale-telling.

Most ignored me. The only one of them who gave some
slight attention to my discreet plea was the one I had to
myself designated their leader. He frowned down upon me.

"Patience, lad," said he. "We'll be off in our own good
time."

"Perhaps, sir, you could prop up the lieutenant so that he
didn't look, well, quite so dead."

At that he let forth a great roar of laughter. "Why, perhaps
we could!"

What followed was minutes of macabre play as they set
about to place him in a sitting position on a step. Yet Mr.
Grimsby stubbornly refused to balance. He would teeter to
the left and totter to the right to the accompaniment of much
laughter and comment from the seamen until at last they had
him properly settled. Then the head of the corpus would flop
back or forward, undoing their careful work and inspiring
further laughter. At one point Harry stood before the dead
lieutenant and gave him a stern lecture on holding his place
like an officer and a gentleman, "for what would people

think of you floppin' and fallin' about like some poor drunken sailor?''

Great gales of laughter at that.

One shook his finger at the bruised and swollen face. ''You must remember your station and keep your position, sir.''

This was finally too much for the belligerent group of onlookers who had gathered to witness this gruesome sport. Two or three of them appeared to be men of consequence. One of these stepped forward and slapped the cobblestoned walk with his stick.

''I wish to inform you,'' said he, ''that I have sent my man to search for a constable. For all I know, you may have murdered this officer. You now mock and jeer at your victim like a pack of savages. What sort of men are you to perpetrate this manner of outrage?''

One of the crewmen, bottle in hand, came to attention and gave a mock salute.

''Royal Navy, sir'' said he, ''His Majesty's Ship *Adventure*.''

''Thank you. I'm sure your captain will want to know of this.''

At that the men from the frigate grew silent, and their leader grabbed off his cap and tugged at his forelock.

''Beggin' your pardon, sir. We didn't mean no harm,'' said he, ''and we certainly didn't do no harm to this here officer. He was found by a boatman and pulled off one of the supports of the bridge yonder—drownded he was. When we saw him, we knew him as one of our own, off the *Adventure*. In truth, sir, he was a good officer, and we respected him, though you might not judge it from our play. This lad here''—gesturing to me—''told us that there was a place nearby where bodies was to be taken. We was haulin' him off when we stopped to rest, and the drink got the best of us.''

''I know of no such place in this environ,'' said the man of substance.

''Oh, but there is, sir,'' said I. ''The Raker's place is only a bit beyond here.''

''The Raker? Good God!''

A shiver went through the man on that hot July day. Nor was he the only one in that small group of onlookers who responded so.

"Well," said he, "if that is so, then be on your way and take these remains with you. At the very least you've shown gross disrespect for the dead."

"And on church property, too," chimed in another. "That counts as blasphemy!"

"Well, sirs," said the spokesman, "you're right, I'm sure. And beggin' your forgiveness, we will be on our way, sirs." He capped his head, and pointed down at the lieutenant's body, which, unattended, had toppled prostrate once again. "Hurley," said he to the man who had saluted and had helpfully supplied the name of their ship, "you take the poor, dear lieutenant under the arms and somebody else take him by the feet."

Without a word of argument, Hurley handed off the bottle for another to carry and did as he was bade. Another took up the lieutenant's feet, and our procession was once more under way. Those who had gathered—and their number had grown—made room to let us pass, and we left quieter than we had come.

As we traversed Fish Street Hill and the approach to London Bridge, I took a long look to my left and attempted to image how it might have looked with houses and shops built upon its length. They had been removed not long before my arrival in London. How curious it must have been to live upon a bridge! Why should anyone wish to do so? I whispered to Tom of this.

The seaman known as Hurley took great abuse from his fellows. His drunken impudence had put them all in jeopardy, and they did not take it kindly.

"Well done," said the big fellow who had spoken for the rest. "Let me tell you, Hurley, if I had Mr. Boone's bamboo stick, I'd give you a blow on the backside with it each step you take."

"Aw," said Hurley, "he will do naught about it. 'Twas but an idle threat."

"We had best hope so."

"Why did ye not give him our names while you was about it, Hurley?"

Et cetera. Hurley grumbled his responses. Yet when, at Graves's Wharf, I signaled that we should turn left again and another was designated to carry the lieutenant's feet, Hurley made no complaint at being made to struggle without relief supporting the trunk as we continued on our way.

"Is that it there?" Tom asked me. "Why, 'tis like a little farm."

"Indeed," said I, "and the field in front is where the bodies of the unknown and unclaimed are buried."

"Sweet Jesus," said he, "is that strong odor what I think it is?"

"Probably," said I, "though they situated the Raker in a space near the Fishmonger's Hall to disguise the stink—or perhaps to mingle the two."

Thus there were further exclamations voiced by those to our rear. Yet all seemed relieved that we had at last reached our destination. We entered through the little gate and made our approach across the field.

"This is a burial ground, then?"

"Indeed it is."

"But there are no markers. How can he tell where to dig?"

"He has it measured off in ways only he knows, says Jimmie Bunkins, so that none but he can tell. He digs deep and stacks the bodies."

Tom sniffed. "This place stinks too."

"Some are buried quite shallow. Watch you do not trip on a nose or a toe."

He looked down in a sudden panic—then up at me in annoyance.

"Was that a joke, Jeremy?"

"Not the sort to laugh at," said I.

I brought them round the little house in which the Raker and his ugly sister dwelt and up to the rail fence behind which were the two ghostly, sick and spavined horses he kept for his wagon. They moved not a muscle but stood, as they always seemed to, with heads bowed.

"Are them animals alive?" asked one of the crewmen.

"I saw an eye move on one of them," said another.

Though I doubted that, I would not argue the point. Instead, I summoned all my strength to shout the Raker out of his grisly barn.

"Halloo! Raker! Are you in there? Come out if you are!" I waited, then shouted again: "*Halloo* in there!"

We waited. There were stirrings within, and at last the man himself appeared. He was as I remembered; there was none like him, after all. His arms dangled as an ape's and seemed near as long as he made his way across the barnyard on his bandy legs. As he came nearer, I heard whispers behind me remarking upon his queer shape, his ill-matched eyes (one much smaller than its mate), his labored walk. Yet they were silent and respectful when at last he arrived.

"I remembers you," said the Raker, fixing me with his full-sized eye. "You're the Blind Beak's young helper. Brought me a lodger, have you?"

"Yes sir, a drowned man," said I, "an officer of the Royal Navy."

"Well, you did right to bring him here, even though I ain't likely to put him under. Why don't you have your chums hand him over the fence. I can take him from here."

Without a word, they complied, even lending a hand to Hurley. They seemed somewhat in awe of the Raker. He took their burden from them and, in a practiced manner, threw the lieutenant's body over his shoulder in a single motion. He then grinned at them in a way meant to be friendly.

"It's right hot today," said he. "You'd be welcome to come into the barn to get out of the sun if you brings your bottles along." He ended that with a mirthless laugh that I found quite chilling.

The six mates from the *Adventure* exchanged glances, then nodded to each other in a sign of assent. A vote had been taken.

"Come along then," said he. "Though I must ask you to come in over the fence, as your friend did. I fear if I threw open the gate, the horses would be gone in the very wink of an eye."

It seemed to me he overestimated their capabilities.

But one by one, the crewmen vaulted the fence, leaving only Tom and me behind.

"Come along," said I to him. "We must go too."

"But *why?*" he responded in a whisper. "I do not like the man, and I have no wish to see what he has there in the barn."

"Nor do I. But we have a task to perform there."

"And what is that?"

"We must undress Mr. Grimsby and examine him for wounds or other marks."

"Why must we do that?"

"Because it is the first question Sir John will put to me when I report the lieutenant's death to him. 'Had he wounds?' he will say. And I must have an answer ready for him."

"Right enough. As you say then."

And so we, too, climbed the rail fence and followed the rest.

"Mind the horse droppings," said I.

They were inside at my next look, near disappeared, it seemed. Yet when we two entered the barn we found that all had gathered to take their ease upon the huge mound of clothing I recalled from previous visits to this unholy place. The bottles had been uncorked and were now making the rounds. I saw that the Raker had dumped Mr. Grimsby's body near the door. There would be sufficient light for us to perform the task that must be done. Conversation had begun as the bottles were uncorked. The seamen from the *Adventure* were naturally (or perhaps morbidly) curious about the Raker's enterprise. They had questions, and he seemed happy to answer them.

"Women on that side, men on this side," he was saying. "Though I vow, it's sometimes a difficult question to settle. I've had men come in who was wearin' women's clothes, and t'other way around, as well."

"You don't mean it!"

"God's truth, I swear. Ah, ye see all in a business such as mine."

Having taken a second swig from the bottle he had been given, he passed it on to the man nearest.

"What's the peculiarest thing ever you seen?" asked the one known as Hurley.

"Oh, well, that," said the Raker. "That's easy enough to answer. That would be one night I was workin' late, puttin' things in order, so to speak, and of a sudden one of me lodgers rises up, throws off the canvas I covered him with, and he says, 'Where is me clothes?' I'd taken them off him, you see, as I do with all me lodgers. You're sittin' on the pile of them."

"Well, was he alive or dead?"

"Oh, he was alive, quite certain. He gave me a start but nothing more. Ye've nicks to fear from the dead. He'd been hit on the head and robbed, showed all signs of bein' dead, but he was just sleepin', so to speak. I fixed him up with a suit of clothes he liked better'n the one he wore in, and I give him a shilling for his trouble and sent him on his way. He seemed well content."

"My God and sweet Jesus," groaned Hurley, "a regular Lazarus."

"A Lazarus he was," the Raker agreed. "Yet if he'd slept a day longer he'd a woken underground."

A hush fell over the troupe of seamen: the unthinkable had been mentioned.

Then spoke up the big fellow who had led the rest on this expedition I had proposed: "Well, that's where us lads got it over the landlubbers. I'll take my watery grave, which I know awaits me, for it's cleaner and it's . . . It's certain."

There was a general chorus of agreement. Bottles were lifted to that brave declaration. One was drained and cast aside.

"Does the stink never bother you?" one wanted to know—or perhaps all wanted to know, for all were alike breathing the same foul air.

"God's truth, I never give it no notice. Ye custom yeself to it."

Of one thing I was certain: Neither Tom nor I would accustom ourselves to the smell of the place. It was the worst I had known in the three visits I had made to the Raker's barn—never before on a day as warm as this one. An effluvium of putrefaction hung over the interior, like a murky cloud of death. If Tom had run from it, I myself would have followed.

Yet we worked as swift as we were able while they talked on in the manner I have described. We stripped Mr. Grimsby's body clean, yet none took but the most casual interest in what we were about. As we went on to the business of inspecting his parts, their colloquy continued.

"Who pays you to do this work?"

"The Cities of London and Westminster," said the Raker.

"How come you by the job?"

"It was passed down in me family. From me father it went, from his father, and from his father before him. 'Twas in recognition of service done in the Great Plague of a hundred year past."

There were no wounds nor marks worth noting on the body's anterior portions, and so we turned him over. Legs, buttocks, and back were clean, but Tom beckoned me forward, and showed me that I must feel his head. Mr. Grimsby's hair was his own, and he had worn it long. It covered a place the size of a guinea that had been crushed in at the base of his skull. I nodded and realized as I did so that not a word had passed between us.

"Indeed ye may give a look to my lodgers if ye've a wish to, though some ain't so pretty, I warns ye. The dead is curious folk," said the Raker. "But it will cost you the little rum that's left in that bottle."

The bottle was stoppered and carelessly tossed to him as the party of seamen rose from their bed of clothing and ambled down the line of canvas-covered corpuses, talking in low tones amongst themselves. The Raker drank from the bottle, giggled to himself, and pushed himself up with a great grunt to his feet. He came over to us and stood staring for a moment at Lieutenant Grimsby.

"Leave him as he is," said he. "You saved me a bit of trouble, you did."

"The Navy will bury him," said Tom. "And a Navy surgeon will visit tomorrow to view the remains. Have his uniform brushed proper, if you would, sir."

"Oh," said the Raker, "aye-aye." He giggled again. "Ain't that how it's said? Aye-aye, sir?"

"We'll be leaving you now," said I to him. "Sir John

will be told of this. Though it is a naval matter, he himself
has an interest in it.''

"Remember me kindly to the Beak, young sir. Tell him I
am his good and faithful servant, I am. Oh, yes, indeed I
am.''

It was going toward dark by the time we reached Number 4
Bow Street, near ten o'clock it was. And we, having eaten
nothing since breakfast, were two hungry young lads. As we
charged up the stairs, Tom suddenly stopped me and whispered urgent in my ear:

"Jeremy, you go into the kitchen first, and if Annie is not
there, beckon me, and I shall follow.''

"And what will you do if she *is* there?''

He frowned. "Dear God, I know not.''

"Oh, come along. You must.''

"All right,'' said he, sighing, "I suppose I must.''

I had noted that relations were most awkward between the
two of them since Annie's return to our household. Tom, in
his chagrin, had little to say in her presence and near nothing
to say direct to her. He avoided her eyes with his own, which
indeed must have been difficult, for hers never seemed to
leave him. They followed him around the room, stared at
him tenderly across the table; at times they seemed to glisten
with tears. During last night's dinner Annie's attention to
Tom had become so obvious that Lady Fielding found it
necessary to speak to her sharply. "Annie, please!'' said my
lady—yet more in exasperation than reproof. Only then did
the young cook lower her eyes to her plate. Yet it was but
a short time until they were raised again to the object of her
fascination.

Thus had it been between them. Hence did Tom now shy
at the door, like a colt at a gate, sensing trouble beyond it.
In the event, there was none to speak of. We continued up
the stairs at a more cautious pace. I heard Annie's voice,
deeper and more womanly than one would suppose from one
of her years, just beyond the door as we approached; it was
raised in song, a sad ballad then popular in the streets. Yet
she ceased as we drew near, and as I turned the knob and

stepped inside the kitchen she was just rising from the table.
Tom followed me.

"Hello, Annie," said I as cheerfully as I might.

"Hello to you, Jeremy, and to you, Tom."

He mumbled a greeting of sorts and kept his place behind
me, as if in hiding.

Something had altered in her. A change had been made,
or at least begun. Her eyes met mine and did not stray to
him who cowered at my rear. She even managed a smile,
albeit a sad one.

"You both must be quite famished," said she.

"Oh, we are," said I. "Bread and cheese will do—even
bread alone."

"I can give you better than that. I've kept your dinner on
a low fire, if stew will do you."

"That would do us remarkable well. But could you hold
it a bit longer? We must talk with Sir John."

"I could, and I would. You'll find him in his little room
up the stairs."

And so saying, she turned to the stove and gave the pot a
stir.

"Thank you, Annie," said I as we made our way across
the kitchen. "Mrs. Gredge never treated me so well."

"And I'm a better cook than she was," said she proudly.
"Sir John told me so himself tonight."

We left her there at the stove. Halfway up the stairs, Tom
stopped me.

"She seems better, don't you think?" he whispered. "Perhaps my mother talked to her."

"Or perhaps," said I, "she's put you out of her mind."

The thought seemed to trouble him. "Oh," said he, "perhaps she has."

We found Sir John sitting in the fading light. The door to
his little study was open, yet I rapped lightly upon it.

"Ah, lads, is that you? Come in," said he. "Tell me, did
you locate our witness, Trindle?"

"No, Sir John, we did not," said I, as we took our chairs,
"but we made a terrible discovery."

"And what is that?"

"Lieutenant Grimsby," said Tom.

"What of him?"

"He is dead," said I.

"You must tell me the story entire."

And between us we did—from our searches through the low Thames-side dens, to the finding of the body the boatman had pulled out of the water at London Bridge, then on at last to the delivery of the remains to the Raker.

"We examined his body there."

"Had he wounds?"

"Well, there were marks upon it, scrapes and such. But as the boatman said, there was no telling how long he had been bumping against the bridge. Yet Tom found something that—"

"Yes sir," Tom put in, "his skull was badly battered in the rear at just the point it attached to the neck. Crushed, you might say, but only at that one spot."

"Just here?"

Sir John turned and touched his head at just the right spot. Then, remembering, he asked, "Or can you see? Are we in the dark? Light a candle, if you like."

"No sir, we can see," said I.

"Yes, just there where you have touched," said Tom.

"How large a wound then?"

"About the size of a guinea," said I.

"Ah, so large! Would you say, Tom, that it might have been inflicted by a bump against the bridge support?"

"Well, it is *possible*, I suppose."

"But you do not think so?"

"No, sir."

"What would you say then?"

"A belaying pin," declared Tom with remarkable certainty.

"Ah, *well* . . ." And so saying, Sir John fell into a protracted silence, musing with bowed head there in the near-vanished light. Tom looked at me, frowning, as if to ask if the magistrate had suddenly nodded off to sleep. I knew he had not. I shook my head firmly. And at last Sir John roused himself.

"Do you recall, Jeremy," said he, "that Admiral Sir Robert was waiting for my return down below when I sent you and Tom off on your search?''

"I do indeed, sir. He seemed most agitated.''

"He was. He brought news that Mr. Grimsby had deserted—left the ship in contradiction of Lieutenant Hartsell's orders and his own. He said Grimsby would be hunted down and court-martialed. Then he demanded to know if the lieutenant had been in communication with me. I told him he had, by letter, and that he had invited us aboard the *Adventure*. The admiral then said he had no right to do that, and henceforward we were not to go aboard unless in his company. All this, of course, we expected, having been lectured by Lieutenant Hartsell upon our departure.''

He sighed and lapsed once more into silence for a moment.

"If Mr. Grimsby was indeed given a knock and dumped overboard,'' said Tom, "then there was a fair chance he would not be found.''

"Except for London Bridge,'' Sir John responded, "he might be floating on still. Yet he told me what he had to tell, poor man, and it could not have been easy.'' He paused. "His death makes one thing certain.''

"And what is that, sir?''

"Mr. Landon must be removed from the *Adventure* at all costs. I believe his life is in danger there, as well. It may mean the Tower Prison for him, but that would be preferable to his present situation. I shall send a letter to Bobbie tomorrow informing of all this and giving him the opportunity to send a surgeon to the Raker's to confirm what you two have found.''

"Who carries these messages back and forth from the frigate to the admiral?''

"I would hazard this one was brought by Mr. Byner. He seems to spend more time with Lieutenant Hartsell than with him he has been appointed to defend.''

Indeed Sir John was right: Annie was a better cook than Mrs. Gredge. Was it her use of good English spices—rosemary, sage, and thyme—which the old cook quite forbore? Her love of onions—which Mrs. Gredge complained caused her gas and consequent flatulence? Was it her boldness with garlic—which the good old lady despised as a foreign intrusion? Or was it simply that Annie gave closer attention to her work? Never a burnt roast. Never a scorched stew. She looked after her own fire and did not, as Mrs. Gredge did, depend upon me to tend it. Annie often said that knowing when to dampen a fire and when to feed it was half the secret of the art.

All this she had proven with the beef stew she had set before Tom and me after our interview with Sir John. It was well seasoned, onioned and garlicked to perfection, and kept at a simmer until the very end when it was brought to a gentle boil. She tasted it as a critic.

"Good as when it was first cooked up," said she with a smack of her lips.

And then, after serving it forth, she had excused herself and gone up to her room. Tom stared after her, quite perplexed.

"She does seem different," said he.

I was too pleasantly occupied with what was in my plate to do more than grunt a few words.

"What was that?" He had not understood.

"Got her pride back," I repeated. "Sir John paid her a great and true compliment. Sincere praise can work wonders. Or had you never experienced that yourself?"

After considering that for a moment, he said quite soberly, "Yes, from Lieutenant Landon."

We may have eaten a bit more solemnly thereafter, though nevertheless just as heartily. We were but lads, after all, and not even a saddening thought could dull the taste of our good dinner.

Only minutes later, we were sopping our plates with bread, when on the stairs below we heard a most frightful racket. Then, without so much as a knock, through the door burst Mr. Benjamin Bailey, the captain of the Bow Street Runners. Such an interruption was so unlike him, who was the most respectful of men (except to malefactors and criminals, of course), that I saw immediately that he was on an errand of extreme importance. I was on my feet as he stood panting for a moment, seeking to reclaim his breath.

"Is Sir John here, Jeremy?"

"He is. I'll fetch him."

I turned and, poised to dash, saw that the man himself was at that moment descending the stairs and making his entrance into the kitchen.

"No," said he, "here I am, here I am. What have you to report, Mr. Bailey?"

"A riot, sir."

"Oh, God help us. In progress?"

"Indeed, Sir John—in progress. What I'm asking for, sir, is your permission to send to the Tower for a company of grenadiers."

"That bad, is it?"

"Sir, it's—"

"No, no, Mr. Bailey, if that is your judgment, I accept it. Send for them, by all means. You will not have to go?"

"I'll send Constable Perkins. He's waiting."

"Go then and put him on his way, then wait for us downstairs. We'll be but a moment."

As he turned to go, Mr. Bailey called out, "It's the crew of that frigate anchored by London Bridge caused the trouble."

According to Mr. Bailey, who told the story as we made our way hurriedly through the streets, this great disturbance had all stemmed from a not uncommon incident at Mrs. Gerney's, a notorious brothel in the Strand. Much earlier in the evening, a seaman from the *Adventure* had, in the course of his visit to one of Mrs. Gerney's belles, discovered he had been robbed. He complained bitterly to the mistress of the house but received no satisfaction. So then, with dire threats, he left her and went immediately to raise a force of his shipmates. He recruited a small army from the dens along the Thames and the dives of Covent Garden. Not only his mates but also their bottle companions and recent acquaintances joined him. Days of drinking and retelling their tales of past battles had put them in a humor for a good fight. As they marched upon Mrs. Gerney's in the Strand, gathering sticks, clubs, and loose cobblestones along the way, the demand for redress was soon altered by the dark chemistry of mob might to a desire for revenge.

They were near a hundred or more in number by the time they reached their goal, where they found but two constables, forewarned and at the door, to oppose them. The mob did not so much do battle with the constables—Rumford and Cowley—as sweep them aside, ignoring their cries to "Disperse!" and "Go home!" What were two men armed only with clubs to do against a hundred?

Through the door the rioters poured, trampling, bruising, and variously abusing the thin line of male defense Mrs. Gerney had hired to protect her and her disorderly house. There were sounds of destruction inside—breaking glass, thumps and bumps of furniture thrown about—and the squeals and screams of frightened women. The action spread upward in the house, which was of considerable size. Windows were broken above, and through them came crashing down to the pavement looking glasses, chairs, bedding, and mattresses. The crowd that had gathered to watch (as crowds will gather to watch anything) ran back in terror from the objects raining down upon them. Smaller pieces sailed out into the broad street, causing confusion and a bit of panic among the carriages and coaches. A coach horse shied and set his partner off, and together they threw their vehicle into rough contact with a hackney carriage. There was a good deal of hot language tossed about between the two drivers as they stopped to discuss the matter; and in stopping they thereby halted the flow of traffic in the street.

And about this time, a line of Mrs. Gerney's inmates and their customers began to run out, seeking safety from the mob. Though none were completely naked, most were in some stage of undress. This added greatly to the entertainment of the onlookers.

It was this scene of near chaos that Benjamin Bailey looked upon when he arrived with three more constables in reinforcement. But these, too, were armed only with stout clubs. The inexperienced Constable Cowley put forward that the rioters might be arrested, one by one, as they emerged from the building. Mr. Bailey saw the folly of that, ordered four of the constables to gather the property littering the walkway and the street together in a single pile and guard it, then left with Perkins to seek Sir John's permission to call out the grenadiers.

The situation had altered somewhat by the time Mr. Bailey returned with Sir John, Tom, and me. As we came down Southampton Street and turned right on the Strand, we saw a great tumult no more than one street distant. But from that great milling mass of people there rose what seemed to be wisps of smoke. Yet as we came closer, and saw plainer by the light of the streetlamps, we noted that they were indeed more than wisps and that there were many of them moving around and about in a design roughly describing a circle. Mr. Bailey informed Sir John of this, then plowed ahead into the crowd. Tom and I exchanged glances, then followed close behind Sir John, who had grabbed hold the constable's belt and thus was pulled along.

"One side, one side," shouted Mr. Bailey. "The magistrate is coming through."

As we pushed roughly through the recalcitrant spectators, I saw the source of the smoke: torches held aloft, carried swiftly back and forth.

"One side for Sir John Fielding, Magistrate of the Bow Street Court."

When it was necessary, Mr. Bailey did not hesitate to use the club he used so well. The most unyielding of the crowd he would knock on the shoulder or thwack on the backside. Thus by his persistence we reached the first row of onlookers and beheld the spectacle that so held them.

The constables, who had done as their captain directed and piled high the property thrown from the upper floors of the brothel, were now forced to defend it as best they could. The rioters had evidently grown tired of their rampage and had trailed out of the building. They then saw the great mound of goods and must have thought what a lovely bonfire it would make—for torches were lit. The constables positioned themselves at four corners from which they might strike out at one who dared approach and put fire to the pile. What ensued was a kind of game—or the sailors must have thought it so; for when we arrived, six of them (I counted six, but there may have been more) were dancing around, torches in hand, feinting with them toward the pile, thrusting them

boldly toward the constables, accepting stout knocks upon
the arms and legs as part of the sport. It seemed to me then
that had they set their minds to it, they could have had their
bonfire and might still have it, yet these bad boys enjoyed
this form of play far more, for it greatly amused the crowd.
There was jolly laughter all round us, occasional applause at
an artful feint or thrust. For this reason alone the spectators
had been reluctant to let us through and make room for us:
they were enjoying the show.

Mr. Bailey had his head close to Sir John's, no doubt
describing this bizarre scene. The magistrate's reply was also
inaudible to me until a roll of laughter came, and he shouted
above it, "How far?"

"Ten paces," came Mr. Bailey's response, also shouted,
"and *no more*."

Then, without hesitation Sir John walked off those ten
paces, whipping his stick in the air before him. This put him
between two of the torchbearers and quite near young Constable Cowley, who watched him in surprise.

The dance came to a halt. The sudden presence of the
blind man in their midst so surprised the performers that they
stood quite still for a moment, looking at one another in a
most doubtful manner. Who was he? What was his intrusion?

Seeing that the frivolity had ended, even if perhaps only
temporarily, the crowd began to boo; there were whistles and
jeers from the rioters who had ranged themselves near the
door of Mrs. Gerney's and beyond. But then, when one—
not the nearest—circled round the pile of goods and approached Sir John, the mob and its audience fell silent, sensing that a confrontation was imminent.

He was a lean man of medium height, one who, like many
seamen, looked older in his face than in his body. Though
his cheeks were lined and darkened by the sun, and he had
not all his teeth, he held his torch up high and until but a
moment ago, he had been capering about with his mates to
the frustration of the constables.

Of a sudden Tom jabbed me in the arm with his elbow.

"It's him, Jeremy," he whispered loudly in my ear, "it's
him!"

I had not the slightest notion what he meant by that, so

deeply was I involved in the drama of the moment. As I made a move to wave him to silence a thought struck me.

"It's *who*?"

"Tobias Trindle," said Tom in that same stage whisper. "I would know him anywhere."

What should we do? Shout the news to Sir John? Rush out and make an appeal to Trindle to bear witness on Mr. Landon's behalf? Quite impossible, of course. All that could be done now was to keep silent and let the drama unfold, for they were about to speak.

"Who be yuh?" Tobias Trindle demanded.

"I am John Fielding, Magistrate of the Bow Street Court. And who, sir, are you?"

He laughed boldly at that. "Wouldn't I be a fool to tell you?"

"Considering what you and your companions have been engaged in during the past hour, I should say that you have already established yourself as a fool—and each of them, as well. So you might just as well tell me the name of the fool I now address."

"Well, I won't do it."

And having said that, Trindle made a swift motion with the torch he held toward Sir John's face. He held it close. Sir John did not flinch. A shocked murmur ran through the crowd. Even some of the rioters fell back at such effrontery.

"Y' *are* blind, ain't ya?"

"Yes, I am. Now remove that burning brand from my face, for I assure you that if you harm me, or any of my constables, you will be hanged. We are officers of the law, and the law must be respected. So far you have shown precious little respect for it. You and your fellows have disturbed the peace. You have done damage to property. And now you play with fire. Arson is also a hanging offense."

Trindle brought back the torch and looked uncertainly at the hundred who had accompanied him to Mrs. Gerney's. Were they with him or not? A few had already begun to drift back, perhaps seeking to make their departure.

"I heard of you. You're the one they call the Blind Beak."

"So I am. And if you have heard of me, then you know my reputation as one who keeps his word. I have given you my promise that if bodily injury is done to me or my constables, you and others will be hanged. I have also promised that if a fire is set, there will be the same result. I now give you another . . .''

He had raised his voice to its fullest. He was addressing the mob as well as its leader.

''I promise,'' said Sir John, ''that if you now disperse and return to whatever pursuits had occupied you before starting out on this mission of destruction, you will not be pursued. You will not be arrested singly or in twos or threes. The place upon which you have vented your rage has given us trouble before. I will consider that rough justice has been done. That is my promise to you. But if, in defiance, you persist, you will be considered in a state of riot.''

Having thus concluded, he turned and, walking to the sound of Mr. Bailey's voice (''Here, Sir John''), returned to us in the first row of onlookers. He waited.

Tobias Trindle threw his torch down to the cobblestones and stamped it out. The others who had played that dangerous game did likewise. They retired to speak with their fellows. They held a council of war—or perhaps one of peace, for it seemed promising that Sir John's reason and promise of leniency would prevail.

I believe indeed that it would have done so, had it not been that at that moment two wagonloads of grenadiers came clattering down the Strand from the Tower. The drivers reined in, and twenty-four red-coated troops piled out, muskets and all. A very young lieutenant had accompanied them on a well-blooded brown mount. The crowd parted, giving them space aplenty to assemble.

''Damn,'' said Sir John, ''they usually arrive too late to do any good. It *would* be tonight that they arrive too early.''

The rioters took the sudden appearance of the grenadiers as a betrayal. They hooted and jeered as the lieutenant lined up his men.

''Take me to him who is in charge, Mr. Bailey.''

Together they started forward, we two again trailing behind. But by the time we reached the soldiers, the lieutenant had his men positioned, in two wide lateral lines, on either side of the heap of property thrown from Mrs. Gerney's establishment. He had his sword out and raised.

"Fix bayonets!" came his command.

Only then did Sir John reach him with Mr. Bailey's assistance. He had in his hand the scrolled document I had fetched for him from his desk in the study.

"Lieutenant!" He spoke most sharply to the young fellow. "What you propose to do is not according to legal process until I read the Riot Act. And I am not ready to do so."

The lieutenant gave another command, and the grenadiers brought their muskets up in sharp precision so that they were grasped behind the trigger and at a midpoint along the barrel; the bayonets, directed outward, shone bright beneath the streetlamps.

"You may read what you like, sir," drawled the lieutenant. "I have orders to put down a riot, and I intend to do that." He raised a white-gloved hand and pointed a drooping finger at the ragged crewmen of the *Adventure* and their chums who had wreaked havoc within the brothel. "I take it that is the rabble against which we are to move?"

"You will move against no one until I tell you to do so. I remind you, young man, that you are under my command here in the streets of London. I am Sir John Fielding, Magistrate of the Bow Street Court."

"I give no particular care to who you are, sir, and I am under no one's command but my captain's. It is he who has ordered me, and I intend to execute his orders. Now, sir, if you will step aside?"

"See here, you young—"

Yet Mr. Bailey, seeing that the lieutenant had every intention of moving his men ahead whether Sir John was in the way or not, pulled him back from the ranged bayonets and then signaled urgently to his four constables to get out of the grenadiers' path; they wasted no time in complying.

The watching crowd of spectators had grown silent in expectation. The mob, by contrast, had become increasingly noisy. Their improvised jeers and taunts were now replaced by a mocking and obscene chorus of "The British Grenadier," which they sang loudly together. There was a bit of bravado in that, for it seemed without doubt that their number had dwindled since last I looked.

"Forward, march!"

The lieutenant's sword came down, and the soldiers stepped out in perfect order, muskets extended, bayonets wickedly aglitter.

Trindle tried to rouse his companions to one more chorus of their song, yet they were no longer so defiant. So much less so, in fact, that they were now in retreat—backing away down the Strand. Their last bold act was to loose a shower of sticks and stones upon the advancing soldiers, which in truth had little effect. Yet they were not yet in full flight— not, that is, until by a series of commands the lieutenant ordered his troops in a single line forcing the remnants of the mob, the rear guard as it were, some twenty yards or more distant. At which time the lieutenant called out, "At the double time, march!"

Then did the last of the seamen turn and take to their heels. The mob had been routed. The grenadiers, weighed down by their muskets and military impedimenta and forced to jog-run in step, were no match in pursuit of the crew, which was now fast disappeared—and Tobias Trindle along with the rest.

All that we had seen we reported to Sir John.

He heard us out and commented that it could have been worse. "That young idiot of a lieutenant might have begun shooting, then gone to the bayonet."

Just then, somewhat in the distance, perhaps down Bailey Alley, we heard the muffled roar of a ragged volley of shot.

NINE

*In which Tobias Trindle
is found, and then
lost again*

The grenadiers' volley killed none but wounded two, neither of them seriously. Both were taken prisoner by the soldiers, as was a seaman who had fallen and twisted his ankle and another who had gone to assist him. As Sir John said before the volley had been fired, it could have been worse.

The arrogant young lieutenant was much too pleased with himself and his handling of the situation to brook criticism from Sir John.

"If there is a specific procedure—a legal process, if you will," said he, as his men climbed back into the wagons which had borne them from the Tower, "then I have never been made aware of it, sir. If you wish my name for purposes of complaint, I should be happy to give it you. It is Thomas Churchill, and I bear it most proudly. As for the prisoners, them I give to you, as well." He made a sharp little bow, no more than a bob of his head. "Good evening to you, gentlemen."

And with that he left us, mounted his horse and rode out into the Strand and stopped vehicle traffic with a wave of his hand that his little caravan might return unimpeded.

Benjamin Bailey watched him go, a deep dislike written upon the rough features of his face. He turned and spat down upon the cobblestones.

"Thomas Churchill," said he then. "He would be one of Marlborough's puppies."

"Some relation, no doubt," said Sir John "How old would you judge him to be, Mr. Bailey?"

"Oh . . . seventeen, nineteen at the most. He'll have a regiment long before he's thirty. It's because of such as him I gave the King back his shilling."

"Ah yes, that's a story you promised one day to tell me."

"And it's a story one day I shall, Sir John."

"Whenever you like. For now, I wish you to oversee transportation of the prisoners back to Bow Street. At least one of them will have difficulty walking, so you may call a hackney—two, if it suits you. I intend to bill Lieutenant Churchill for incidental expenses—including medical. Fetch that fellow Carr, the one you said had Army experience. He should do."

Mr. Bailey saluted sharply. "Yes sir."

So saying, he wheeled about and went off to join his five constables (Mr. Perkins having returned) and their prisoners.

The walkway before Mrs. Gerney's, now nearly empty, had only a while ago so teemed with footloose men and women of dubious character that the crowd overflowed into the broad street. The drama had ended. Their entertainment was done. All who remained were of Mrs. Gerney's company; they labored to return the bedding, mattresses, looking glasses, and other odds and ends back into the house.

"Lads? Are you still with me?"

"Both of us here, sir," said I.

"Then let us return," said Sir John. "It has been a long night, and I am exhausted—as you must be, too." He sighed. "Point me in the right direction, will you? It's all been so back and forth here that I have quite lost my bearings."

And so, with Tom on one side and me on the other, we set off toward Bow Street, retracing our path down the Strand. Sir John walked silent and at a slower pace than was his usual. He seemed somewhat disheartened by the turn that events had taken there at Mrs. Gerney's. Though not wishing to add to his discouragement, I felt he should be apprised of Tom's discovery.

"Sir," said I, "Tom has something to tell you about the

seaman you dealt with before the grenadiers arrived.''

"Oh? The fellow who near burned my nose off? What about him, Tom? He was not among the prisoners, I understand.''

"That was Tobias Trindle, sir.''

"Oh, *damn!* Our witness, eh? Then our Lieutenant Churchill spoiled even more than I realized. What bad fortune!''

Again he lapsed into silence. Yet gradually, as we approached Southampton Street, his pace quickened. His lower lip jutted forth, and he began nodding to himself in such a way that I was sure that his confidence had returned.

"We may yet be able to turn this to our advantage,'' said he. "Tom, it is true, is it not, that Tobias Trindle was aware of Lieutenant Landon's predicament?''

"Oh, yes sir, all of us knew by the time we dropped anchor. The news went around the ship like a flash of lightning. There was nothing else we talked of.''

"Yet Trindle, perhaps the only true witness to what had happened except Mr. Landon himself, did not come forward. Tell me, was Trindle in that first leave party—the one with which you yourself arrived?''

Tom took a moment to be certain. "Yes sir, he was.''

"The admiral made an appeal there on Tower Wharf for any who knew something of the Landon matter to step forward. Yet Trindle did not—nor did he later visit the admiral in his office. Nor did he contact me. That much is certain. I must ask you, Tom, why has he remained silent?''

"Fear of retribution,'' said Tom, "fear of the captain's revenge.''

"Yet Trindle's testimony, together with other information that has now come to light, could destroy Lieutenant Hartsell utterly in a court-martial. He must know that. He was certainly a bold enough fellow when he talked to me not long ago. Why should he quail before a court-martial?''

Tom Durham took a long moment to answer, and when he did, it was with obvious reluctance: "Sir, the men of the *Adventure* give Mr. Landon no chance at all before a court-martial. They would count any effort on his behalf as wasted.''

"Including our Mr. Trindle?''

"Oh, certainly, sir."

"Including you?"

If Tom had seemed reluctant a moment before, he now seemed quite torn in two: "I'm . . . I'm afraid so, sir."

We had by then turned down Southampton Street which, unlike the Strand, was near deserted. Our footsteps echoed hollow across the night for a good many steps before Sir John spoke his response.

"Have you so little faith in His Majesty's Navy?" said he in a manner most grave.

"Perhaps in its justice, sir."

"Well, no matter," said Sir John, "for I have a plan by which Tobias Trindle may be made to testify at the court-martial. I shall put out a warrant for his arrest. I shall say he fomented a great disturbance of the peace. I shall say there was damage to property. I shall say a good many other things—*except* that he led a mob in riot, which of course he did. But in saying that I should have to pass him on for trial at Old Bailey, and I want this to be a matter between Tobias and me. When he is apprehended, as I'm sure he will be when I put my constables out after him, then I shall have something to hold over his head. I daresay he will then agree to testify at Lieutenant Landon's court-martial."

He picked up his pace again, his stick now making a sharp click-click-click upon the cobblestones.

"Yes," said he, "I daresay he will."

Tom was thrown into a great turmoil by this conversation. He groaned and complained of it to me until long past the time the candle had been blown out and we should have settled down to sleep.

"But don't you see the position this puts me in, Jeremy?"

"Of course I do," said I into the dark. "You have made it clear."

"But they are my shipmates!"

"I understand, Tom."

"Tobias Trindle is my shipmate."

"Yes, I see that."

"How can I assist in a search for him when I know what Sir John has planned?"

"Yes, but what he has planned is merely to force him to

do the decent thing. But tell me true, Tom: Was not Lieutenant Landon *also* your shipmate?''

''Certainly, yet he is . . .''

''He is what?''

''He is past saving.''

''So you said. I think you fail to give Sir John his due. He has worked wonders in the past.''

He said nothing to that, and so I shifted in the bed in such a way that sleep might come soon. I was breathing deeply and about to doze, when Tom sat up in bed of a sudden and pounded his pillow with his fist.

''Those men are my shipmates!'' he wailed.

''You're repeating,'' said I. ''Now, go to sleep, Tom.''

And at last, after another such protest, that is what he did, leaving me to wonder just how dependable he would prove to be during our search the next day.

I was in no wise encouraged by our conversation, after breakfast, when he took me aside and asked where the four prisoners from last night might be held. I was surprised at that—surprised that he had taken such little notice of the working of the court and constabulary which were below.

''Why, in the strong room,'' said I. ''You must have seen it. It is a cage with bars and a door that must be opened with a key.''

''I suppose so,'' said he. ''Indeed I may have been kept in it but cannot remember. I have blotted all that court business of three years ago from my mind.''

What an odd thing to say, thought I then, and an even odder thing to have done. Would that I could expunge from my memory much that I had seen and experienced during my last years.

''I was wondering, Jeremy, if you would go down and inquire how they are getting on. I would count it a great favor if you would do so.''

''But why do you not yourself go down and greet them? No doubt you know them. You could give heart to them. Tell them they may expect fairness and more from Sir John.''

''Have you understood nothing of what I have been telling you?'' He managed somehow to shout in a whisper. ''I do not wish to set myself apart from my shipmates. I do not wish to show myself as being one with the power that holds them prisoner.''

What power? The law? Then, with a bit of a shock, I divined his intention.

"You mean . . . *Sir John?*"

"Yesss!"

The hiss of his whispered answer seemed to linger in the air between us. I knew not what to say.

"But Tom," I managed at last, "Sir John Fielding is the fairest, the decentest of men. Why, you owe him your life, if I have heard the story aright."

"Oh, indeed I do—as my mother has reminded me at least a hundred times since my arrival. But if I owe him my life, as you say and I allow, I also owe it to two—no, three of my mates on as many separate occasions on the *Adventure*."

"So for this you would deny Sir John to your shipmates?"

"No, I would not! That is why I am asking you, Jeremy, to go in my stead and make inquiries as to their condition for me. Don't you see? I do not wish to be put in a place where I am asked to deny him."

My own poor head was quite split asunder by Tom's divided loyalties. He had not even mentioned Lieutenant Landon, whom he admired, nor would I mention him, for the complexities of Tom's situation were already enough; I dared not plague him with more. Of course I did in the end agree to call upon the prisoners taken last night and agreed, also, to make note of their names. How could I, considering Tom's dilemma, have done otherwise?

And so it was, leaving him to pore further over Lord Anson's *A Voyage Round the World*, I descended through the kitchen and down to the warren of rooms and alcoves set back behind the courtroom, searching for Mr. Marsden, the court clerk. I found him engaged in conversation with Mr. Fuller, the day constable, as he enjoyed his morning puff on his pipe of clay. He sent a great billow of smoke into the air, then gave me a wink.

"What have you on your mind this morning, young Jeremy?"

"I was merely wondering, sir," said I to Mr. Marsden, "if I might speak to the prisoners." So saying, I nodded beyond Mr. Fuller toward the stoutly barred cage which we named the strong room.

"I've no objection so long as Mr. Fuller has nothing against."

I looked hopefully toward Mr. Fuller. "Sir?"

Though Mr. Fuller bore the title of constable, he was in matters of general duties a jailer, for he had the responsibility of maintaining the prisoners, conveying them to the bench, and thence to Newgate or the Fleet, should that be Sir John's disposition. I got on less well with him than with the rest of the Bow Street Runners, for he suspicioned my friendship with Jimmie Bunkins and put no store by his reform. "Once a thief, always a thief," he had said to me on more occasions than one.

At this moment, however, he seemed inclined toward leniency—perhaps because Mr. Marsden was present.

"I trust you've some purpose," said he, "and it ain't mere curiosity urges you on in this."

"Oh yes, Mr. Fuller," said I, "for Sir John has appointed me to find one of the crew of that frigate—those who were involved in last night's trouble. I thought to question the prisoners as to the man's whereabouts."

(That was the answer I had prepared for Mr. Fuller to meet his expected challenge. There was, after all, the possibility that I should find out something regarding Tobias Trindle—though in all truth I thought it unlikely.)

"In that case," responded Mr. Fuller, "I could have no objection."

So, giving my thanks to both, I proceeded past them to the strong room. Glancing back, as I should not have done, I noted Mr. Fuller looking after me most sharp. Not knowing quite what sort of face to show him, I attempted to smile reassuringly and offer a confident wave—no doubt thereby awakening even greater distrust in him.

There were, as we had been told, four prisoners in the strong room. To my surprise, two of them were known to me from my visit with Tom and Bunkins to the Gull and Anchor.

"Old Isaac," I called quietly. "How do you fare?"

I had captured his attention. He rose from the bench where

he sat, all morose and dejected, and hobbled over to the place where I stood at the bars, looking in. Was he wounded? I thought not, for there was no trace of blood on the bandage that was bound tight about his bare ankle. One of the two he had left on the bench had sat at the table with us, yet whether he was Bristol Beatty or Trotter Tim I could not be certain, for I had made no sure distinction betwixt the two when first we met.

But as Old Isaac approached, he seemed to recognize me, for though he could not quite manage a smile, he brightened somewhat and began nodding like the wise old fellow he pretended to be.

"I knows you," said he. "You come with Tom Durham and the little lad who proved hisself a proper guzzler. What's your name?"

"Jeremy," said I. "Jeremy Proctor."

"Well, it's glad I am to see a familiar face."

"What happened to you, Isaac?"

I pointed down to the ankle, which was wrapped so thick his foot was near too big for the shoe he had squeezed upon it.

"Well," said he, "I was merely strollin' along tryin' to clear my head of the gin I drunk during the day. Uh, Bristol Beatty was by me side he was. When of a sudden, and quite without warnin' it was, a great troop of men come runnin' down upon the two of us. I says to Bristol, I say, 'Why, them's our mates from the *Adventure*.' And Bristol says to me, 'So they are. Where can they be off to in such a hurry?' So we tries to stop one to inquire of him, so to speak. Yet he would not stop, indeed he knocked me down and another stepped upon my ankle, causing me great pain. Now, how is that for mates? I ask you. Anyways, as they were past and Bristol was helpin' me to my feet, the two of us seen what it was caused the great panic: a squad of grenadiers it was, with bayonets fixed come down the dark street at the double. Before we could move out of their path, they was upon us. 'Twas a sergeant arrested us, Bristol and me, for it seemed the other lads from the *Adventure* was involved in some manner of disturbance. But not us, oh, indeed not Bristol and me. We was just walkin' by."

It would have been impertinent of me to voice my doubts—yet I had them. Had I not seen Old Isaac, or someone quite like him, among those grouped in the doorway of Mrs. Gerney's establishment? I believed I had.

"Well," said I, thinking only to make an agreeable response, "I'm glad you were not wounded. I heard the volley fired by the grenadiers and feared the worst for all."

"They had no call for that," said Isaac darkly. "It was that little pissant of a lieutenant ordered it. But the mates was then so distant and scattered that they did little harm to us."

"How many were hit?"

"Two. But it weren't bad for either one. Henry Bladgett got a finger shot off. He could've got away, but he stayed to look for it and got arrested. Damn foolish thing to do— not like a surgeon could stick it back on and make it work like new. And Fat Paddy, the cook, got shot in the arse. That's him stretched out on the other bench; can't sit down, but he can walk right enough."

I had learned from Isaac all that Tom had asked me to discover. Wondering then how I might take my leave, I looked right and left, hoping for a proper excuse. I wished not to leave a man cold in such sad circumstance.

But then Old Isaac spoke up again: "I'll do a bargain with you, lad."

"What sort of bargain, sir?"

"My nose tells me there's tobacco bein' smoked down the way. Ain't that so?"

He meant Mr. Marsden, of course. The aroma of that strange weed had wafted down to the strong room. Isaac was quite in ecstasy for a moment as he sniffed the air. He produced his own pipe and offered it to me.

"Now, if you'll take my pipe and beg a fill for me, I'll tell you something will interest you, I swear it. Might interest that blind fella we're to see later on today. What say to that?"

I took the pipe from him and was surprised at its lightness in my hand.

"I'll see what I can do for you," said I.

Hastening back to Mr. Marsden, I wondered what it was Old Isaac had to trade. Would he know where Tobias Trindle had now gone to hide? Perhaps—and perhaps not. He might simply be gulling me for the pleasure of a morning pipe. But if that were the case, it would count against him, he must know that. And Isaac seemed much inclined to ingratiate himself.

Mr. Marsden, who had by that time gone to his desk in the alcove, was occupied with the routine of court business. Mr. Fuller was then noplace about, for which I was grateful: he would surely disapprove any such favor to a prisoner.

After hearing me explain my mission, the court clerk took the clay pipe and began filling it from his pouch, as all the while he kept his long churchwarden clenched between his teeth.

"What have we to lose but a bit of tobacco?" said he, handing back the filled pipe. "And you may tell him there'll be more good Virginia for him if what he has to offer is of value." And with that he winked.

Giving him my thanks, I made my way back to the strong room, where I found Isaac waiting patiently by the barred door. Patience slipped swiftly to impatience as he grabbed the pipe from my hands and began fumbling with his tinderbox. Only when he had the pipe lit and had exclaimed enthusiastically at the quality of the tobacco would he deign to discuss other matters. He beckoned me close and began whispering.

"I remember you three lads was lookin' to find Tobias Trindle."

"Yes," said I most eagerly. "Do you know where he might be?"

Isaac shook his head in something akin to annoyance.

"That ain't the point. What I got to tell you is this: There's others looking for Tobias."

"Oh? Who?"

"This is how it was, like. A long time after you come by, there was another come asking the same sort of questions— where is he, where might he be, and such like. Only us three at the table, we told him nothin' at all, considerin' who he was."

"But who was he?"

"Aw, 'twas that little shit, Mr. Boone, the midshipman—

the one you sent flying down the poop deck ladder. Damn, we did enjoy that!'' He ended in a cackle, revealing gums, stumps, and a few whole teeth.

"But what would he want with Tobias Trindle?''

"Have you no sense, boy? It's the captain sent him to find Tobias. Boone even said as much, he did. 'The captain wants him,' said he. 'Tell him so, if you see him.' Oh, we nodded, gave assurance and all. But when he left, we agreed amongst ourselves that if the captain wanted him, it was for no good.''

"And what did you tell Tobias?''

"Oh, we told him the captain wanted him, right enough, and that he'd sent snotty Boone to find him. But we advised him to stay well hid till after they got done hanging Lieutenant Landon. That's what it's about, ain't it? I mean, it was well known in the fo'castle that Tobias had a view of it when the captain—Captain Markham, I mean—went overboard, and according to him, it happened just as Mr. Landon said. But we all kept still about it.''

"But why?''

He looked at me in dismay and shook his head as if marveling at my ignorance.

"You ain't got the littlest notion of what it is to ship aboard in His Majesty's Navy, have you?''

"No,'' said I in a manner suitably grave. "But tell me, you said that it was some time after we came to the Gull and Anchor that Boone came by. Could you be any more exact about when it was?''

"Sorry, lad, drinking the day away with no ship's bells to ring the watches, you lose your sense of time, in a manner of speakin'. Yet it seems to me it must have been gettin' toward dark. For not long after it was that Tobias hisself came by, and we—'' At that point he stopped, realizing perhaps that what he had been about to impart would impeach the tale of innocence he had earlier told.

"Was that when you let Tobias Trindle know that Boone was searching for him?''

"Well, you never mind when one thing happened and then another,'' said he, most suddenly peckish. "I done what I said I'd do. I told you what you wanted, and it weren't for the tobacco I told you, neither. It's because Tobias would be better off with the blind man than if the captain got hold of him.''

"Lieutenant Grimsby was pulled from the river," said I.

"That's what I mean. We got word of that. So did Tobias."

"Where is he? You must know."

"I mustn't no such thing. He's a fair bright man, so he would have sense enough to stay hid. If you want him, you must search him out—and pray you find him before Boone does."

He held the pipe up to me and waved it in a great fit of pique.

"Now look what," said he. "All this talkin' with your questions and all, and my pipe's gone out on me."

He fetched out his tinderbox once again and began the business of lighting the pipe all over again.

"One thing I will say," he muttered through clenched teeth. "Tobias said he'd had his fill of high-priced whores. You'll not likely find him around Covent Garden. Look where you was lookin' on the docks. He could've holed up with some wharf doxy in her crib, paid her well, and sent her out for food and drink. That's what I would do if I was him: keep low and let the ship sail without him. There was one he was lookin' for from years back—Black Emma or Black Ella, some such name. Anyways, she was mixed blood. He likes them so."

He shook the pipe in disgust. Ashes flew.

"Damned thing won't light, all smoked out."

"Don't worry, Isaac," said I, backing away from the bars. "I'll see you get more tobacco—a good deal more. I promise."

The question was this: Had last night's notable occurrence at Mrs. Gerney's constituted a riot, or merely a disturbance of the peace? If the latter, then the matter would be heard and judged by Sir John Fielding alone. It would go no further than his Magistrate's Court. If, however, he ruled that riot had taken place, any and all who had participated would be bound for trial at Old Bailey, for riot was a hanging offense. It was an interesting question, one whose answer attracted quite a crowd on what would otherwise have been a slow day in court. In point of fact, no other cases were to be heard that day. Ordinarily, that would have made for a short session, as well. The court crowd expected no more than a brief entertainment, a bit of diversion at the expense of a few unruly sailors. Yet it became clear that Sir John meant to treat this as a far more serious matter. To that end, he had put me to work for a good hour or more in his chambers, looking up law and reading cases to him from the dusty collection of books on the shelf behind his desk. He had also assembled diverse witnesses for examination in the matter.

So it was that the Bow Street Magistrate's Court convened at its usual hour, well filled with spectators. The prisoners, bound only in wrist irons, were marched into the courtroom by Constable Fuller. As Mr. Marsden read off their names— Timothy Beatty, Henry Bladgett, Patrick McGough, Isaac Tenker—they answered right sharply. All were then told to seat themselves, and all did, save Patrick McGough, who asked if he might remain standing due to the nature of his wound. There were titters and a few guffaws at that. But Sir John gaveled the room to order and granted permission to the prisoner to stand, if he chose, and went so far as to say that should he grow tired, he might take a place next to Mr. Fuller and lean against the wall. It was then time to make a proper beginning.

"We are here to determine the nature of the incident which occurred last night at Number Seventeen in the Strand," said Sir John, "and having made a determination on that matter, to make some disposition of the four prisoners taken there." He paused at that point and told Mr. Marsden to call the first witness.

The first witness was Constable Cowley, at twenty the youngest of the Bow Street Runners yet more than an apprentice, for in size and initiative he compensated for what he lacked in experience. As the first officer at the scene, he had the earliest look at the situation and had seen it through to its end. He had been notified of a great gang of men on the march down the Strand, and thinking they could be up to no good in such number, he hastened to intercept them. When he reached Number 17, he found them arrived and the first of them ready to push through the door. He yelled at them to halt, desist, disperse. Yet no attention was paid to him, nor to Constable Rumford, who arrived upon the scene but a few minutes later.

"Did you and Constable Rumford attempt to use physical means to prevent their entry into the house at Number Seventeen?" asked Sir John.

"We did, sir," said Mr. Cowley, "but it was quite useless. We tried to block the door, but they pushed us aside. We beat upon a few with our clubs, but they just ignored us. Laughing they was, having a great time of it. They paid us no mind at all."

"Were they acting as drunken men? Would you characterize them as a drunken mob?"

"Well, they weren't staggering or nothin', but yes sir, I would say they'd probably been drinking right through the day, for the smell of gin and rum was strong upon them. I would say they was drunk, but active drunk—oh, right active, if you get my meaning."

"I do indeed. And at what figure would you put their number?"

"Sir?"

"How many of them were there?"

"Near a hundred."

"Very well, continue your story."

And so he did. Constable Cowley said that upstairs windows were broken and that objects of all kinds began to fly out to the pavement—as Mr. Bailey had earlier described. The captain of the Bow Street Runners had come on the scene with Constables Perkins, Sykes, and Cummins.

With that Sir John dismissed Mr. Cowley, and the court clerk called Benjamin Bailey, who continued the tale from that point, describing the events much as I have earlier done. Only two matters stand out as noteworthy. As I sat listening to Sir John's questions, recalling the cases he had asked me to read to him earlier, I sought to discern some pattern from them. Yet from Mr. Bailey's answers none seemed to emerge.

Sir John interrupted his chief constable as the latter told

of his urgent visit to summon Sir John to Number 17 in the
Strand.

"Let me ask you here, Mr. Bailey, when you came to me,
how did you describe the trouble you had witnessed?"

"Well, I told you what I'd seen, sir."

"Indeed you did, but what term did you use?"

"Well . . ." He hesitated, evidently uncertain as to what
he should say. Finally: "I called it a riot."

"On what did you base that?"

Again he hesitated. "The size of the mob," said he at last,
"the destruction of property, and the commotion caused in
the street."

"And you recommended that troops be called from the
Tower."

"Yes sir, I did."

"And I accepted your recommendation without hesitation.
Now continue, Mr. Bailey, please."

He resumed his narrative and came swiftly to the peculiar
behavior of the crewmen of the H.M.S. *Adventure* as they
danced about that great heap of goods thrown down from
Mrs. Gerney's upper stories. Sir John allowed him to give a
full description of the poke-and-parry that they practiced with
their torches much to the distress of the four constables that
Mr. Bailey had left on guard.

Sir John held him again with a wave of his hand.

"Mr. Bailey," said he, "you described the activity of
these men to me then in unusual words. Do you recall what
you said to me?"

Benjamin Bailey took a moment to think on that; then said
he: "I believe I told you, sir, that they was playin' a game
with the constables, that all they had to do was toss a torch
on the pile if what they wanted was a fire."

"Exactly," said Sir John, "and then what happened?"

"Then what happened? Well, you went bold as brass and
offered a bargain to the rowdies."

"Yes, please tell us what was said and done by me and
by him who spoke for the mob."

In that part of his testimony the chief constable seemed
somewhat hesitant, for he wished to be accurate in quoting
the magistrate, most particularly in this matter. When he con-

cluded, he was offered Sir John's congratulations.

"That is exactly as I recall it. There are but a few more details I wish from you, however. First of all, the man with whom I spoke—would you, from your experience in such matters, say that he was the leader of this band of near a hundred?"

"I would say so, yes sir."

"And is his name known to you?"

"Yes sir, his name has been given to me as Tobias Trindle."

"Excellent, Mr. Bailey, and as you said, he conferred with his fellows on the offer that I had made. What happened then?"

"Why, the grenadiers came in two wagons, led there by a certain Lieutenant Churchill."

"Thank you, Constable Bailey, that will be all for the present."

All eyes in the Bow Street Court rested upon the young gentleman who had quietly taken his place among the constables. He stood out from the rest of the assemblage as a proud red-feathered peacock might from a homely group of woodcocks. There seemed to be a general expectation that Lieutenant Thomas Churchill would be the next summoned.

But he was not. As Mr. Bailey retired from his place before Sir John's bench, Mr. Marsden called for Constable Oliver Perkins to appear as a witness. Upon hearing his name, Mr. Perkins jumped to his feet and made his way swiftly to the station his captain had left. He was a bit shorter than the rest of the Bow Street Runners; moreover, the left sleeve of his coat was empty—pinned up it was at the elbow, for he had lost that arm in the line of duty a year before. Thus he appeared somewhat different from the rest, though I knew him to be unsurpassed in courage and resourcefulness. But were his lively manner, his modest stature, and his empty sleeve reason to laugh? Nevertheless, a long chorus of idiot laughter rang forth out of the crowd from the moment he showed himself.

(Mr. Marsden later suggested to me that firstly, they had anticipated Lieutenant Churchill being called and were therefore surprised when Constable Perkins came forward—a

common response to surprise being laughter. Secondly, said
he, they had been bored by the proceedings up to that time,
for they had not been near so entertaining as expected, and
seized upon the constable of a sudden as an object for de-
rision. Perhaps the presence of a one-armed constable was
thought amusing by them. "He ought not to take it personal," concluded the court clerk.)

Yet take it personal he most certainly did. Mr. Perkins
turned angrily upon the courtroom and might have shouted
back at the crowd had not Sir John silenced them all with
his gavel. The magistrate conferred briefly with his clerk to
the reason for the disturbance. Mr. Marsden may have then
advanced to Sir John the very reasons he offered me later.
In any case, after a brief discussion, Sir John let fall the gavel
one more time.

"Any more such disturbance, and I shall have the room
cleared," he announced. And he was answered with absolute
silence. He listened carefully to it for a few moments, then
nodded in satisfaction.

"Mr. Perkins," he began, "I have but a few questions for
you. Mr. Bailey sent you to the Tower with a request that
troops be sent to Number Seventeen in the Strand, did he
not?"

"Yes sir, he did."

"You made all haste?"

"I did, sir. I ran to Russell Street, and caught a hackney
carriage. In point of fact, I climbed up on the driver's box
and urged him faster all the way."

"Very good. And you asked your way to the barracks of
the grenadier guards? They were cooperative?"

"They sped me on my way. In no wise was I impeded.
They treated it as an urgent matter, as it of course was."

"And who did you speak to once you reached your destination?"

"To a Captain Weybright, sir."

"And was Lieutenant Churchill present?"

"Is he the officer now present in the courtroom?"

"Yes, Mr. Perkins, just behind you, I believe."

Constable Perkins turned and glanced back at the young
red-coated officer.

"Yes, sir, he was one of three other officers who was engaged in a game of cards with the captain. He jumped up from his chair and said, 'Let me go, Captain!' "

"And what did the captain say to him?"

"That I wouldn't know, sir, for at that point I was invited by the captain to leave. 'That will be all, Constable,' said he to me. I offered to show them to the place on the Strand, but the captain just repeated, 'That will be all.' Quite frankly, sir, I was hopin' for a ride back with them. But I left and went lookin' for another hackney. You have to stretch your legs to find one on Tower Hill that time of night."

"Now, Mr. Perkins, I would like you to think carefully before answering this question, for I would like you to respond accurately and with perfect honesty. The question is this: When you described the situation at Mrs. Gerney's establishment in the Strand, what word or phrase did you use?"

Constable Perkins did give the question serious consideration. He lowered his eyes, scratched his chin, and said at last: "I told the captain that it was a serious disturbance that was more than the constables present could handle. I told him I had been sent by your request and that you would be at the scene when the troops arrived—as I understand you was, sir."

"Those were your words?"

"As I remember them, sir."

"You did not use the word 'riot'?"

"No sir, I did not."

"Thank you, Mr. Perkins," said Sir John. "And Mr. Marsden, you may call the next witness."

The next witness, of course, was Lieutenant Thomas Churchill. He stood before Sir John Fielding, his tricorn tucked under his left arm, in the military attitude known as parade rest. He was the very picture of a young officer of great promise. Putting aside his name, his family connections, and his wealth, it was possible to look upon this young man and know he would go far in the military. Capability and confidence showed forth from him in near visible measure. And indeed he had the night before demonstrated those qualities beyond doubt. All that had been missing were proper judgment and respect for authority.

After identifying himself by name, rank, and unit, he waited silently for Sir John's questions. If he was nervous, or even uneasy, it was impossible to tell.

"Lieutenant Churchill?"

"Sir?"

"Will you tell the court your part in putting down the trouble at Number Seventeen in the Strand?"

"That I can do in brief, sir. Upon arriving at said number, I assembled my men in the street, ordered them to fix bayonets, and marched them toward the entrance of the house whereat the mob was assembled. They threw sticks and stones at us, but we carried on until they broke and began running in a westerly direction along the Strand.

"At that, I double-timed my men in pursuit of the mob and turned them down a side street, little more than an alley, thus continuing in pursuit. There we took our first prisoners—an old fellow who had fallen and twisted his ankle and another who had stayed to help him. Since we had stopped to take them, I ordered the men to shoulder and present fire— a single volley, no more. It wounded but two and killed none, but we took those two prisoners, as well. Since the mob was dispersed, I sent the men about-face and marched them back to the wagons. We did then depart."

"I congratulate you, Lieutenant," said Sir John. "An excellent summary it was—brief but truthful, for it revealed an omission on your part in the matter of procedure. You've been apprised of this, have you not?"

"I have, yes sir, by Captain Weybright."

"And what did you learn?"

"I learned, sir, that while the tactics I used to disperse that great body of men were right enough, I was a bit hasty in putting them to work."

"And specifically?"

"I did not wait until the Riot Act had been read."

Then did Sir John address the court: "You present here may not be aware of this nicety of English law, so it were better perhaps if I make a short explanation. When a disturbance is of such proportion that troops must be called, it is

the magistrate's decision to call them. Their mere presence—
the threat of bayonet and bullet—is usually sufficient to disperse the mob. If it is not, the magistrate has one last re-
course, and that is the reading of the Riot Act to those
causing the disturbance. Even here a brake is put on the use
of the military force. For by custom, after the Riot Act has
been read, those who have made the disturbance are given
an hour to disperse. If they are not then gone, they are only
then considered in a state of riot, and all means necessary—
bayonet and bullet—may be used to clear them from the
area. Prisoners taken are to be considered rioters and tried
as such.

"Now," continued the magistrate, "you can tell from
what I have said so far how reluctant were the Members of
Parliament who framed this act to allow the military to take
the initiative in its enforcement. At each stage, it is the civil
authority, usually the magistrate like myself, who must make
a determination on the use of military force. He calls them
to the scene of the disturbance; he threatens their use; he
reads the Riot Act to let the unruly mob know of the dire
consequences should their continued destructive behavior
continue. As regards the military, the disturbance is not to
be considered a riot until the magistrate has named it such
with the reading of the act, and has after due pause given his
permission to proceed against the rioters. It is a clear instance
of the preeminence of civil authority over the military, a
principle upon which the laws of our Kingdom rest.

"As I said in the beginning, we are here to make a determination as to the nature of last night's trouble. As we have
heard from the testimony given thus far, it is a matter on
which reasonable men may differ. When he came to me describing the situation in the Strand, Mr. Benjamin Bailey did
not hesitate to characterize what he had seen as a 'riot'—
and he gave good reasons for doing so. Constable Oliver
Perkins, who was sent to the Tower with a request for troops
in my name, described what he had seen as a 'serious disturbance' that was beyond the power of the constables to
handle."

By this time the crowd had grown restless. There was
probably not one in ten among those who had come in from

the street capable of following Sir John's discourse. The remainder did not dare express their dissatisfaction by noisy comments or other rowdy behavior, yet express it they did with much restless shifting in their seats and beating of their feet upon the floor. Yet Sir John pressed on.

"Then, too, there is the matter of intent," he declared. "The law takes it into account in many ways. For instance, homicide lacking the intent to kill is not murder but manslaughter. And if, at the end of a long coach ride, a man takes another's portmanteau which is quite like his own, that is not theft but merely a mistake. So since it was generally agreed among the constables that this mob had a proper leader—which in itself is unusual—and his name as given by Mr. Bailey was Tobias Trindle, I think it important that this Trindle come before me as a witness that I might examine him as to his intent in this matter. Therefore I shall issue a bench warrant for his apprehension and detention as a material witness in this matter. I should like, in other words, to continue this question of riot versus disturbance to a later date when I may gather more testimony to come to an informed decision.

"Yet what am I to do with these four men before me now as prisoners? If last night's disturbance is found eventually to have been a riot, then they must be passed on for criminal trial, but I cannot hold them indefinitely without charge. Perhaps a lesser charge would do. If you four would come up and face me now?"

Up they came, looking glum, fearing the worst. In spite of his wound, Fat Paddy, already on his feet, led the procession; Old Isaac, hobbled by his twisted ankle, was the last. They ranged before him, a good space between them and Lieutenant Churchill.

"Now, Constable Cowley has already given it that the mob which entered Number Seventeen was heavily under the influence of alcohol. Constable Bailey?"

Mr. Bailey shot to his feet and responded in sharp, soldierly manner.

"No need to approach the bench. It must be getting a bit crowded up here," said Sir John. "Since you accompanied the prisoners to this place and oversaw their detention, perhaps you could give me your opinion as to their condition?''

"Their condition, sir?''

"Were they drunk?''

"They were drunk, sir. Been drunk for days.''

"Thank you, Mr. Bailey.'' To the prisoners he then posed this pregnant question: "Would any of you care to deny this?''

They hung their heads and mumbled in the negative.

"That being the case, I find you all guilty of public drunkenness and sentence you to seven days' incarceration in the Fleet Prison. If, by any chance, the *Adventure* should make ready to sail and the case is not yet resolved, I shall make some arrangement. Now, gentlemen, the Fleet is fundamentally a debtors' prison, and though it may seem paradoxical, you will need money there, particularly since three of you four are in need of further medical attention. I know not your financial state, nor do I wish to, but I do believe there is a way to allow you some modicum of comfort there.''

With that, Sir John shifted bodily in the direction of the lieutenant.

"Lieutenant Churchill,'' said he, "are you still with us?''

"I am, sir,'' came the reply.

"Good, for by your own admission and description you acted against the law in proceeding as you did against those who caused such trouble in the Strand. For that I find you guilty of discharging firearms illegally in the City of Westminster and, by so doing, causing bodily harm to two men.''

"But sir,'' objected the lieutenant, "I carried no firearm. I had no pistols by my side. My only weapon was my sword!''

"Come now, Lieutenant, I thought better of you. You know very well that the firearms I refer to were the muskets of your grenadiers, and they were discharged at your command. And for this the court fines you five guineas.''

"I shall have to borrow it.''

"Then borrow it. Now if I may continue, this fine will go toward easing the stay of the four prisoners at the Fleet and paying their medical bills. None of it, however, is to pay for alcoholic drink. If any is left over after they have served their sentence, it is to go into the general fund.''

And having so said, he slammed a great blow with his gavel and bellowed, "This court is dismissed, the matter continued."

Whether it was late at night or early in the morning, I was unsure. I knew only that it was deep dark at an hour of no moon and that we had been exploring the dens of St. Catherine's Street through the evening. They were, as Black Jack Bilbo had assured us, far worse than those in the area of the Custom House. There were none of the dirt-floored gin dives which lacked all furnishings but bar and bottle, yet those through which we had passed on that night seemed distinctly worse, even when well appointed, due to an oppressive sense of evil which seemed to permeate them all.

How might one describe such an air of malevolence? No doubt the same sinful pursuits were available in Covent Garden to those who wished them, yet I then always thought of it, and today think of it still, as a jolly place, one given more to frivolity than conspiracy. Yet in place after place there on St. Catherine's, we were met by a sudden hush as we entered; eyes narrowed watchfully; and when conversation resumed, it was to be heard in a whisper. And the appearance of those who threw conspiratorial glances about and buzzed who knew what dark plans to their fellows seemed of a somewhat satanic cast. Lean and hungry they were—hags young and old—and hagridden men. They looked the sort who, given equal opportunity, would rather do harm to a man than good.

I believe I might not have survived my tour of that dark underworld (as indeed I nearly did not) had it not been for Constable Oliver Perkins. Now that I, like Tom Durham, could recognize Tobias Trindle on sight, there was no point in the two of us searching in concert. Moreover, had we located him, we could have done nothing but attempt to persuade him to give himself up—neither of us had the power to arrest him, after all—and so each of us two was paired with a constable who carried a warrant for Trindle's arrest. It fell to Constable Perkins and myself to search the riverfront beyond the Tower, which included the gloomy dens along St. Catherine's Street.

It seemed a bootless task. We entered one dark place after

another—the Pig and Whistle, the Green Man, the Quarterdeck, it was all the same—whereat I would look through a
crowd gone suddenly quiet and carefully observe their sullen
faces. Mr. Perkins would, in the meantime, engage the innkeeper in conversation at the bar, displaying his red waistcoat
prominently (which identified him as a Bow Street Runner),
as well as the brace of pistols he wore in his belt; he mentioned the names of Tobias Trindle and, at my suggestion,
Black Emma or Black Ella. He learned nothing of either, and
for my part, I saw neither Trindle nor any of the others from
the *Adventure* I had come to know in the past few days.

At one point, as we passed from the last to the next, Constable Perkins gave out a groan and shook his head in a great,
slow gesture of discouragement.

"I vow he ain't here," said he. "I would wager him to
be across the river in Southwark or Bermondsey. That's
where I'd hide—another world entirely over there."

"Perhaps you're right, sir," said I. "I've never once been
to that side."

"You've no need to go, lad. It's a bit fouler than here,
though there's not so much of it." He walked along in silence for a bit. "But we'll do the job, will we not? If they
wish us to search this nasty stretch, we shall give a good
effort to it. You're holding up well?"

"Well enough."

"Good lad."

It may have been at our next stop, or perhaps the one that
followed it—yet not long afterward a break came in the dis-
appointing pattern that had thus far been established. I recall
well the name of the inn that marked our change of fortune,
for there seemed something prophetic in it: the Queen of
Sheba it was called, after the Ethiopian queen who led old
Solomon such a ramble.

I had completed my inspection of those at the tables—
drinkers, smokers, gamblers at simple games of chance—
searching for the sharp-featured, leathery face of Tobias
Trindle; all without result, of course. Yet returning, I noted
Mr. Perkins standing near the door and saw him gesturing
sharply for me to hurry. I was with him in a trice.

"What is it, sir?"

"Come along," said he. "I'll tell you as we walk."

Stepping outside, the constable surprised me by taking us back the way we had come. He was angry, properly seething, cursing under his breath. I thought it best to put no questions to him until he had cooled down a bit. Yet it did not take long until he had regained control of himself and blurted it forth.

"It was the innkeeper of that last place. He was no better than the rest of them, but he did have something to say when I brought up your Black Emma woman."

"What was it?" I asked, of a sudden taken with excitement.

"Well, he said, 'She don't come here no more.' And I said, 'But she used to?' And he said, 'Aye, she used the rooms upstairs.' Never mind what for, lad. I'm just tellin' it as it was told to me. So I says to him, 'Where does she go now?' And he says, 'The Green Man'—and that's what makes me so damn angry."

"I don't understand, Mr. Perkins. Why should that anger you so?"

"Because we were in there eight or ten places back, and the fella there said he never heard of her, that's why! Thinks he can trifle with a one-armed man, he does. Well, I'll show him Oliver Perkins is not to be dallied with, not to be mocked. No indeed, I shall *not* be lied to."

Thus with muttered threats and imprecations the constable led me the long way back to the Green Man. Though not much taller than myself, and with legs not much longer, he nevertheless kept me at a jog-trot as I continually attempted to catch him up. I hesitated but a moment as he burst through the door and into the place; then I plunged after him. Yet in that moment, he had whipped out his stout oak club and cleared three men from the bar and then emptied it of bottles and glasses; they were still skittering left and right as I entered. He then threw down his club upon the bar and dove across it, grasping the cowering innkeeper by the collar, and pulling him back by the strength of his single arm, he stretched him forward until they were face-to-face.

Then said Constable Oliver Perkins to the innkeeper in a

voice which, though quiet, filled the room: "You lied to me."

One of the three men who had been at the bar began moving slowly sidelong toward the door. Seeing him, I took a position near it, reached into the pocket of my coat, and brought out the pistol that Mr. Bilbo had given me the day before. I showed just enough to prove that I was armed. That proved sufficient. He returned to his former place, and his fellows had noted my demonstration. As I returned the pistol to its place deep in my pocket, I continued to hold it tight by its handle.

"Now," said Constable Perkins to the innkeeper, holding him as before, "I shall ask you again. What do you know of a whore named Black Emma? Where . . . is . . . she? And if you tell me you do not know, sir, you will regret it."

The innkeeper's answer came in a whisper, whether because Mr. Perkins had him so tight by the collar or because of his shame at snitching I cannot say. Yet even though I was not far distant and the room quite silent, I could not make out the exact words of his reply. It was not lengthy, but it proved to be precise.

Having heard him through, the constable gave him a great shove, propelling him back across the bar and sending him down in a heap behind it. He grabbed up his club and moved past me to the door.

"Come along, lad," he called. "We must hurry."

And hurry we did. He resumed at an even faster walking pace—so fast, indeed, that I was obliged to go at a run to keep up with him. Nor would he allow me to fall behind. He urged me on with a steady stream of curses well mixed with encouragement.

"I've need of you," he declared. "Someone looked after my back in the Green Man, and I believe it was you. I'll not ask what you have in your pocket, but by God wave it if you've need and use it if you must."

"Where are we going?" I gasped.

"To Black Emma's. She has a lodging down Pillory Lane."

"But why this great rush?"

"Because that fool of a fellow behind the bar said that

another had come only minutes before and bribed the right answer from him.''

''Bribed? That does not sound like Trindle.''

''Nor did the description he gave.''

We had turned down Pillory Lane. I liked not the name of the street, though I knew not its history. There were many great buildings in it of a simple kind I took to be storehouses and magazines.

''It should be an easy matter finding the place. He said that it—'' Constable Perkins stopped and pointed down and across Pillory Lane. ''See it, lad? Stuck there between big boxy structures? It's the only lodging house on the street.''

''I see it, Mr. Perkins.''

''Here is what I wish you to do. If it is like most such places, it is a warren of small rooms, top and bottom, with a way out the back. The woman's crib is on the upper floor. I will enter by the front and find it. Yet it will take a bit of noise to do so, and our man may hear and scarper out the back. That is where I wish you to be. Should he come, do all you can to stop him, short of shooting him dead. Don't worry. If shoot you must, then I'll take the blame upon myself. Now come along.''

We proceeded in a diagonal course across Pillory Lane. He moved as stealthily as he had moved swiftly but moments before. He held his hand to his lips, signaling quiet, then pointed left around the side of the old house where a path led to the rear. He then gestured that he would go through the door immediately before us, where a single candle burned. It was, as near as I could tell, the only light in the street.

I nodded my agreement and started down the path as he had directed. The stench of it near drove me back. Many a chamber pot had been emptied out the windows this side of the house. I would have stepped careful had there been light enough to do so, yet there was naught but a dim glow from one of the upper windows. I tripped once but did not fall.

Little more than halfway to the rear of the house I heard a small explosion, a loud report—a shot! I started to run down the path, unable to see much beyond my hand before my face. I bumped into I knew not what on my left, careened into the wall of the lodging house on my right, just as I heard the clatter of footsteps above. I had near lost my balance completely as I came at last to the rear of the house. Thus stumbling awkwardly about in the dark, I was ill prepared when, with no more warning than a grunt from above, a man dropped down, not quite on top of me but against me in such a way that I was knocked off my feet. I rolled so as to take me away from him. Yet in doing it, I lost my pistol. I began groping the ground most frantically for it, feeling this way and that.

For his part, my assailant paid no attention to me, nor to my searches. I sensed rather than saw (so dark was it) that he had recovered his feet and was thrashing forward—that is, away from the lodging house.

Just as I found my pistol, I heard a voice cry out from that rear:

"This way, sir!"

Still down on the ground, I had the presence of mind to pull back the hammer. I raised to my knees, peered hopefully into the darkness, and by some faint glow, perhaps radiated from distant streetlamps, I caught the movement of a dark-clad figure some thirty yards away.

"Stop or I'll shoot!"

"Shoot away, lad!" came Mr. Perkins's call from above.

Aiming low at the ill-defined target, I pulled the trigger. There was a great flash. The weapon jumped mightily in my hand. This one was no dueling pistol but a serious firearm from Black Jack Bilbo's dark past.

Mr. Perkins discharged his weapon at nearly the same moment.

Yet great was the disappointment we shared when we heard the footsteps resume farther and continue yet farther away.

"Step away," called the constable. "I'm jumpin' down."

Light on his feet he was, and he landed easy just to my right.

"Go up and secure the room—up above, last on the left," he yelled to me. "I'm off to give chase."

But he was already on his way—and I on mine. I went to

the front of the house and through the door. The curious had popped their heads out their doors.

"Back inside," I yelled at them, then hopped up the stairs two at a time. They were out and milling about on the upper floor. I still held the pistol in my hand, and though it was empty, I knew it to look quite formidable. I waved it about in a threatening way.

"One side," said I, putting a growl in my unsettled tenor. "Back into your rooms. This is a matter for the Beak-runners."

They fell away, men and women, dressed and undressed, giving me an easy passage down the hall. Had I counterfeited authority so well, or were they simply fearful of a pistol that went this way and that in the inexperienced hand of a lad so young? Whatever the reason, I must have enjoyed the moment of strutting command that I was given, for at the end of my long walk I was emboldened to shout rather roughly at those who had crowded about the open door of the last room on the left, push my way through them, and brandish the empty pistol one last time.

"Away, all of you!" I yelled. "Back to your rooms! Be-gone!"

Then I slammed the door in their wantonly curious faces and returned the weapon to its place in my pocket. As I turned to survey the room, any pleasure I may have taken in my performance immediately vanished, for my eyes went swift to the bed whereon the body of a man rested, half covered by a dirty sheet. Though his face was besooted with gunpowder and a bloody hole had been crushed into the skull between and above the eyes, I recognized him to be Tobias Trindle.

He was dead. Of that I was sure. I stood staring, unwilling to touch him for fear of disturbing something materially ev-idential. And staring, I pondered the fate of Lieutenant Wil-liam Landon. Could he now be saved? Could anyone, even Sir John Fielding, help him?

I know not how long I stood so, but gradually, I became aware of a certain small sound, irregular but continual. I looked about the room. It was near bare but for the bed. There were two chairs and a chest; upon the latter were the leavings of a meal. What was that sound? What did I remember it to be?

Taking the pistol from my pocket, I moved quietly to the only place from which that half-familiar noise could have issued. There was an antechamber to the room, no doubt a closet, separated not by a door but by a thick curtain.

I threw back that curtain and exposed a sobbing woman dressed only in a shift. Though far from black in hue, she was of a darker color than any I had seen, save for the Lascars on the H.M.S. *Adventure*.

This was surely Black Emma.

TEN

*In which Lieutenant
Landon tells his story
to Sir John*

Being as incapable as any other male in dealing with a
weeping woman, I pocketed my pistol and persuaded
her forward with soothing words to one of the room's two
chairs; I had the foresight to turn it in such a way that once
seated, she was facing in a direction away from the bed. She
wanted not to look upon the body of Tobias Trindle, and I
saw no reason why she should be made to do so.

Seated as she was, it was not long until the small hiccup-
ing sobs ceased. She raised her eyes to me. Though tearful
still, they shone with rage.

"Bloody hell," said she in plain London speech, "I saw
the bastid put him down. If I'd been there, he'd a done the
same to me."

"But where were you?"

"In there," said she, jerking her head toward the closet
from which she had emerged, "on the pisspot. I peeped
through the cloth when I heard him and held my water. He
had his other pistola pointin' my way, so I knowed he musta
heard me. He woulda come for me were it not there was
someone bangin' up the stairs."

"Would you know the man? The room has but a candle
for light. How well did you see him?"

She looked at me with sudden suspicion. "Who're you?"
she demanded.

"I'm with the Beak-runners." Was that an outright lie? I hoped not.

"No you ain't. You're just a kid."

She had quite a deep voice for a woman and a most commanding manner. She seemed much less intimidating when she was weeping. What was I to say to her now? Yet I was saved from attempting to explain my relation to the Bow Street Runners, or fabricating something on the spot, as it were, for after a moment she resumed, apparently indifferent to any response I might give.

"Toby was a rum joe," said she. "He shoulda had better. I knowed him from years back, I did. He come to me, and he says, 'Em, you be my moll slavy for a week, and I'll give you a quid a day.' So I made the bargain, bought us bub and grub and kep' the rest. He set up here with me just like we jumped the broom together. But he told me the Runners was after him. He gets put down in his sleep, then you comes and says you're with one of the Blind Beak's. What'm I supposed to think?"

"Think what is reasonable," said I, at last stung to protest. "He was wanted alive, not dead. We wanted him as a witness. Dead men can give no testimony."

"So you say."

"There was one who did want him dead, however."

She nodded wisely at that. "There was one he feared more than the hornies."

"And who was that?"

"He did not say his name, but 'twas someone on his ship. Of that I'm right sure."

I should have liked to pursue this further with her. Yet at that moment came a pounding at the door. I jumped up, the pistol in my hand, ready to turn back any intruder, but then in walked Constable Perkins. We met at the door. Sweat stood upon his brow.

"Ah, you did well," said he. "The halls were clear, and—" He hesitated but the briefest moment as he spied her in the chair. "This would be Black Emma, would it not?"

"It would, sir."

"Well, I shall talk to her about our friend there on the bed."

"She saw it done," said I.

"Did she now? Perhaps she had a hand in it herself. It does make you wonder, don't it? Her surviving the assassination in such good health?"

"She tells a good story."

"She'll have a chance to tell it to me now. But you—your name's Jeremy, ain't it? I've seen you about, of course, but we were never properly met. You did a man's work tonight, lad, but now you must do a bit more. As you have no doubt concluded, I failed to catch the visitor. There was two of them, as it happened."

"Yes, I heard one call out to the other," said I. "The voice was familiar to me."

"Well, tell that to Sir John. There was two ways they could've gone. The one would have taken them through Goodman's Wharf, then up Butcher Row, which I thought most likely and followed in pursuit. The other would have taken them through St. Catherine's Churchyard and on to St. Catherine's Street, yet the only place to go from there is to the Tower. Could the two of them have gone to the Tower—or, say, to the Tower Wharf?"

"They could have, yes." Indeed they could!

"Well, tell that to Sir John too. What I'm saying, lad, is that you must go fetch him now. Remember this here location—the only proper house on a street of magazines—Pillory Lane."

"Right, sir."

He pointed down at the pistol, still in my hand.

"Have you reloaded that blunderbuss?"

"No sir. I lack the necessary."

"It is not your own then?"

"No sir, it was loaned to me."

"By . . . ?"

"Someone."

"Mmmm. Well, may I examine it?"

I handed it over to him, pleased at his interest. He took it, weighed it in his hand, and sighted down the short barrel at the floor.

"Well, I can't help you. It takes a bigger ball than mine do, but it's got a frame that will handle a good-sized charge.

I saw the visitor by the muzzle flash from this pistol. He was set to return fire when I shot at him. I doubt either one of us hit our man. That's why you must always move away fast when you shoot a weapon in the dark. They shoot back at the flash.''

''I'll remember that, sir.''

He handed it back to me.

''It's a grand weapon for close-in fighting,'' he said. ''I never saw the like. Pull it out and wave it if anyone accosts you on the trip back to Bow Street. That ought to be enough to frighten anyone. Have you enough for a hackney, should you be lucky enough to find one at this late hour?''

I nodded.

''Well, on your way then. Don't leave by the back, though. There's a porch, but the stairs rotted away long ago. Hence, all this jumpin' about.''

He gave me a pat on the back to send me on my way, then turned toward Black Emma. ''Now then, my good woman,'' said he as I departed, ''I wonder would you tell me what you told that fine young lad?''

My return to Bow Street was blessedly uneventful. Somewhere along the way on those deserted streets a hackney carriage came plodding along behind me. I heard it on the cobblestones long before I saw it, and prayed that it was for hire. Though the driver was near as sleepy as his horses, he seemed glad for the fare, and glad also to wait at Bow Street when we arrived, for I assured him I would be returning to Pillory Lane with a party of some number.

But that was not to be. I sought Sir John and found him in hushed conversation in the alcove with Mr. Bailey, Mr. Baker, and Tom Durham. I liked not the tone of it. There was defeat in the air—and thus far all they would know was that Tobias Trindle was not to be found. It now fell to me to announce that he had been found and was dead, murdered in his bed by an assailant as yet unidentified.

I was greeted soberly by the four, made my announcement in brief, and promised the details on our way to the house on Pillory Lane in the hackney which now waited at the door. Sir John showed little emotion as he rose heavily from the court clerk's chair. The others, who had been standing about, made ready to go.

"Mr. Bailey will go with me," said Sir John. "Tom, Jeremy, go to your bed. You've had a long day, both of you." Then he added quietly, giving expression to his deepest feelings: "And the day ends bitterly for us, does it not?"

"But sir," said I, "you will need me to show you the place, surely."

"I think not. Mr. Bailey, do you know Pillory Lane?"

"Quite well do I know it, sir," said he. "I know the very house Jeremy has described, for wedged as it is between those great storehouses, it seems not to belong."

"Then let us be off and through this ordeal as quick as ever we can."

"But sir—" I had in mind to make one last bid to accompany them.

Yet he would not hear of it: "No, Jeremy," said he, interrupting me most firm. "This is something Mr. Bailey and I will attend to. Constable Perkins awaits us there?"

"Yes, sir."

"Then he will provide the information you promised. You've done a good job, and I thank you. But now you must go to bed."

He stepped out into the long corridor as we gave space for his exit.

"Mr. Bailey?"

And the two made their way swiftly to the street door and the waiting hackney.

Tom, who had spoken not a word, gestured me toward the stairs leading up to the kitchen. I said my goodnight to Mr. Baker. He nodded and gave me a wink of encouragement.

"Sir John is right, lad. This is man's work that may take the rest of the night. Be grateful you have someone to look after your interest. You, too, Tom Durham."

"Yes sir." In chorus.

And so, without another word, I followed Tom up the stairs and into the kitchen. A candle burned on the table. Annie had put out beside it what was left of a mutton roast and a near-full loaf of bread, each wrapped in cloth.

"Hungry?" asked Tom.

"Famished," said I.

And so we set to. On thick slices of bread we laid over generous portions of mutton and slathered all with hot mustard. Water was needed to wash it down and extinguish the mustard-fire. Ah, but we did enjoy it. What a feast it did seem to two hungry boys.

Once we had satisfied our first ravenings, we settled down to serious, steady chewing, content to savor our food a bit before we swallowed it.

"Good of Annie to leave this out for us," said Tom.

"For Sir John, too," said I. "We'd best leave some for him."

"Oh, aye. He likes his mutton—and his beef."

"And his veal and his lamb and his pork and his cod and his—"

Then did we two burst out laughing, for indeed Sir John was a great and enthusiastic eater and a man of considerable girth. It may seem odd to you, reader, that Tom, who had just lost a shipmate, and I, who had seen that shipmate dead in his bed, might carry on so lightheartedly, but so is it with boys of the age we were then. They have a great love of silliness, and it does find expression, sometimes at the most inappropriate moments. Yet having had our laugh together, we seemed somehow to have purged ourselves and were now able and willing to talk of the subject that had brooded over us since we entered the kitchen.

"Who did it?" asked Tom of a sudden; there was no need for him to be more specific.

"Hartsell and Boone," said I.

"You're sure of it?"

"I heard a voice, and I recognized it fair sure as Boone."

"Boone could not pull the trigger. He is a coward—a bully and a coward."

"No, it could have been Hartsell—or one he had hired. Whoever it was did the deed near jumped on top of me, knocked me over he did, he was that close. Yet it was so dark I could not see well enough to be sure certain 'twas him. Constable Perkins had a glimpse of the assassin when I fired a shot as he ran. Mr. Perkins took a shot then too."

"Did you hit him?"

"Mr. Perkins thinks I did not, nor did he. He gave chase and lost them. It seemed to him they must have made for the Tower."

"Or the Tower Wharf," Tom suggested.

"Exactly."

We remained silent for a bit, ruminating the consequences and circumstances of Tobias Trindle's death. When we had finished our midnight supper, we took care to wrap the meat and bread in order to leave it as we had found it.

"Should we keep the candle burning?" asked Tom. "It's gone fair short."

"No need, I suppose. Whether it would be ten candles or none, it would make no matter to Sir John when he enters, for none is what he would see. Can you find your way in the dark?"

"I'll stay close to you."

So saying, he bent and blew out the flame. The room was flooded in darkness that was not quite complete, for a thin crescent of moon had risen sometime in the past hour. It gave a ghostly light to the familiar objects in the room, one that made them seem somehow less substantial than they were.

"Jeremy?" Tom's voice stopped me near the stairs.

"Yes?"

"Someone sold him."

"Trindle?"

"Of course," said he a bit snappishly. "Who else would I be speaking of?"

"Well, the innkeeper at the Green Man admitted he took money and sent some unknown person to Black Emma's just before Mr. Perkins squeezed the same information from him. And that had to be the assassin."

"But someone had to have given her name to the assassin—to Hartsell—just as Old Isaac gave it to you."

"You're right, certainly, and perhaps sent him direct to the Green Man, as well."

"I think it was Isaac sold him twice—once to you for a bit of tobacco and once to the captain for an easy berth."

"You do him an injustice," said I. "He gave forth to me because Boone had come around asking exactly the sort of questions we had asked. He said it were better that Sir John

got him than Hartsell. I told you that, and it was what decided you to put aside your scruples and rejoin the search
for Trindle. You said so yourself.''

"Aye," said Tom, "and perhaps I did wrong to be any
part of it."

"You make no sense at all." It was a very harsh thing to
say, but I felt harshly toward him at that moment.

"Did he not demand tobacco before he would speak?"

"He did not demand it. He asked for it. He would have
spoken up in any case."

"So you say. Yet he must have suspected that some hint
as to Tobias's whereabouts would put him in good stead with
Sir John. Did you not tell Sir John the information *and* its
source?"

"Of course I did."

"You see? He accomplished his purpose."

"You have my head spinning with all your suspicions. I
know not what to say."

"There is but one way to settle this. Does that prison
wherein he is confined—What is the name of it?"

"The Fleet Prison."

"Would the prison keep a record of his visitors?"

"Perhaps," said I. "No, probably." Then I admitted: "I
don't really know for certain."

"Well, if they do, and Mr. Boone is on the list, I'd say
there was a good chance I was right, wouldn't you?"

I said nothing.

"Wouldn't you?" Tom repeated.

"I'll have no more of this talk," said I. "All I want now
is to go to bed."

I at last prevailed. We climbed up the stairs, I leading the
way and Tom close behind. As I thought back later upon
this conversation it seemed oddly significant to me that it
had taken place in the dark.

As I arose early next morning to make the fire in the kitchen
stove, I found Sir John sitting at the table. He was hunched,
with head bowed, over a plate of mutton and bread. Had I
known it to be his habit, I should have said he was saying a
prayer over his meal. Yet his lips did not move, and his deep,

tranquil breathing made it plain he had fallen asleep at the table. But how long ago? If he had fallen asleep but minutes ago, it might be proper to wake him and urge him up to his bed. Or, if he slept as deep as he seemed to, it would be best perhaps to leave him undisturbed. Yet the fire had to be built. The porridge must be cooked and the tea made. Annie would be down in a short time. What was I to do?

In the end, of course, I did what I had done all those mornings before, but did it much quieter. I cleaned the ashes from the grate and made rid of them, then very quietly placed the logs and the kindling, and over and among them I sprinkled wood shavings and torn paper. Finally, fetching down the tinderbox, I sparked the brimstone match and waited till it burned a good flame and lit the bits of paper till all blazed well. I saw the shavings catch fire, and also the kindling; then I knew the job had been done. All this I managed so quietly and well that Sir John ne'er stirred. I was quite proud of myself.

Yet when Annie came clopping down the stairs in her clogs, I thought it certain she would rouse him, and so I rushed to silence her. I caught her at the last step but one. She looked at me most puzzled when, instead of my usual morning greeting, I met her with a finger to my lips, then pointed into the kitchen at the dozing Sir John. She nodded, sat down on the step, and removed her clogs.

"The poor man," she whispered. "How long has he been like that?"

"I've no idea," said I. "Tom and I went late to bed. He may have been out the entire night. He was just so when I came down and fixed the fire."

"Best to let him sleep."

"I thought so."

"Was there a great crime?"

"Yes, murder—and worse, for it was murder of one we sought as a witness."

Murder she understood quite well. The rest, I think, was beyond her. Still, she nodded soberly, rose, and entered on silent bare feet. She swept about the kitchen, doing all that had to be done, yet managing it remarkably quiet.

It was, at last, the smell of cooking bacon that roused him.

Annie had cut a full eight rashers from the flitch and laid them in the pan: once they began popping and sizzling they gave off such an aroma as would have raised the dead from a churchyard. Sir John was most assuredly not dead, but only sleeping. His bowed head raised a bit, then a bit higher, and at last he twitched his face and turned about.

"Ah," said he, inhaling most deep, "bacon!"

"So it is, Sir John," said Annie, "and would you like a hen's egg or two to go with it?"

"I would, Annie, for if a man be denied sleep, he ought not deny himself food, for strength to meet the day must come from some source."

With that, he stood and stretched and tested his neck, which seemed a bit stiff, this way and that. He was in remarkably good spirits for one who had slept so little—and that in a chair: remarkably good, as well, for one who had lost his last hope to save one whom he deemed innocent.

"Then, after a good breakfast, sir," said Annie, "you may go up and have a nap. Do you good, sir. I hear Lady Fielding stirring about now. I'm sure she'll agree it's what you need."

"Much as I should like to do so, I cannot, for I have a busy morning before me. But who knows? Perhaps later, after my court session."

He turned his head about until it was fixed right square in my direction.

"Jeremy," said he. "You are here, are you not?"

"I am here, sir."

"Get the razor and the bowl—and strop the razor good. I'm in need of a clean close shave today, for I must look my best. And so must you, boy, since we are off this morning to pay another visit to Vice-Admiral Sir Robert Redmond. Indeed I hope it shall be our last."

Whilst I had been told by Sir John that I might expect Lieutenant William Landon to be present during our time with Sir Robert, I had no idea he would arrive in the company of marine guards. There were three: one on either side of the prisoner and a third to shout commands at them. We encountered this curious quartet as we alighted from the hackney in which we had been driven from Number 4 Bow Street.

They marched up Tower Hill, having traversed the moat bridge down by the river. Sir John had succeeded in getting an order from the admiral to have the prisoner installed in the Tower Prison following the death of Mr. Grimsby, even though Sir Robert, in a brief inquiry (which consisted of an interview with Lieutenant Hartsell), had determined that Grimsby had fallen overboard in a state of drunkenness in the middle of the night at a time when the attention of the deck officer (Mr. Boone) was otherwise engaged.

By his keen ears, Sir John was made aware of their coming before I so much as glimpsed them. Stepping down from the conveyance, he cocked his head and took a moment to listen.

"I hear three men marching in good time and another walking indifferently," said he. "Would that be Mr. Landon conveyed by a guard party?"

Turning, I looked in the direction he indicated—toward the Thames—and noted that he had "seen" them perfectly with his ears.

"Yes sir," said I, "it is."

"Is he in hand irons?"

I looked closely and saw arms and hands swinging freely.

"No, sir."

"Well, thank God for that. They have at least allowed him that shred of dignity."

In point of fact, Lieutenant Landon looked quite relaxed in this odd company—and in some peculiar fashion, amused. He blessed us with a wry smile as the hackney pulled away, and we waited for them to pass. I thought it odd and commented upon it to Sir John.

"He is a strange young man," said he. "I know not precisely what to think of him. At times he seems to me almost to be seeking martyrdom."

Sir John pointed after them with his stick, and we set off together. Clearly, he intended that the marines and their prisoner should arrive first in the admiral's office. He dawdled. We waited. The marines, re-formed into a single column with their prisoner in the second place in line, continued up the stairs and into the building, then up and up the wide stairway—while all the while we followed them, impatient that they might get on with this strange ceremony. When they

entered Sir Robert's office, Sir John held me back at the top
of the stairs until the marines emerged and took their places
in the hall, standing at rest arms. All this he knew and understood by the information given him by his ears. At last
he nodded, and we proceeded past them and through the
door.

"Sir!" shouted Lieutenant Byner in his exaggerated sergeant major manner. "The admiral awaits you within in
company with the prisoner."

"Very good," said Sir John. "I take it that you, as the
prisoner's counsel, will also be present during this interrogation?"

"With your permission, *sir!*"

"Permission granted, certainly. It should be we who ask
you."

Having no response for that, Lieutenant Byner simply
bobbed his head in an exaggerated manner, walked stiffly to
the door, and threw it open. We entered. The lieutenant followed. There were handshakes all around—though none for
me, as a minor, of course. Sir John rather pointedly sought
out Lieutenant Landon and made an offer of his hand, which
was solemnly accepted.

"I understand, Sir John, that it is you who is responsible
for the change in my accommodations," said Mr. Landon.

"It is in a sense, I suppose," Sir John responded, "for I
made the suggestion. Admiral Redmond granted the necessary permission, however."

"Well, I thank you, sir, for I am more comfortable in that
ancient and notorious old prison, odd though that may
seem."

"I'm happy for your comfort, Lieutenant, but it was your
safety I had in mind. I feared you might meet with an accident, as Lieutenant Grimsby did."

"Jack," said Sir Robert, "there is no need to go into that.
I've inquired into the matter, as you know, and satisfied myself as to the cause of his death."

"So I heard," Sir John replied to the admiral. Then to Mr.
Landon: "I thought also that you might speak more freely,
given the chance, away from the H.M.S. *Adventure.*"

At this point, nephew and uncle exchanged looks, as they

had before in the lieutenant's cabin on the frigate. On this occasion, however, what they communicated with their eyes was altogether different and much easier to interpret. Sir Robert threw him a strong challenge, but Mr. Landon met it and returned him one of his own. There was a prolonged moment of silence as each continued to stare at the other. It was Sir John who broke that silence.

"Lieutenant," said he, "will you speak?"

"That I will."

"Then let us sit down, for a magistrate's hours are never well fixed, and I have had a hard night of it, this one past."

"I prefer to stand, if I may," said Mr. Landon.

"Then stand, by all means," said Sir John, sinking into the chair to which I had guided him, "but let us proceed."

I took my usual place behind it. On this occasion, I placed my hand upon his shoulder so that a signal might be passed between us when the time came. He had assigned me a role to play. Though unrehearsed, I was certain I could act it well as any at Drury Lane.

"Lieutenant Landon," said Sir John, "what sort of officer was the late Captain Markham?" Then he added hastily: "Before you answer that, let me ask Mr. Byner, do you have a writing instrument in hand?"

"Yes sir, a pencil."

"Probably best. And something to write upon?"

"Yes sir, a quantity of paper."

"Good. Make special note of my question, for when it comes time to interrogate him in court, those you ask him should be, like mine, broad enough to allow him to tell his story. And listen well to the answers he gives now, for you must never ask a question of a witness in court to which you do not already know the answer."

"Sir?" Mr. Byner seemed puzzled by that, though it seemed perfectly sensible to me.

"Exactly so. There should be no surprises." Again to Mr. Landon: "Now, sir, if we may begin again, with my apologies for the interruption, I shall put the question to you. What sort of officer was the late Captain Markham of His Majesty's Ship *Adventure?*"

There was a pause as Lieutenant Landon stood briefly,

facing Sir John, apparently organizing his answer. Sir Robert Redmond sat uneasily at his desk, leaning forward as if fearful of what the prisoner might say. Lieutenant Byner was hunched in his chair, scrawling on a block of folded paper he balanced upon his knee.

"From the first day out of Portsmouth," Mr. Landon began, "it was evident that Captain Markham drank to excess. At our first mess at the captain's table, he alone downed two bottles of claret—seemed to guard them as his own, leaving two more for the rest of us to share out amongst ourselves. He then consumed half a bottle of brandy, grew increasingly drowsy, and fell asleep at table.

"This became the pattern on those occasions when he did appear at his own table, which occasions became rarer as the ship progressed south. Likewise, his appearances above decks were correspondingly rare. He took little part in charting the ship's course, though I understood he kept a record of it for a time in the log. He knew none of the officers but Lieutenant Hartsell by name, and him he knew because he more or less left the running of the ship to him. By the time we were well along the coast of Africa, Lieutenant Hartsell was acting in the role of captain as Captain Markham remained in his cabin, presumably drunk."

"Very good," said Sir John. "You have answered the question. End your response there. In court, you must try to avoid phrases such as 'more or less' and such terms as 'presumably.' Be as exact as it is possible to be. We already have it on record in a statement from the ship's surgeon, Mr. MacNaughton, which will be read at the court-martial, that the captain was in a state of near-perpetual drunkenness during those hours, and indeed days, when he was incommunicado. It will not be necessary for you to presume."

Mr. Landon, who had stood rather rigid while answering Sir John's question, relaxed somewhat during this criticism, nodding his understanding and acceptance of the points made against him. He then seemed more, rather than less, confident when Sir John posed his next question.

"Will you give us your memory, Mr. Landon, of the pertinent events of April 12, 1767?"

"We were but two days out of Cape Town, as I recall,

where we had taken on stores, when a storm of a magnitude I had never before experienced caught us and held us for most of a day and part of a night. It grew quite dark. There was heavy rain. But the worst was the sea itself, for there were swells as tall as any church tower in London. We were thrown up and down, battered port and starboard, in a most frightful way.

" 'Twas I who brought Lieutenant Hartsell the news, in the midst of all this, that the foremast was showing signs of splintering and might not hold through the storm. I asked him should it be taken down. And he said that was not his decision but the captain's, and that I was to fetch him. Then he—"

Sir John interrupted: "What was your reaction to that order from Mr. Hartsell?"

"One of surprise, sir," responded the lieutenant, "for Mr. Hartsell had captained the ship in all but name for a good two weeks and had certainly made all decisions so far that day and had managed well to keep us afloat. In point of fact, I had not even seen Captain Markham for three days. He had put in a brief appearance on the quarterdeck during our stay in Cape Town. I wondered, considering all this, why Mr. Hartsell had grown suddenly shy of command."

"In what condition did you find Captain Markham?" asked Sir John.

"In a frightful state. He seemed more dead than alive. He had been drinking, certainly, for he had a near-empty bottle by him in his bed. There was fresh vomit there, too, and the smell of spirits was heavy in the air. Yet he seemed more than drunk. I have heard of men, through illness or injury, falling into an unnaturally deep sleep for days, weeks even. So he seemed to me. I simply could not rouse him. And so I returned to Lieutenant Hartsell on the quarterdeck and told him I could in no wise rouse the captain. His response was that I must do it nevertheless, but that I was to take him to the poop deck, where the two of them would also inspect the mizzenmast. That was his order. I had no choice but to do what I could to carry it out. And so I returned to the captain's cabin, pulled him bodily from his bed, and began dressing him in whatever manner I could. I recall throwing a cape around him and tying it, yet leaving him bareheaded, thinking that the wind and the rain might do something to bring him to consciousness. Before taking him above to the poop deck, I tried walking him around the cabin for a minute or two. I believe I did get some response from his legs, but his head slumbered on, just as before. But in the end, I managed, by supporting him, to get him up the ladder to the poop.''

At this point, Lieutenant Landon paused in his narrative, apparently in need of a brief rest from the rigors of such recollection. I have known it to be so, reader, that in recalling and retelling events of great stress a man may find himself caught up in them once again, enduring the same feelings, the same strains as before. Thus it seemed to be with Mr. Landon, for sweat dripped from his face in that room which was not uncomfortably warm, and he seemed somewhat short of breath.

All this Sir John seemed to perceive, for he waited an interval before putting his next question to him.

''What did you find when you arrived on the poop deck?''

''It was a question of what I did not find,'' responded the lieutenant, a smile of irony upon his lips. ''I did not find Lieutenant Hartsell there as he said he would be. The poop deck was empty but for me and the man I bore as a burden. It is, of course, the uppermost deck, and as such is a dangerous place in such a violent storm as that one. The ship was plunged down in a trough. I managed to catch hold of the rigging of the mizzenmast while yet keeping my grasp upon the captain. In that perilous posture, I caught sight of Mr. Hartsell below on the quarterdeck, clinging tight to an eighteen-pounder which was well secured. He raised an arm and beckoned us down. At the bottom of the trough the *Adventure* righted herself, and I thought it possible to risk it to the starboard ladder. I had near reached it with my arm about the captain when we were thrown hard along to the starboard quite of a sudden, and the violence of the motion tore him from my grasp. He landed against the taffrail just opposite the ladder, yet at the same time, the ship continued to slip starboard, and he began to topple overboard. I reached out to grasp him, but he continued his slide and passed through my arms into the sea, and I was left holding his shoe—as I believe I told you before.''

"Now, Lieutenant Byner," said Sir John, "my next question will have to do with motive—important to cover this, for none can be attributed to Mr. Landon.'' He paused, then began again in his court voice: "Tell me, sir, were you and Captain Markham on good terms?''

"Neither good nor bad," replied Mr. Landon. "I honestly do not believe he knew my name, so slight was our acquaintance. I am not sure I ever had occasion to address him directly, except when I was introduced to him at the beginning of the voyage—that is, until I sought to rouse him during the storm.''

"Yes, in content that will do well," said Sir John to him, "but do not use that phrase 'neither good nor bad.' It seems to imply indifference. Find some other way of saying the same thing, Mr. Landon. I shall now ask you another question to make the matter more explicit.'' Again, he paused; then: "Had you any reason to wish Captain Markham dead?''

"None, absolutely none.''

"Did you, in truth, cause the death of Captain Josiah Markham by pushing him into the sea?''

"I did not—absolutely not.''

Turning toward Mr. Byner, who continued to write feverishly upon the sheaf of papers on his knees, Sir John called attention to his last two questions. "They must, no matter what the circumstances, be asked. Is that understood?''

"Understood, sir.''

Through all this, Vice-Admiral Sir Robert Redmond had listened carefully, and as he had done so, the severe expression he had earlier worn softened somewhat. Yet as the next line of questioning developed, it returned to his face, so that he appeared both apprehensive and disapproving.

"Did Lieutenant Hartsell discuss the matter of the captain's death with you immediately afterward—say, within the next twenty-four hours?''

"Only in the most general way," said Mr. Landon. "He said what was obvious—that with the death of the captain he would serve as acting captain and that I should correspondingly consider myself acting first officer. Then on the day after the storm, he held his first captain's table and explained all this to the rest of the officers, reassigning duties and so on, all quite unnecessary, of course, for in practice we had done without a captain from the beginning of the voyage. Some sort of memorial to the captain was attempted at that occasion. Lieutenant Hartsell said something brief which I recorded in my diary. Then Mr. MacNaughton informed us of the captain's con—''

"Just a moment," said Sir John, interrupting. "You kept a diary?"

"I did, yes."

"You have it now?"

"No, sir. I surrendered it to Admiral Sir Robert Redmond. I trust it is still in his possession."

Sir John responded with silence. Beneath my hand I felt his shoulder tense.

"No accusation of murder came from Mr. Hartsell immediately following the captain's death then?" said Sir John after near a minute's delay.

"None, sir."

"When did Mr. Hartsell first inform you of his charge of murder against you?"

"Late in the afternoon, the day before we anchored at London Bridge. We were in London roads waiting to enter. Members of the crew speculated as to the reason we had not proceeded to Portsmouth. They wondered would this mean shore leave in the great city, and so on their behalf I asked Mr. Hartsell. We were on the quarterdeck at the time. I recall his words exact. He said, 'Mr. Landon, we are putting into London so that you may be tried in court-martial for the murder of Captain Josiah Markham. And now that you know, I think it only fitting that you confine yourself to quarters. Go to your cabin. Your meals will be brought to you there.' "

"And what was your reaction?"

"Amazement. I was quite overwhelmed. Having served under him for over two years, I knew it was no joke. Besides, there was another matter between us with which this fitted."

"What was that other matter?"

"I had made a threat against him."

"For what cause and of what nature?"

"In general, Lieutenant Hartsell was a good officer and played the part of captain very well. Having had a command in the French War, he brought authority to the position. He was a good sailor and calm in battle. Yet as a man, Mr. Hartsell's conduct left much to be desired. His ascent to full command allowed him to give full rein to his unnatural propensities."

"Be careful with your accusations," the admiral warned his nephew darkly.

"I would make none," said Lieutenant Landon, addressing Sir Robert directly, "had he restrained himself to his liaison with Mr. Grimsby, but he began to prey upon the midshipmen—upon mere children! I heard him boast of it to Mr. Grimsby. He called them his harem."

"I will hear no more of this," said the admiral, pounding his desk with his fist.

"The threat!" shouted Sir John over the admiral. "What of the *threat?*"

"Yes, yes, the threat," said Mr. Landon, himself near shouting. "Mid-shipman Sample came to me, told me of acts that had been forced upon him by Lieutenant Hartsell. He had appealed to the Reverend Mr. Eagleton and got no satisfaction. The boy, who was but thirteen, asked me to intervene. I went to Lieutenant Hartsell and warned him that if he did not cease these acts with the midshipmen, I would bear witness against him on the matter when we returned to Portsmouth. That, I believe, is when he fabricated his charge of homicide against me in a letter from India, whose contents Sir Robert has made known to me. All this is recorded in my diary—including the death of Midshipman Sample who, one week after his conversation with me, fell or was pushed by Mr. Boone from the fore-topsail yardarm to his death— he may even have jumped. I was belowdecks at the time and did not see. And did Mr. Hartsell cease his practices after my threat? After the child's death? He did not. He was only more secretive in them."

"Enough, Lieutenant," said Sir Robert, jumping from his chair. "We have heard quite enough. Mr. Byner, take him out. Tell the marines to show him back to the Tower.''

Byner jumped to the order, scattering his pages over the floor, grabbing Mr. Landon by the arm and jerking him with unnecessary roughness toward the door.

Sir John called after him: ''Thank you, Mr. Landon. Now at last we have the full story, and you told it well.''

The lieutenant's reply was naught but a grateful look as he was pulled through the door.

The admiral had circled round the desk. He confronted Sir John, hands on his ample hips, bending angrily to Sir John, who remained seated. They were thus face-to-face for a long moment before the admiral spoke in what was not much more than a whisper.

''You are satisfied, are you, Jack? Now you have the *full* story, as it were? What is it that has driven you on but morbid curiosity—that and a desire to sully the reputation of an institution you once claimed to love! You wish to befoul the name of the Navy in repayment for the loss of your sight. I understand it now—you, who were once a hero to me, to all of us.''

Sir John then spoke evenly, calmly, and coldly: ''I wish only to see justice done for that innocent young man who is your nephew.''

''Yes, he is my nephew, and I love him well, but I love the Navy better. Jack, there have always been such as Hartsell in the service. These things happen, but in the larger sense, they do not exist. They *cannot* exist, for England believes in its Navy, has always believed in its Navy as in no other institution. To let such a scandal as this out would besmirch it in such a way that fathers would never again send their sons to be midshipmen. Worse, the Navy would be held to ridicule, to contempt. Don't you see?''

During this heated oration, Mr. Byner reentered the room, yet so quietly that I was not sure that Sir John had noted his presence. I gave a slight squeeze to the shoulder beneath my hand. Though I was sure he had caught my signal, Sir John gave no sign.

''I recall,'' said he, ''that you pled with me to find witnesses, teach Mr. Byner my 'tricks,' as you called them, do anything necessary to save your nephew. Now I find 'any-

thing necessary' excludes the truth. How has it come to this?
There is even a diary kept by him which would corroborate
all that he has said. You have it. It must be entered as evidence under the rules of any criminal proceeding, even the
Navy's. Do you intend to withhold it?''

That last question brought forth a gesture from Sir John,
a hand extended to the admiral, which he returned sharply
to his chest, slapping the fingers of my hand as he did so.
With this, he returned the sign to me.

I doubled over of a sudden as if in great pain, recovered
a bit, then whispered in his ear. Having listened, he turned
to me in annoyance.

"But you said you were done with that," said he gruffly.

"I know, but . . ."

I grimaced then and held my belly.

"The lad had a touch of diarrhea last night. It seems
now to have returned. Could you . . . ? Could Lieutenant
Byner . . . ?''

The admiral sighed. "Yes, yes, of course. Lieutenant, see
the lad to the necessary down the hall. Wait for him. We
cannot have boys of such an age wandering around the halls
of the Navy Board alone.''

And so out I went, Mr. Byner all but taking me by the
hand. I played my role throughout, continuing to grimace,
doubling over once or twice more along the way. In all modesty, I thought I did quite well.

In any case, Mr. Byner seemed convinced. He hurried me
along down a long hall and around a corner, threw open a
door and pointed inside.

"In here," said he, "and be as quick as you can.''

He slammed the door after me.

The place was lit by two candles set in holders against the
wall. Though small, as such rooms always are, it was quite
the best of its kind I had seen since my time in Lord Goodhope's residence a year or more before. This one was also
equipped with a cistern and had a proper washstand, as well.

I waited inside near five minutes, counting the minutes out
by sixties. Sir John had reckoned this about the maximum
length of time our stratagem might be made to work. He had
devised it as a way of speaking at greater length to Sir Robert

without Mr. Byner present or listening at the door. He did not trust Mr. Byner, not in the least.

When the time was up, I pulled the chain and set the cistern going with a great sustained splash. As I left the room I fumbled with the buttons on my coat, as if putting myself back in order.

"Come along," said Mr. Byner.

And that I did, hopping along beside him, as a sick man might when suddenly made well.

Whatever more had been discussed between admiral and magistrate had not taken as much time as expected, for I found Sir John waiting for me in Mr. Byner's outer office, my hat in his hand. The door to Sir Robert's larger office was now closed. I knew not quite what this meant.

He said a civil, though far from warm, goodbye to the lieutenant, and we started off down the stairs. He cautioned me with a finger to his lips against speaking inside the building. Only when we emerged onto Tower Hill did he speak—and then in the gravest tones.

"Ah, Jeremy," said he, "what an infernal matter this is. It is worse than I thought and as bad as ever I feared."

ELEVEN

*In which the court-martial
of William Landon
takes place*

Iⁿt is no short stretch between Tower Hill and Number Four
Bow Street, and in the late morning, with dray wagons,
carriages, and coaches plodding through the teeming streets,
our route along Thames Street, Fleet Street, and the Strand
moved so slow that there was naught for our hackney driver
but to permit his two nags to plod along slow with the rest.
Thus had Sir John more than ample time to relate to me the
content of the conversation as it continued between him and
Sir Robert in the absence of Mr. Byner, to comment upon
it, and to rail against it. He seemed to hold nothing back
from me. So much was said, reader, that I feel it best to
summarize the greater part of it and quote him only where
it does seem pertinent in some particular way.

Sir John brought up the death of Lieutenant Jonathan
Grimsby. What could that have been but murder? In spite of
the official findings of his inquiry, Sir Robert had tacitly
admitted the likelihood of homicide by consenting to move
Mr. Landon to the Tower. And why should Mr. Grimsby
have been murdered? Because he communicated to Sir John
the true situation aboard the H.M.S. *Adventure* as regards the
midshipmen; all that he said there confirmed what was said
minutes ago by Mr. Landon. And Grimsby offered to testify
on Landon's behalf.

(Sir Robert objected that such testimony would be tainted
by the fact that Grimsby, according to Mr. Landon, had en-

gaged in unnatural relations with Mr. Hartsell. Sir John
brushed this aside.)

Then there was the matter of the counsel appointed by Sir
Robert. Lieutenant Byner was at best incompetent and at
worst traitorous. Sir John pointed out that Mr. Byner was
present during the interrogation of the ship's surgeon in
Portsmouth; he had heard from his lips that the helmsman
on the fateful day when Captain Markham was lost, one Tobias Trindle, had given out that though Mr. Landon had made
a great effort to save the captain, nothing could have been
done to bring him back once he had begun to slip over the
taffrail. This account conformed perfectly with Mr. Landon's
description of the action. Tobias Trindle would have made a
strong witness for Landon's defense, but he was murdered
the night before, shot between the eyes as he lay in bed. Sir
John declared that he had withheld the name of Tobias Trindle from others; that he would vouch for his young assistant,
Jeremy Proctor; and that surely Sir Robert would do nothing
that would so brutally hamper his nephew's defense. That
would leave only Mr. Byner who had heard the name of the
potential witness from Mr. MacNaughton, and it would seem
likely that he had passed that name on to another; and that
other would have caused that potential witness's murder. Sir
John urged Sir Robert to be careful what was said and entrusted to Lieutenant Byner.

(Sir Robert declared that Mr. Byner was his executive officer and that of course he trusted him and would continue
to trust him. As for the death of Tobias Trindle, it was probably a personal matter—some low, seaman's quarrel that resulted in his murder, over a woman no doubt. He thought it
unlikely that it had anything to do with the coming court-
martial. And by the by, it was doubtful that a seaman would
be permitted to testify in contradiction to his captain, doubtful that a seaman would be permitted to testify at the court-
martial of any officer.)

Sir John said there was another whose name he could give
as a potential witness—that of the chaplain and schoolmaster, the Reverend Mr. Andrew Eagleton. Yet Mr. Eagleton
would only testify were he summoned by subpoena—and
then not dependably. He was, Sir John declared, frightened

half out of his wits by Lieutenant Hartsell, and in fear of him had probably distanced himself a hundred miles from London, not to return until the court-martial be done.

(Sir Robert responded that for all the reasons Sir John had given, there was really no point in summoning Reverend Eagleton.)

Here, reader, I shall begin to quote Sir John as he spoke to me in that slow-moving hackney carriage, in order that you may grasp the intensity of his passion in this matter:

"At this point, Jeremy," said Sir John to me, "I challenged Bobbie. I said to him, 'You seemed earlier to have a wish to save that young man. Now you have set a course against him. How comes it that you have so altered in a few days' time?'

"He said to me then, 'Jack, I have never changed in this, for when I first heard from my nephew this matter of Lieutenant Hartsell and the midshipmen, I forbade him to speak of it to anyone else. And I told him that under no circumstances could it be brought up in the course of the court-martial. But the lad seems *determined* to tell his tale of Hartsell and the midshipmen.'

"Bobbie said that his nephew derived satisfaction from telling his tale this morning to me, that he may be tempted foolishly to try to spread it further. He insisted that the lad had a chance in the court-martial if he restricted his testimony to the matter of Captain Markham, but none at all if he bladdered on about Hartsell. And then he added that we would soon find out about that, for the panel had been chosen. An admiral and a captain are traveling up from Portsmouth tomorrow. The court-martial will take place in but two days' time."

"Two days!" said I to Sir John. "But is that regular, sir? The *Adventure* has been at anchor less than a week."

"Whatever they may determine is regular," said he to me. "That is a truth about the Navy that I seem to be learning late in life, lad. It is disheartening to understand how little I knew about it during those four years I served. It seems the Navy is a law unto itself, a country all its own in which the ordinary rules of conduct and procedure need not apply.

"Did you note what Bobbie said to me, accusing me of

wishing to sully the reputation of the Navy in revenge for my lost sight? How dare he say such a thing? How dare he?''

Sir John brought his stick down sharp upon the floor of the carriage in a rare display of anger.

''Indeed, sir!'' I was truly filled with indignation on Sir John's behalf. ''I loved the Navy as no other did. If asked beforehand, I would have said, 'Yes, I will give the Navy my eyes. I will give it my life!' When I think now of the years I pined for my lost career, how I took as second best the life in the law that my brother gave me—I do wonder at my own stupidity, truly I do! I see now that I was made for the law, and if I came to it by a somewhat devious path, then that is unfortunate; yet the important thing is that I came to it. By God and by Jesus, I love the law, and she's a better, fairer mistress than the Navy ever was. If Bobbie thinks that he may frighten me away by mouthing such grossly untrue suppositions in my face, then he has the matter dead wrong. He should not be trying the case in the first place because of his relation to the accused. He has meddled in it as no judge should. He has seized Mr. Landon's diary—not as evidence pertinent to the trial but to sequester it that it may never be introduced. Yet, by some means, Jeremy, I promise I will see some justice done for that young man.''

When at last we arrived at Bow Street, there was naught for Sir John but to rush inside and call his court to order. He had, however, given me my instructions as we drew close in the hackney, and immediately I had seen him inside the door at Number 4, I set off to the house and court of Mr. Saunders Welch. I knew the way well, having gone there but a few short days before. And on this occasion, as on that one, I was bearing a request from Sir John that Mr. Welch might hear Sir John's cases two days hence. He felt assured that his request would be granted, for after all, the tally was still uneven.

As it developed, Mr. Saunders Welch, Magistrate of the Hanover Street Court, objected less to the content of the request than to the form in which it was sent.

He, having heard his cases for the day, allowed me to be admitted to his chambers. This setting differed greatly from

that rough and dusty place in which Sir John drank his beer
most afternoons following his court session. Mr. Welch's
quarters were well lit; there were pictures upon the wall, a
rug upon the floor, a good many stout chairs about, and a
heavy oaken desk behind which he sat. He was engaged in
counting money, his collection in fines levied that day. It
was said that near any offense but murder could be settled
by means of a fine in the Hanover Street Court; and there
were rumors that even an occasional homicide might be for-
given as accidental death with the offer of a fine large enough
to suit Mr. Welch.

As I entered the room, he held his hand up to keep me
silent at the door. Then, finishing his count of shillings, he
entered a number in a ledger and beckoned to me, and I came
forward.

"You're the boy from Bow Street, are you not?"

"Yes, sir."

"What have you for me?"

"A message from Sir John Fielding, sir."

He extended his hand across the desk. "Give it me," said
he.

"It is a message by word of mouth, sir."

He frowned at me quizzically. "His word? Your mouth?"
he then asked, in a manner somewhat exasperated.

"Yes, sir."

Silence. Then: "I am not sure I like this at all. It does not
seem right to me that the business of the Magistrate's Courts
of London be entrusted to the memory of a street urchin like
yourself."

I took this ill, reader, as indeed you would also have done
if you had washed as careful as I had that morning and put
on your best duds to meet the admiral. Street urchin indeed!
I thought myself a proper young gentleman, at least in appearance.

"Why did he not send a written message, as is his usual?"

"He had not time, sir."

"Ah, well, indeed. No time, is it? It's true that our duties
do oft press hard upon us, but surely he could have found
time to dictate a letter and sign it with that blind man's
scrawl of his."

Now I was truly offended. He could say what he liked about me, and I would hold my tongue, but to mention Sir John's affliction in a manner so crude and callous seemed to demand some retort from me.

"Since it is to me he dictates his letters, more often than not," said I, with all the dignity I could muster, "he no doubt trusted my memory in so small a matter as the message he gave me for you."

"All right," said Mr. Welch, "I'll hear the message, then judge myself if it be a small matter."

"Well and good," said I. "Sir John asked me to go and seek you out and ask if you would take his cases on the day after the morrow. Mr. Marsden will deliver the docket. And the prisoners will be brought by Mr. Fuller of the Runners."

"What he proposes will mean twice the work, twice the time for me! I took his docket but a few days ago. Who but an ignorant boy would call this a small matter?"

"Why, *you* would, sir," said I, most innocent. "If I may quote in part your letter to Sir John of last May . . ." I cleared my throat and began: " 'And if you will oblige me in this *small matter*, I should be back from Bath in a week's time more fit than ever for my duties and always ready to fill for you if and when you should ask.' "

(In truth, I know not whether I quoted his words exactly, yet I had read the letter aloud to Sir John and taken his dictation on the one in response, and I knew that in Mr. Welch's was a promise to do the same for Sir John whenever called upon. And so I recited what I remembered firmly and confidently, as if it was of such import that I had committed it to memory.)

Mr. Saunders Welch stared at me long and hard without a word spoken. I began to wonder if perhaps I had not gone too far, and if it might not be proper to offer an apology at this very moment. I was, in fact, framing one in my head when Mr. Welch began to laugh. He laughed, in fact, long and quite uproariously in the way of a man who had just heard a great joke. At last he contained himself sufficient to speak.

"You are an impudent boy," said he to me, "but I know when I have been bested. Go now before I decide to be

angry, and tell Sir John Fielding that I will certainly handle
his docket along with my own two days from now. But remind him, his Mr. Marsden, and Mr. Fuller that *my* court
begins at ten. Now, off with you.''

I made my way to the door at something between a rapid
walk and a run.

"Thank you, sir,'' said I, as I swung the door wide.

"Not another word!''

And so, in less than a minute I was back on the street and
glad to be, swearing to myself I would never again play so
bold in matters that concerned Sir John. It was a promise
which, in general, I kept.

Having at that moment nothing urgent to attend to and
knowing, too, that my route homeward might be bent in that
direction, I decided to call upon the residence of Black Jack
Bilbo and rid myself of the burden I carried in my coat
pocket. That pistol with which he had entrusted me had stim-
ulated much interest in Constable Perkins. I wondered at its
origin. I wondered at much about Mr. Bilbo.

The grand house in St. James Street, where I had spent
some time and Annie Oakum a great deal more, rose up
before me at the end of my long noonday walk. I knew the
secrets of that house, or some of them, and perhaps my friend
Jimmie Bunkins had learned them all by now. I saw little of
Bunkins in those days—less and less since Mr. Bilbo had
taken over his tutelage. He was learning discipline, right
enough, from his "cove" and wished to please him, yet as
was proven by poor Bunkins's misadventure during our
search for Tobias Trindle, he had yet to learn discipline of
his self. It must be difficult, I thought, for him to give up a
way of life he'd learned so well.

Thus had I been thinking of him when my knock was
answered and he opened the heavy door.

"Hullo, pal,'' said he, "enter and welcome.''

He threw open the door, and I stepped over the threshold.

"How're you keeping, Master Bunkins?'' I asked of him,
entering somewhat into his free and easy style of speech.

"Well and good, Master Proctor. You've come to return
a barking iron, I'll wager.''

"So I have, so I have. Is the cove of the ken up and about?"

"That man snoozes less than any I've knowed, he does. Tom—your brother or cuz or chum, whatever he may be to you—he has been by to see him on the very same errand as you. The fact is, you just missed him by a bit."

"A pity and a shame," said I.

"Tom said 'twas you found the joe you two was nosin' for."

"Found him dead," said I.

"He was sure someone snitched him over. Went off to Fleet Prison to talk to that someone, he did." Jimmie Bunkins gave a great shiver of disgust. "Brrrr," said he, "that strikes me as right queer—to step a foot inside a jail without bein' pushed."

"Well, he has his suspicions," said I, "and welcome to them."

He gestured me to follow, and just as we started on our way down the long central hall, the door to what had once been Lady Goodhope's sitting room flew open and a woman popped her head out—and quite a pretty head it was, with curls piled upon it and rouge applied upon cheeks and lips most artfully.

"*Ah, Monsieur Jimmie,*" said she, wagging a finger at him, "*vous partez! Mais non, non! Revenez pour la leçon!*"

Bunkins sighed and pulled a face. "This here is Madame Bertrand," said he by way of introduction. "She's a right rum blowen, but I'll never learn her Frenchie talk."

She opened the door a bit wider and offered a most charming smile to me. She had won me altogether. I bowed waist deep, hand upon heart.

"*Enchanté,*" said I, knowing it to be the proper thing.

Wherewith she loosed a torrent of French upon me, the like of which I had not before heard and the sense of which eluded me completely. Very sweetly it was said and very musical it sounded, however, to my untrained ear; yet I could do naught but bow once more and step away down the hall.

"That's right, chum," said Bunkins to me. "Take yourself down to the cove. He's where he always is—in that room with all the boats on the wall. You know it from before, ain't I right? I got to *continuer avec la leçon.*"

So saying, he surrendered himself to Madame Bertrand. She took him in hand and, with a pleasant nod to me, swept inside her classroom. I believe I envied him.

I gave a stout knock upon Bilbo's door but waited to enter until an invitation was called to me from inside. He seemed happy enough to see me and urged me to a chair opposite him. Before seating myself I drew his pistol from my pocket and laid it carefully upon the desk whereat he sat.

"I understand that it has been fired," said Mr. Bilbo.

"Yes, it has, sir."

"It was an unavoidable circumstance, was it?"

I sighed. "Yes, sir. I called, 'Stop or I'll shoot!' And the constable I was with ordered me to shoot ahead."

"Who was the constable?"

"Mr. Perkins."

"The one-armed fellow? He's a sensible man. And did you hit your target?"

"I think not, sir. I aimed low so as to wound. Constable Perkins also shot from the light of my muzzle flash. It was his opinion that neither of us had hit our mark. It was very dark."

"Just as well you missed. You can do terrible damage at short range with this thing."

"Constable Perkins thought it a most fearsome weapon."

"Did y'tell him whence it came?"

"No, sir."

"Good boy," said he. Then, picking it up from his desk, he hefted it, examined it, tugged back the hammer, and, pointing it down at the floor, pulled the trigger; the hammer snapped sharply forward. "Always best to be sure. Now, since it has been fired, it must be cleaned and reloaded. Stay and we shall talk a bit whilst I attend to it."

He then rolled up the sleeves of his handsome shirt and took from a drawer in his desk tools and materials he would need for the task and spread them out before him. He went at it with a practiced hand, working swift and efficient. Breaking the pistol down into its parts, he went at them one by one.

"It is not the usual to clean a pistol so thorough as I clean this," said he, "but it needs a good going over."

I nodded and merely continued to watch, most fascinated.

"So you found your witness a dead man? That is what Tom told me. He had a tale of betrayal he recited to me— dark suspicions it was—how one fella had sold Sir John's witness to another."

"Tom is more certain of that than I. This is, in truth, a most troubling case. I . . . I would say that it is not going well."

"What troubles you about it, Jeremy?"

"Well," said I, "for one thing, I do not understand it wholly."

"Continue." All the while he went on with his task.

"Sir John and others involved in it refer again and again to what they call 'unnatural practices' and 'unnatural propensities.' It looms large in the case. I asked Sir John to explain to me what was meant, and he put me off. In truth, he seemed somewhat embarrassed by my question."

Black Jack Bilbo nodded. He rubbed his beard as he considered the matter for a moment.

" 'Tis a matter that may cause embarrassment to some," said he, "and reasonably so, I allow. No blame to Sir John in that. Yet before we delve into this matter of unnatural practices, tell me, Jeremy, what do you know of natural ones?"

"Sir?"

"What do y'know of what takes place between a man and a woman, of what makes babies and so on?"

He put it to me so calm and direct that I felt no need to lie or exaggerate my knowledge.

"I know some," said I, "but not all. I know there are diseases may come of it—the pox and the like—and I know that babies come of it, too. But I don't know what *it* is."

He nodded. "Well and good," said he. "You are of an age when you should know these things, so I shall tell you. And perhaps Sir John will tell you later. But if he does, do not stop him, saying, 'I have heard it all from John Bilbo.' This will be between us. Is that agreed?"

"Agreed, sir."

"Have you ever looked upon a woman naked?"

"Uh, once, sir."

"Then you must have noticed that there was something missing on her body that you have and I have and all men have."

"Yes, sir," said I.

"Well, here," said Mr. Bilbo.

And quicker than I could tell it, he had the pistol reassembled, but still unloaded, and had pulled a holster from another drawer. He held both up, one in each hand. Then, with a swift, sure motion, he plunged the pistol into the holster. The barrel disappeared right up to the trigger guard.

"Do y'see how neat this pistol fits into the holster?"

Thus with that demonstration began my instruction in that information which all men and women must gain by whatever means. I had questions. He answered them. At last, having satisfied me and said all he had to say on the matter of natural practices, he went on to the unnatural and quite astounded me.

"Now, in my experience," said he, concluding that part of his lecture, "a man will not turn to what is called unnatural acts so long as there is a woman available to him—though some say different. Some say it is in the nature of certain ones. But where it's known most common is when men and only men are close together for long stretches of time—such as in prison or on shipboard. It is better known on shipboard than most would know or care to admit."

There seemed to be an opening there for me to put a question to him. But how might I put it without telling too much? Perhaps in the form of a supposition.

"Mr. Bilbo," said I, "let us suppose—only suppose—that one in high authority, the highest authority say, upon a ship, were to force others in . . . unnatural practices, and that these others were much younger, boys only, uh, midshipmen. What then?"

I realized I had phrased it so clumsily and plain that he would see through my "supposition" with no difficulty. But just as he trusted me, I trusted him. He made no deeper inquiry into the matter but answered my question forthwith.

"That would be a very grave offense for two reasons."

Mr. Bilbo did not usually make use of such terms, nor did he often talk so solemn. "First of all, if forced or not, boys the age of midshipmen have not the age and experience to say yea or nay, so any sort of act done with them would be forced in that way. And second, it would be a terrible use of authority on the part of the captain—let us call him the captain—a *misuse*, it would be. For boys of that age are given to the captain in trust. They are his responsibility. It would be for him like the breaking of a most solemn vow."

"Would such be a hanging offense?" I asked.

"Why, that I couldn't say, Jeremy. I am as ignorant of the law as the next man, perhaps more ignorant than most. I know only that I would not care to die with such an offense upon my conscience."

He gave a wink of his eye to me then and a sad sort of smile and a shrug of his great shoulders.

"Here," said he, "we have talked a long while of these great matters—and they are great, have no doubt of it. More foolishness, meanness, and plain nastiness have been done in the service of natural and unnatural practices than anyone but God will ever know. Yet, or so I've been told, love comes of it too. And even such an old sinner as I am looks for that and hopes one day to find it. As you grow to be a man, Jeremy, I hope it does not escape you altogether, as it has me."

This bold, fierce-looking man whose dark history had inspired so many rumors and so much conjecture could not have said anything that would have surprised me more than this, had he told me that he wished to grow wings so that he might fly. (In a sense, I suppose, that is what he did tell me.)

"But you must go now. I've kept you far too long as it is. Sir John will have things for you to do, I'm sure. But do not stay away, Jeremy. You're a good lad to talk to, and Jimmie Bunkins needs you more than you know."

The next day was a busy one for Sir John Fielding. There was much going and coming. Visits were made to him. An air of secrecy hung over these proceedings that I was unable to penetrate. He left early in the morning with Constable Perkins and did not return until shortly before his court session began. Waiting for him then was the petty officer who served as footman to Vice-Admiral Sir Robert Redmond; he had a letter in hand which I thought surely to be from the admiral. Yet Sir John did not ask me to read it to him. He simply tucked it away and sent the fellow off empty-handed.

Then, later in the afternoon, Mr. Marsden entered his chambers, stayed for some time, and upon leaving, directed me inside. They had prepared a letter between them which I was to deliver.

"Will there be an answer?" I asked Sir John.

"None that I expect," said he, as he offered it to me.

I looked at the letter and saw it was addressed to the admiral.

"Take it there by foot," said he. "Return at your leisure. But give it to no one but Bobbie, certainly not to Lieutenant Byner. If you must wait for the admiral, then wait, but put the letter in his hand only. If you cannot do that, then return with it."

He was seldom so explicit. Naturally, I wondered at the letter's contents. Yet asking no question, I said my goodbye and turned for the door.

"Jeremy, there is one more thing you probably should know."

"What is that, sir?"

"The admiral who came up from Portsmouth to serve upon the court-martial board brought with him promotion papers for Lieutenant Hartsell. He is hereafter to be known as *Captain* Hartsell."

"But what does that mean, sir? That is, coming at such a time as this?"

"Indeed, what does it mean? Why, among much else it means that throughout tomorrow's proceedings he will be referred to and addressed as 'Captain.' Any reminder that during the action covered by the court-martial the accuser and the accused were of the same rank will be erased. It means that all of Hartsell's decisions are certified as justifiable and right in retrospect. It means that by the means of this promotion the proceedings have been weighted hopelessly in favor of the prosecution. It means that Lieutenant

Landon has not a chance in this world. It means they intend
to hang him. That has been foreordained.''

All this was said in a quiet voice, as if explaining to me
one of his rules of court. Tears welled in my eyes. I dabbed
at them, glad that Sir John could not see.

"How can they do that, sir? That is not justice."

"He'll get no justice from the Navy." He sighed deeply,
then gestured toward the door. "But on your way, Jeremy.
We'll talk of all this sometime in the future."

And indeed I went on my way, though my heart felt quite
as heavy as my feet on that long walk to Tower Hill. As
must surely be evident to you, reader, Sir John Fielding was
to me at the age I was then something more than a hero and
little less than a god. To see him despair so, to see him
defeated, made me near as sad as to contemplate the fate of
Lieutenant William Landon. That he be distressed and angry
as he had been yesterday seemed far better than to see him
in this state. Surely something could be done, would be done,
by him.

To arrive at the Navy Board thus in such a sad and listless
state in no wise prepared me for the reception I received
there. I found, first of all, that without so great a personage
as Sir John by my side I was made to feel not near so welcome as before. When the boatswain at the door heard I had
a letter for the admiral, he demanded it from me. Yet I would
not give it. It seemed so likely that he, a large man, would
grab me by the scruff of the neck and take the letter from
me that I retreated quickly some steps away from the door.

"Here, you, boy, come back here with that letter. Give it
me."

"I was instructed by him who sent it to put it in the hands
of Admiral Redmond, and in his hands only."

"And who is that who sent it?"

"Sir John Fielding, Magistrate of the Bow Street Court."

Whether it was the name, the title, or the office that impressed him or the concatenation of the three—whatever it
may have been—the boatswain relented and, leaving the
door open, tempted me inside with a promise to send me
upstairs with a seaman to the admiral's office. He was as
good as his word and appointed one of the three lounging

about as my guardian to the floor above. Once at the admiral's door, there took place again that strange ceremony of knocking and shouting back and forth through the door. When at last it opened, the lieutenant was there, frowning at me most critically.

"What is it you want, boy?"

I had anticipated a wrangle with Mr. Byner over possession of the letter, yet in the event, it lasted longer than I could have expected, certainly longer than was necessary. And all this was carried on at the very threshold of the office; I was not invited inside nor did my guardian leave me there. All the while, too, I heard a hum and hubbub of voices inside raised in jovial discussion behind the closed door that led to the admiral's private office.

At last the lieutenant saw he could neither bully nor wheedle the letter from me; and so, signaling to the seaman that I was to remain where I stood, he left me and went to knock lightly upon the admiral's door. A moment later Sir Robert Redmond appeared, listened to his lieutenant, looked at me, and nodded. Yet in that moment, with the door briefly open, I heard something that quite chilled me.

The admiral came forward to me. Between the time he had first made his appearance and his arrival at the threshold, his face had gone quite somber.

"I believe you have a letter for me from Sir John."

"Yes sir, I do. And here it is."

So saying, I pulled out the letter from my pocket and laid it in his open hand. With a nod, I stepped back and showed my intent to go.

"Were you not told to wait for a reply?"

"No, sir."

"Well, though I have not read his letter, I have one for him nevertheless. Tell him for me that I deeply regret losing his friendship over this matter, but duty dictates, and I must obey." He looked at me most severely. "Do you have that?"

"Yes, sir."

"You may go."

And indeed I went, quite distancing my assigned companion on the stairs and running out the door to the street. I did not even pause to shake the dust of the Navy Board from my shoes, though I thought to do it, for what I had heard when the door to the admiral's office was opened still sounded in my ears. The words did not matter, for they were a mere fragment of a sentence—"... though some may find it so"—followed by laughter from others. It was the voice in which they were spoken that gave me such upset: a nasal drawl it was, and unmistakably that of Lieutenant, now Captain, Hartsell. His promotion was cause for celebration, of course; the toasts were drunk in the admiral's office.

When I reached Number 4 Bow Street, I was glad to discover Sir John away, gone out once again on one of his mysterious errands, this time in the company of Mr. Fuller. I had no wish to add to his burden by telling him what I had learned. And by the time I did see him at dinner that evening I had decided to say nothing of it at all. I merely delivered the message the admiral had given me for him. He listened. An ironic smile played upon his lips.

"Duty dictates, eh?" said he. "No doubt in the voice of some lord—an earl, a baron, perhaps the Lord High Admiral himself."

We all sat round the table in the kitchen. Tom's eyes met mine. His mother's rested uneasily upon Sir John. For her part, Annie seemed happily oblivious of the nature of the silence that hung over the rest of us, or perhaps she wished only to divert us.

"I used something new for flavor in the chicken stew," she announced in a spritely manner. "They call it papricker, or papricka, or some such. Walked down to the spicemonger's on the docks for it. I saw your ship there, Tom. 'Twas pointed out to me. Looked ever so big."

"It is big, Annie," said he, "though many are bigger."

"The chicken is quite wonderful, Annie," said Sir John. "Nothing helps so much as good food to raise the spirits when they are low."

"Thank you, sir."

"Jeremy?"

"Yes, Sir John?"

"I shall need you with me a good part of the day tomorrow. That letter you delivered to Sir Robert was a request to be given permission to attend the court-martial. Though it is certainly not a trial open to the public, he will not deny me in this—notwithstanding the finality of that message he had you deliver to me. Oh, I am sure he will find room for us there.''

In truth, reader, I had no wish to attend and could not suppose why he had decided to do so. If it was as certain that Lieutenant Landon would be found guilty as Sir John had said, then why be witness to such a miscarriage of justice? Why be present to see him wrongfully disgraced? Yet of course I had no choice in the matter. If I was needed, of course I would go.

''Certainly, sir, I shall be ready whenever you wish.''

Silence reigned once again at the table. Annie's chicken stew may have raised Sir John's spirits, but it did nothing to uplift mine. I dipped a bit of bread in the sauce and chewed it idly, tasting it not at all.

Tom cleared his throat in a manner most tentative. Then said he: ''I reckon that Sir Robert will not be of much help now in getting me an appointment as midshipman.''

''No, Tom, I would say we can count on little from him now in that regard.''

''But Jack,'' wailed Lady Fielding, stricken of a sudden by the import of what he had just said, ''that is *terrible!* Does that mean Tom must return to the ship with that man as captain?''

''All that is uncertain now, Kate. You must leave it that I will do all that I can to help the situation.''

''All that you *can?* You have done all you can to help that lieutenant, and you now say it is likely—even sure—that he will be found guilty.''

''Kate, I will do *all I can* for Tom. More I cannot promise.''

''That isn't good enough, Jack. That man will learn Tom's relation to you—if he doesn't know that already. He will punish him for it. He may have him killed. He may—''

At that point she broke off, rose from the table, and threw down her napkin. She was quite near tears.

''No, Jack, that isn't good enough.''

She left the room then, marching up the stairs to their

bedroom. Sir John heard her go. He shook his head sadly as if at a loss as to what he might say.

Then: "Tom, go up and see what you can do to comfort your mother, will you?"

"I will, yes sir."

There were but three of us at table after Tom had left. Annie and I exchanged looks; she rolled her eyes in such a way to express alarm.

"Would anyone like more chicken?" she asked. "There's ever so much left."

The trial by court-martial of Lieutenant William Landon for the murder of Captain Josiah Markham, both of His Majesty's Ship *Adventure*, commenced promptly at nine o'clock at a hearing room known to Sir John in Whitehall.

Besides Vice-Admiral Sir Robert Redmond, the panel of judges consisted of Rear Admiral Charles Semloe, on permanent duty in Portsmouth Naval Stores, and Captain Thomas Bender, of the H.M.S. *Bristol*, a ship of the line recently anchored at Portsmouth. An unidentified lieutenant, who looked quite young, assisted the judges by reading aloud what had to be read, and keeping a record of the proceedings in shorthand at a small desk off to one side.

The accused was present of course, as was his counsel, Lieutenant Richard Byner. The accuser was also present, in the company of Midshipman Boone. So, too, were a small number of observers and interested parties seated there. Apart from Sir John and myself, all but one were junior officers in uniform—"sent by their superiors," Sir John muttered to me; he who was in plain dress—well clothed, properly bewigged, and in age about fifty—may have been a civilian member of the Navy Board, again according to Sir John. These, except for the trio of marines who had two days before brought Lieutenant Landon from the Tower to Sir Robert's office, were all who were present in that room in Whitehall. Yet they filled it, for it was not large—no more than twenty-five feet by fifteen—and as that July morning wore on, the place became close and exceedingly warm.

Vice-Admiral Sir Robert Redmond called the proceedings to order and introduced the other two judges. Then, at a nod

from him, the anonymous young lieutenant stepped forward
and read the statement of charges against Lieutenant William
Landon. It was quite remarkable. The crudely written indictment of no more than a paragraph in length that had been
framed nearly a year before in Bombay by then Lieutenant
Hartsell had grown in length so that it covered ten foolscap
pages and took near a quarter of an hour to read aloud. Yet
in substance it said the same thing: that in the course of a
storm of unusual proportions Mr. Landon had pushed Captain Josiah Markham overboard into the waters of the raging
sea, where he had thus, necessarily and inevitably, suffered
death by drowning.

Sir Robert then directed Lieutenant Landon to stand.

"Have you heard the charges?"

"I have, sir."

"And how plead you, guilty or not guilty?"

"I plead absolute innocence in this matter."

"Guilty or not guilty?" repeated the admiral.

Lieutenant Landon hesitated; then said he in a voice so
quiet it struck us in the back row as nearly inaudible: "Not
guilty."

Then was Captain James Hartsell called. He stood from
his chair and strode in a confident manner to the table
whereat the three judges sat. Clasping his hands behind him,
he stood facing them, his back to us. After identifying himself as "the present captain of His Majesty's Ship *Adventure*," he launched into the tale he had told that day aboard
the *Adventure*, yet told it with an ease that suggested repeated
rehearsal and told it, as well, without the challenging inter-
ruptions Sir John had earlier made. (Quite unintentionally,
Sir John had strengthened Hartsell's account, for where he
had found inconsistencies previously, these had been artfully
covered over so that as delivered to the panel of judges, there
was a smoothness to it as to a report of established fact.)
Thus, so polished was Hartsell's performance that the body
of his testimony lasted a comparatively short time—com-
pared, that is, to the statement of charges, which was longer
in the reading than his was in the telling. He concluded with
a curt nod of his head but remained standing in the same

posture, available to the judges for whatever questions that
they might have.

Captain Bender of H.M.S. *Bristol* whispered something to
Sir Robert and received what seemed obviously an affirmative reply. Then said he in a most commanding voice: "Captain Hartsell, you mentioned in your account of these events
that upon seeing Captain Markham go overboard in those
high seas, you put a boat over the side to seek his rescue.
Was that wise? Could he have been saved?"

Hartsell remained silent, head bowed for a moment, as if
carefully considering his reply. "Probably it was unwise on
my part," said he, "for it resulted in the loss of four men
and a boat. Could he have been saved? I know not the answer
to that, nor can I be certain that I even considered it when I
gave the order to drop the boat, for my only hope at that
moment was to rescue one of the finest officers and grandest
men it has been my privilege to serve under. I knew him but
a short time, yet I profited greatly by his wisdom. At that
awful moment when I saw Captain Markham pushed into the
sea, I simply refused to accept his loss."

"I quite understand, Captain Hartsell," said the questioner. "Thank you for your frank reply."

And Sir John, beside me, gave a great "Hrrrumph!" causing a number of heads to turn our way. Let them gape,
thought I, but if they only knew all which that man who
addressed the court had done, they would recognize that such
rank hypocrisy as he now mouthed was the least of his sins.

"I have a question for you, Captain," said Sir Robert.

"Yes, sir?"

"There is a considerable discrepancy between the date
upon which you have said these events took place and the
date upon which you wrote the letter reporting him. Further,
I have searched carefully through the ship's log, which is
here before me in evidence for the examination of the others
on this panel—I have searched carefully through it, I say,
and find no mention of the captain's loss as homicide, neither
on the date which it took place, nor any time thereafter. How
do you account for a delay of months in reporting so grave
a matter? And why was no mention made of it in the log of
the *Adventure?*"

I give Sir Robert Redmond credit. It was a proper question, one that demanded answer in any proper trial procedure. Hartsell had dismissed it earlier when it was put to him by Sir John, saying that he had to be certain in his own mind of what he had witnessed. That, I was sure, would seem a weak answer to put before any court, even this one, yet I could not have conceived of the mendacious manner in which it would be given support.

Far from causing evident difficulty to him who was asked it, the question seemed almost to give him pleasure, for Hartsell had a ready reply. Said he: ''To answer first the question of the ship's log, it seemed not a fitting place to record more than the loss of Captain Markham, which I did enter there. The ship's log is not secure and cannot be kept secure. The other officers, and at that time there were three besides myself, had occasion to consult it and occasionally as deck officers make entries. Had I kept a diary—and kept it under lock and key—I would have noted it there, but such has never been my habit.

''Now,'' said he, continuing, ''as to the greater question of delay in reporting the matter, I brooded over what I had seen for quite some time, asking myself if I had truly witnessed what my eyes told me I had. As has been pointed out to me, a swift movement to pull the captain in could be seen as a swift movement to push him overboard. I considered this possibility and for a period I would say that my feelings in the matter amounted to more than suspicion and less than absolute certainty. What was prominently missing was any reason why Mr. Landon might so want the captain dead that he would attend to the matter himself. I could think of none. But then I was approached by one of the midshipmen. He told me that—''

''I must interrupt you, Captain Hartsell,'' said Sir Robert. ''Was that midshipman who approached you Midshipman Albert Boone?''

''It was, sir.''

''And is he here to testify?''

''He is, sir.''

''Then let us hear from him what he told you. We shall call him as the next witness. I take it that what he communicated to you gave you a greater sense of certainty in the matter?''

''It did, sir.''

''Well and good. Then we shall hear it and better understand, ourselves.'' Sir Robert seemed about to dismiss Hartsell when apparently struck by something suddenly remembered. ''Ah!'' said he. ''I believe this is the time that I ask the counsel for the defense if he has questions for Captain Hartsell.''

Sir Robert looked up and about the room. ''Mr. Byner?''

''*Suh!*''

''Have you questions?''

''Suh?''

''For Captain Hartsell?''

''Oh no sir, none, sir.''

''Very well, then. Captain Hartsell, you are dismissed. Will Midshipman Albert Boone come forward?''

He did come, a slight swagger to his walk. He seemed inordinately proud to have a part in matters as serious as these. He looked about the room almost arrogantly as he made his way forward, seeming to falter only when his eye caught that of Lieutenant Landon. Boone looked away quickly. Mr. Landon continued to follow him, staring openly at him even after the midshipman had assumed the place of Captain Hartsell before the panel of judges.

Asked to identify himself to the court, Boone saluted and blurted out his name in a manner not entirely appropriate to the proceedings, adding, only after prompting from Sir Robert, ''Midshipman, His Majesty's Ship *Adventure*.''

Then Sir Robert prompted him again: ''Will you tell us, please, young man, what it was you had to tell Captain Hartsell regarding the death of Captain Markham?''

''Oh yes, sir, I will, sir.''

And then, simply put, reader, Boone told a lie. It was not only a great lie, it was also quite plainly a lie, for not content with simply presenting whole cloth, he felt called upon to embroider it with moral indignation and self-righteous anger. It was also greatly deficient in detail.

The lie was this: that at some uncertain time before the day of the great storm, Mr. Landon had expressed to Midshipman Boone his hatred of Captain Markham. "He had an evil smile upon his face when he said it, sir," declared Boone, "like unto the Devil hisself. He said he had been insulted by the captain and would somehow get revenge upon him. He frightened me, he did. I protested to him, I did, sir, I said what I knew to be true, that Captain Markham was a good officer and a just man, though sickly. Then said Mr. Landon that mattered naught to him, for he would have his own back, no matter what."

Having had his say, he gave a nod that was meant to convey an attitude of great certainty. He shifted his feet as if eager to be gone. Yet Sir Robert, perhaps insulted by the crudeness of this attempt to attribute a motive to Lieutenant Landon's alleged actions, put to him a series of questions that confused Boone and the answers to which seemed to embarrass all those who heard them.

"Can you be more specific to when Lieutenant Landon made these remarks to you?" asked Sir Robert.

"Uh, not exactly, sir. Just that it was before the big storm."

"What was the occasion of these remarks?"

"Sir?"

"Surely he did not simply walk up to you one fine day and say, 'Oh, by the by, Midshipman Boone, I hate the captain and will have revenge upon him.' Are you telling the court that this is how it occurred?"

"Uh, no sir."

"How then?"

"Well . . ." Boone delayed a long moment, trying to give some substance to his fantastic tale with an imagined detail or two. Finally: "It was at night, sir."

"At night, was it? And you two were alone?"

"Yes, sir, on the quarterdeck."

"On the quarterdeck? What about the helmsman?"

"He was there too."

"Did he hear Lieutenant Landon say all this?"

"No sir, because Mr. Landon whispered."

"I see. Did you say something to him that drew from him the sinister remarks you have quoted?"

"Uh, no, well, all I said was I liked the captain."

"And that was sufficient to inspire such sedition?"

"Sir?"

"Oh, never mind," said Sir Robert. "But let me hear from you why you waited so long to inform the acting captain. You yourself said that this alleged conversation took place before the great storm. Yet it was not until months later that you reported it. Why was that?"

"Because, sir, I was frighted of him—of Mr. Landon, I mean. He come up to me one day after the storm, and he said to me, 'Tell no one of what I said, or you will get the same as the captain.' "

"And that was sufficient to buy months of silence from you?"

"Sir?"

"Stay where you are, Midshipman Boone. There may be more questions for you." Sir Robert looked about the room. "Captain Hartsell, will you rise, please? Keep your place, but tell me, was this boy's story truly what swayed you to write that letter of accusation against Lieutenant Landon?"

"It was, sir," said Hartsell in a forthright manner. "He was truly frightened of Mr. Landon when he came to me, and the threat made to Mr. Boone by Mr. Landon seemed to carry with it a confession of guilt in the matter of the captain's death."

"You were satisfied that the supposed insult by Captain Markham provided Lieutenant Landon with all that he needed by way of a reason to kill the captain?"

"I was, sir."

"Did you confront Lieutenant Landon with Mr. Boone's story?"

"I did not, sir."

"Did you make known to him your own suspicions?"

"I did not, sir."

"Did you mention the matter at all to Mr. Landon?"

"No, sir."

"You chose, rather, to send the letter accusing him of murder?"

"Yes, sir."

"And why was that? Why did you not attempt to convene a court-martial in Bombay?"

"For two reasons, sir. First, there were not at that time—
nor, I believe, at any time while we were in Indian waters—a
sufficient number of ships of the Royal Navy to provide senior officers for a panel of judges. Most of the time we in the
Adventure were all alone there with naught but the East India
Company's merchantmen to keep us company. And second,
sir, having lost the captain, we could not afford to lose more
of our complement of officers. In point of fact, we did lose
another officer, Lieutenant Highet, not quite a year later.
Lieutenant Landon's performance as an officer on the *Adventure* was satisfactory in every way but one: he had murdered Captain Markham.''

Sir John and I had heard this little joke of his before.
Hearing it again annoyed me. What annoyed me further was
hearing a number of those present, including Captain Bender
of the *Bristol*, break into laughter at it. Hartsell waited for
the laughter to subside.

"That was why, in short," said he, "that I chose to defer
the matter of Lieutenant Landon until our duty was done.''

"In fact, you waited until you had come to your present
anchor before informing him, did you not?'' asked Sir Robert.

"It was, in truth, the night before.''

"You may seat yourself, Captain Hartsell.''

He looked right and left to his fellow judges. "Are there
any questions for Midshipman Boone?'' Receiving no positive response from either Rear Admiral Semloe, nor from
Captain Bender, he called out, "Mr. Byner, have you questions for Mr. Boone?''

"None, sir.''

"Very well, you may go, Mr. Boone.''

And indeed he quite fled. No longer so pleased with himself, he returned with his head low to his chair next to Hartsell's and simply sat down.

"Lieutenant William Landon, please present yourself,''
spake Sir Robert.

And forth went Mr. Landon to the table whereat the panel
of judges sat. After saluting and identifying himself, he
adopted the same pose Hartsell had taken before the judges—
feet planted wide and hands clasped behind him. I noted that

in one hand he held a sheaf of foolscap rolled tight. Upon Sir Robert's order, he launched upon his version of the events in question which occurred on April 12, 1767, the day of the great storm off the Cape of Good Hope.

It was essentially and in most of its particulars the tale he had told two days before in his uncle's office at the Navy Board. It was clear that he had meant to report it in as cold and forthright a manner as his adversary, Hartsell, yet he could not. He faltered as he approached the climax, that moment upon the poop deck when Captain Markham slipped from his grasp and was propelled by the motion of the ship to the taffrail. As he attempted to describe his final efforts to save him, holding him, feeling him pulling away, Mr. Landon gave in at last to tears. Such displays of emotion were and are, of course, considered quite unseemly among officers of the Royal Navy; and when he blurted out, ". . . I was left with his shoe in my hand," and quite lost control, sobbing and sniveling as any child might, a disapproving murmur went round the assemblage. The judges themselves averted their eyes.

"You have done then, Lieutenant Landon," said Sir Robert. It was no interrogative but a statement, near a command.

Mr. Landon lifted his head. "No . . . sir, I . . . have not done. I have more to tell, of how this perfidious charge came to be lodged against me, of how—"

"Lieutenant, *you have done!*"

"But I must—"

"You must *nothing* more—unless the other judges . . . No? Mr. Byner, have you anything to ask within the limits of this inquiry?"

"No questions, sir," said Mr. Byner, "but a statement to be read in support of Lieutenant Landon."

"What? Oh . . . oh yes, from the ship's surgeon, not so?"

But of a sudden Mr. Landon had turned round and seemed to be addressing all present, waving the sheaf of foolscap he had kept tight in his hand all through his testimony.

"*I* have a statement!" cried he. "It is set forth in plain English what iniquitous, unnatural acts were perpetrated by that man!" He jabbed a finger angrily in the direction of Hartsell.

"Let me have that!" Sir Robert had risen from his chair. "I demand the right to read it out in this court."

"I must look at it first to determine its relevancy."

Mr. Landon looked wildly about for a moment, as if searching for some higher authority to whom he might appeal. Finding none, he weakened. When he spoke next, it was in a smaller voice, and in a tone near pleading.

"Or at least, sir," said he, "let it be inserted into the record of this trial."

With that, Mr. Landon threw down the wadded and rolled sheaf upon the judges' table. Sir Robert picked it up, unrolled it, and, still standing, gave it but a moment or two of his attention.

"This will not do," said he.

And having said it, he set about to rip those papers into small bits and pieces. Mr. Landon watched him do so, and of course made no movement to stop him.

"You are no better than any of them," said he to his uncle. "It is not in my nature to curse, but I call down God's judgment upon you all."

He went to his chair against the wall between the two marines and sat down, staring blindly ahead.

A silence of considerable duration followed. I, for one, was aware of the quick, heavy breathing that seemed to come from the judges' table. Sir Robert still stood, yet with difficulty. He supported himself but barely by his two arms. He was red-faced and panting. But he managed to gain control of himself and eased himself back down into his chair.

"Mr. Byner, read the statement from the surgeon."

He proceeded to do that. Though I had been present as it was drafted, I found that I bare remembered it. Mr. Mac-Naughton's words seemed not to be his own, as I indeed knew them to be. What he had insisted was an addiction to alcohol had become "a strong propensity to drink"; what he had diagnosed as a liver distended by alcohol was now "an abdominal swelling." It had in such subtle ways as these become denatured, weaker. It did end, however, with a eulogy to Mr. Landon as "the finest Christian gentleman I have ever had the honor to know," and a statement of certainty that Lieutenant Landon could never have committed the act of which he had been accused. "Surely a mistake of judgment has been made."

Coming, as it did, after the drama that was played out before us by nephew and uncle, there was something anticlimactic about it all, not least because Mr. Byner read the statement aloud in a monotone and mispronounced the surgeon's name when he had done.

"That will do to be inserted into the trial record," said Sir Robert, now somewhat recovered. "Pass it to the clerk, Mr. Byner."

Vice-Admiral Sir Robert Redmond looked left and right at his fellow judges, and then addressed them as follows: "You will note that the statement just read is somewhat at variance with the testimony given us by Captain Hartsell. No mention was made earlier by Captain Hartsell of Captain Markham's 'propensity to drink,' nor of the latter's frequent long absences above decks which Mr. MacNaughton attributed to that propensity. No doubt it was Captain Hartsell's generosity of spirit that prevented him from mentioning these as faults of his former captain. However, Mr. MacNaughton's opinion, as a medical man, should probably be given greater weight.

"Having noted this for the record, I believe we have heard as much testimony as we need to make our decision. We shall absent ourselves for as long as it takes for us to reach it, and then we shall return with our verdict."

He rose then, Rear Admiral Semloe and Captain Bender with him, and the three filed through a door at the rear of the room to the hall.

"Jeremy," said Sir John beside me, "I should like you to see me down the stairs, since I know not the way, and then I want you to return here."

He rose from his chair. I saw others stand and stretch, but we were the only two in the room who made for the door. As I moved him along to the nearby stairs, and as we descended them, he continued his instructions to me. And though they puzzled me somewhat, I asked for no explanation, since I perceived a sense of urgency in what he said to me.

"Once the judges return, and their decision is handed

down, you must not let Hartsell and that young idiot Boone
out of your sight. If they take this route, which I expect they
will do, then simply follow. If they take another, then stay
with them long enough to be sure of their path, then run to
me and tell me where to look for them. Is that understood?''

''Uh . . . yes sir.''

''Good. Now here is the door, is it not?''

He leaned forward and fumbled at it, searching for the
handle. Finding it, he swung open the door—and there, to
my surprise, standing quite nearby, was Benjamin Bailey,
captain of the Bow Street Runners. Behind him I glimpsed
Constable Perkins, which surprised me further.

''I'm here, Sir John,'' said Mr. Bailey.

''Good. Now, Jeremy, you must return. But one last word:
Do not let Boone get away.''

Boone? thought I as I jog-trotted back up the stairs. What
importance had he? What had been planned? Could they not
have trusted me sufficient to include me in their strategy?

I felt much confused and a little hurt as I reentered the
hearing room and slipped into the chair by the door which I
had left only a minute or two before. Those who had stood
were still on their feet. There was some discussion between
two or three, which was carried on in low, quiet tones. None
made so bold as to walk about. Hartsell and Boone sat together; not a word passed between them. Lieutenant Landon
was but a few feet away. His eyes were open, yet somehow
blank; it was as though he had removed himself from this
room, in which he had been so humiliated and abused, and
taken himself away to some friendlier place where justice
and charity ruled.

We had not long to wait. It could not have been much
more than five minutes when the door to the hall reopened
and the three judges returned through it and made their way
back to their table. They remained standing.

''Will the prisoner come forward?''

It was necessary that one of the marines prod Lieutenant
Landon to return him to the proper time and place, so far
had he gone. Yet once back, he responded in the approved
manner and presented himself to the judges of the court-
martial. He saluted.

Vice-Admiral Sir Robert Redmond said as follows: "Lieutenant William Landon, you are found by the judges of this court-martial guilty of the murder of Captain Josiah Markham by means of drowning. You are hereby sentenced to be hanged by the neck until dead at Execution Dock one week from today. Corporal of the guard, return the prisoner to the Tower." At that Mr. Landon saluted once again, which quite amazed me.

The rest was all carried out with great swiftness. The marines surrounded the lieutenant; and the corporal, barking out a series of commands, moved the entire party down the aisle past me through the door. Mr. Landon gave me no sign of recognition as he went by. Though I had been prepared for this outcome, I was dumbstruck nevertheless.

First to their feet were Hartsell and Boone. The newly made captain turned and looked about as if he expected to receive congratulations. He got none. Those who had assembled, for whatever reason, to witness these proceedings turned away from him as if from a leper. The judges of the court-martial disappeared through their portal at the far end of the room. Others followed them out. A few trailed out the door just to my right, among them Hartsell and Boone. The captain paid me no mind; the midshipman, however, gave me a scowl which, I believe, was meant to frighten me. I allowed one or two to get between me and them so that my pursuit would not seem obvious.

Thus we went down the stairs, and thus we exited through the door into the warm July morning. I came through the door just in time to hear Mr. Bailey say, "Captain Hartsell?"

And the foolish man looked up, smiled after his fashion, and said, "Why, yes"—as if he believed he was at last about to receive the recognition he was due for his daring and cleverness.

"Right this way, sir."

Curious, he followed Mr. Bailey toward the waiting coach. Neither he nor Boone noticed when Constable Perkins and I fell in behind them.

"Just inside, sir," said Mr. Bailey, most polite. "The coach will take you to your destination."

Satisfied with that, Hartsell took himself up and was nearly inside, when (as I later learned) he spied Black Emma and the innkeeper from the Green Man awaiting him, alongside Sir John.

"That is the man," said Black Emma.

"Aye," said the innkeeper. "That's him."

"You are under arrest, sir, for the murder of Tobias Trindle," said Sir John.

Then tried Hartsell vainly to clamber out. Mr. Perkins dealt him a great blow upon the backside with his club, and Mr. Bailey picked him up by his trousers and threw him bodily inside.

That left Boone for me. He turned, wild-eyed, and looked where he might run. He found no place, for I delivered him a stout blow in his midsection for which he was in no wise prepared. He doubled over, and I gave him another in the face.

"That'll do," said Mr. Perkins to me.

And indeed it would, for Mr. Bailey picked Boone up then and with no trouble at all threw him atop his master. Then he jumped in after them both.

"You'd best ride up top, Jeremy," said Mr. Perkins. "It may be a bit rough inside."

Then he, too, ascended into the coach and slammed the door after him.

The footman, quite unknown to me, gave me a hand up and made room on the seat. The coachman urged the four horses into motion and we were off—I knew not where.

A small crowd had gathered to gape at our departure.

TWELVE

*In which an end is at
last put to
the matter*

The coach, I was quite amazed to learn, was Black Jack Bilbo's. Four horses pulled it. The compartment below contained seven at that moment—though perhaps not in great comfort. My seat above, praise be, was equipped with a strong handle that I might grasp to keep myself from flying high and wide off the seat and onto the cobblestones, for the driver hurried the horses on to Mr. Bilbo's residence.

All this I learned from the footman who rode beside me. He was a jolly sort, all "begod" and "bejesus," as he shouted out to me all the preparations that had been made by the "cove of the ken." Quite proud he was of their part in the successful abduction of Hartsell and Boone.

The driver reined up the horses before the great house.

"Down you go, lad," said the footman.

I started my descent, feeling with careful feet for each rung below.

"We'll be right here a-waitin'."

By the time I reached the pavement, half our company was inside, Mr. Bailey pushing Hartsell forward with no difficulty, and Mr. Perkins followed close behind, gripping Boone by the collar. It was remarkable how swiftly the two culprits had taken on the appearance of common street criminals now that they were in the hands of the law: Hartsell had lost his tricorn in the coach, and his wig was askew;

Boone was whining and squealing as loudly as any seven-year-old might.

Sir John paid them no mind. Assembling the rest of us, he moved forward with my help through the open door, Black Emma and the innkeeper from the Green Man close behind. Mr. Bilbo was there at the door and slammed it shut once all were within.

"Right down at the end of the hall, Sir John," said he. "I believe you know the way."

"I do indeed, sir. Come all, and follow me."

He led our procession, sure enough, wishing no guidance from me, running his stick along the wall on the left until he came to the open door.

In the room, the constables waited with their prisoners, so Mr. Marsden also waited upon Sir John's arrival. A sufficient number of chairs had been ranged about facing the large desk. In one of them sat a familiar figure, puffing on a pipe; Old Isaac it was, and beside him, arms folded and a frown upon his face, sat Constable Cowley.

Mr. Marsden hastened to Sir John's side and moved him up to the place that had been prepared for him at the desk. The two sat down side by side and conferred.

"Come, Jeremy, take this chair next me, and we shall see this through together."

It was Mr. Bilbo pounding the chair beside him; I took it, and looked about to see if others of his household had come to witness these proceedings. There were none. The door to the hall had been shut tight.

"If you're searching for Bunkins, you'll not find him," said Mr. Bilbo. "I sent him off on an errand that should keep him the rest of the morning. The rest I told to keep away. Sir John wanted this kept private."

"Secret?"

"Private, was what I said."

Sir John Fielding beat thrice loudly on the top of the desk with the flat of his hand. What whispering there was in the room ceased.

"The Bow Street Court will come to order," said he in a proper, solemn tone. "We meet here in special session on this day, the twenty-fifth of July, 1769, at Number Twelve

St. James Street for to hear testimony on a single matter. That which is before us now is the murder of Tobias Trindle, able seaman late of the H.M.S. *Adventure*, just after midnight two days past. The acting captain of the *Adventure*, formerly Lieutenant and now Captain James Hartsell, has been detained in this matter. Will he come forward now?"

Hartsell remained seated, grasping tight to the arms of his chair.

"Captain Hartsell, come forward," repeated Sir John.

Mr. Bailey, beside the prisoner, rose and ripped him bodily from his place as easily as he might a bird from his perch. He marched him up to Sir John at the desk and held him there.

"Captain Hartsell, you will save us considerable trouble if you now admit your guilt in this matter. So tell us now, prisoner, how do you plead? Guilty or not guilty?"

Now somewhat recovered and thus emboldened, Hartsell declared: "I do not plead neither, for I do not recognize this court. I am an officer in His Majesty's Navy and can only be tried in a naval court-martial."

"Captain Hartsell, you may not recognize this court, but this court recognizes you, for the crime for which you have been detained was committed within its jurisdiction and be you admiral or general, it is all the same. One who is accused of a crime committed in London will be tried by a London court. I will explain, however, that this court will not try you for the said crime of murder. It will but weigh testimony and evidence to determine if they be sufficient for you to be bound over for trial in the felony court at Old Bailey. So now I put it to you again: How do you plead? Guilty or not guilty?"

Hartsell remained most belligerently silent.

"Mr. Marsden, put it down that the prisoner refuses to plead, but we shall continue as if we had heard a not-guilty plea from him. Return, Captain Hartsell, and Midshipman Albert Boone, come forward."

Boone did not resist. He came hopping eagerly to the desk.

"Not guilty," cried he, impatient to be asked. "I only done what he told me to, sir, and he's my captain, so I had to do it, sir."

"Not quite so impetuous, Mr. Boone. Let me inform you of the charge on which you have been detained and explain it to you."

"Yes, sir."

"You are supposed to have aided and abetted Captain Hartsell in the murder of Tobias Trindle, to have acted as his accomplice in it. Now, to have been so involved in a capital crime is itself a capital crime—that is, punishable by death. Now, having heard, how do you plead? Guilty or not guilty?"

"Not guilty, sir, not guilty, for as I said, I only done what he told me."

"Return to your place. Now, Mr. Marsden, call the first witness."

The clerk called Isaac Tenker—Old Isaac, as I knew him—and the weathered seaman approached Sir John somewhat less than confidently. The story that he told confirmed Tom Durham's suspicions. He admitted a bit shame-faced to Sir John that after he had told me in general where we might look to find Tobias Trindle, and with whom, he had been visited in the Fleet Prison by Midshipman Boone, to whom he had given the same information.

"Exactly the same?"

"Not exactly, no. I told him as how ol' Tobias said something about lookin' for the black woman at a place downriver called the Green Man. I would've told your boy the same, except I only remembered that part after I talked to him."

"Such a pity," said Sir John. "Mr. Trindle might be alive today, had you remembered. But tell me, Mr. Tenker, why did you tell Midshipman Boone anything at all? Had you special fondness for him?"

"Uh . . . no sir. It was just, y'see, he said he had come on the authority of the captain, and he was speakin' for the captain, and a man can't go against his captain, now can he?"

"I find no need to answer your question," said Sir John, "and so I shall ask you to return to your place. Mr. Marsden, call the next."

Call him he did, loud and clear: "Seth Tarkin, come forward."

The name was unfamiliar to me. Yet I was not surprised to see the innkeeper of the Green Man rise and take the place before the desk vacated by Old Isaac. His part in it I knew already, for Constable Perkins had threatened it out of him in my presence. He told willingly to Sir John what he had done: that for a bribe of a guinea (twenty-one pieces of silver, not even thirty) he had told "that man there" (Hartsell) not only where to find Black Emma's lodging house, but the exact location of her lodgings, as well ("top floor, last on the left").

Sir John did not discuss with him the propriety of his act. He simply asked him if Captain Hartsell was alone when he entered the Green Man to glean this information from him.

"No, sir, he weren't alone. That boy there was with him."

And with that, the innkeeper turned and pointed direct at Midshipman Boone.

"That will be all. Mr. Marsden, call the next witness, please."

"Constable Oliver Perkins."

Constable Perkins came up and explained that he had, with me, toured a great number of inns and gin-houses in the district, and on information given him by another innkeeper, returned to the Green Man. "I persuaded Mr. Tarkin to tell me the same that he had told the earlier visitor. He also told me that there *had* been an earlier visitor, only a few minutes past. Young Mr. Proctor and I hurried to the location. I instructed Mr. Proctor to go to the back, whilst I would enter through the front."

"May I ask, Mr. Perkins," said Sir John, "what was Mr. Proctor to do to stop the . . . visitor should he have made an exit through the rear—which, as I recall, he did."

"Nothing at all, sir. I told him merely to call out to me, should he come. I told him to stay hid. It was a very dark night, sir."

"I see. Continue."

"Well, sir, when I was halfway up the stairs and running, I heard what was a pistol shot, most certain. I hurried on my way, my pistol out, then saw a figure leap through the door I was headed for and out the back. He must've got a surprise there because there was no stairs in the back—they's rotted away. With me behind him, he had no choice but to jump. When I appeared, he took a shot at me, and I fired back at the flash.''

"Thus accounting for the three shots heard by the inmates of that lodging house."

"Yes sir. Well, he ran. I jumped down and ran after him, first instructing young Mr. Proctor to go to the room of that woman to see what had been done and to secure it."

"Those in the lodging house said the boy who had come down the hall ordering them back into their rooms wielded a pistol."

"Ah, yes sir, before I sent him into the lodging house, I gave him the pistol I had fired—empty, of course."

"Of course. It would not do to give a loaded firearm to a lad so young. Go on, Mr. Perkins."

"Well, Sir John, I gave chase, though there was no sound of steps to follow. There was two ways to take, and I must've took the wrong one, for I lost the trail."

"I see. And where would the other way have taken you?"

"Toward the river and the Tower."

"Well and good, Mr. Perkins: I believe I shall have Mr. Proctor take up the story at this point."

Just as I was making to stand up, Mr. Bilbo grasped my arm and whispered in my ear, "I believe we're off the hook, lad. My thanks to Mr. Perkins."

I returned his wink as Mr. Marsden called out my name.

"Now, tell me, Mr. Proctor," said Sir John to me, rather severely, "after you rampaged through that lodging house threatening its residents with an empty pistol, what did you find when at last you entered the room at the end of the hall?"

Thus I told him what I have already told you, reader, and no need to repeat it now. My testimony was brief, and Sir John did not ask me to enlarge on any part of it. I described the condition of the body of Tobias Trindle. I described the condition of the room. He ended my part of the tale at the appearance of Black Emma.

"Call her, Mr. Marsden," said Sir John.

"Emma Black, come forward now."

She rose but remained reluctantly where she stood.

"That ain't my name," said she most firmly.

He looked down at the paper in his hand and back up at her.

"It is not your name?" said he. "Well, what is?"

"Black Emma," said she. "It's the only one I ever had."

He frowned at that, leaned over, and entered into a whispered discussion with Sir John. Then, with a nod to him, he returned to her.

"Would you care to choose a surname now?" asked the clerk.

"You mean a name like Smith, or Jones, or Tatersby?"

"That's right."

"Well, I ain't sure." She thought upon it for a moment. "Say my name like you said it before."

"Emma Black!" Though he did not shout it, he let it ring out a bit.

"I like that well enough. Leave it so."

"Then come forward, please."

That she did, and if Hartsell had previously held some hope that the weight of testimony against him was not so great (for neither Mr. Perkins nor I had claimed to see the face of the man who had fled), then it was dashed utterly by the recital of Emma Black. From her perch on the chamber pot, she had seen a man enter the room, pistol in hand. He stepped over to the bed where Tobias Trindle slept and, putting the barrel of the pistol close to his forehead, pulled the trigger. She heard the loud report of the shot. She saw Trindle's body jump convulsively and sprawl across the bed. She saw his murderer then turn toward her hiding place and pull out another pistol. But, hearing the approach of another, he turned away and ran swiftly out the door.

"How was the man dressed?" Sir John asked her.

"It were not easy to tell, sir," said she. "He had on a black cloak that covered him, shoulder to boots. But when he pulled out that other pistol, I did see the flash of something could've been a brass button."

"I see. Then there was light in the room?"

"One candle was burning, my side of the bed."

"Could you, by the light of that single candle, see his features clearly?"

"I could, sir, for when he bent over Toby to do his nasty act, the light from the candle showed his face clear."

"So you then saw him well enough to identify him now?"

"Oh yes, sir, indeed I can."

"Is that man here in the room now?"

"He is, sir. He is sittin' right there."

And turning, Emma Black pointed directly at Captain James Hartsell.

"Thank you, Miss Black, that will be all."

"Thank *you*, sir."

With that, she curtseyed, after her fashion, and returned to her chair.

"Prisoners, come forward again," Mr. Marsden called out.

And forward they came, Boone quite willingly, and Hartsell somewhat reluctantly though not forced; they were accompanied by Mr. Bailey and Mr. Perkins. Sir John was most solemn in mien and demeanor as he waited upon them and then addressed them once again.

"Captain Hartsell and Midshipman Boone," said he, "as you have heard, there is more than sufficient testimony to bind you over for trial in felony court. Have you now anything to say? Mr. Boone?"

"Just what I said before. I only done what he told me."

Hartsell turned and gave Boone a withering, contemptuous look. Yet Boone was not withered; he returned a defiant look of his own.

Sir John, who was quite naturally oblivious of this unspoken exchange, simply inclined his head in the direction of Captain Hartsell and asked if he now had anything to say.

"I have nothing to say," responded the captain, "for the reason that I do not recognize you or the authority of your court over me."

"We have already discussed that. You are obviously not averse to repeating yourself. I, however, am. The governor and warders of Newgate jail will now have authority over you until the time of your trial—and, no doubt, for a short time afterward. You may argue your position with them, if you like. Do not expect them to be sympathetic to it.

"Midshipman Boone, since you seem to feel yourself a victim of the captain and apparently wish to end your association with him, I shall help you make a first step in that direction by sending you to the Fleet Prison, rather than Newgate. It is principally a prison for debtors, and they may treat a lad of your years more gently than would the hardened criminals who make up the better part of Newgate's population.''

''Oh, thank you, sir, thank you,'' wailed Boone.

''Don't mention it,'' said Sir John, in an expression of generosity somewhat tinged with irony. ''Now, Mr. Bailey and Mr. Perkins, you will accompany Captain Hartsell to Newgate forthwith. Mr. Cowley and Mr. Proctor will see Midshipman Boone to the Fleet and return Isaac Tenker there, as well—but not until a bit later, for I have matters to discuss further with the midshipman. The rest of you may now go with my thanks. Mr. Marsden will provide you with a shilling each for your return to your lodgings in a hackney carriage. Yet please remember that you will be called upon to testify when the date of the trial is set at Old Bailey.''

By the time Sir John Fielding had done with Midshipman Albert Boone he not only had from him an agreement to testify against his captain, which he gladly gave in exchange for Sir John's promise to recommend transportation for him, rather than hanging; he had also secured his signature on two copies of a document written out by Mr. Marsden in which he freely admitted that he had given perjured testimony in the trial by court-martial of Lieutenant William Landon.

The trip to the Fleet Prison in Mr. Bilbo's coach-and-four was quite uneventful, save for Constable Cowley's frequent yawns, which put me in fear that he might doze off and the two prisoners might take it in mind to scarper; since he was armed and I was not, there was little I could have done to prevent them. Yet Mr. Cowley, in spite of the fact that he had spent the night patrolling the streets of Westminster, managed to keep awake the length of the drive. And in truth, neither Old Isaac nor Boone showed any inclination toward bold action. The seaman grumbled sullenly on and on that he would now be held as a material witness after his chums had been let go; while the midshipman said ne'er a word, so plunged into gloom was he by the contemplation of his future.

The transfer of the prisoners to the warders at the gate of the Fleet was managed without incident. As instructed, I told them that Sir John had specified that Boone be kept separate from the other prisoners from the H.M.S. *Adventure*; and I was assured that his wish would be respected. There was left naught for Mr. Cowley and me then but to be returned in great style to Number 4 Bow Street. He had to be shaken there from a deep slumber, for he had given in to sleep the moment he had reentered the coach and settled again upon its soft cushions. But upon our arrival he came awake and staggered down. We called our thanks to the driver and footman. Constable Cowley parted from me there to labor back on wobbly legs to his lodgings nearby.

I entered at Number 4 to find the place all topsy-turvy. Papers were scattered about ahead. I saw Constable Fuller's keys upon the floor. I heard a hubbub of shouting back and forth in unfamiliar voices. Had I better sense, I should have turned round at that moment and made my way out softly at the door where I had come in. But driven on quite irresistibly by curiosity, I went cautiously forward.

Just as I was approaching the empty strong room and reconsidering my decision, a marine stepped out from whence I least expected him and leveled his musket at me. There was a bayonet fixed at the end of the thing.

"Corporal," he yelled, "I got one here."

Indeed he had. I stood rooted, more fearful of the bayonet than the musket to which it was fixed. I doubted he would shoot me, but he might stumble and stab me by mistake. He looked a clumsy fellow.

From out of Mr. Marsden's alcove came the corporal, followed by another marine who, like the fellow who held me at bay, hauled with him a musket with a bayonet affixed. They shuffled over through a great litter of paper which had been emptied onto the floor from Mr. Marsden's desk and storage boxes. The corporal scrutinized me and turned away in disappointment.

"He ain't nothin' but a boy," said he. "Put him over with the other one and tell the lieutenant."

Thus I was marched over to Mr. Marsden's alcove where I joined Mr. Fuller, who, with a forlorn expression upon his face, greeted me in a voice that suited his face. There was a guard for us both.

"Hullo, Jer'my. I could do nothin'. They come runnin' in here with bayonets fixed before I could grab a pistol and challenge them."

"No one could blame you," said I. "They surprised me, as well." Not quite true, but it seemed the decent thing to say.

"I feel quite disgraced."

"For no reason. But how many of them are there?"

"Five or six—six, counting the corporal—and a Navy lieutenant in charge. They thought to find Sir John here with his court in session, but I told them, I did, that he went off to a court-martial. That made the lieutenant quite furious, it did. He kept shouting at me, 'Where is Sir John then? And where is Captain Hartsell?' Jeremy, who is Captain Hartsell?"

I heard and recognized the lieutenant some moments before I saw him. He came thundering at us in that sergeant major's voice of his which could be heard from some distance away. Lieutenant Byner did indeed sound angry.

"I believe I know *that* boy," he bellowed. "Take me to him."

And then he confronted me, hands on hips. He stamped his foot once, presumably to gain my attention, which of course he had already.

"Yes, it is you, isn't it?"

That struck me as a singularly unanswerable question, yet I tried my best: "Yes sir, it is."

"I have some questions for *you*."

"Well, I shall try my best to answer them."

"First of all, why are there no papers in Sir John's chambers? No records—and no memoranda on present inquiries. By God, there must be memoranda. In the Navy, we keep memoranda on everything!"

"Sir John keeps no memoranda, sir, no records of any sort."

"No diary?"

"None, sir."

"No records? I found every drawer in his desk quite empty. How do his investigations proceed?"

"He keeps it all in his head, sir. I should think it would be obvious why you found no papers."

"Oh? How so?"

"He cannot read."

"Cannot read? And he a magistrate?"

"No, sir, he cannot read because he is blind."

"Oh." The lieutenant put hand to chin and thought upon that for a moment or two. "Strange," said he, "but one never thinks of him quite so."

"Will that be all, sir?" I moved as if to go.

"By no means! Where is Captain Hartsell?"

"Why, I suppose he might be aboard his ship." And of course he might not be. Actually, it seemed a very slim possibility, considering what Sir John had said and that the captain had left Mr. Bilbo's in the company of two armed constables.

"He was seen to leave under duress in a coach. We believe that Sir John Fielding was in that coach, and that he has abducted him to hold him prisoner on some technical charge."

"Oh, well, there I might be able to help you, Lieutenant Byner. Sir John left before the verdict was handed down."

"I know. I saw him leave with you—then you returned."

"Yes sir, he asked me to report the verdict to him when he returned."

"Returned from *where*, damn you, boy."

"From the Lord Chief Justice, sir. He said that the Lord Chief Justice was sending his coach for him, and that he would wait there at the entrance for it."

"You mean to say that was the coach of the Lord Chief Justice into which the captain was forced?"

"That is certainly a possibility, sir—even a probability."

Again he stroked his chin. "Hmmm, well, the Lord Chief Justice, is it? I don't like the sound of that. Perhaps I'd best go back and . . ."

"The Lord Chief Justice lives in Bloomsbury Square," said I, "at Number Seven. You might find Sir John there now. Or perhaps you and your marines might wish to wait for him here?"

"No . . . uh, no . . ." He looked about and found his man. *"Corporal!"* said he in the voice of command. "Assemble your party and make ready to go."

"Aye-aye, sir," said the corporal, and gave a smart salute.

There was a good deal of shouting from the corporal as he formed the five into a single file.

"Yes, well," said Lieutenant Byner to me, "thank you for the information. Very interesting it was, very interesting. Well, carry on. Sorry for the mess."

To me he gave a vague sort of wave then.

"Corporal! Take them out!"

Commands. And soon the marines were marching toward the door, muskets on their shoulders, bayonets now removed and tucked away. Even so, I doubted they would get through the door with their muskets so high—yet somehow they managed. Mr. Byner followed them out and shut the door behind him.

I looked at Mr. Fuller. He seemed quite overcome by the experience—not shaken as by fear but rather downcast by shame. He sighed.

"There was little I could do when they come down the hall as they did—nothin' at all, really."

"Nothing at all, Mr. Fuller," I agreed.

"And when they went upstairs, I—"

"Upstairs!"

I had not thought they would dare, yet—

Assuring Mr. Fuller I would be back to help him clean up the litter on the floor, I ran to the stairs and up them. I burst through the door and into the kitchen—and narrowly missed a braining by Annie as she swung a heavy iron skillet at my head.

"Jeremy!" she screamed. "I could've hurt you!"

"You could've killed me!"

"But I thought you were one of them come back. I fought two off with this well enough, they took my word there was none here but me."

"I'm sure you did quite well with that. You—"

A great commotion of voices from below interrupted me.

Mr. Marsden, usually the calmest of men, was quite beside himself, hooting his indignation at the top of his voice. I heard Sir John's low rumble and Mr. Fuller's keening tenor join in.

"Come along, Annie," said I. "You may as well see what they did downstairs and give your report to Sir John."

By the time we had descended, Sir John had stilled them all and was listening to Mr. Fuller's doleful tale. Mr. Marsden wandered about, picking up odd sheets of paper and shaking his head sadly. Sir John bolstered the constable with a few words of commendation; then, with undisguised amusement, he heard Annie tell of her battle in the kitchen, and her he commended, as well. Yet when it came my turn, he seemed to treat me somewhat more severely, reminding me early on that the prudent thing would have been to depart when I heard strange voices. Yet I made no excuses and continued, identifying the leader of the group as Lieutenant Byner (this brought a grunt from Sir John). I then told him that I had told Mr. Byner a lie in hopes of getting rid of him and his party of marines.

"Oh? A lie? What sort of lie?"

"I'm afraid that I led him to believe that the coach in which Captain Hartsell departed belonged to the Lord Chief Justice. He seemed sure you were inside it, as well."

He considered for a moment. "And how did the lieutenant react to that?"

"It seemed a bit more than he expected, sir."

"He left right swift, Sir John," said Mr. Fuller, "him and his marines. The corporal formed them up, and out they marched. They wanted naught to do with the Lord Chief Justice."

"Well, Jeremy, sometimes—though not often—a lie told in a good cause can do better than the truth. Yours has put me in mind of a plan. Mr. Fuller, those papers you have collected from the floor already, I wish you to throw them back as you found them. You say your keys were there, too? Throw them also on the floor, just as they were. Mr. Marsden, though it may pain you, we shall leave all as it was for a bit, for you and I are off to visit the Lord Chief Justice. He must see this."

When, in less than an hour, the two returned, they had in
tow William Murray, the Earl of Mansfield, Lord Chief Justice of the King's Bench. That august personage seldom
deigned to visit the Bow Street Court, and when he did, it
was usually with some complaint to nettle Sir John. Sympathy was quite the last thing one expected from him, yet
sympathy he gave in abundance to Mr. Marsden; and to Sir
John he gave a pledge that the felony court would in no wise
give way to the Navy on this Hartsell matter.

"You say you have a chain of witnesses to give testimony
that includes one who viewed the act and an accomplice who
is willing to testify against him?"

"I have, my Lord," said Sir John.

"Then, captain or no, he shall be tried like any common
criminal. We cannot have one law for the Navy and another
for the rest of us."

"No, indeed we cannot."

"Yet why would they cause such havoc? What were they
looking for?"

"For the most part," said Sir John, "I believe it was ordered done in a fit of pique by the officer in charge of the
invading party. He expected to find me or Captain Hartsell,
or both of us. And finding neither of us, he ordered the marines to create this disorder."

"Reprehensible! Intolerable!"

"My young assistant also informs me that they were
searching for notes, memoranda, anything pertinent to recent
investigations. In my view, they were after the names of our
witnesses against Captain Hartsell."

"Indeed! Well, they shall not have them. If must be, then
those witnesses will have the protection of the court."

Thus began one of the greatest and truly earnest games of
tug that London has ever seen. Vice-Admiral Sir Robert Redmond wanted Captain Hartsell. The Lord of the Admiralty
wanted him. It seemed that the whole of His Majesty's Navy
wanted him. Against them all stood the Lord Chief Justice.
It was generally agreed of William Murray, the Earl of Mansfield, that by nature he had one outstanding characteristic,
and that was stubbornness. By others it was judged either a

failing or a virtue, depending upon whichever side of the Lord Chief Justice they might find themselves in any particular disagreement. Yet he was one who would hold firm on what he judged to be a question of principle, no matter what the cost and no matter what forces were ranged against him.

The Lord of the Admiralty came calling upon him and came away cursing him for a pigheaded fool. The Prime Minister invited him for a visit that they might discuss the Hartsell question; the Lord Chief Justice wrote him that there was no reason to make such a visit, for there was nothing to discuss. It was said that even the King had made discreet inquiries into the circumstances, then quite sensibly decided to allow the two warring parties to battle it out, each with the other. As by rumor and titbits dropped in the columns of two of the newssheets the matter became known to the public, it also became widely discussed; the opinion of the public was staunchly with the Lord Chief Justice. I doubt, however, that he knew this, nor knowing, would he have cared a farthing. What mattered to him was that he had set the date of the trial at Old Bailey for the thirtieth of July, just five days following the indictment handed down by Sir John Fielding at that special session of the Bow Street Court; and that he, as chief judge, would preside. That was *all* that concerned him.

Though in all the furor, it might have seemed that the cause of Lieutenant William Landon was lost and forgotten, this was not so: Sir John had not forgotten him, nor did he deem the cause lost. I know this to be so, for on the day following that one of great excitement whereon the lieutenant was convicted, I was summoned to take a letter dictated by the magistrate, then sent to deliver it to Vice-Admiral Sir Robert Redmond. Because Sir John had not been specific as to what matter he wished to discuss, the recipient must have supposed it was what concerned him most: the question of Captain Hartsell. So enlivened was he by what he judged an opportunity for conciliation that he made ready to leave immediately for Bow Street. He called for his coach to be brought round and, as a gesture of his optimistic good feeling, invited me to come along. (It is worth mentioning at this point that his order was conveyed to an unfamiliar younger lieutenant; Mr. Byner was conspicuous by his absence that day.) But because as we waited for the coach, the admiral questioned me without success on Sir John's state of mind, I was made to ride up top next his murderous footman. Nevertheless, I was glad to ride that long walk back from Tower Hill—and glad, too, to ride it in silence.

The arrival of Sir Robert was well noted by Mr. Fuller, who may have expected an even larger detachment of marines to enter behind him, and by Mr. Marsden, who interrupted his continuing work of sorting and filing to stare at him resentfully as he passed by. Sir Robert ignored them, as admirals will, and asked me simply which was Sir John's door. I pointed it out to him and offered to announce him, but he waved me aside and charged on, straight through the door, leaving it open.

I will not say that it was my intention to eavesdrop, curious though I may have been. Nevertheless, reader, as it was my habit to sit upon the bench outside the door to Sir John's chambers that I should be at hand for whatever errands or tasks he might have for me, I saw no reason to break that habit. And, taking my usual place beside the open door, I happened to hear every word that passed between them.

"Jack, Jack," said Sir Robert, in a most effusive manner, "I was so happy to receive your invitation that I rushed here immediate. I was about to write you and ask that I might come, hat in hand, to present my apology."

"I concede that one is due me," said Sir John.

"A terrible mistake was made yesterday. Lieutenant Byner far exceeded his brief. I understand that he left this place in a terrible state. For that you have my sincerest and most profound apology. It was an insult to you, and for that I am most deeply sorry."

"I accept your apology."

"He has been relieved of his duties. He will be disciplined in some way, probably sent off to sea. Would you believe it? The fellow has not had sea duty since he was a midshipman."

"Yes, I would believe that," said Sir John. "But Bobbie, the fact remains that he was sent to the Bow Street Court with a party of marines, and I can only suppose that their purpose was to free a prisoner—namely, Captain James Hartsell—by force, if necessary. Was that not why they were sent?''

"Well . . . yes, Jack, it was."

"That, you may believe me, was a greater insult to my court and to the entire body of law upon which this nation is founded than you will ever know."

"But you must realize our position. Captain Hartsell is a naval officer, and therefore he must be tried by a naval court-martial. We will deal with him, believe me. You will see how sternly and swiftly naval justice can work."

"I have seen naval justice, Bobbie, and I was not favorably impressed."

"Ah, Jack, that unfortunate business—let us put it behind us. Believe me, I did what I could to save that boy." (This, reader, in a most plaintive voice.) "I did, truly."

"I give you credit," said Sir John. "I believe that within the limits you had set for yourself you did the best that you could. You questioned Hartsell closely and, I thought, well on the matter of his tardy accusation. You sought to expose Midshipman Boone's story for the preposterous tale that it was. I am sure, too, that in deliberation with the other two judges you argued for acquittal, yet gave in to them when the vote was cast."

"I did! I did!"

"Yet it was not enough to save him."

"No," said Sir Robert bleakly, "it was not."

There was a pause. I heard a drawer open and shut.

"I believe, however, that this will be."

"What is this?"

"It is a document witnessed by me and my court clerk and signed by Midshipman Albert Boone wherein he admits giving perjured testimony in the trial by court-martial of Lieutenant William Landon, and of having done so at the instigation of Captain—then Lieutenant—James Hartsell."

Silence. Sir Robert cleared his throat. Then further silence.

"I must give this some study."

"Indeed, you may have it. I have another copy, equally valid—worded exactly as this one is, witnessed, and signed in the same way. I want you to take it, and use it as the basis to declare the trial by court-martial invalid and drop all charges against Lieutenant Landon,''

"Jack, I am not sure I could do that. I am not sure I have that power."

"And why not? You served as chief judge in the trial. You saw through the boy's testimony. That much is evident from the trial record. I should think you would welcome this."

"I do, I do, but . . ." There was another long pause. Then, of a sudden, Sir Robert spoke up in a cautious, knowing manner: "Now, Jack, I think I see your game."

"My game? What could you mean? I have no game."

"Oh, perhaps, perhaps, but it seems to me that what has been suggested here very quietly is a kind of trade—Landon for Hartsell. Well, let me say that such an arrangement might indeed be a possibility. I shall have to confer with my superiors, of course, but what you suggest is certainly not beyond the realm of possibility."

Another silence, yet on this occasion it was Sir John who was slow to respond. Then at last: "You have misjudged me entirely. Let me assure you that if you fear that you have not the power to declare Mr. Landon's trial invalid, I am *certain* that I have not the power to alter Captain Hartsell's status. He has been bound over for trial in the felony court. The date of the trial has been set. Nothing can change that—nor should it."

"But surely, Jack, if you could talk to the Lord Chief Justice it would—"

"Would do nothing at all. Your captain will be tried here at Old Bailey and there is no way round that. But good God, Bobbie, I thought you would be eager for this document I have given you. You can save Mr. Landon with it. He is, after all, your nephew—or need I remind you of that? And you know him, as I do, to be innocent of the charge on which he was convicted. And you have it before you, he was convicted on the testimony of a perjurer and a murderer."

"Ah, there, Jack, now you take too much upon yourself. Captain Hartsell has not yet been convicted. Innocence is presumed, guilt must be proven. Even I know that much about the law."

"In this case, you are merely quibbling. You may be as sure of it as it is me before you now that he will be convicted and that he will hang."

Then, without a word of goodbye, Sir Robert came through the door he had entered only minutes before. He moved less swiftly, however, and much less surely, and I noted that in his hand he held the confession of perjury signed by Midshipman Boone.

Next day, in the midst of all this, Tom Durham received a letter that quite changed his life. When it was put in his hand it puzzled and then astonished him (as he told me later), for it bore the Royal Seal. It was, in effect, a communication from the King, and indeed it bore the royal signature at bottom. It was a "King's letter," appointing him midshipman in the Royal Navy.

Unbeknownst to me, for the pertinent pleas had been dictated to Mr. Marsden, Sir John had taken the advice given him by Sir Robert when first the matter was discussed. He had made formal application for Tom for a King's-letter appointment, and at the same time had written a more personal note to Queen Charlotte asking her swift intercession on Tom's behalf; he had merely pointed out to her what was true—that though well educated, Tom was a court boy, and that he had distinguished himself in his service on the H.M.S. *Adventure*, rising from galley scullion to ordinary seaman during the term of the frigate's tour in Indian waters, and that he was known for his bravery in battle and steadfastness in executing all orders given him. Tom Durham's success proved the worthiness of the scheme to which she had so generously given her royal support; to recognize him with a King's-letter appointment as midshipman would give it further distinction and dignity; and what was more, Sir John had added quite prophetically, young Mr. Durham would make a superb naval officer.

Thus it had been accomplished. Though the matter had not slipped from Sir John's mind certainly, he had refused to offer the appointment by the King as a possibility to Lady Fielding and Tom, for as he had occasion later to instruct me, it is always a risky matter to depend upon royal favor in any matter. He thought it best not to raise their hopes, so that they might not later be dashed.

It was, of course, cause for great celebration. I was sent forth to buy Mr. Tolliver's best beef roast. Annie cooked it worthily and served it in the dining room complete with a pudding made from its drippings; she was invited to sit with us there, as she always did in the kitchen, and for the occasion she had put on her best frock.

There were but two matters that marred that festive evening. The first was Tom's early departure. A note accompanying the King's letter stipulated that he must leave the following day and report to Portsmouth for duty on the H.M.S. *Leviathan*, a seventy-gun ship of the line which would sail in a week's time for service in the Mediterranean. He would have just enough time to be fitted with his midshipman's uniform and learn his new duties.

Sir John's mood also cast some gloom over that evening. I knew him to be most pessimistic, following the admiral's visit, regarding Lieutenant Landon's chances of escaping hanging at Execution Dock. Yet, I thought, surely these grand tidings for Tom, which Sir John himself had brought to pass, would at least temporarily raise his spirits. Yet I had reckoned without a full appreciation of the deep sadness that the entire affair had caused him.

He had raised his glass and drunk with the rest of us when, after we had eaten, Lady Fielding proposed her toast to a long life and a great career for her son. Yet then he remained silent, offering no toast of his own, sinking down, rather, into that deep, contemplative silence into which I had seen him slip before in his darker moments. I, of course, was not the only one at table who noticed.

"Jack," said Lady Fielding, "are you not happy at Tom's good fortune? Of all of us here you should be most pleased, for it was you brought this about." Then she raised her glass again. "All of you, I give you my husband, who can work wonders, a man who makes the impossible possible and gives hope to the hopeless."

While what she offered was well intentioned, it was not the sort of tribute to enliven the spirits of one who feared, with good reason, that a great injustice was to be done, one who believed he had used up the last chance to halt the march of an innocent man to the gallows. Yet he rose and took up his glass.

"I admit to feeling of two minds on this occasion," said he. "For while I well know that Tom looks forward to a better berth than the one he had, and more, that his experience of the last two years and his native intelligence will make him a fine officer, I am sad that in these last days I have lost all faith in the service to which he now prepares to devote his life. Though I know he will not do so, I would not blame Tom, nor criticize him, if, knowing what he knows of one who sits condemned in the Tower, he would decline the honor that has been bestowed upon him by the King and depart the Navy as swiftly as I could arrange it. But, as I said, he will not do that, for I know he loves the sea as I did when I was his age—and I pray God he will have the opportunity to continue to love it all his life long. And so, Tom, I drink to you and offer you but two cautions. The first is that as a midshipman and as an officer you always hew to what you know is right and just and not be swayed by those voices around you that urge what is expedient and easy. The second is this: that you never mention my name nor my relation to you to your shipmates, to your fellow officers, nor to anyone who wears a naval uniform. Tom, I drink to you, and may God bless and protect you."

We all, save Tom, stood and emptied our glasses. Then we all sat, save Sir John, who tossed his napkin down on the table.

"If you will forgive me now," said he, "I think I'll be early to bed. I hope I shall be granted the sleep I need. It has not been easy the last few nights."

I moved my chair from the table and made ready to assist him.

"No, no, Jeremy, don't get up. I have not had so much wine that I cannot find my way to bed. Tom, I shall say a proper goodbye to you on the morrow. Good night, all."

And thus he left us. We did not stay long at table afterward. Annie and I cleared the dishes and did the washing up. Tom and his mother took the candles and went into the parlor, where they talked long into the night. I know that to be so, for though I read till late, he had not made an appearance in the attic bedroom we shared.

It had been decided that Lady Fielding, and she alone, would accompany Tom to the Portsmouth stagecoach, and so we gathered in the kitchen to say our goodbyes to him. Annie he kissed boldly on the cheek, thrilling her and quite confounding his mother. From Sir John he received a manly hug, a warm shake of his hand, and a few solemn words whispered in his ear. They must have affected him deeply, for by the time he came to me, his eyes shone with tears. He took my right hand and shook it vigorously.

"Jeremy," said he, "my brother, keep on the path you have chosen. I know it is the right one for you. I shall miss our talks at night."

I was so overcome that he should call me his brother that I was scarce able to say the few simple words I had prepared. Yet I ignored my own tears, cleared the phlegm from my throat, and brought my left hand from behind my back. I offered him the book it held.

"What is this?"

"Anson's *A Voyage Round the World*," said I. "You had not the chance to finish it. I thought you should have the opportunity. Keep it, Tom, for it is my gift to you."

"I know not what to say. I shall keep it always and read it, and reread it, then reread it again. And each time I do, I shall think of you."

Then, picking up the proper portmanteau that Lady Fielding had rushed out to buy him the day before, and nodding dumbly at us all, he went through the door and started down the stairs. His mother followed.

Of Tom's departure, there is but one more thing to add. Well over an hour later, as I had returned from my buying in the Garden, I was once more back in the kitchen. Annie had gone out for a walk, wishing, I think, to be alone with the sorrow of Tom's leaving. As I was putting away the vegetables in the bin, I heard steps on the stairs and thought it might be Annie returning. It was, however, Lady Fielding who came through the door. I greeted her, then returned to finish what I had been doing.

"Jeremy," said she to me, "I have something to say to

you." There was a slight tremolo in her voice.

"Yes, my lady," said I, coming to her.

"I have withheld from you something you need, withheld it because I, unsure of my own place in this household, was unsure of your own, as well. I knew not how I should behave toward you. Jeremy, I have withheld my love from you. But my Tom called you brother, and that can only mean that I—" She broke off in a sob. "That I am your mother. From this day, I shall withhold nothing from you. You shall have all the love from me you deserve and want. From this day I shall be mother to you, too."

With that, reader, she opened her arms to me, and I fled into them. And as you may suppose, we both of us wept copious tears—as I weep them now, remembering that moment.

Neither Sir John Fielding nor I attended the trial of Captain James Hartsell, so what I now give to you, in brief, has been gleaned from reports of it in the newssheets, and from one whom I met later in life who indeed was present.

Captain Hartsell was provided by the Royal Navy with proper counsel in the person of Sir Richard Calper, a distinguished and most successful barrister. He had a few cards to play, and one of them he played immediately. Sir Richard contested the composition of the jury, saying that in this case, "a trial by a jury of his peers" could only mean that Captain Hartsell must be tried by twelve others holding the naval rank of captain; he proposed that the trial be delayed until such a jury could be assembled. The Lord Chief Justice dismissed this argument, saying firstly that it was impractical, for such a jury as he proposed would be difficult to put together—"and might be damned impossible, which I suppose, Sir Richard, would suit your purposes well." He added, too, that he liked not the reasoning that underlay it. "Are we to try by occupation? For make what you will of the rank of captain in the Royal Navy, it is but an occupation like any other. I daresay you would not care to be tried by a jury of your peers if that meant that twelve other barristers would sit in judgment upon you." At that a ripple of laughter went through the courtroom. "No, I disallow your argument. The crime with which Captain Hartsell is charged was committed in London, so he may be tried before twelve ordinary citizens of our city. Let it be so.''

The trial proceeded, apparently along the lines of the hearing in Sir John's Magistrate's Court, except for the addition of two new witnesses. The first of them was Mr. Singh, the Lascar seaman of the *Adventure* to whom I had talked that day of our second visit to the ship. The barrister objected that in appearing before the court he was in violation of orders that he remain aboard the *Adventure*; he was, in effect, a deserter, and a man in such a state should not be allowed to testify in a court of law. The Lord Chief Justice informed Sir Richard that Mr. Singh had come at the invitation of the court, and the court's wishes superseded naval regulations. Free then to have his say, Mr. Singh gave it that he was one of a crew of Lascar seamen who had rowed Captain Hartsell and Midshipman Boone to the Tower Wharf on the night of the crime; that they had waited over two hours for their return, which was after midnight; and that on their way back the two had talked openly of the murder of Tobias Trindle, how his body jumped when the shot was fired, and afterward, how cleverly they had eluded their pursuit.

In cross-examination, the barrister tried to suggest that the two villains would never talk so openly before others. ''Why should they do such a stupid thing as that, Mr. Singh?''

''Because they think we only Inja boys and cannot understand English. But I understand all they say. Oh yes.''

Then came Seth Tarkin, the innkeeper of the Green Man, to tell his Judas role in Hartsell's murderous enterprise. He told also that Mr. Boone was next the captain when he made his inquiry regarding Black Emma's lodgings.

Next, of course, Emma Black was called—she the most important of all to the case, for hers was eyewitness testimony. And at that point, Sir Richard Calper played his last card.

''M'Lord,'' said he, ''I object to the appearance of this woman as a witness as she is a criminal, currently and actively engaged in crime. She is a known whore, m'Lord. She was called such by the last witness. Prostitution is a crime, and therefore she is a criminal.''

The Lord Chief Justice was forced to give this some consideration, yet it ended in this colloquy between judge and witness.

"Miss Black, are you currently and actively engaged in prostitution? You must remember that you are now under oath."

"No sir, I am not. I am a resident of the Magdalene Home for Penitent Prostitutes, learning the trade of seamstress."

"So you say you *were* a prostitute but are no longer. Is that so?"

"Yes, sir. If you knew the truth, half the women in London sold themselves one time or another, including the married ones."

"While I suspect and hope your estimate is a bit high, I accept the principle of what you say, and I am satisfied you are not currently and actively so engaged. This witness may testify."

And once she had done so, Captain James Hartsell was a doomed man. Then came Midshipman Albert Boone and made it all the more certain. He told of his visit to Old Isaac, what he had learned from him, and how the plan of murder had been hatched and executed. He told of their escape and confirmed their discussion of the crime on their return to the *Adventure*.

"You admit then that you were Captain Hartsell's accomplice in this act?"

"I do, m'Lord, but I was only following orders."

"Have promises been made to you for your testimony?"

"None sir, except Sir John, the blind one, said he would make recommendations."

"He has done that. The court will take them under advisement when you are tried. You may step down."

It is interesting to note that the matter of motive was brought up neither by the prosecution nor by the defense. The prosecution had no need to, since the weight of testimony against the captain was so strong. The defense did not challenge this, for of course the Navy had no wish to make his motive in all its details known in court as part of the public record.

The jury went out and returned within minutes. The verdict was guilty.

The Lord Chief Justice sentenced Captain James Hartsell to hang in two days' time.

That afternoon, late, Sir John dictated a letter to Mr. Marsden and entrusted it to me to deliver. I ran most of the distance to Tower Hill and at the desk I was told that the admiral was still in his office but had left word that he was not to be disturbed under any circumstances. I had no choice but to leave the letter with the petty officer in charge.

What was in it? I know not for certain. I can only guess that in it he pointed out that now it was certain that his nephew had been convicted on the testimony of a perjurer and a murderer, for Captain Hartsell had been convicted. I am sure he made a final appeal for the life of Lieutenant Landon. Yet, as I say, I know not its contents for certain, since Mr. Marsden took Sir John's dictation.

Midshipman Albert Boone was tried the following day. All the witnesses who had appeared at Captain Hartsell's trial again appeared at Boone's trial, with the addition of Old Isaac Tenker. Boone could simply have pled guilty and relieved them of this trouble, yet he insisted on pleading not guilty, with the defense he had simply been following the captain's orders and had been made to help in what he knew to be a wrong and unlawful act. Yet he was convicted by the jury. And the judge who heard the case, who was not the Earl of Mansfield, took into consideration Boone's testimony against his captain and followed the recommendation of Sir John Fielding. He condemned the convicted felon to transportation to the colony of Georgia and ten years' hard labor there.

As fate had it, Lieutenant William Landon and Captain James Hartsell were hanged on the same day, August 1, 1769. By all reports, Captain Hartsell gave the better show. During his ride in the tumbrel to Tyburn Hill, he snarled, cursed, and spat at the jeering crowd. Pushed up upon the gallows platform, he kicked so vigorously at his executioner that his feet, too, had to be tied. Yet hanged he was, bobbing and choking on the rope, gasping until his tongue lolled from his lips.

Lieutenant Landon, on the other hand, went to the gallows on Execution Dock with solemn dignity. He blessed the executioner and forgave all who had wronged him. He died, they say, like a true Christian gentleman.

Now available in hardcover

PERSON
OR PERSONS
UNKNOWN

A Sir John Fielding Mystery

BRUCE ALEXANDER

Putnam